Ghosts of Tokyo

Christopher J. Smith

Meredith-Smith

For Gadget

First published in 2012 by Meredith-Smith Pty Limited

Copyright © Christopher J. Smith 2012

National Library of Australia
Cataloguing-in-Publication entry

Smith, Christopher J.

Ghosts of Tokyo / Christopher J. Smith.

ISBN 9780987463302 (pbk.)

A823.4

First Edition 2012

The characters in this book are fictitious and any
resemblance to real persons, living or dead is purely
coincidental.

www.ghostsoftokyo.com
www.christopher-j-smith.com

Author's Note

Ghosts of Tokyo is a work of fiction and for the most part the novel is set in Japan. The idea for the book came to me one night while dining at the top of the Roppongi Tower, with the vast city of Tokyo spread out before me like a blanket of light stretching to the horizon. I was moved to consider the Japanese culture, sub-culture and the very underbelly itself and so I just started writing. It should be noted that in the writing, I have endeavored to achieve some degree of geographical accuracy regarding the layout of various cities and their buildings, subway and railway systems. However I have taken some liberty with certain buildings and locations in the interests of the story. It should further be noted that I hold no qualifications in any of the sciences involved in this book, so if you do and, in turn, find fault with my logic or theories... keep it to yourself. I am not a scientist, I am a storyteller, and on that basis I beg your indulgence. As I have said... this is a work of fiction.

Acknowledgements

I wish to express my gratitude to the following people for the parts they have played in turning 'Ghosts of Tokyo' into the book you now hold. To my panel of readers, Vicki Roney, Quinton Smith, & John Dudley.

To my son Zane Smith who provided invaluable assistance and enthusiasm for this book, and to my partner and editor Lynn, without whose support, tireless devotion and attention to detail this book would probably not exist.

1. UNDERGROUND

The present...

The first time I saw him, I mean really saw him, was actually the second time. The first time... the real first time I saw him, was deep down in a green phosphor lit tunnel about three layers below the very lowest subway line.

It was a dream of course, but when I turned that last corner, drawn along by the hissing green, there he was. I didn't talk to him. I just stood there rooted to the wet ground. He was looking at me... right at me... without even seeing me, without even knowing I was there. He was against the rock wall, twisting and convulsing like a dying caterpillar hung on a thread... too busy by far to acknowledge me. I heard a strange hissing noise behind me, but I was petrified... too scared to look back. Then I felt a strange sensation that rose up deeply from my feet. I felt I was being turned inside out. From over my head came a malicious green mist, a thing at once holy and evil. The mist hung over the boy, his eyes wide with fright. He opened his mouth to scream and the mist drove downwards into the boy's mouth. I fell back against the dank wall of the tunnel and fought off clutching nausea. I couldn't open my eyes. It was like they were sewn shut. After a minute or so my eyes slowly focused on the boy. As I watched, I swear I saw his soul tear itself out through his gaping mouth and stream off along the tunnel roof and then, with a sucking noise like the last foul breath from a crone's maw, it found a crack in the rock face and was gone. He crumpled down the wall and collapsed onto the wet ground. The pain fled his contorted face and as he closed his eyes he released a great sigh... which woke me!

But back to the present...

I'm on Koshu Kaido, the bridge outside the south exit of Shinjuku Station, and my eyes are being drawn to a figure making its way through the throng just below me on the street.

His hair is three colours; blond on the tips, green in the middle, and native Japanese black at the roots. It is teased high on his head, but spills spear-like, down his face, almost covering his eyes. There's a large metal stud to the right side of his bottom lip, and his eyebrows have been shaved off and replaced by two sharp pencil lines peaking at the centre like a child's drawing of Mount Fuji. He's wearing a black hoody with white lining and black formal pants. He's got on a blue t-shirt, with the number 26 printed on a torn, winged heart, and a large silver padlock on a heavy chain around his neck.

I see all this easily, digest it quickly. It's the boy from the tunnel... the boy from the dream. I'm frozen to the spot, now I'm stirring from my stupor with the sharp pain in my fingers and looking down at my hands, I see I'm clutching the railing so tightly that my fingers are cramping. I release my grip and look back down into the crowd... straight into the searching gaze of the boy. He has stopped moving and is staring straight up at me. Those lifeless eyes can clearly see me now. A sickening grin forms round the edge of his mouth and spreads like hoar frost across his face. He points up at me and screams.

"I KNOW YOU!!"

The bile wells in my throat and my legs start to buckle, but I run... stumbling at first like a damned crab, but then stronger, until I'm into the ground floor of the Takashimaya store complex. I look back and see him even closer, maybe now only thirty metres back. He's cruising and I'm running as fast as I can, but still he's gaining on me. How can that be... this is no dream.

But *this* is...

I was back in the tunnel. I had moved forward, nearer to the sleeping figure of the boy in a dark puddle at my feet. I was petrified but strangely calm, and while he slept I was able to study him more closely. He was clearly a rent boy, but I had no idea of his gender preference. I guessed that there was probably a clue in his dress or maybe the trinkets on the silver chains that hung round his neck or disappeared into his right pocket. Of course I'd seen guys like him before, in every Japanese city I'd ever been in as well as a few other places like New York and Toronto. They're sort of nocturnal. One minute the streets and shop arcades are full of shopgirls and salarymen and the next minute the rent boys can be seen trawling through the early evening crowd. Just cruising, and always in groups of four or five, their handlers, watching from back in the shadows.

I told myself this was a dream and that I was safe in my bed at the Sunroute Plaza, so nothing could happen. I was still telling myself this when the boy opened his eyes. His hand snaked out to grasp my leg, but I was just beyond his reach. He collapsed face first into the rank puddle, his left eye just visible and its gaze fixed on my foot. I knew then that he was calculating the success of another strike and just as surely I knew I had to get out of there, dream or not. I turned to run and doing so grazed my forehead on the edge of the low hanging rock arch. I travelled quickly back through the tunnels, ever upward, my sense of direction keen. Finally I saw the light cracking around the last door that I knew brought me out onto the brightly lit lowest platform of the new south exit. I slowed my breathing, calming myself. After all, it was just a dream. I pushed on the door and found myself back in my bedroom in the hotel. Sure I was surprised, but this sort of shit happens in dreams; so I dreamt that I climbed back into my bed and slept, without any more dreaming.

2. THE STAMPEDE TO CALGARY

The not too distant past…

I remember I'd just finished my last show in Jasper, Canada. It was spring, but up there the highest peaks are still white and the glacial air can still freeze your damned face off once the sun goes down. I'd gone upstairs into the cold night, leaving the band to pack up the gear, and my manager to fight with the promoter over my fee. We'd driven up here after finishing some pretty good shows in Vancouver. I'd done small venues in places like Kamloops and Lake Louise. I'd played to an audience of about thirteen people in Banff and, to top it off, tonight some drunken moron had climbed on stage and demanded I sing something by Johnny Cash!

I was over it and I was claustrophobic. That's right… up there in those wide open spaces with the grandeur of the Rockies all around… I was claustrophobic! The problem was that you can't stand back and get a good look at one mountain without backing into another one. Just one morning I'd like to have woken up in a hotel room that didn't smell like damp leather and open the blinds onto a balmy beach view. I'm a water person… I need to be near the water to survive; liquid type water, not frozen water, and those damned mountains seemed to creep in closer every time I turned my back.

"So… Calgary then?" said Nick.

Nick was my manager. I hadn't heard him come up. I'd wandered over to the railway line and was sitting on a rock wall outside the station, looking up at some kind of totem pole.

"Nope, Calgary's off. I've had enough," I said. "The only reason I'm going to Calgary is to get on the first available flight home."

"But we've got bookings," he said.

I turned to face him and was struck by how old he looked; or maybe that was just me.

"You're not listening Nick," I said quietly. "Find me a decent gig somewhere where there's less bears and more people... people who like my music. People who like my music and have wallets."

I'd left Jasper early the next morning and driven straight through to Calgary Airport, leaving Nick to sort out the cancellations. There was a New York flight early the next morning, so I'd checked into the airport hotel and spent about an hour in the shower trying to get warm. Not my body... my soul!

When I had finally flopped on the bed, I checked my cell and found three missed calls and two messages from Nick. While I debated checking the messages, the phone rang again. I stared at it blankly then pushed the off button and swiped my finger across the screen, sending Nick's final call into oblivion. I'd slept.

I'd got home to my apartment in the village, and I'd slept again. This time I'd warmed my soul with the best part of a quart of vodka. When I woke up I was so warm my head hurt!

3. WHERE THE SILENCE WAS DEAFENING

The distant past...

There was a dream. The most vivid and powerful dream I have ever had.

I remember my nose bled.

In fact... in all the carnage of that dream, that's the most vivid memory I have. It seems I had just left a friend's house and was walking back downtown when, into the stillness of a quiet Sunday morning, came a great rending crash. A great, almost deafening crash, followed by the sound of an over-revving engine that seemed to fly above me. Instinct saved my life. I looked up, and above me, corkscrewing through the air was a red and white sedan. I dived clear as the sedan crashed down sideways onto the step of the corner walk-up. I was looking at the underside of the car for just a second, then it rolled back on its roof blocking the door to the building. Inside I could see two guys. One was spread across the upturned roof lining like a discarded ventriloquist's dummy and the other was up on his hands and knees, clawing at the broken seats hanging above him. He was bleeding heavily from a large gash across his forehead and screaming over and over... "Vince... Vince... where's Vince?"

Time was flowing like treacle. On the other side of the street another car was rolling to a stop against the curb. The front was crushed in and upwards about two feet, but miraculously it was still rolling. When it finally stopped moving there was silence for what seemed an eternity, but I guess it was more like ten seconds. I could see two people in the front seat. They looked totally wrecked, but my eyes were drawn to the road in front of the car, where I saw the body of a young child limp on the asphalt, surrounded by shattered glass and twisted chrome strips. I started to walk towards the body. Now I could see it was a young Japanese boy. As I approached him he opened his eyes and looked right at me, but it was like he wasn't seeing me. Like he was looking right through me. I don't know why, but I leant down to take his little hand. As I reached out to touch it a great spark of electricity jumped between those tiny crumpled fingers and mine. I jumped back startled.

"Vince... Vince". I turned back to look at the other car. The bloodcurdling screams made even more so by the blood coursing down the guy's face and bubbling out of his mouth, while he screamed for Vince. But Vince was dead and as I watched, his friend sank down, sobbing onto the roof lining. Instantly it was quiet. The sensation of silence was both overwhelming and clearly emotional. It was like someone had turned down the volume on my life. I could see people running down the street. I could see flashing lights bouncing off the window of the deli on the opposite corner. I could see two people screaming mute obscenities as they tried to clamber out of the smashed front door of the walk-up and over the upturned wheel of the wrecked sedan. I watched as policemen wrenched open the passenger door of the blue Ford and carefully laid a woman on the sidewalk. From where I stood I could see she had long blond hair and was well dressed. Police already... how long had I been standing there staring? The policeman draped his own uniform jacket over the woman's head and shoulders. She had left the scene of the accident.

Both cops turned their attention to the driver still trapped in the car.

I saw a silent ambulance arrive on silent, screeching tyres.

Suddenly the sound came crashing in and I fell back clutching my ears against the clamour of sirens, the screaming of instructions, the gasps of the onlookers and the giant sobs heaving up from the upturned car across the road. I turned back to the child... there was nothing but the pile of shattered glass and twisted chrome. I looked everywhere... there was no child. I sank down to sit on the curb in front of the mangled Ford. I felt like someone had just kicked me in the head.

Somebody touched my shoulder.

"Which vehicle are you from?" asked an ambulance attendant.

"I'm not from any vehicle" I said, "I was just…"

I stopped talking. I had a strong metallic taste in my mouth and felt the drained liquid of a fresh kill around my nose and mouth. I realised my nose was bleeding… badly. The medic clearly had seen the blood and assumed I was a victim; and I was… even then, but not the way he thought.

"Are you okay son?"

"Yeah, sure," I said, "It's just a nosebleed."

"What about that burn on your hand?" said the medic.

I looked at my hand and saw an angry blister swelling on the pad of my index finger. It was punctuated by a great black sooty flash that ran up, over the heel of my hand and onto my wrist.

"No I'm fine. It's nothing," I said backing away.

I was pretty dazed, and wandered off a short distance to deal with my nosebleed. As I pinched my nose shut, the blood ran down my hand and wrist, painting patterns in the carbon flash. The bleeding continued for about fifteen minutes and then stopped as suddenly as it had started. I felt light headed. Loss of blood maybe but, there was something else. Something had died. I don't mean the piles of lifeless meat left by the crash, I mean something else… and something had been born.

I woke up. I was light headed and dizzy. I went to the bathroom and splashed cold water on my face. The end of my index finger was sore. I flexed my fist a few times and it went away. Must have been sleeping on it.

4. SOMETIMES IT TAKES A KNOCK ON THE HEAD

The present...

I'm lying awake in a hotel room in Tokyo and I'm thinking... jesus, get a grip. Too much convenience store saké and vending machine coffee are giving me bad dreams. I'm staring out the window at the expanse of glass about twenty feet away, that makes up my view, when I notice a group of giggling office girls looking down at me from the lift lobby opposite. As my eyes adjust I now see that about half the windows opposite are occupied by viewers. Some have coffee, some wave. Some laugh when I climb out of bed naked to pull on last night's clothes. Oh well... story of my life. There's two empty 'One-Cup' saké flasks on the table beside the bed... and a clock that says 8.35am. What! I need food.

Over the road there's a Family Mart convenience store. Hotcakes; two for a buck, washed down with a Boss black, then back to my room for a shower. I hit the light switch and walk into the shower pulling my t-shirt over my head. Oh shit no! No, no, no... it just can't be. As the t-shirt pulls off my head I'm looking straight in the mirror and there on my forehead is a graze. A fresh graze. A fresh graze done on a low rock arch in a sodding dream! Okay so now I'm backing out of the bathroom and I'm trying to convince myself there's a logical explanation for this. But I find myself staring at the dirty brownish bloodstain on my pillow and I'm telling myself... no there's not!

My gaze is drawn to the windows opposite and there he is. The rent boy with the blue t-shirt with the number 26 printed on a torn, winged heart, and a large silver padlock on heavy chain around his neck, and he's staring right at me. As I grab for my t-shirt and run for the door, I see him turn and run to the lifts behind him.

Now I'm out on the street. I race across the road and back into the Family Mart. I'm hiding behind the first row of groceries when I see the boy run past in the direction of Shinjuku station. I make my way quickly out onto the street where I can see him now, slowing down. I duck behind a vending machine as he turns and looks back the way he has come. Satisfied he's not being followed, he turns back and strolls, almost casually across the street and along to the south entrance of the station. I'm up as close behind him as I dare get. I watch as he makes his way through the station and turns right, heading for the stairs that lead down to the Narita Express platform. I follow him down at a safe distance.

He's on the stairs about twenty metres ahead of me when all of a sudden he turns and looks straight at me. His eyes strike me like a solid punch and I stagger back a step or two trying to regain my equilibrium. It was a second, maybe two, but when I looked back at him I was looking into the space where he used to be. There is at least another dozen people on the stairs, but nobody else seemed to have noticed anything odd. I continue on to the open air platform and scan every possible direction finding no sign of him. I'll say I was defeated again, but in reality I'm petrified and I'm happy to make my way back to my hotel.

Back in my room, I go where I always go when I'm hurt or confused, to my music. Pulling my Martin from its case I just start in with some finger style exercises, then move straight into the opening notes of Georgie, the warm up number from my current show set.

I get a few bars in when a sharp pain indicates a blister on the end of my index finger. Sometimes when you've been off the instrument for a while, a right handed player like me will maybe have the odd problem with the fingers on his left, or fret hand, but I've never had a problem with my right, or picking hand. Must have been quite a show last night. I'm glad I was there.

5. ALL THE LITTLE BIRDS ARE DEAD

Almost as far back in the past as we need to go...

Martha Bird was not pretty, nor was she ugly, she just was, that's all. She smelled of mothballs and urine and her hair was black and straight, even lank. She always looked old. Her head was old. Her head was too old to be on the shoulders of a primary school kid. Whenever you looked at her she smiled, but shyly. Martha Bird always seemed to be alone in the playground. She seemed to have no friends. She was always on the edge of a group as if she wanted to break in, but did not have the confidence to do so. There was something about her that made people shiver. People know odd when they see it!

It was 1959.

In 1959 Sally Pepper was just seven years old and went to a different school to Martha Bird. Her parents had some money from somewhere, but little Sally Pepper was an only child and she got lonely. Her mother worked in an office in Vancouver and her father was some kind of executive who drove a flash car. Near the back door of her house was a little cactus in a red pot, and underneath the red pot was the backdoor key. After school, little Sally Pepper was supposed to come straight home, let herself in, grab a cookie and a glass of milk and wait for her mum to come home about two hours later. But little Sally Pepper got lonely and on the way home she used to pass an old rundown house, old paint curling off ancient grey boards. Often there were four or five kids playing in the front yard. Screaming, shouting, laughing and just being kids, so each day little Sally Pepper took longer and longer to walk past that house, barely moving while she imagined herself in that yard laughing and playing... imagined herself laughing and playing like she belonged.

One day little Sally Pepper was walking slowly past the old rundown house when Martha Bird, who was the oldest of the four kids and the same age as little Sally Pepper, ran up to the fence in hot pursuit of a coloured ball. From that day on, little Sally Pepper and Martha Bird became close, but secret, friends. Little Sally Pepper knew that her mother would never approve of her mixing with other neighbourhood kids, especially the Birds. So almost every day after school, little Sally Pepper would stop off and play with Martha and her two little sisters and her little brother, making sure she beat her mother home afterwards.

Mrs. Pepper never found out until one day she came home and found the back door ajar. Little Sally Pepper never left the door open, she was under strict instructions to lock it behind her and let nobody in but her mother and father, so, alarmed, Mrs. Pepper ran into the house calling Sally's name. Sally was not in the kitchen; she was not in the lounge where she sometimes listened to the radio. Mrs. Pepper ran to the back window but there was no sign of little Sally. She was getting worried, on her way up the hall she was checking the bathroom when she heard pathetic whimpering coming from Sally's bedroom.

Mrs. Pepper sprang through the door to find Sally face down on her bed with her bottom in the air and a pillow over her head. Great sobs came from under the pillow along with dreadful whimpering and gurgling sounds. Mrs. Pepper knelt down beside the bed and laid her hand on Sally's heaving back. Little Sally Pepper scampered sideways like a frightened lamb and jammed herself hard against the wall like she meant to pass through it. Her mother sat beside her on the bed and gently removed the pillow from her head. Sally's sobs got heartbreakingly louder, and Mrs. Pepper tugged her into her safe arms.

"Oh my heavens Sally," she said. "Whatever is wrong?"

Sally's sobs died to a jerky crackle and then a fast breathing. She turned to her mother. She was as red as a late season peach and there was snot and drool spread all across her contorted little face. The rapid breathing finally slowed and Sally turned to her mother and said.

"The... the birds. The birds have (sob) died."

"There there," said her mother. "Sometimes God takes pretty young birds up to heaven to sing for him."

"No no no... you don't understand. All the little Birds are dead!" cried little Sally Pepper.

6. COULD THIS BE THE FUTURE MRS. SINGER?

The present...

I decide to practice with a plectrum for a while, because the end of my index finger is throbbing to a strong beat all of its own. I run through the whole set and it takes my mind off all this other stuff. I'm three nights in to a twelve show tour, sometimes headlining, sometimes not, but the money is great and I love Japan, so I've got no complaints. Tonight I'm headlining at Eggman, and it's a good venue with a great crowd. It's also just up the road from my hotel in Shinjuku, so it's handy for my afternoon sound check.

The sound check done, I'm about halfway back to the hotel when the heavens open. Like daffodils on the first warm day of spring, the whole city sprouts umbrellas. I'm ducking for cover all the way back to the hotel, but I make it in one piece, get to my room and go online to check my emails. Presently I notice that my right index finger no longer hurts. There's no sign of the blister... gone!

I've got an email from Nick. He's been in Osaka organising promo and wants to have a meal when he gets back. He tells me he'll be at Shinjuku south exit at 6 pm, so we'll have three or four hours to chill before the gig. I hit the lobby bar for a couple of drinks. Whisky I think; there's a good selection here. I settle for a ten year old Laphroiag, one ice cube. I lean forward on the bar and drop my chin on my fists to watch the magic elixir splash down across that mini berg... I wait for the crack. While I watch I'm trying to make sense of the day. Sure, the morning started weird, but the rest of the day went smooth, so maybe I've just been imagining things. Bad dreams, delayed jet lag... I don't know. Sometimes I wake up in a hotel room and for about ten minutes or so I have no idea where I am. This is not my beautiful house... then when I figure I'm in a hotel, another ten minutes to figure out which city in which country. But give me a break… tunnels, weird rent boys, green mist, man I've got to get sorted.

"You're the singer right?"

I turn toward the voice and there she is… the future Mrs singer!

I'd like to say she was a vision of beauty, unmatched by any other. But she wasn't. What she was, was the most naturally pretty woman I had ever laid eyes on. She had great big honest eyes. She was smiling… I was probably staring. God, how long had she been standing there like that, waiting for me to actually notice there was more of her below the neck, and that one of her hands was out waiting for me to shake it?

"Yes, I am," I finally answer, taking her hand and shaking it.

"I'm sorry," she said, "I've disturbed you. I'm Yuka Sasaki from Radio 3…."

But I had already stopped listening. I was lost in those eyes.

"… I wanted to arrange an interview with you before Osaka. Your manager told you about me right?"

"I'm sorry," I said, finally getting my feet back on the ground. "No… but I haven't spoken to him for a few days. I'm meeting him soon for dinner. Ah… perhaps you would like to join us?"

"Wow," she said, "That was quick. I mean I've heard about you musicians but that was one of the quickest pick-up lines I've ever experienced."

"Shit… I'm sorry. I just meant…"

"Forget it!" she said laughing (and making my poor heart ache). "I'm just kidding; I'd love to have dinner with you and your manager. I've got to be in Sendai tomorrow afternoon, so it may be our only opportunity to do the interview face to face."

And what a face, I thought to myself, finally snapping out of it and coming back to my senses.

"Okay then... we have an hour or so to kill, how about a drink?"

"Whisky... please," she breathed, "whatever you have there is fine."

I'm sliding the Laphroaig across in front of her when I sense something behind me. Just a feeling, like when you wake up at night in a room that is pitch dark and sense a spider close on a wall. Like a tiny smell... almost not there, that brings back the crashing memory of something you can never quite put your finger on.

Anyway it's there, this feeling, right behind me. And in front of me the first woman I've been interested in since my wife decided not to be my wife anymore. Another story, but right now I have to choose between the woman of my dreams and the horror that I sense is lurking behind me. I'm telling myself that if I don't look around there won't be anything there, but I'm just not convincing myself. Yuka has this puzzled look on her face, but I tear myself away from those big eyes and slowly turn toward the window that runs the full length of the bar and looks out onto the street. At first all I can see is the reflection of the bar and the other patrons. Slowly I make out my own reflection... out there on the street looking straight back at me. Then slowly, as if time was winding down... out from behind my reflection steps the rentboy. He's wearing a black hoody with white lining and black formal pants. He's got on a blue t-shirt with the number 26 printed on a torn, winged heart, and a large silver padlock on heavy chain around his neck. He's there... he's real.

7. STAN AND ELAINE GET A NEW CAR

The past...

Stanley Robertson worked for a tool manufacturer. Forged spanners and chrome socket sets, that kind of stuff. Stanley sold their quality tools all over the state. They had just replaced his old company car with a brand new Ford Falcon sedan.

Man, Stanley loved that car. Powder blue with a big wide chrome speedometer and white-wall tyres. On Sunday morning Stanley had loaded his sample boxes into the spacious, rubber lined trunk of the powder blue Falcon, and run over it just one more time with the genuine 100% cowhide chamois, that came as a free gift with his company's 8-piece ring spanner set. Stanley's wife Elaine was inside getting ready for church. She placed her best Sunday hat (a small grey shape sprouting coloured berries and small flowers, and topped with a grey mesh) on her head and smiled contentedly at her image in the mirror. Every Sunday Elaine and Stanley went to church at 10am.

While Stan always asked God to help him make his sales targets, Elaine always prayed to the same God to give her the child she longed for. She knew in her heart that her and Stan would make terrific parents. She knew that God would finally answer her prayers.

But God wasn't listening, or worse... there was no God. That week Stanley would miss his sales targets and poor Elaine wouldn't talk to her God.

Stanley squeezed out his free chamois and went inside and washed up. Then he put on his tie and suit coat and grabbed his prayer book from the mantlepiece, where it lay unopened from one Sunday to the next. He told Elaine he would see her in the car, then went back out onto the drive and climbed behind the big plastic and chrome steering wheel of the powder blue

Falcon. Stan lost himself in the gleaming metal, fake leather and vinyl infused '*new car*' smell. He was roused from his reverie by Elaine sliding in next to him across the two tone blue vinyl seat. She smiled at him and leaned across and pecked him on the cheek. She was so proud of Stanley and his success at work. He was so perfect that as they pulled out of the drive she could imagine him hurrying home each night to play with the children she knew were coming.

As they drove along their street, they both sat up straight so as to be clearly recognised in the gleaming new powder blue Falcon.

. . .

Vincent Morelli wasn't going to church, but he was halfway to heaven on top of his girlfriend Amanda. They had been going out together for about three weeks, and when Vincent wasn't working as an apprentice painter or arguing with his father, he was inventing novel new ways of getting into Amanda's pants. But Amanda wasn't giving in so easily, and that morning was no different, so Vincent made a strategic departure, happy in the knowledge that he could try again tomorrow night and that eventually Amanda would succumb to his advances (actually he never thought 'succumb'. He didn't even know what the word meant. He just thought she would eventually crack under the pressure) and he'd have his way. Underneath all the Brylcreem and bravado, Vincent was a fairly decent guy and he really did like Amanda. In fact he felt she might even be 'the one'.

Vincent also drove a Ford, but it was an old beat-up thing with red fender panels. Vince left Amanda's house and picked up his pal Terry from about three blocks away. They drove to the Esplanade and sat on the sea wall, smoking cigarettes and throwing rocks at the seagulls. Finally they climbed back in the car and headed into the city looking for some kind of action. Five miles away Stanley and Elaine were coming off the highway headed for the cathedral. Elaine liked her churches serious and the city cathedral was her church of choice. The big chrome speedometer sat on thirty five miles an hour as they cruised down the street.

Vincent, meanwhile wheeled the old red and white Ford downtown, and then slowed to watch his own reflection in the department store windows. He stopped at a red light and sat tapping his fingers to the tune on the radio while Terry slouched on the passenger side reading the Sunday paper.

Stanley's powder blue Falcon cruised down the steep section of roadway and into the city. He veered away as the road split into two and became one way... and suddenly Stanley caught sight of something in his rear view mirror.

. . .

The light turned green and Vincent Morelli eased the old red and white Ford away and into the intersection.

There it was again! Something in the back seat. Stanley looked up into the rear view mirror and was looking straight into the sad eyes of a young Japanese boy. Stanley shouted in panic and Elaine followed his gaze into the back seat.

Vincent was halfway across the Murray Street intersection.

Elaine screamed a scream older than religion itself and Stanley's foot went right to the floor as the little boy's sad smile became the last thing Stanley and Elaine saw in this whole world. They were still looking back when the powder blue Falcon, with the big, wide chrome speedometer, now reading 58 miles per hour, tore through the side of Vincent Morelli's red and white car.

As Vincent's car left the road and climbed skyward, his head was whipped this way and that, severing the spinal column right up high, and rendering poor Vincent dead before the first pieces of cheap chrome and plastic tore into his face and body. Terry was thrown down into the footwell by the impact and suffered a broken leg, collarbone and ribs, along with a ruptured spleen. But by the time the red and white car came to a rest upside down in that doorway, Terry's heart was broken too. Vince was his best friend!

Stanley Robertson never made target that week and Elaine Robertson never knew the unconditional love of a child of her own. And God, if he really existed, never saw them in the cathedral that day.

8. ONE DOOR CLOSES AND ANOTHER OPENS

The past...

Patrick Leroux slid the carton of envelopes under the counter and looked up at the old wooden clock on the wall... 11.47am.

The morning had dragged on like a latin mass and Patrick was bored. Being the Postmaster in a small village in rural France really was the perfect job for someone as lazy as Patrick. There were only about two thousand people in the village and surrounds, and he pretty much opened if and when he felt like it. But then, so did almost every other business in the village.

He flopped back in the beat up old office chair and picked up yesterday's Le Monde. In true Patrick Leroux style, he scanned the newspaper carefully, avoiding any articles that looked long and taxing. Felice Gimondi of Italy wins the Tour de France. Presidents Giuseppe Saragat and Charles de Gaulle are due to open the Mont Blanc Tunnel in a few days. Patrick tosses the paper back on his desk and contemplates sliding the lock on the front door. That would involve getting up and walking around the counter and he just couldn't summon up the strength. He slid further down into the ancient leather and horse hair chair, flung his feet up onto his desk and closed his eyes. Soon Patrick Leroux was snoring away with his head flung back and his big slack mouth wide open and dribbling. He stepped off the train and down into the brown water at the base of the reed bed. Parting the tall reeds with his hands, he moved deeper into the pond. He heard the tinkling of a bell somewhere off in the distance and strained his ear to find the source. Moving through the reed bed he came across a group of people feasting around a formal dining table. As he approached, the diners all turned to face in his direction. The man at the head of the table wore a red topcoat and a filthy ruffled shirt. He reached down and picked up a small bell, shaking it daintily.

"Ladies and gentlemen... I think our dessert has arrived."

And with that he put down the bell and picked up a large carving knife and fork. He made towards Patrick as the other diners likewise waded in Patrick's direction. Patrick turned to run, but the swamp water seemed to have turned to molasses. His legs struggled to move through it. He felt the first hands grasping at his clothing as he fell backwards, landing on something solid. He kicked out at his pursuers and felt his feet sink even deeper, before striking the bottom of the pond. As he thrashed around he suddenly became aware of a young boy, maybe ten or eleven, standing quite still beside him.

The boy had oriental features, and for some reason Patrick felt this child could save him from the diners. He reached out and grabbed the boy by the elbow. The boy remained impassive... just staring down at him. Patrick let go the boy's elbow and grasped his hand. It was like he had grabbed a red hot poker. He felt the searing pain and smelt the sickening sweet odour of burning flesh. He let go the boy's hand and opened his mouth to scream, but all that came out was the distant sound of a tinkling bell. Patrick woke with a start and in a muck sweat. Embarrassed, he half expected to see someone at the counter.

Daydreaming is one thing, but nightmares in the middle of the day... merde! He grasped the arms of his old office chair to hoist himself upright and yelped in surprise, as a burning pain snatched at the palm of his right hand. He let go the chair and turned his hand palm up to see a series of angry red blisters forming across the heel of his hand and his fingertips. There was a black scorch mark ran across his wrist and up his forearm. Patrick Leroux stared at his hand and felt an unreasonable fear creep through his bones. Patrick Leroux now did all he could think of to do under the circumstances... he cried.

About an hour later, the Postmaster arrived at the doctor's office in the next village, which was about five miles away. His right hand was wrapped in a towel. He explained to the nurse on the front desk that he had burnt his hand badly (he didn't say how). He got into the doctor's room almost immediately and he winced as the doctor unwrapped the towel.

"This is some kind of joke yes?" said the doctor. Only he actually said it in French.

Patrick Leroux opened his eyes and looked at his right hand. Not a mark… then he groaned (in French of course).

· · ·

Six years to the day after Patrick Leroux's bad dream, Jennifer Beale stood with her best friend Lizzie Morgan, outside the gates of the CBS Soundstage 2 at the CBS Studio Centre in Los Angeles, California. They were to be part of the live audience at the filming of the Mary Tyler Moore Show. Lizzie was the big fan, but she'd talked Jennifer into going with her. At around 7pm, the studio gates were unlocked, and the studio audience was allowed into the seats on Stage 2. The filming didn't begin immediately. Actors were still in their dressing rooms running over their lines. A person who introduced himself as David Lloyd was the audience warm-up guy. He told crappy jokes to put the audience in a good mood, and then answered audience questions. About ten minutes in, Jennifer was bored to tears. She didn't like the show and in fact she really didn't like television much at all. Eventually, Mary Tyler Moore came out and was introduced. After the applause died down, she introduced all the other cast members and finally, the filming began.

After each scene ended, there were mind numbing repeats of certain lines to create close-up shots, with each actor repeating only the words and action to be seen in the close-ups on the final episode. While this was happening Jennifer noticed a teenage boy standing beside one of the scene flats or prop walls. He was Japanese and he was dressed in very weird clothes. She couldn't figure out what he was doing there. The next scene was a long shot of Mary Tyler Moore entering her boss, Lou Grant's office and it was shot from inside Grant's office. As the door opened and Mary entered from the back of stage, there was the boy, clearly framed in the background. Jennifer was momentarily distracted when the guy on camera two held up his hand and called the director on set. When Jennifer looked back, the boy was gone and the cameraman was being chided by the director for suggesting there was an unknown person on set. With the episode being shot in film, there was no way to check. Two other cast members and a crewman who had also seen the boy, decided that saying nothing was the best course of action. It seems the rest of the adoring audience were focused on their idol at the time so the shot stayed in. Finally the show and filming ended and Jennifer breathed a great sigh of relief, before grabbing hold of Liz and heading home.

"What was all that with the Japanese kid I wonder?" Jennifer said as they walked to the parking lot.

"What Japanese kid?"

"The Japanese kid in the funny clothes who just kind of turned up on the set. I don't think he was supposed to be there. Probably a messenger or something who took a wrong turn," laughed Jennifer. "Most exciting part of the whole show."

The following morning the editor and director were rolling through the rough cut which had been trimmed down from about an hour of film footage, when the director called a halt at the office scene.

"Who the hell is that?" he yelled.

"Dunno," said the editor. "But I do know there is no other take on this scene and, there is no suitable spill from either of the other two cameras. I've already clipped it down pretty close, but if I go any further I'll be clipping Mary's dialogue. Who is the kid anyway?"

"No idea, but I think I owe camera two an apology," said the director.

He ran his fingers through his hair.

"It doesn't matter. If it has to stay it has to stay."

9. AN INCIDENT IN AN IZAKAYA

The past...

Akira Matsumoto and his wife Sato looked at each other across the table in the izakaya. Akira didn't know whether to laugh or cry and Sato was just plain bursting with happiness.

"You're sure?" spluttered Akira, his saké cup paused midway between the table and his mouth.

"Yes of course I'm sure," laughed Sato. "I've been to see Dr. Yoshida."

Akira slowly came to life like a frozen lizard waking in the sun. He looked down at his hand as if seeing the saké cup for the first time, then quickly drained it and, now grinning like a fool, held it out to Sato to refill. With Akira's cup filled, Sato put down the flask and picked up her own cup, holding it out to Akira.

"No no," said Akira, "pregnant women shouldn't drink saké. Especially when they are carrying my son," he said with exaggerated pride. "From now on you need to obey your husband and eat and drink only what is good and healthy for you."

Sato reached across and filled her own cup, covering her mouth with her left hand, she giggled.

"Oh... so who made you the emperor; and what makes you think it will be a boy?"

Putting her cup down, she knelt up straight and reached across to take Akira's hand and draw it toward her stomach. Wide eyed, Akira strained to flatten his hand on her stomach.

"Feel see, it's a girl... sweet and delicate and feminine."

Suddenly Sato grabbed Akira's hand with both of hers and doubled over, her face contorted with pain. A loud moan escaped through her clenched teeth. Akira yelled in shock and pulled his hand away as if it was burning.

"My god, what's happening?' quivered Akira, looking at Sato's pain, "your stomach is red hot."

"I... I don't know," said Sato breathing fast and shallow. "It just came from nowhere and now it seems to be going just as quickly... maybe just a cramp."

"A cramp?" said Akira. "What about the burning stomach? I swear you were red hot."

Suddenly the door to the booth slid back and the manager was there on his knees.

"What's going on?" he stammered. "Is everything okay?"

"Yes, everything is fine. It was nothing, just a sharp cramp. I'm so sorry to disturb you," said Sato lowering her head in a bow.

"Okay then, if you're sure," said the manager. But he seemed unconvinced. He looked at them both and then slowly slid the door closed.

Akira looked at Sato and put his fingers to his lips. He could still see the manager's shadow through the shoji. Presently the manager's shadow stood up and moved slowly away down the hall. Sato hadn't breathed since the manager arrived in the doorway. Now she clawed a great breath into her lungs and picked up and drained her saké cup in one swift movement. She looked across at Akira who sat there with a startled expression on his face.

"Sato... " he started.

But she cut him off and insisted that they forget the cramp and just enjoy the moment. There was, after all, cause for celebration regardless of whether it was a boy or a girl. The rest of the evening passed without any further incident and by the time Sato and Akira paid their bill and went downstairs to look for a taxi, the incident was all but forgotten.

At six weeks, Sato and Akira had gone together to see Dr. Yoshida. They had already argued about doctors. Akira felt that Yoshida was too old and set in his ways, but Sato had insisted she wanted to remain with her family doctor. As old as he was, Dr. Yoshida had insisted on an ultrasound, with the first one at eight weeks.

"No," said Sato, "I do not want an ultrasound."

Akira was taken aback, but the doctor was insistent.

"But Sato, there is nothing to fear from an ultrasound. They are now quick, sophisticated and both painless and harmless to your health and the baby's. The benefits of discovering any abnormalities at an early stage far outweigh any inconvenience."

Sato turned and glared at Yoshida.

"It's got nothing to do with inconvenience. This is my baby and…"

Akira went to speak, but Sato cut him off and snapped…

"…and my body. Do you both understand that… *my* body."

For the next six months or so, Sato enjoyed a fairly normal pregnancy. The strange thing was that every time she and Akira discussed the baby's gender, she had cramping episodes of ever increasing strength. Dr. Yoshida could find no problem during his normal physical examinations and tried again to talk her into an ultrasound. Failing that, he suggested that maybe it was a psychological issue and could be dealt with by counselling. But

Sato knew different. She knew something was not quite right, but she hid her concerns from Akira who, was delightfully happy in his new role as father-to-be. Her dreams were increasingly strange and frightening. She feared sleep each night, as it led her into some strange netherworld in which she was falling and then searching endlessly for her lost child... a child that was yet to be born.

She looked up at Akira, who was slouched in his chair watching one of his strange quiz shows. Look at him, she thought. How can I spoil everything for him? After all, I might be wrong, thought Sato, maybe the doctor is right. Maybe it is just me. The baby in her womb kicked out and Sato struggled up out of her chair and quickly left the room to hide the coming cramp from Akira.

. . .

Seven weeks later, Sato lay staring up at the blinding overhead light, while Akira stood beside her gripping her hand and talking gibberish. *What does he mean by breathe* she thought? *I do that every day.* Sato never swore out loud, but right now she was wishing Akira would take his patronising platitudes and piss off. She was breathing and she was totally calm, because this was all happening as it did in her dream. She now knew, with total conviction, what was about to happen and she accepted that knowledge with a grim, but calm resolve. What else could she do? She now knew the total wasteland of her future. She had seen it in the dream and that dream was converging rapidly with reality. The nurse avoided her gaze, but Sato could tell it was her. She recognised her even with the mask.

When the doctor told her to push, she responded with a half hearted effort, but only for Akira's sake. Suddenly she felt the thing inside her slide effortlessly out. The whole world went quiet, stopped what it was doing... and then with a quick breath everything returned to normal. She didn't need to look at the doctor, or at Akira. She already knew. To them, everything seemed normal. The doctor handed the healthy baby boy onto Sato's stomach while the nurse tied and cut the umbilical cord. The doctor tried to place the boy in Sato's arms, but she swatted it away, reacting, as though it was a spider.

"Get them away from me. Get them away from me." she screamed

And the nurse wrapped the tiny boy in a sheet and hastily removed him from the room.

When they wheeled her back to her ward, Akira remained in the delivery room, stunned beyond comprehension. He never even saw her go.

Back in her room Sato waited calmly while the nurse pulled up the covers and straightened the room, chattering on about what a wonderful moment this must be... what a wonderful, beautiful boy.

She ran through how the rest of the day would go... when Sato could see her child. You'll feel better soon. That sort of thing; but Sato wasn't listening.

When the nurse finally left, Sato slipped quietly out of her bed. She was shaky on her feet, but totally calm as she slid back the glass door to the balcony, took two steps forward, looked back briefly at the door, climbed the railing and stepped out into oblivion.

. . .

"But I'm telling you, she just appeared... out of nowhere, right in front of me," said the driver of the black Honda Accord. "There was nothing I could do... nothing. I barely had time to brake."

30

The young policeman watched as the ambulance attendants lifted the lifeless form of the woman in the hospital gown, down off the bonnet of the Honda, and zipped it into the body bag.

. . .

Upstairs in the hospital Akira had walked zombie-like to his wife's room. When he arrived the bed was empty. They must have taken her somewhere, he thought. *I'll just wait here.* He heard the screech of tyres and the dull thud out on the road in front of the hospital. It registered, but only just. *Some poor sod just got hit by a car. Still, at least they are close to a hospital.*

Akira Matsumoto was Shinto. In the days following the death of his wife, through his crushing grief, he adhered the rituals of the Shinto Buddhist cremation ceremony and allowed Sato's remaining ashes and bones to be buried in her family's ancestral plot on the hillside below Kiyomizudera, the Pure Water Temple high on the hill behind Kyoto City.

A square, clean grey granite stone thrusts up among the stones of the ancestors like a new tree in the forest.

In Japan the name Kioshi means quiet. Since the day he was born, the boy had not made one single sound. Not a cry or a whimper... nothing! Akira found himself resenting the child. He blamed the baby for the death of his beloved Sato. He wanted nothing to do with it. On the twelfth day of his still short life, Akira's baby son was handed into the care of Sato's family. Everybody believed that Akira would come to want and love his son in time. He just needed to grieve. The child had still not made a sound, and so it was that the child was named Kioshi. Kioshi Matsumoto... the quiet son.

In the following twelve months, Akira Matsumoto's life changed even more. He became the butterfly that morphed into a slug. He had been a man in love, with a beautiful wife, a new son and a junior executive position at Dai Nippon Cable. Now, just twelve short months later he was a broken man. No wife, no son, fired from his company for drunken behaviour, and nothing to look forward to but the cold alleys of Osaka as a place to live.

. . .

On a particularly cold night, Akira's cousin Miyuki was walking back to her hotel with a group of friends. She was enjoying a weekend in Osaka and she and her friends were taking a shortcut through Shinsaibashi Suji after a great night out. The arcades were almost empty. Most of the stores were closed. Every so often the arcade would echo to the great rattling cacophony of someone entering or leaving a pachinko parlour. Miyuki was happy. She liked Osaka. It was different than Kyoto where she was fairly rigidly bound by the restrictions of her family life and surroundings. But tonight was different. No need to think of any of that.

The shuttered service entrance to Daimaru Department Store was home to two men. Street people. Their meagre belongings piled under them in plastic bags and their filthy bodies part covered by stiff cardboard blankets. Two doors further down she saw another sleeping form. This one looking more comfortable than most in a warm sleeping bag. As Miyuki drew closer to the sleeping figure, she felt some kind of familiarity with that dirty, smudged head and filthy hair.

She slowed behind the group and let them walk on ahead. She was inexplicably drawn toward the prone figure in the doorway; both fascinated and horrified in the same instant. She didn't know what was drawing her on, but she knelt and trembling, carefully pulled back the edge of the sleeping bag, to reveal the startled face of her cousin Akira. They had been great friends before the tragedy had seen Akira cut himself off from his family. Sato's family didn't want to see him. They now blamed him for their daughter's death and resented his attitude to the child. His own family understood his grief and wanted him back home in Kyoto where they could watch over him and take care of him.

But on this night, Miyuki had finally persuaded Akira to come with her to her hotel, where she had smuggled him in to her tiny room. He now sat propped between the bed and the wall, unsure of what to say or do. He drained the last of the coffee Miyuki had bought him. He was embarrassed that she should see him like this, but the strong bond between them had got him this far.

"I'm so happy to see you," said Miyuki. "Nobody knows where you are. Nobody has heard from you for months. Your mother has been so worried."

Akira opened his mouth to speak, but just a squeak came out. The tiniest noise like a small bird caught deep in a thorn bush. He had not spoken to anyone, not used his voice for such a long time. The only noises out of him had been hollow sobs like the sound of boulders settling in an empty desert. He tried again.

"I don't know what to do," he croaked haltingly, "Sato has gone and Kioshi won't leave me alone."

"I can't pretend to understand how you feel," said Miyuki, somewhat taken aback by hearing Akira use the name of his son. "The memory must be unbearable. You must miss them both so much."

Akira just stared at his empty coffee can. Presently he spoke again.

"I miss my beautiful Sato," he said, "but I want the boy to leave me alone."

Miyuki felt the room go cold.

"You may never get over this," said Miyuki, "but I'm sure the pain of the memory will fade with time."

"No, you don't understand. It's not the memory. It's Kioshi... every night and every day I feel his presence."

"Now now," said Miyuki. "I want to take you home. Will you let me do that Akira? Will you let me take you home to your family?"

Akira tried to speak, but his voice wouldn't work. He started to tremble, and Miyuki watched as a tear broke from her poor cousin's left eye and traced a clean swathe down across his filthy cheek.

All he could do was nod. But that was enough.

10. DON'T THROW THE BABY OUT WITH THE BATHWATER

The past...

Osaka may stay up all night, but after ten it was almost impossible to buy new clothes anywhere in the city, so Miyuki had to content herself with getting Akira to take a long overdue shower, then slide back into his smelly old clothes. He emerged from the bathroom looking only marginally better but, with his hair slicked to one side and some of Miyuki's eau d'cologne splashed on, he would do. By the time she had calmed him down and talked him into returning to Kyoto with her, it was five in the morning, but finally, he relaxed enough to sleep. He was sitting on the bed when suddenly he just fell sideways. It reminded Miyuki of something out of a cartoon or an old comedy and she stifled a giggle as she hauled his feet up onto the bed. She settled herself into the tiny bucket chair and managed a bit of disturbed sleep before the sound of Akira stirring woke her.

She was concerned that if she left him alone for too long, he would disappear again, and while she desperately wanted a shower, she made do with a quick splash from the cold tap. Gathering up her belongings, she told Akira to follow in two minutes and wait for her on the street. She went down to the lobby to check out. While Miyuki was at the desk, leaving messages for her friends, she tried to divert attention from the bum who walked out of the lift and across the lobby. The desk clerk called out to Akira to stop, but he just kept walking until he was through the door and onto the street. As she followed him out, the morning sun fought it's way down between the buildings and spread it's weak light across the forlorn figure of Akira Matsumoto, waiting there on the sidewalk.

Fate is like a bulldozer. An analogy of course, but, like a bulldozer, fate moves on inexorably; pushing everything in its path, crushing the slow and relocating the more vigorous. Every event no matter how seemingly insignificant is linked in a timeline, and fate controls this timeline. So what transpired next didn't just happen by chance. It started way back in the beginning of time itself, where two independent event lines, insignificant in themselves, pushed out across the planet and the moment they started, they set in play their own inevitable intersection... and this , this is the stuff of fate!

And so it was that as Akira sat on the train, watching his own reflection speed between Osaka and Kyoto, the infant Kioshi made his first noise. After twelve months without so much as a whimper, Kioshi started to scream. And this was a scream that came from the depths and carried with it the penance for the sins of all mankind.

Sato's mother jumped out of bed and ran to Kioshi's side. The child thrashed about like a trapped animal, his eyes wide open and staring off into some other place.

On the train to Kyoto, Miyuki saw Akira clutch his head in pain, his eyes screwed shut, his teeth clenched in his jaw.

Sato's mother leant down to pick up Kioshi and comfort him, but as she did so his head snapped around to face her and he stopped screaming as if it had never been. All that remained was the echo of something not right. Sato's mother shook herself to be rid of the cold, unreasonable fear that had enveloped her. She sat with the child for almost two hours, never taking her eyes off him. Finally, content that the child was settled she stood up and went to the window. Outside all was normal. The cleaners and street sweepers went about their business, and the first threads of traffic started weaving its procession past her window.

She turned back and looked at the wall clock. 7.13am. By the time she bathed, dressed and had breakfast, it would be 8 o'clock. Then she could call Dr. Ohno at the hospital. He had always told her to contact him immediately if there was any change. If Kioshi ever spoke or just made any kind of noise. And now, it had happened.

When she arrived at the hospital with Kioshi, she had waited only a short while outside Ohno's office, when she was approached by a nurse who greeted her by name and reached down and took young Kioshi from her arms. That was odd. The boy would never react with anyone else, and he seemed almost pleased to see the nurse. In the instant before she handed him to the nurse, she could have sworn he actually recognised her.

"Dr. Ohno wants the boy to have a thorough physical check up before he sees him," said the nurse. "It won't take long, maybe fifteen minutes."

As the nurse turned away with Kioshi, Sato's mother was overtaken by a feeling of dread. It was like the world had slipped sideways about a meter and left her behind. In a split second she had caught up to the world again, but the sensation left her dizzy and disorientated. And there was something else. Something disquieting.

While she was getting her bearings, the doctor's door opened and Ohno stepped out.

"Oh!" he said. "I thought you were bringing the boy with you."

"Yes... I have," said Sato's mother. "Your nurse has taken him for the check up you wanted."

Ohno's eyes widened in surprise.

"My nurse... check up," he said. "I have no nurse and I ordered no check up."

The hospital where Ohno held his clinic was a small inner city hospital, and it took less than fifteen minutes to establish that the boy was no longer in the hospital and that Sato's mother's description of the nurse matched no current staff members.

Kioshi was gone!

As Akira stepped off the train he turned to Miyuki and grabbed her by the arm, pulling her close.

"Kioshi is gone," he whispered through his teeth, flecks of spittle forming at the sides of his mouth. "He's lost... forever."

Miyuki watched, almost frightened, as Akira's head slumped down on his chest. He was sobbing. She couldn't understand what he was saying, and sought only to comfort him when she said...

"It's okay; Kioshi is with Sato's mum. We'll get you cleaned up and sorted out, then maybe tomorrow we can arrange for you to visit him."

Akira turned on her, eyes burning like a madman.

"Why don't you listen? When will everybody understand? The boy is not normal. Sato knew that, even before he was born. That's why she..." His voice trailed off again to a whisper, like he was talking to himself.

"It doesn't matter now," he said, "he's gone... maybe it's for the best."

He looked up at Miyuki, who was standing stock still. Stunned.

"I'm sorry," he said. "Thank you for trying to help."

And he wandered off along the platform, and was soon swallowed up by the throng of people coming and going at the station.

11. MY FEET HAVE A MIND OF THEIR OWN

The present...

He's smiling at me... the kind of smile that says one thing and means another entirely. Somewhere off in the distance I can hear Yuka calling to me. I think she is asking me what is wrong. One minute I'm in love, the next minute I'm ignoring her. But I can't help it.

My gaze... no, my whole being is centred on the boy. I can't take my eyes off him. It's not bravado... it's fear. If I look away what might happen? Clearly he's following me, but why? He's getting bolder, much bolder. But through my fear I feel my feet slide off the stool rail and make contact with the granite floor. I feel them moving, one after the other, one in front of the other, across the floor of the bar and out into the expansive foyer. They're working on their own, taking me towards the automatic door. Through the glass my eyes are still locked on the boy's face. He's standing stock still, only his head turns, following me as I make my way outside. Now I can see a look of uncertainty in his eyes. I break and run for the main door. It's not glass, but solid panel and I lose sight of him for just an instant. I careen into the doors, too fast for the automatic sensor to get them moving. When they finally open, they slide apart with a theatrical 'swishing' noise, like the sound of a magician's wand passing through the air. And, like magic... the boy is gone. I run across the forecourt to the footpath and look both ways, but I see no sign of him.

Finally I turn back toward the hotel. I see Yuka framed in the big bar window. She shakes her head in disgust and fixes me with that '*I should have known better*' look, and... like the rentboy, she too has disappeared before I can get back to the foyer.

Great... story of my life. But every cloud has a silver lining and this one has two glasses of Laphroaig, so I head back to the bar and reach out for the closest glass. It's only then I notice that my hands are shaking uncontrollably. I also noticed the blister on the pad of my index finger is back, and it is punctuated by a great black sooty flash that runs up, over the heel of my hand and onto my wrist.

. . .

Under the city, the boy makes his way back to the tunnels beneath Shinjuku Station. He is weakening. He has been on the surface too often and for too long. He would normally go only where his soul took him, but this was different. He felt a connection to this man. He didn't understand it. He felt he knew him. He felt maybe this man could help answer the questions that crowded his mind. The rest of the boys exhibited no such doubts. This was his burden alone. He held snatches of memory in the deepest recesses of his mind and he had found no answers. But now, with this man, maybe there could be some answers.

12. WHO'S THAT THERE BEHIND THE GREEN DOOR?

The past...

The nurse left the waiting room and headed down the short corridor to the back entrance. She stopped, checked behind her to be sure she was not being observed, then stepped quickly through the door to the women's toilets.

Once inside she placed the child on the floor of a cubicle and recovered the bag she had hidden in the cleaner's closet. In the cubicle she quickly peeled off her uniform and shoes and pulled on a floral dress and blue coat. Finally, she stepped into a pair of heels, picked up the child, left the cubicle and, carrying the bag across one arm and young Kioshi in the other, she opened the door a crack to see if the corridor was empty. Seeing that it was, she slipped out and made briskly but calmly for the rear door. Once outside she headed straight for the station and down onto the Shinkansen platform for Tokyo.

A few hours later, a bullet train pulled in to Shinjuku Station. Anyone watching the platform carefully would have seen a woman in a floral dress and a blue coat, step off the train carrying a small child. They would have also noticed that the woman in the floral dress and blue coat paused briefly until the last passengers were off before she turned against the flow of the other passengers, and made her way to the far end of the platform. She paused again at a green metal door then, content that nobody was watching, she slipped through the unlocked door, turned and locked it behind her. She was in a broom cupboard. She went to the right hand wall and pushed, and the side and back wall slid away to reveal a door and stairs on the other side. She started down the stairs.

The woman made her way down, down, down, ever downwards, until she came to a dimly lit corridor that led to an old machinery room of some sort. In here there were a number of tall, grey metal lockers. The woman in the floral dress and the blue coat made straight for the one on her right. It was no different from the others in the room, but the woman reached around beside it and pulled. It swung easily outward, revealing a white metal door. This one had a small shuttered spy hole at eye height. She tapped out a code on the cold metal door and presently, the spy hole shutter slid back. A pair of disembodied eyes stared out at her with no emotion. The eyes came closer to the opening and flickered down to the child she was carrying. Then the spy hole closed. Suddenly the door swung open and the woman was ushered into a small room finished in bright, white tiles. The room was sparsely furnished, containing only a simple wooden table and a simple wooden chair. There was another plain white door opposite the one through which she had entered. The man with the eyes wore a dark suit. He indicated that the nurse should sit at the table, then he stepped forward and took Kioshi from her arms. He stepped through the other door. She had no idea what was behind that door and she didn't care. Her arrangement was a simple one. She received her instructions by telephone.

They told her when a baby was to be collected and she collected it. She brought it here as instructed and left with her money. No questions asked. She had brought five babies here, the first four close together, nearly a year ago, but this one had been different. It had not gone to plan. When the mother had stepped off the balcony, it had drawn attention to the child and she had been unable to get this infant out of the hospital. She didn't know what to do, so she did nothing.

Finally they had contacted her and told her to wait for further instructions. Those instructions were almost nine months coming and she was angry that she had not been able collect her fee. Once things had died down and the police had seemed to lose interest in the other disappearances, they told her to get this last infant. It had taken another two months of watching and waiting for an opportunity, but now finally here she was. She was startled from her reverie when the white door opened again and the man in the dark suit stepped back into the room. He placed a thick white envelope on the table. She knew it contained ten million yen. Briefly, she considered asking for more, due to the problems on this job, but one look at the man in the dark suit and she decided against it.

She stood up to leave.

"We will be in touch," said the man in the dark suit. But then he always did.

He opened the outer door for her and she stepped through. As it closed behind her, she shouldered the metal cabinet back into place. Sometime later, she emerged back onto the far end of the platform. She cracked the door slightly, then peered out to ensure she would not be observed. Then she slipped through and quietly closed the green metal door behind her.

Had she re-opened the green metal door she would have found it was just a small services cupboard again, going nowhere and containing just a fire extinguisher and couple of old buckets and brooms. But she didn't re-open the door. Not just because it was locked behind her, but because the woman in the floral dress and blue coat was halfway down the platform, daydreaming about how she would spend the ten million.

Over ninety feet below the ground, the infant Kioshi was carried down a clean, white tiled corridor and into a room fitted with all manner of medical equipment. The infant was placed gently on a raised bed with lift up chrome rails and crisp white sheets. The man in the dark suit stood for some time looking down at the child. Presently he turned from the bed and walked to a desk against the wall. He picked up the telephone handset and spoke into it.

"He's here," he said.

13. JUST ANOTHER SLICE OF Pi

The very distant past...

It was August 1955. It was around 9.45 in the evening and it was warm; almost 23 degrees. The woman wandered across the grass and into the shadows by the bamboo stand. She was dressed in a drab blue shift or housecoat of some kind, and she was apparently pregnant. She seemed disorientated. She was panicked and struggling to understand. Suddenly, like a marionette dropped from it's strings, she folded sideways on the grass clutching her stomach. Almost immediately she felt the baby coming. She breathed hard and when she felt the time was right, she rolled on her back and pushed harder.

She felt the baby slide out of her onto the grass, but there was no joy in her eyes, and no longer any panic. In fact, there was nothing much human about her. She gave one great rending shudder and reached around to jerk on the tie of her gown, until it tore from its anchor point. Then she groped down between her legs and hauled on the umbilical cord. When she was a girl she had seen puppies born on her uncle's farm, so she knew what she had to do. The woman avoided looking at the baby and craned her neck to look more closely at the cord. It had stopped pulsing and there was a lighter area appearing at one point. She tied the gown cord tightly around the umbilical then strained even harder until she could reach it with her teeth. She quickly chewed through it, then pushed herself back away from the tiny clump of life now squirming on the grass. Wiping her face with the sleeve of the gown, she pushed herself upright. The placenta parted and the woman staggered away into the shadows, where she stopped and finally looked at the child. Then she was gone.

The baby, a boy, was found on the lawn outside the hospital by a groundsman about five minutes later. He was rushed into the emergency room of the hospital where, after whatever tests that could be done, were done, he was found to be in good health.

When the child had been brought in by the groundsman, the police had been called. An extensive search had failed to find any trace of the mother. The only proof that she ever existed were the newborn child and the placenta found on the grass near the child. All the hospitals were checked and the nearby neighbourhoods were canvassed by a police van with a blaring tannoy on the roof. But the woman was never found, and nobody came forward to offer any assistance or explanation.

It was finally assumed that the child was the result of an unwanted dalliance, maybe a young, unmarried mother unable to live with the shame. Or maybe the child of an Hibakusha, an 'explosion affected' person. It was almost ten years to the day since the atomic bomb had been dropped on Hiroshima and it seemed the number of Hibakusha grew bigger every day. Unfortunately, some Hibakusha women felt that, while they were dying, their child would stand a better chance of survival if raised by someone else. However, this child's subsequent tests showed no sign of the horrid ailments found more commonly in the children of Hibakusha, and so he was not classified 'Nisei Hibakusha' or second generation A-bomb victim. He was finally classed as an orphan and, after some fifteen months, was made available for adoption.

During the early days he was kept at the hospital. Maybe there was some emotion involved because he had been found in the hospital grounds, so he 'kind of' belonged. From the very beginning it was obvious this child was a survivor and in the ensuing weeks, his every action, albeit those of a new born baby, was evidenced with resolve. He did not seem a happy baby. Not necessarily unhappy, but definitely focused. And so, when his birth certificate was prepared by the hospital, he was named Tetsuya.

Tetsuya was adopted by Noriko and Hiromitsu Hiroko.

Noriko was thirty nine and a physics teacher. Hiromitsu was a biologist, a serious man who escaped into his own world of science fiction novels, of which he owned a vast library. Having had no children of their own, they had decided that Noriko would leave her job and they would pursue adoption.

That they loved Tetsuya, there could be no doubt. But they had no experience in child raising, and did their best with whatever resources they had at their disposal. From an early age, Noriko occupied an inquisitive young Tetsu with basic displays and experimentations in physics.

Hiromitsu was at first uncomfortable with the child, but as the boy grew older he dropped the 'kiddie' bedtime stories for something a little meatier. At age three, one of Tetsu's favourite stories was 'Urashima Taro', an ancient Japanese legend about a fisherman who rescues a turtle. He is rewarded for this with a visit to Ryugo-jo, the palace of Ryujin, the Dragon God, under the sea. The fisherman stays there for three days and, upon returning to his village, finds himself three hundred years in the future.

Young Tetsu, went on to devour his father's expanding collection of science fiction. He was strangely drawn less to the more obvious and colourful, and more to the thoughtful writings of authors like Jules Verne, H.G. Welles, Franz Kafka and H.P. Lovecraft. Welles' '*The Time Machine*' was a favourite as was Lovecraft's '*The Unnamable*'. Anything that dealt with the notions of expanded time, or the manipulation of time, became epistles for a young furtive imagination. In 1969 his father bought him Kurt Vonnegut's latest novel, '*Slaughterhouse Five*', and the fourteen year old Tetsuya found accord with Billy Pilgrim.

So Tetsuya immersed himself in a world of how. How to combine the fantasy of time travel with the science of physics? He was bright... and he knew there was something missing from the equation that was his life. He felt it, but it was not until he turned eighteen and, was preparing to enter his first year of university, that his father and mother sat him down and explain to him that he had been adopted. They explained how and where he had been found. They told him honestly about the search for his mother and father, at least as much as they knew. And that was all it took. The circle was complete. At eighteen years of age Tetsuya Hiroko had his life's quest laid out before him. It all fit.

Tetsuya Hiroko became a study machine... at the expense of all social mores. At university he found answers, then questions, then better ways to ask new questions, that resulted in more expansive answers. He didn't mix easily with other students, male or female. He simply felt superior. What looked like awkward was in reality lack of interest. What looked like geek... was really focus. Most of the information was there and he gathered it mercilessly from books, lectures, lecturers and other students. By the time he left university he had completed multiple Bachelors, Masters, and Doctoral programs. But, more importantly, using the university facilities he had begun experimentation into the management or expansion of time and space.

Of course, very early in the piece, Tetsu had satisfied himself that he had exhausted every possible avenue to track down the truth of his past. He was ruthless in his quest, but he was also aware that to find any answers in the conventional manner would somewhat undermine his motive for future experimentations with time. Following his historical searches, he started examining the dearth of time/space theories. There was no shortage of theories. After all, this was the seventies. 'What ifs' and 'wormholes' were standard topics of conversation at office water coolers and artsy parties. Science Fiction was becoming an important genre. But to Tetsu, this was serious stuff. He looked carefully at each theory, crackpot or otherwise. He mapped them out on paper, drew diagrams and extruded equations as, one by one, he whittled his group of possibles down to a mere few.

One of Tetsu's student group had set himself the impossible task of working out the number of decimal places possible in Pi. Normally this was written as approximately 3.14159. Tetsu knew the guy was wasting his time and that the decimals were infinite. He knew because he had tried this himself when he was younger and had got to around a million places, deciding wisely that he would never live long enough to complete the math. He realised he only had one lifetime and so he needed to find shortcuts to problems.

Faced with three or four possible time theories, Tetsuya thought now of the Pi problem. He instinctively knew that if he tried to chase down three or four theories and by chance started at the wrong end, he could simply run out of lifetime to complete. So for a scientist, a professional skeptic, he did the most unscientific thing imaginable. He went with his instinct. His gut feel. There was one theory that seemed more plausible than the rest. Just seemed mind! With a bit of tweaking here and there he could imagine that this broad theory might just be progressed from the theoretical to the practical.

Once he had made his decision; this great unscientific leap of faith, he excised all notion of the proprietary name given to this theory. After all, he reasoned, I have grown it and will grow it even further. It will not be the same. Over the coming weeks he visually tested 'his' theory. He needed to start basic. Only when he had a finished sketch of what his time theory looked like could he get down to business. His final sketch reminded him of a documentary he had seen, where a factory produced various pastas in commercial quantities. As the sheet of pastry emerged from the final set of rollers, and prior to it being cut, the machine housing the rollers moved back and forth in each direction, and this caused the pastry to fold backwards and forwards upon itself, like a long flat serpentine snake. It folded out flat, touching, but separated by, a thin film of flour, from the layer beneath. When the machine reached the extent of its travel, the pastry formed a nice clean arc as it turned back in the other direction to repeat the process.

Tetsuya Hiroko made a quick trip to the market and bought himself a block of ready made pastry and some plain flour. Back at home, he searched around for something with which to roll out the pastry. A large bottle of Asahi beer was pressed into service and with a thin dusting of flour on the table, Tetsu set to work. He ended up with a narrow piece of pastry about as long as his arm. He took the pastry and held it up in one hand. He brought it down on the table and then folded it back and forth making sure to dust between each layer. Sure, his pastry didn't look as precise as the factory job, but with a bit of refolding and general manipulation he was happy with the result.

He sat back and studied his creation for a long time, then he got off his stool and dug a toothpick out of his cabinet drawer. He pushed the toothpick slowly down through the first layer of pastry. Getting down on his haunches and up real close, he could see the toothpick straining to pierce through the top layer, and pushing down into the next, as it sought to break through the pastry. Once it broke through, he observed it separating the two top layers and pushing down on the second layer, creating tension before it finally pierced that layer too. He also observed that the pastry seemed thinner where it made the fair radius to turn back on itself. Each layer touched the next, but was separated only by the thin dusting of flour. The flour separated the layers, prevented them from joining or mixing, but did not prevent intrusion from one layer to the next. Also, what happened on one layer could clearly impact on other layers without full intrusion, but only at the exact adjacent point. If he pierced only halfway through a layer, and then peeled that layer back, it revealed the memory of the event in the next layer. Déjà vu... maybe!

So... Tetsuya Hiroko had his theory. In his theory, time existed in parallel layers of specified length separated only by a thin, effective but penetrable medium. Then Tetsu did something he rarely did; in fact something he had not done for some time. He laughed. He dug out his camera and took a photo of the pasta model... for posterity. Then feeling the pangs of hunger, he dined on his raw pastry model washed down with a warm bottle of Asahi beer. Delicious!

After finally exhausting his studies at university, Tetsu was snapped up by an astrophysics company with a division involved in the study of space and time. Tetsu brought to the company a new and flexible attitude to the boundaries of physics and as a result, the company was hastened down the path to the marketing of several lucrative commercial applications. Within a few short years, Tetsuya Hiroko was given project head status. Whilst being readily available as an extra 'head' or advisor on other projects, and within certain established guidelines for commercial reality, he was free to pursue whatever projects he wished. He was essentially a one-man think tank with a huge research resource at his disposal. He also had at his disposal, some of the finest mathematical minds in Japan, as well as a troop of assistants, undergrads, interns and tech aids.

Tetsu created various projects as a blind for his major, private focus. These projects were generally components of his big picture and some would lead to commercial application. Others were classed as pure research into space/time. The founder and President of the company had a personal and philanthropic interest in the area of space/time, and was actually a bit of a closet science fiction addict. It wasn't too hard for Tetsu to push the speculative science research projects into the queue.

So now Tetsuya Hiroko had a motive, a theory and a means to try and prove that time travel was possible.

The motive was of course contrived. He never really entertained the idea that he would find his real parents, but time travel... now there's a motive for you. The parent thing was really just a means of picking a date to target. He had to start somewhere, it may as well have some relevance. At least this is what he told himself. However there was still something. A feeling of emptiness and it wasn't longing for his parents... it was something else. Tetsuya Hiroko pushed on into the unknown. By 1987, Tetsuya Hiroko was close. His theory was beginning to bear fruit. He now thought he had nearly as many knowns as unknowns. Of course it was still just a theory.

He had started out by having his team develop an exhaustive global data base of what he referred to as unexplained paranormal events or UPE's. A UPE was anything from a well documented déjà vu case, to a full blown alien encounter. In between were tens of thousands of credible but unexplainable hauntings, mind readings, time travel experiences and psychic happenings. Of course there were also tens of thousands of other events that went in what the younger techs called the 'wacko' basket. It took five years for the team to bring the database all the way from the first recorded event to the present day. Not full-time of course, but near enough to it. They had managed to turn up one or two commercial possibilities along the way, but nothing that would really justify the expenditure. And even though Tetsuya's theoretical mind was producing bankable results on other projects, company middle management was starting to sniff around the project which was becoming known, less than affectionately, as Hiroko's Black Hole. Fortunately for Tetsu, at this point he was able to cut back on human resources. Tetsu's cover had held, but it was starting to fray around the edges.

Of course a decent number of current events continued to roll in on a daily basis and so, while most of the team were now transferred to legitimate company projects, a small group was maintained to keep the records up to date. These current events were fresh. Not so much time for the trail to go cold, and so they tended to allow the team to drill down further into the available data. From this point on, his mathematicians had become involved, and they had spent over two and a half years converting credible information, which was a very small percentage of the overall information received but still a huge final database, into mathematical formulae.

Finally after seven years, certain numbers started to stand out in the random streams generated. 36, 72, 108, 144, 180, etc. All multiples of 36, but 36 appeared around fifty times more frequently than any of the multiples and the multipliers seemed to drop away with a nice even scale rate. In addition, as the multipliers stretched out, the event impact weakened. When the computers worked backwards from these weakest impact events, they almost invariably located incidents at each 36 year interval. On more than one occasion, subjects who reported an incident in their youth, when interviewed by the team, reluctantly admitted the existence of another incident that they had left unreported 36 years later. In their middle age, some people were more circumspect about admitting any involvement with strange paranormal incidents.

And so the original scientific model for Tetsu's space/time theory held up. It was possible to pierce multiple layers of pasta and just leave a slight impact in a subsequent layer. After seven years work, Tetsuya Hiroko was prepared to deduce that the length of each parallel strand of time was 36 years. He was also prepared to deduce that time travel was theoretically possible provided it was undertaken forwards or backwards in increments of 36 years. In other words, if you wanted to be there live for the legendary Evel Knievel's attempt to jump the Snake River Canyon in Twin Falls Idaho on September 8th. 1974, you would have to travel from September 8th. in the year 2010. But, his team argued, wouldn't you have to start out from Snake River Canyon in 2010 to arrive in Snake River Canyon in 1974. Half the team were of the opinion that yes, you would have to. But this raised even further questions concerning the earth's rotation and its orbital position at 36 year intervals. It's all very well to start out in Snake River Canyon, but where in space was Snake

River Canyon relative to the earth's rotation, and its revolution around the sun, 36 years ago.

Half the team thought the position of the planet was irrelevant because theory was just that; theory. In all those years, and with all those resources the team was no closer to finding a trigger for time travel. The evidence that it could occur was overwhelming, and the cycles seemed undeniable. But what event or circumstance could form the bridge between time parallels remained a mystery. This was an area of personal interest to their boss, Dr. Tetsuya, to such an extent that he spent many hours interviewing a small percentage of the people on the database who had at least two credible experiences.

The 'think tank' sessions with his team were spirited and rewarding. Tetsu sat in on these sessions not as a leader, but as a participant. This was as close as he ever came to sharing a familial experience in his adult life. He was not aware that these sessions were the only thing that kept many members of his team on the project. Here, he became one of them. Excitable, argumentative... almost playful at times. Quite the opposite of the repressive slavedriver that normally pushed them beyond the bounds of reason. One or two of the team were quite brilliant theorists. Almost, he said to himself, but not quite, as brilliant as he was.

One undergraduate in particular, was becoming a standout. He was Hideo Tanaka, and Tetsuya sometimes thought if you opened the top of his head it would be full of wires and solid state components. He was that rarest of humans for whom the word 'faith' did not exist. He would accept nothing at face value. It was all science to Hideo. He was on the way to becoming that most perfect of scientists, the absolute sceptic.

When Hideo was a child growing up in Ashoro, a small town on Hokkaido, his father once took him ice fishing on Lake Akan. It was January and the ice was thick. It was dotted with many tents and fishermen. Deep fried tempura smelt were one of his father's favourites, and the smelt were made all that much sweeter by his catching them himself. But the nine year old Hideo would not venture onto the ice. He tried to explain to his father that it was just frozen water... it could break. There definitely was a point at which it would crack. His father had pointed out all the fisherman already on the ice, but this just hardened Hideo's resolve. He explained to his father that they themselves, might be the final additional weight that caused the ice to crack.

That day his father fished for smelt alone, while Hideo read books and sometimes watched out the window of the lodge at Akankohan. That evening Hideo went to bed hungry. His father's lesson was meant to deny him the tempura smelt because he had not aided in their capture. It didn't matter. Hideo went to bed hungry but happy. He had had a wonderful time in the warm lodge reading about the workings of volcanos and maybe, just maybe, he had saved the lives of his father and all the other fishermen by not adding his critical weight to the ice on Akan.

Tetsuya came to value Hideo's opinions and thought of him as a younger version of himself. He took upon himself the role of mentor to Hideo. He even entertained the thought that he and Hideo could at some stage become friends. After a particularly invigorating session with the team, Dr. Tetsuya Hiroko M.Sc. Ph.D. took Hideo aside from the group and told him that he had decided to publish. He was both surprised and disappointed by Hideo's response. Hideo questioned the validity of publishing. He submitted respectfully that even though he was just an under graduate, he felt it was too early. There was too much supposition, too much work left to do.

Tetsuya knew it was wrong to publish early, but he was excited. He was so convinced that he had found the answer to the space/time question that he would publish regardless. After all, he knew he was right. He had the answer. To him, the testing and workings were a secondary issue. It was the same at school. He always knew the answers to the tough maths and science questions, but was always marked down because he had no workings. No step by step test and proof. He arrived at a certain point then proceeded on instinct and he was always right. He was right now. He would publish.

He knew it was a little different to school. He would need the workings this time. This was possibly one of mankind's greatest discoveries. He could manipulate space/time and he knew it to be a truth. He would work backwards from the answer and provide all the supporting workings and test data necessary to publish.

Who would know?

14. COLD KARAGE ON THE DOCTOR'S PLATE

The past...

It was 1987 when it all went off the rails, but at the same time, it all seemed to come together. One door closes, another opens; or in this case one door opens and another one closes.

Hideo Tanaka had decided to leave early. Budding scientist or not, there were some things in life that were just as important as physics... well almost. Aiya Matsuda was the President's personal secretary. She was three years older than Hideo but, ever since their atrocious duet at a staff karaoke night six months earlier, they had been lovers. Well maybe not lovers. They were really two lonely hearts that got together regularly to make love. Well maybe not to make love, maybe just to thrash about on damp sheets for an hour or so until Hideo's body was sated and his mind turned to new issues. Often, as Aiya lay in bed with the sheets tugged up around her chin she was overcome with feelings of incredible guilt and shame. She thought Hideo's actions indicated similar feelings. But Hideo was actually fraught with feelings of complete indifference. He would never love anybody. It was unscientific. To him, the relationship was purely physical, but gradually it occurred to him that Aiya's position of trust with the President may be of some use.

During the more recent stages of the paranormal event research, the team had conducted lengthy interviews with a fifty one year old man named Ken Hayashi. Mr. Hayashi's case stood out for many reasons. He had multiple event experiences from which to draw information. Many of these were matching sets. At the age of 6, young Ken Hayashi suffered what could be best described medically as a seizure. From all the information available, the team had been able to piece together a detailed account of what had happened.

In the middle of a reading class, young Ken's eyes had rolled back in their sockets and he had dropped sideways from his chair to the floor like a sack of rice. The teacher rushed forward to assist him and found him absolutely rigid with a hideous rictus expression on his face. He slowly arched up off the floor then, suddenly slopped down and lay on his side. The teacher said that at this point Ken looked peaceful, as if he was asleep. Slowly he regained consciousness, but as his eyes opened he was clearly distressed and disorientated. He cast about with eyes wide, muttering something about bookshelves. It had seemed to take him a little while to remember where he was, but doing so just made him more distressed. He was taken to the infirmary, and the teacher had called a doctor. The doctor had found no evidence of any physical damage. Apart from being clearly over excited and somewhat distressed, a slightly fast pulse was the only apparent after effect. The school had telephoned Ken's mother and the doctor suggested she take Ken along for a thorough check up, and a series of tests to make sure there was no chance of epilepsy. The doctor had turned to speak to the teacher, but she had left the room. That seemed to be the extent of it.

However, during the course of a personal interview with Tetsuya, Ken Hayashi had provided the name of both the teacher and the doctor. Mr. Hayashi had gone on to develop a very successful publishing company and still lived in the same ward. In fact, he had moved back into the family home after the death of his parents. Ken's teacher had left the school shortly after the incident and had died mysteriously not long after. The doctor, who had been quite young at the time of the incident, still practiced in the ward. Tetsuya's interview with Ken had been so compelling, that Tetsu wanted to speak to the doctor personally about his recollections of the incident.

They now sat opposite each other in a small restaurant near the doctor's office. The doctor was waving a piece of karage around with his chopsticks and Tetsuya was half expecting it to fly off and do someone an injury.

"I'm a pragmatist," warbled the doctor around a mouthful of deep fried chicken. "I tell it like I see it, and that's how I saw it."

"Yes of course, I'm sorry," said Tetsuya. "It's just that it was a long time ago and I just want to be certain. It's not that I don't believe you, it's just my job to question... you know; cover off all the details. Would you mind going through it again... from the beginning?"

The doctor softened a little.

"Okay, you're paying for lunch, so I guess you're calling the shots. So... I remember it was a Friday morning, because I was looking forward to leaving early. I was called to the school around eleven as I recall. The child was in the infirmary with his teacher. The boy was very animated. His pulse was a bit fast, but other than that he seemed fine. There was no physical injury, no evidence of concussion, no nausea... nothing. The teacher on the other hand... well the teacher was very distressed. I turned to speak to her but the boy blurted out this fantastic story about how he had closed his eyes and his classroom had changed. He said it was the same room, but suddenly it had soft carpet on the floor and rows of desks with funny little grey televisions on them. Behind the desk were three or four rows of new wooden bookshelves. He had looked out the window. The temple on the hill was still there, but now it was part obscured by a tall building, maybe five or six storeys high... with his own name right there on the side... Ken Hayashi Publi... publi something. The boy said he had blinked again and then he had found himself on the floor with the teacher leaning over him. He was very confused because the room was back to normal. He said he had looked out the window again. The temple on the hill was clearly visible and there was no tall building."

The doctor paused to select another piece of karage. He stuffed it in his mouth and followed through with a mouthful of rice. Tetsuya's meal sat before him untouched.

"Please... go on," he said to the doctor.

"Well, of course as I said, I thought the boy was talking rubbish. That is until I tracked down his teacher. She had left the infirmary while I spoke to the boy. So after telling the mother that she could take her boy home, I went looking for the teacher and found her in the staff room.

As I entered the room the teacher looked up at me, startled. She looked like a scared rabbit caught in headlights."

The doctor stopped chewing. He put his chopsticks down. He looked decidedly unwell. He was staring down at the table top.

"I'm sorry, I didn't think this would affect me so much after all this time, but something unexplainable, maybe something evil, happened in that classroom on that day."

Slowly his head lifted up in small jerky movements. He looked Tetsu in the eye. When he spoke Tetsuya sensed fear in his lowered voice.

"Like I said earlier, I'm a pragmatist and I know when to be scared Professor. I'll never forget what happened next. As I started across the room towards her, the teacher jumped up and backed into a corner. She knocked several cups off the counter, but didn't seem to notice when they smashed on the floor. She held her arms out towards me, looking at the back of her hands with a frightful intensity. Slowly she turned her hands over, palms upward and, just before she crumpled down the wall, I saw that both hands seemed burnt and blackened. Of course I thought she had fainted, but as I knelt down to help her I noticed she was staring straight at me. Her eyes were so wide it seemed that they would pop out of their very sockets."

The doctor had found himself back in the moment. He gave a great shudder and shook himself out of it.

"When I looked at her hands I found she had blisters on most of her fingertips. The blackening was more like a scorch. There was lots of loose carbon like material that rubbed off on my hands. When she spoke I could barely hear her. She told me... and I'll never forget this. She told me when she went to help the boy that, as soon as she touched him, she burnt her hands. She said that, in the instant she touched him, she felt her hands had left her body and gone somewhere else. Then she claimed she had seen his soul... that's right, his soul, flow back into his body. She was saying over and over... 'His soul was somewhere else, his soul went away and came back.' She told me that when he regained consciousness, his eyes were fixed on the window.

I'm telling you professor, this was no crazy woman. This was a well balanced, well educated, middle aged woman from a stable family and the reason I was so shocked was that she was kind of... you know, collaborating the boy's story. Anyway, I administered a mild tranquilizer, prescribed a salve for her hands and organised for another female teacher to take her home."

The doctor looked down at the table again. Tetsuya sensed he wanted to say more, but was holding back. Tetsuya let the silence hang in the air like the single strand of a spider's web. Barely there but still connected. After about a minute, the doctor raised his eyes and looked at Tetsuya.

"I know it wasn't my fault. I mean she wasn't even my patient."

He looked back down again. This time Tetsuya broke the silent thread.

"What wasn't your fault?" he said.

"That woman, the teacher... I should have seen it coming. I mean I'm supposed to observe symptoms."

He picked up his chopsticks and shuffled some fried chicken around his plate.

"She lived alone. Her friend, the other teacher, took her home. She sat her at the table and made her tea. She wrote her phone number on a writing pad and put it on the table in case the teacher wanted to contact her. She said she seemed distant but okay. She left her there at the table with a cup of tea in front of her and returned to the school. On the following Monday at about 10 o'clock I had a call from the police. They told me the teacher's address and asked me to meet them there immediately. It was not far from my office and I got there about fifteen minutes later. Her friend the other teacher was outside and she was upset and crying. The police took me inside. The teacher was sitting bolt upright in a chair. She was dead, but her eyes were wide open and staring down at her hands. On the table in front of her was a cold cup of tea... and a note. The police motioned to me to read the note without touching it. The note simply said, 'Tell the doctor to look at my hands.' Her hands were clean. There was no scorching, no blisters, nothing. I estimated she had been dead less than twenty four hours, so it seems that she had just gone home and sat there for two days without moving. She had simply faded away sometime on the Sunday. There was no autopsy but it didn't matter. They wouldn't have found anything."

"So what do you think?" Tetsu asked the doctor. "Do you think it was something evil?"

"No, I don't actually. She certainly did, and at that point I think I did too, but then about a week later the boy's mother brought him to my office. Because I had examined him at the school, she wanted me to see him. She said the boy, named Ken, had told her and her husband this amazing story about how the room changed and how a building with his name on had grown up outside the window and then disappeared again. The tests had shown nothing, and her own doctor had laughed off Ken's story as the result of an overactive imagination. She was worried that he might have a mental condition. I spent over an hour talking to him and listening to his amazing story in great detail. In the end I was convinced that Ken Hayashi was one of the sanest and brightest young boys I had ever met. I believed that he had seen what he had seen. Does that make me crazy too professor?"

"You already know the answer to that," said Tetsu. "I presume you've been back to the school in recent years?"

"Oh yes," said the doctor, now more animated.

"I met Ken Hayashi again when he invited me to the inauguration of the new school library and reading room that he had donated. I didn't know why I was invited, but just before the little ceremony, he came up and shook my hand warmly. He took me to the end of the room and showed me the brand new wooden bookshelves, packed with children's books. In front of these were a number of tables with computers on them. Then he took me to the centre of the room and asked me to kneel down and look out the window. You know, I'd travelled through that neighbourhood plenty of times over the years as it grew and developed, but without really noticing. When I knelt down and looked out the window there, almost obscuring the temple on the hill, was a hi-rise building. On the side of the building in tall metal letters it read 'Ken Hayashi Publishing'."

So Tetsuya Hiroko had a neat collaboration for Ken Hayashi's story. For his part, when asked directly if he thought he had travelled in time, Ken was evasive. He cited the 'chicken and the egg' scenario and said he believed that Chinese horoscopes often proved correct because of the recipient's own psychic energies pushing them along that pre-mapped path. He said he thought maybe he had tailored his life to fit the vision he had had in that classroom that day. Who knows?

Well... thought Tetsuya Hiroko, there's a dead schoolteacher who might know.

15. HAPPY BIRTHDAY KEN

The past…

Ken Hayashi was a romantic. During his college years he was into everything. Nobody danced weirder than him, nobody sang louder, nobody partied harder. He was always the centre of attention, surrounded by a large group of friends. After college he had met the woman of his dreams and everything changed. Ken was head over heels in love. He switched all his attention to his new love and gradually drifted away from his group. He spent every waking minute and more with his new love. It was like they were joined at the hip… inseparable. After just nine months, the pair had decided to marry. The girl had been raised by her elderly grandmother who had now passed on, so together with Ken's parents they planned a traditional shrine wedding.

Ken's fiance had spent her final night away from Ken, at his parent's house. In the morning, Ken had arrived early at the shrine and was in the dressing room waiting for his bride-to-be, when the three people he most loved in this life were cruelly taken from him. Ken's mum and dad and his bride-to-be had stepped off the curb to cross the road in front of the temple, when they were struck down, all three, by a speeding truck. His mother and father went under the truck and his bride-to-be left this world in a more spectacular fashion. She described a near perfect arc, as she flew through the air to finally rest lifeless on the head of the large bear statue 'higuma', in the front of a nearby saké house.

Ken Hayashi knew this before they came to tell him. In the precise instant that his love had landed on the head of the bear, he had felt the whole planet stop turning. The jolt of it had rocked him forward like when you're standing up on a bus and it stops suddenly. After a respectful minute to mark her passing, the world started turning again. This time the jolt almost unnoticeable to Ken as his life took another turn.

It was nearly forty eight hours before Ken re-surfaced. Nobody could get near him in that time. He never cried, but he did consume an almost unreasonable amount of beer and saké.

He found his parent's house exactly as they had left it. Clothes left scattered around as they had made their hasty preparations to get to the shrine. In his old bedroom he could smell his bride-to-be… on the bedclothes, the curtains, all around. He opened her suitcase and on the top was a picture of her with a large colourful bouquet of flowers in her arms. It was a retouched studio photo, intended for him as a gift. In the photo his bride-to-be was a beaming six or seven year old beauty. This was the face he would remember, not the tortured visage hanging upside down on the bear's head. He took the photo to the lounge room and placed it on the dresser, then, like a robot, he went out to finalise the details for this part of his life and set in motion the plans for the next part.

And so over the years, Ken Hayashi had become almost reclusive. In time he turned his interest in books and reading into a handsome business venture. With no interest in anything else to distract him, he spent his days driving his business hard and his nights sitting at home reading beside the picture on the dresser. He had finally acquired the site on the verge opposite his old school and he had set about working with the architects to design the building and the signage on it. They could do what they liked inside, but he was completely inflexible on the details of the outside.

Following the eventual completion of his building, he had approached the school to provide them with funds for a new children's library and reading room. His only stipulation was that it must be housed in his old classroom. The one he was in when he was six years of age.

There was a small dedication ceremony to open the new reading room and Ken had arranged for the doctor who had treated him that day all those years ago, to attend. Everything went as planned and Ken ended the day feeling a little foolish. Nothing had happened. Maybe it was all in his mind. Maybe what he thought he had seen out the classroom window all those years ago was simply a trigger. Something that spurred him on to achieve what he had. After all, he had even taken a six year old child's vision of a building and forced that vision on the architects. And what if he had let them design the exterior. In fact, what if he hadn't worked so hard at buying that land in the first place. He was both disappointed and relieved. For thirty six years he had carried that haunting vision around with him. They had kept the teacher's death from him back then. Made sure he didn't know. He was nearly fourteen when he found out about her and the image of her horrible death had blended with the original incident to fuel the fire. Now it turns out it was just well… one of those things.

The following day was Ken Hayashi's birthday. He would be forty two years of age. He had accepted an invitation to read to the first class of six and seven year olds to use the new facility. When he entered the reading room, he cast a glance over the expectant faces of the thirty or so kids who stood and bowed deeply to welcome him. He returned their bow, then as their teacher got them all settled down, he turned and walked to the window. As he stared up at his building, and the edge of the temple beyond, he smiled to himself. So it was all over and done with. Time to read to the kids.

One little girl had been chosen to present their benefactor with a lovely bouquet of flowers and now as Ken stared out the window, she came and stood nervously behind him. Ken turned from the window and looked straight down into the beaming face of the little girl behind the flowers. My god, the similarity! He couldn't take his eyes off the child. Waves of nausea swept across him and he stumbled forward like a robot, with his arms outstretched, calling the name of his dead bride-to-be from so many years ago. Then he pitched forward, scattering the children

and the furniture and he felt like the top of his head had just...
well just blown off. He hit the floor hard and everything swirled
into the blackest black. The children's screams faded off into
silence as Ken Hayashi went stiffer than a day old tuna. Then he
arched up off the floor, supported only by his heels and the back
of his head. He collapsed sideways onto the floor. When he came
round he was looking straight up and out of the window. There
was the temple... unobscured. There was no hi-rise building, no
Ken Hayashi Publishing. Then someone touched him and it was
like a great jolt of electricity coursed through him as he looked
up into the terrified eyes of his old teacher. He felt something
flowing up and out of him, through the top of his head, then the
blackness came back and through the blackness came the far off
sound of children screaming and sobbing. He was back... his
building was back.

16. RETURN OF AN ANGEL

The present...

Up in my room I shower and scrub at the black mark on my hand and wrist. The harder I rub... the more it just stays right there. I finish up, dress and head out to meet Nick at Shinjuku south entrance.

I'm pretty edgy now, half expecting to see the boy at every turn. I'm searching faces in the crowd, but there's nothing. I'm not sure if I'm relieved or disappointed. When I get to the station entrance I find I am a little early. I walk past the entrance and onto the overhead to look down towards the Green Peas Pachinko building. I scan the faces in the busy space between me and the building, but again I come up blank. After a few minutes I turn and walk back to the entrance.

· · ·

From high in the Times Square building, the boy watches me go. He turns and makes his way back down to street level, then crosses into the south entrance to Shinjuku station and starts his descent into the safe haven under the station. When he finally makes it to his nest, he puts his back against the wall and slides down into a sitting position. What is this feeling, what is happening to me?Eventually... his heavy lids drop across his burning eyes and he no longer has the strength to open them. With the final thought that this man may be nobody at all, unconnected, he sinks down into a deep sleep. With an arcane, death-like tremor, his soul shakes itself loose from his body and wafts along the rock wall, seeking its own nest in the rock crevice and... with an obscene sucking noise, it was gone.

· · ·

"So Nick... how was Osaka?"

He turns at the sound of my voice.

"Hyperactive as always," he laughs, slapping me on the shoulder, "but I got you Osaka Jo."

Osaka Jo, or Osaka Castle Hall, is one of the biggest concert venues in Osaka. It holds about thirteen thousand people, so I'm already doing the math in my mind. I'd done Osaka twice before, but Osaka Jo would be the biggest venue I have ever played as top of the bill.

"Way to go Nick, so how hard was that?"

"Not hard at all, they jumped at it. It seems you're becoming something of a star. Well, in Japan at least," he laughed. "The band is all sorted. All the usual crowd, plus a pretty tight string section if you're sure it will work."

"Of course it will work. I keep telling you Nick, I hear the instruments when I'm writing the songs and I often hear strings. Once we sort the playlist I'll know how many numbers need them and I think they will really flesh out the sound for Osaka Jo."

"Okay, so where are we eating?" he says.

I hadn't made a booking, but I told Nick I wanted to eat at one of the cool, modern restaurants at the top of Sumitomo building.

"Right... mind if I drop off my bag and freshen up at the Sunroute on the way?"

We always used the same hotel, it was central and reasonably priced, but if Osaka went well, maybe next time in Tokyo we could stay somewhere like the Park Hyatt in the skyscraper district.

At the hotel Nick collected his key and headed for the lift. I collected my thoughts and headed for the bar. I decided to stick with the Laphroiag, and was about to take my first pull, when all of a sudden, there was that voice again.

"I'm sorry. I guess I over reacted."

I turned to face her.

"Yuka... I'm sorry too, I thought I saw someone I knew out there. I know it was rude and I apologise."

"Yes, it was rude," she said, "but then who am I to complain. It's not like we're married or anything. We just met and I had no right to get upset."

Those words circled around in my head... *It's not like we're married or anything.*

"I'm glad you are here. If the invitation still stands I'd like to join you and your manager for dinner."

I can feel myself melting again. Get a grip boy. What is it about this woman?

"Great," I blurt out. "Nick is upstairs getting ready, so while we wait, let's try again to have that drink together."

I order another Laphroaig and watch her as she takes the glass in her slender fingers and raises it to her lips. That image... right there, would push Laphroaig sales through the roof.

But I remind myself there's a serious side to this. While I study her sweet face, I ask myself; should I confide in her. Should I tell her what is going on, or will she just think I'm some crazy gaijin? While I was walking back from the station with Nick I was asking myself the same question. I had decided to tell him over dinner that night. A problem shared is a problem halved, or something like that. Yes, I was going to tell Nick. After all, he was invested. He would probably be involved. If it was real, maybe he could help. If it wasn't real, then he could visit me Sundays when they let me out on the lawn under close supervision. But Yuka... no, it was too early. I think I had made up my mind that I really wanted this woman. I don't mean wanted, for a night or so, as a distraction while I was here. I mean wanted to be with her for the rest of my life. I wasn't going to do anything to jeopardise my chances with her.

Yuka could feel my eyes on her and turned towards me with an enquiring look. But just then Nick walked in. I stood and introduced him to Yuka.

"Yes... Nick, we've spoken on the phone," she said.

"Yuka! Of course we have. I've not had a chance to tell our star here about the interview, but it seems..."

I cut him short.

"That's alright, it's under control. Yuka is going to join us for dinner. That way we get some cultured female company and Yuka gets her interview."

17. WHAT'S FOR AFTERNOON TEA MRS. ANTONELLI?

The past...

It was cold even for this time of year, freezing cold in fact.

On her way to school, Martha and her sister had played in the frozen puddles. There was no concrete curbing or guttering in this part of town, just dirt ditches that served as gutters to keep the water off the dirt back streets. Normally, in the bottom of the deeper gutters, bright green, smelly grasses bent their blades in concert with the flowing water. But that day... in fact for weeks, the water didn't flow in the gutters until the sun reached down into the ditch. The drains were part frozen. Up on the road, shallow puddles that had formed in potholes, were frozen over. Some clear and crisp, others cloudy and cracked, with maybe the odd twig or piece of litter poking through.

Martha and her sister would play at treading on the frozen skin to see if it could hold their weight. It never did of course and Martha and her sister generally arrived at school with wet, frozen feet, encased in their cheap black leather lace ups. Martha's sister was lucky. She sat close to the long, low, black electric radiator that ran along the wall by her desk. She was able to kick off her wet shoes and twist her legs around so her feet rested on the perforated metal skin. Sometimes she got caught. It didn't matter.

Martha didn't care about the heater in her classroom, and besides she was two rows away from the wall. Martha had decided that her life was to be devoted to God and so if she felt pain, then that was God's will. If Martha had been able to fully understand her own feelings, she would have realised that to her, the service of God meant an escape from the poverty that enveloped her family.

Her father was a shoemaker. He was out of work, but spent almost every day in the city turning his hand to whatever piece work he could find. Her mother was a seamstress. She had a job in a factory, but laboured long into the evening after she got home from work, mending or altering other peoples things. There was never enough money for food, heating or clothes, and the family was forced to live off the charity provided by neighbours and the church.

Every time someone handed them a food parcel or a 'hand-me-down' dress after Sunday mass, Martha's resolve strengthened. Martha was old beyond her years. She looked up now from her reader, at the chubby little red faced Irish nun whose life's work it seemed, was to make Martha's life a misery. No, no sign of hunger there. Fat little belly rolling around under her nun costume. Martha Bird was no fool. She would be a nun.

She turned her attention back to the book on her desk. It was about another saint, suffering for the cause in far off France or somewhere. Martha would be a nun... or even a saint. So she thought she understood that the path to glory lay in pain and she thought she understood that God would send her a sign. Like this Bernadette at... where was it... yes, that's right, Lourdes.

The day was like any other. While Mr. & Mrs. Bird were at work, Mrs. Antonelli, the next door neighbour, would look after the two younger children. Martha and her sister would hurry home from school so that Mrs. Antonelli could leave and cook dinner for her own husband. Mrs. Antonelli normally left some bread and jam for the children, but today she was distracted. She hurried out as soon as Martha arrived. She wanted to get to the butcher shop and pick up a ham hock, so it had time to cook for dinner.

Martha always looked after her two young sisters and baby brother, but that day, Martha too was distracted. As soon as she got in the door, she left the younger children to play in the kitchen, while she went to the bedroom they all shared. She sat on the bed and was opening her school bag when she was startled by a noise. She looked up to see a small boy, maybe three or four years old, standing on the bed opposite.

He looked different somehow. Where had he come from? Suddenly Martha Bird knew. God had sent her a vision. Was this a miracle, could this be the young Jesus? He did look a bit like the young Jesus standing beside Joseph in his workshop in the picture book she had. Martha threw herself down on her knees and made the sign of the cross. The boy didn't move, he just stood on the bed looking down at her. His eyes moved up to the Canadian flag on the wall behind her, then back down again.

Suddenly Martha Bird jumped up and ran from the room to the hall cupboard. She grabbed her father's Box Brownie camera, one of the family's most prized possessions. She was not allowed to use it unsupervised, but this was different. This was a miracle and Martha needed proof. Back in the bedroom the boy remained motionless on the bed, just his eyes growing wider as Martha held out the black box in front of him. Martha Bird pulled down on the little lever and the boy blinked once and suddenly disappeared. Gone! My God, my God, a vision from God, and she had proof, right there in the Box Brownie. Martha Bird would do God's work. Martha Bird would be a saint.

Martha knelt on the floor clutching the Box Brownie to her chest. This was probably what they called a sacred moment. Martha was aware of some strange noises coming from the kitchen, but nothing was going to spoil her sacred moment, but then another boy appeared in the bedroom... at the door. It was her little brother and there was blood flowing from his mouth, eyes and ears. In an instant he reached out to Martha, then collapsed on the floor convulsing. Martha leapt up, swept him up off the floor and struggled out into the kitchen where she was horrified to see her little sisters prone on the floor. One was bloodied but not moving, and the other was lying on her side, wide-eyed and vomiting. Between them sat a cardboard box and a breakfast bowl with the remains of whatever rat poison the children had not shoveled into their mouths. Martha took it all in. The chair up to the top cupboard, the cupboard door ajar. Martha knelt with the now lifeless body of her little brother draped across her lap. Both her sisters were now still.

Martha had not taken a breath since her little brother had appeared in the bedroom doorway. Now she sucked in a great gulp of air. Martha bird was older than her years... too old in fact. Her God was calling her. Her brother's limp body slid noiselessly onto the cheap lino floor as she shuffled forward to pick up the box of poison. She shook the last of the green granules into the bowl, then lifted the bowl to her mouth.

About forty five minutes later, little Sally Pepper crossed the un-mowed lawn of the Bird house. She picked her way around the rusty bikes and garbage and, arriving at the kitchen steps, called to her new playmate Martha Bird... no answer. She climbed the steps and called again through the open kitchen door... no answer.

She tip-toed over to the door and looked in, her eyes becoming accustomed to the gloom.

And right there, Sally Pepper lost her sweet innocence!

. . .

Sally's sobs died to a jerky crackle and then a fast breathing. She turned to her mother. She was as red as a late season peach, and there was snot and drool spread all across her contorted little face. The rapid breathing finally slowed and Sally turned to her mother and said.

"The... the birds, the birds have (sob) died."

"There there now," said her mother. "Sometimes God takes pretty young birds up to heaven to sing for him."

"No no no… you don't understand. All the little Birds are dead!" cried little Sally Pepper.

18. THE BLACK BOX RECORDER DOES ITS STUFF

The past...

The funeral was gut wrenching, two tiny white coffins, two baby birds.

Mrs. Pepper had arrived breathless at the Bird's house right after Mrs. Bird had arrived home. From the path to the front door, Mrs. Pepper heard the screaming coming from inside. She stopped at the front door which was closed, then went back down the three front steps and around to the backyard. The back door was open, and in the gloom, Mrs. Pepper could see Mrs. Bird hugging the limp forms of two of the children as she rocked back and forth wailing mercilessly.

Mrs. Pepper turned and ran the two blocks to her own house and grabbed at the heavy black phone on the kitchen bench. She was so proud when they had it installed, the first in the street. Now she struggled to get her fingers into the little holes and jerked up and down impatiently while the round silver dial span ever so slowly back to the stop.

Turned out Mrs. Pepper wasn't as ditzy as she looked. She arrived back at the Bird's house and took charge. Poor Mrs. Bird was now prone on the floor with all four children gathered up to her. She was jelly. The screaming had given way to the wailing, and now the wailing had given way to sobbing. The police arrived before the ambulance, which was close behind.

It turned out that Martha and her baby brother were still alive... just. Accidental child poisonings and the treatment and applications of the vitamin K antidotes were known and recognised. Martha and her baby brother pulled through, and they were mercifully still in the hospital when the funeral took place. So was Mrs. Bird.

After the funeral Mr. Bird stoically hosted a kind of wake in the side room off the church hall. When the tea urn was empty and the last of the scones and sponge cakes had been cleared, he made his way slowly along the road and down the hill to his house. Anyone passing might have thought he was drunk.

Usually, unless it was after eight in the evening, from the front door you could always hear the noise of the children... laughing, screaming, fighting... but not today. Today there was nothing. Just the deafening silence of his own grief, bearing down on him like the weight of all time. He unlocked the front door and went straight to the children's bedroom. He sat on the bed that Martha shared with one of her sisters and stared at the crayon pictures cello taped on the wall. God he thought. How many times do I have to tell those kids. He turned to look behind him. There was the flag he had given Martha, telling her the story of how he had come to Vancouver from London before she was born. He was proud of that flag... so much like the Union Jack, but now he reached up and tore it from the wall, wishing he had never come to Canada.

Then he cried. He cried off and on for over an hour. Gaining his composure then loosing it again, as the memories flooded back like sand into a loose hole. He just couldn't stop it, so he gave up trying.

Finally, the shuddering slowed and stopped and he sat there staring at the floor. It was only then he noticed his camera. His prized Box Brownie under the edge of the other bed.

Mr. Bird scooped up the camera and stood for while, turning it over in his rough hands, trying to figure out how it got there. He finally concluded it had something to do with the tragedy. The only person who knew where the camera was kept was Martha and she was a good girl. She wouldn't touch it without permission or use it when he was not present. Through the tiny magnified counter window he could see the number nine. He kept a record because, even though the price of developing was included when you bought the film, the film was expensive and use was confined to special events only. There were maybe three shots left, but he knew he had only taken eight shots since he last wound on a film. He snapped out the little rotating handle and wound the film off, unconcerned now about wasting the last few shots. Focused only on knowing what the mystery photo could tell him, he left the house and headed directly into the village to the local chemist. The chemist took the film roll and dropped it into a little pre-addressed bag and handed a receipt slip to Mr. Bird.

Ten days later Mr. Bird stood stock still in his kitchen. His wife was back at work at the garment factory. She should be home soon. Two of his children were in the hospital... two weren't.

In his trembling hands he held the paper photo wallet. There should be nine photos inside.

He opened the wallet. The first two pictures had been taken by his wife and were pictures of the house. The next three were pictures of his daughter's birthday. There was his sweet little darling beaming out at him from behind a birthday cake. Mr. Bird smiled at the memory, then a more recent and horrible memory overtook the first. Mr. Bird lowered himself slowly down onto the yellow vinyl and chrome dining chair. The same chair his baby girl knelt on to blow out her four candles.

Next there were two photos of the family at a rocky beach. Photo eight was a picture of Martha and her mother on the first day of the new school year. Mr. Bird wiped his right eye with the heel of his rough, shoemaker's hands and slowly separated photo eight from the one he knew was underneath. Suddenly the kitchen door opened and his wife came into the room. He turned the last two photos face down on the table.

"What have you got there?" asked Mrs. Bird.

She looked haggard. Her hair was lank and messy and her clothes seemed to hang off her shrunken frame. My God! What has happened to us, he thought.

"It's the photos... from the Brownie."

"I don't know why you're..."

"I need to know," he said, cutting his wife off. "There's something here, I... I know it, something that might tell us why this has happened."

His wife moved closer to the table. She stood behind her husband and held fast to the cold chrome chair back. She watched while his rough hands reached out towards the photos on the table. His big calloused thumb found the edge, and slowly he turned the last photo over.

"Who's that then?" he whispered, almost to himself.

The photo showed a little boy with dark hair, standing on one of the beds in the children's room. The photo was dark, but if you peered closely, you could see the kid's crayon drawings in the background and, you could just make out the child's features. His eyes seemed wide open in surprise.

"I don't know... but he looks Chinese or Japanese or something."

19. DINNER FOR THREE

The present...

We are leaving the hotel on our way to the Sumitomo building. A light rain has started falling. Not too bad, but enough to help me be brave in company. As we near the corner, I suggest it might be better to get into the pedestrian tunnel. Besides, at this time of night it's easier.

In the back of my mind I am thinking the boy might be watching, following me. With three of us together, I feel braver and so might get a chance to learn more about him. As we make our way along the tunnel we pass through areas where homeless men are preparing meals and getting ready for the night ahead. There is quite an encampment down here. I understand every now and then the police drive them all out, with the result that the camp city in Yoyogi Park grows into a mini metropolis.

But tonight, all is clean, quiet and ordered. Nick is chatting with Yuka and I'm using the distraction to look about for the boy. Nothing!

We clear the tunnel near the entrance to the building and head straight up to the restaurants. We settle on Ajito, a modern kind of 'Izakaya' style with separate rooms, each housing a couple of tables in separate niches. I've been here before and they remember me. This gets us a great table right up against the windows. Full length glass abuts the end of our table and the incredible vista of Tokyo at night is spread out before us. The boy is out there somewhere in the night, maybe above ground, maybe underground.

"Saké, I need saké," says Nick, shaking me out of my reverie.

The saké choices are vast and after a few samplings we settle on one of my favourites, *Tsukinowa* from Iwate Prefecture. It is refined and complex.

"That's like chilled velvet," says Nick. "Beats the heck out of One Cup."

Yuka laughs. "Everything beats the heck out of One Cup Nick," she says and turns to me.

"Seems you know your saké. It is one of the best. It comes from Iwate like me."

"So that's at least two wonderful things that come from Iwate," I say trying to sound cool, but ultimately sounding pretty corny.

Nonetheless Yuka blushes slightly and looks down. Then she looks me squarely in the eye and says…

"I think we had better get down to business."

She takes a small notepad and a pencil and asks me the usual stock questions about what got me started and how long have I been playing and writing. That sort of stuff. I'm a little disappointed. I don't know what I expected, but this woman struck me as so different, I guess I expected different questions. I welcome the distraction of the waiter coming for our order. We let Yuka take charge and, after checking our likes and dislikes, she orders a varied selection.

Nick is filling me in on the details of the Osaka concert and Yuka is taking notes, when the first courses arrive. Suddenly I realise how hungry I am and, I lose myself in the incredible selection of bite sized delights laid out before me. Nick and Yuka are talking and eating more slowly. Clearly both of them have had lunch!

Finally I come up for air and rest my chopsticks across the rim of my bowl. I drain my saké cup and hold it out for Yuka to fill. This she does with studied skill, whilst all the time maintaining eye contact with me.

"I'd like to get past the stock questions and ask you about what influences your songwriting. It... It's difficult, but I mean, where do your songs come from?" she says.

"Yes, it is difficult. And it's difficult to answer as well. I rarely sit down and say... I think I'll write a song now. And if someone asks me to write a song about something, that is hard too. In fact, even if I decide that I would like to write a song about something, say some place I happen to be, maybe Florence, or even Tokyo, the thought just remains somewhere in my head. At some stage in the future days or weeks, maybe even months later, the song comes," I answer, knowing both how confusing and pretentious this sounds.

"I don't understand," says Yuka, moving closer to me around the table.

"Well," I stammer, looking for the right words, "this may sound a bit weird but, in a way, the songs just write themselves. I might wake in the middle of the night with a few words or a line or two, or be tuning a guitar and some odd chord mix will lead to a lyric. Generally I guess it's something that's on my mind, either consciously or subconsciously."

"Okay, so what happens next? How do those few words become a song?"

"Well, that's the best bit. Then I get to fill in the blanks. Sometimes it's not until I get right to the end of a song that I fully understand what the song is about. Sometimes that realisation leaves me stunned because, I suddenly recognise it as something that has been on my mind."

Yuka looks at me strangely, then turns to looks at Nick as if for assistance.

"Don't look at me," says Nick, "I've already had this discussion with him and I still don't understand."

"Well no," says Yuka, "I've heard about this before, about how songs sometimes write themselves. The artist says he is really just the... what is the word?"

"Conduit!" says Nick from around a mouthful of prawn.

"Yes," says Yuka, "the conduit. I once read how Michelangelo claimed he would look at a block of granite and know what beautiful form lay inside. It was simply his job to bring out the beautiful shape that was already there."

"It's something like that I guess. Look, if the song is something meaningful, it will happen that way. A lot of my songs have some kind of message in them. A lot are based around true life and events. Others are just songs for the sake of music."

"Can you give me an example of a song that, as you say, writes itself?"

I think about this for a minute, searching my catalogue for a good example. I want to get this right. Just when things are starting to go well for me I don't want to come of sounding like some zealot.

"Okay," I say to Yuka. "Let's look at two songs. "The first is *'Can't Get Over You'*. This is just a blues song about a barfly whose woman leaves him and, how he handles it. I had the idea driving home in the early hours after a show. I wrote most of it in my mind while driving. No big message, no divine intervention, just a good song wrapped around some good music. Anybody who has been in the situation will recognise the feelings of guilt and blame that the lyrics evoke. But that's it, kind of a Brill Building song, written to fill a mood and an album.

The second song is called *'When You Were Susan'*. It isn't released yet so you won't have heard it. What happened there was I woke at about 2.30 one morning with two lines of lyrics. They were...

'I cut myself and I'll bleed for your forgiveness.
To feel your breath on my cheek and the violence of your love.'

I grabbed a pen and paper and wrote them down. I really had no idea what they meant, so I went straight back to sleep. When I woke in the morning I found the lines and read them over and over, trying to figure out what they meant. I finally gave up, put the piece of paper in my wallet and forgot about it."

"Until?"

"Until about six or seven days later I was stuck in traffic on a bridge and, suddenly I felt I had to get that paper out. As soon as I was able, I pulled off into the emergency space at the end of the bridge lane and pulled out the paper and a pen. Within ten minutes I had written the whole song. I had written it... but it wasn't until I read it from the beginning to the end that I knew what it was about. I was only about ten or fifteen minutes from my studio, so I turned around and drove straight there. As I had been writing the lyrics I instinctively knew what the music would sound like. I heard the chanting and the stilted piano, all of it. So when I reached the studio, I had it sung and recorded within about two hours."

"I think I understand what you mean, but I would love to hear it. So what is it about?"

All of a sudden this wonderful woman was asking all the right questions and for all the right reasons.

"It's a strong emotive message song," I reply. "It's about a man who is drawn to and, ultimately falls in love with, an astonishing and innocent young woman. Having won her heart he then proceeds to mould her into something entirely different, to satisfy his wants. All too late he realises what he has done, and laments the loss of the 'real' Susan; the Susan he fell in love with."

"Wow!"

"Wow? That's it... wow!" I say, feigning disappointment.

But Yuka just laughs. Out loud like a sweet bell, then turns to face me with that incredible big smile.

"Someone who writes like you do can't be all bad," she says.

Suddenly I'm overtaken by something like early teenage awkwardness.

"So... if I'm possibly not all that bad, does that mean I might ask to see you again. I... I mean outside of office hours so to speak?"

Mercifully the smile remains.

"Maybe," she purrs. "Let's just see how things pan out."

20. I HAD A DREAM LAST NIGHT

The past...

The dreams had been getting stranger and stranger. Tetsuya had been having the dreams almost as long as he could remember. They came and went at the same time each year, always around his birthday, and lasted for about two weeks. Each night for two weeks the dreams were identical and, when they returned the following year, they picked up exactly where last year's had left off. They were always very short, seeming to be just seconds long, and they were always set in a hospital; the same hospital. Tetsuya always viewed the scene from up high, close to the ceiling... looking down. He never saw his own reflection in a window or mirror and never saw his own shadow. He had the definite impression that he possessed neither.

Each year as his birthday approached, Tetsu became increasingly anxious and withdrawn. At first he had put this down to his orphan status and, a subsequent longing to know his birth mother. Then he became unsure if the anxiety was caused by the dreams or, the dreams were caused by the anxiety. Over the years Tetsu had come to attach more importance to these dreams. In fact he had stopped thinking of them as dreams and started thinking of them as episodes. When he pieced all the episodes together, Tetsu had witnessed a woman give birth to a baby. At first he thought the woman must have been his mother; he felt such longing when he saw her face. Then he realised the hospital was too modern, the equipment too state-of-the-art for it to be his birth in 1955.

The following week was his 36th. birthday and, he had begun to feel increasingly empty and anxious during the day. He knew the dreams were coming. He rooted around in his top drawer until he found the red notebook. He took it out and opened it at the bookmark. He didn't need to, he knew what it said word for word. For the last few years he had taken to writing these episodes down as soon as he woke. And that was another thing. When he woke he was always sitting up naked on the edge of his bed, minus the boxers that he had gone to sleep in.

He climbed into bed and read the entries from the last few years...

1987 - The doctor places the new baby on the mother's chest but she rejects it, pushes it away. "Get them away from me" she screams.

1988 - A nurse takes the baby, wraps it in a blanket and leaves the room. By the door calendar shows year 1991. This is impossible. Can't see day or date.

1989 - Another nurse wheels the mother out of the delivery room. A man seated in the room, presumably the husband, doesn't even appear to notice she is gone. On the wall in the corridor, a cleaning roster is posted for 10 August to 17 August. Can't see year.

1990 - The mother arrives in her room on the gurney trolley. The nurse speaks to her kindly and fusses over her. The mother does not react.

Tetsuya knows that soon he will make another entry and, through his anxiety, he senses more than ever that these episodes are somehow a part of his life.

He digs out a pencil and puts it on the bedside table with the red notebook, then he turns off the light. Lying there in the darkness he can hear the silence. He can hear the planet turning with a soft whirring and finally, over all that noise he can hear his own heart beating.

He's floating near the ceiling and below him he sees the nurse leave the woman's room. The woman remains motionless for just a few seconds then as if in a trance, she pushes back the covers and slips out of bed. She slides back the glass door, then steps onto the balcony. Tetsuya hovers lower to see out onto the balcony. The woman has stepped across the balcony and has straddled the railing. She lifts her last leg over and falls sideways out of view. Where she just was, Tetsuya can see the Kyoto skyline. There's Kyoto tower right there. He wants to go out and look over the balcony but he can't, so instead he sits naked on the edge of his bed.

. . .

Tetsuya Hiroko sat naked on the edge of his bed for a long time... motionless. After an hour he finally moved. He had gone over the thing again and again, and had reached no conclusion. He ran his hand through his damp hair and, reached for the red notebook to update the entry. It would be the last. The dream only happened once that year and then just stopped.

21. ET TU BRUTE?

The past...

Tetsuya Hiroko put down the handset, stood up and walked to the mirror on the stark white wall of his long office. At one end, the room was furnished with a desk, a chair, a small bookcase and the mirror. At the other end was a side table cabinet and a round meeting table with chairs. The only other things in the room were two grills at opposite ends of the ceiling. One took stale air out and the other delivered clean fresh air from over one hundred feet up... at street level.

Tetsuya stood in front of the mirror watching his reflection, watching his face. He breathed deeply... in out, in out. This had to be the one. He could feel it. Besides, he was running out of options. Based only on what he had learnt from his dreams and noted in his diary, he had narrowed the time and place down to sometime in August 1991 in a hospital in the city of Kyoto. He was well aware of how unscientific this all was, but he knew beyond all doubt that these dates were critical. There were six male babies born in that period. He had already acquired and tested four of these babies and whilst they would all be of some use, none of them was the one he sought. This one was number five. Number six had died of lower respiratory infection. Tetsu steeled himself for the task, then turned away from the mirror, and opened the door to the corridor. He closed the door behind him and leant back on it, as if delaying the moment might somehow alter the outcome. He went through it all again in his mind.

The dream episodes had stopped when he was thirty six years old. He felt that the woman and child from his final dream were somehow central to his life and, by definition, his research. Every single paranormal episode seemed to throw up 36 year cycles and multiples thereof. He now believed that the secret to manipulating time was hitting the cycle. The trigger was

89

emotional trauma and the key was the soul. This was where Tetsu's theory differed from others... this aspect of the soul being the trigger.

Tetsu was not religious and as a scientist it was unlikely he would connect the soul with any form of spirituality. Whether his notion of a soul, or what he called the soul, was anything like anybody else's idea of a soul, just wasn't important to him. To him the soul was simply the essence of life. The electrical energy that resided in every living thing and, with the right set of circumstances, the soul could leave its container and cross the divide in time and space. Tetsuya was aware that in lots of Japanese literature, souls could act independently of the host body. When he was young he had read '*Tales of Genji*' and, had just thought of it as fiction, but suddenly it seemed there was strong evidence to support the supposition. Isn't that why he had published prematurely? Wasn't he convinced? Of course he was concerned that somebody else would beat him to it. Time travel... this would be one of man's greatest discoveries and he had no intention of letting the kudos slip through his fingers. He had after all created his own demons. There were people on his own research team who had the ability to beat him to the goal and, there was one... Hideo Tanaka, who also had the imagination... and that worried him.

It turned out that Tetsu had both over and under estimated Hideo. First he took him into his confidence and, only shortly after did he discover that Hideo had a conscience. Actually it happened that poor old Tetsuya was confusing conscience with raw ambition. Hideo knew where his bread was buttered because he had buttered it himself.

He had blown the whistle big time on Tetsuya.

Thinking she was headed for a starring roll as the future Mrs. Tanaka, Hideo's girlfriend had managed to provide him with project budgets and copies of Tetsuya's monthly test reports.

Tests which of course had never occurred, and the results of which were manufactured. Even though these tests were manufactured backwards from very solid theory, Tetsu knew that the results would stand up if the time consuming, laborious and expensive testing had actually taken place. So did Hideo. But this clear evidence of fraud and misappropriation coupled with Hideo's proximity to Tetsuya on a daily basis gave him all the proof he needed. Hideo was content to bide his time. He waited until Tetsuya was published, then he went to company and handed over copies of his own very detailed project notes.

Of course Hideo had two sets of notes. The first set was safely hidden away in his apartment. These would be essential when he had removed Tetsuya from the picture. The second set were carefully engineered not only to discredit Tetsuya, but to deny the existence of any possibility that time travel could be realised.

Hideo also possessed the gift of exquisite timing, and he used this gift to ensure that Tetsuya Hiroko fell from the absolute pinnacle. And so while Tetsuya basked in the glory of his incredible discovery, fielding global media interviews and harbouring visions of the Nobel kind, Hideo was busy tabling the evidence that sent shockwaves of fear rippling through the company. The company was heavily subsidised by government funding and, was both unwilling and unable, to withstand a scandal of these dimensions. Their reaction was swift and predictably premature. The budget misappropriations were easily proven, as was the falsification of test results. Had they investigated further, the company would have found the true depth of Tetsuya's remarkable discovery. But no... that was not the Japanese way. The Japanese way demanded swift and decisive action, but even that came at a price. And that price was the huge financial payout to Tetsuya to avoid the further scandal of a long and protracted legal battle. The company's audit procedures, and checks and balances on its use of public funds, were clearly questionable. Press releases were hastily prepared and a media conference was called. The company advised the gathered global media that Tetsuya Hiroko's findings were flawed. The Professor, they said, had been working under incredible stress for the past four or five years and, had simply collapsed under the strain. He had left the company voluntarily to seek treatment in a private facility. The company apologised in the grand tradition with lots of bowing and supplication, and a massive sigh of global disappointment rent the planet. There was simply no such thing as time travel.

And so Tetsuya Hiroko's moment in the limelight was just that; a brief moment. His fall from grace was however, cushioned by a huge pile of money. That money would set him up to continue his research. Strangely but perhaps predictably, Tetsuya was unconcerned by his public crucifixion. It barely dented his ego. After all, he had always been an outsider. Now he had both the funds and the obscurity to move into the practical application stages of his life's project. He simply needed to find a suitable location that could supply secrecy along with the kind of resources he needed.

He was however, shaken to the core by Hideo Tanaka's betrayal. He had thought they could be friends. He thought they were kindred spirits. He hated that he had been wrong... really hated it! He decided that Hideo would pay the ultimate price.

22. HIDEO TAKES A HOLIDAY

The past...

Tetsuya knew that Hideo Tanaka was going to his parent's home in Hokkaido for a short holiday. He had approved the leave himself. He knew that Hideo would be travelling home on the Shinkansen. This would give Tetsuya an opportunity to dispose of his betrayer somewhere far from home, where no suspicion could attach to him.

At the Shinjuku Station in Tokyo, Tetsuya slipped off the Shinkansen from Kyoto. For a man with such an orderly mind, his plan to kill Hideo was remarkably short of detail. In fact, that was almost the plan in it's entirety.... to kill Hideo. The only other planning had involved making a reservation on the first Shinkansen out of Kyoto on the day he knew Hideo was also travelling. He would make his way to Shinjuku Station in Tokyo and wait, all day if necessary, until he saw Hideo arrive on the platform from Kyoto. Somehow, somewhere in Shinjuku Station, he would kill him.

He had used a false name to make the booking and because it was a cold day, he arrived at the station hunched up in a large trench coat. He was excited by the prospect of the days work. He felt seriously mysterious, and he felt that murdering Hideo would be like a baptism for what lay ahead.

And so Tetsuya Hiroko took his first steps into darkness.

As pure chance would have it, as he made his way through the entrance to the Kyoto Station, he had spotted Hideo amongst the throng of people heading for the platforms. He had praised himself for remaining alert, hunched himself further down into the collar of his trench coat, and followed Hideo onto the train to Tokyo. Once on the platform he had experienced a moment of panic as he realised that the position of his reserved seat might give him away. But again, chance was on his side, and he found himself at the back of the same carriage as Hideo. He had peered out from behind his newspaper as Hideo had jammed his backpack into the rack shelf at the front of the carriage, and had heaved a great sigh of relief as Hideo swung into one of the seats at the front.

Hideo had got up just once during the journey, to stretch his legs or maybe go to the toilet, but Tetsuya had remained resolutely hidden behind his newspaper. As the train had rolled into Tokyo, Tetsuya realised that he had reached the extent of his planning. From here on in, he knew he would simply have to await his opportunity. He was sure there would be an opportunity and, in the event, it had proven remarkably easy.

Tetsuya had hung back until he saw Hideo heft his backpack, and then he had made his way carefully out onto the platform. As he made his way around a kiosk stand, Hideo had caught his backpack on the edge of a cleaner's trolley and broken one of the shoulder straps. Tetsuya had slipped behind the kiosk while Hideo stopped and knelt down to tie the two broken pieces together. Up ahead, the last of the straggling passengers made their way to the surface, leaving the platform deserted, but for the hunter and his prey. Without breaking stride, or really giving it too much thought, Tetsuya pulled a small shovel from the cleaner's trolley and, in one swift motion, swung it over his head and advanced on Hideo.

Hideo sensed rather than heard the sound behind him. A tiny swishing sound like a scuttling crab on a beach. He rose and turned toward the sound. It was coming from a small steel shovel which sliced through air. It struck him in the thin layer of flesh over the bridge of his nose, and carried on into the bone which exploded into the front of his brain. The force of the blow knocked his feet out from under him, and he landed with a sickening thud flat on his back on the platform... already dead. Tetsuya leant down to retrieve the little shovel of death and found he had to plant his foot on Hideo's throat and jerk hard to pull it free. He took hold of Hideo's legs and dragged him the short distance to the edge of the platform. He rolled him off the edge and watched him fall, lifeless, down onto the tracks. It was so easy, so final.

Tetsuya had straightened at the sound of approaching voices and, had run back along the platform, searching for a hiding place. Ahead there was an alcove and in the alcove a rusty old green metal door. He was surprised to find it unlocked. The hinges were rusty but they gave in with some effort and the door jerked back far enough for him to squeeze through. As quietly as possible he pushed the door closed, and stood with his back to it, breathing heavily as his eyes became accustomed to the darkness. As he waited and brought his breathing under control, he heard shouts from out on the platform, but he felt sure he had not been seen. Slowly his eyes detected a dim orange glow. He had thought he was in a small room, but now he could detect that the glow was coming from an open door on the opposite wall. He made his way across the small dark space and stood looking through the doorway. There was a short landing, lit by a single low voltage light, behind an orange grill, and stairs that disappeared off down into total darkness. Next to it was a large old rusty contact switch. It was open. Tetsuya took hold of the handle and pulled it down into the contacts… nothing! He pulled it in and out a few times, dislodging stubborn rust flakes, until suddenly an orange glow cast away down the staircase. As he peered down he could see that many of the lights were not working, but there was enough to light the way downwards, so downwards he went.

It was difficult for Tetsuya to determine how far down he had gone. By counting the steps as he descended, he could guess that he was at least eighty or ninety feet down before the stairs leveled out into a short corridor. At the end of the corridor he had found himself in a room crammed with old machinery. In the dim light, he could make out a large pipe bending machine and some kind of cable splicer. Against one wall was an old metal locker, and on the floor lay two more. Everything was covered with a thick layer of dust and spider webs. Dead end. Clearly nobody had been down here for many, many years. Tetsuya could hear what sounded like rats squealing. He cupped his ear to try and zero in on the direction of the sound. It seemed to be coming from high on the wall near the locker. Maybe the rats lived in the locker… creepy. He turned to go then noticed a large spider web reaching from the corner of the locker into the darkness of the wall behind. What had attracted his attention was not the spider web, but the fact that the spider web seemed to be moving; ever so slightly, back and forth like a living breathing thing. Tetsuya climbed around the old splicing machine and peered up. He could just make out a ventilation grill at the other end of the spider web. It was almost completely clogged with dust and thick webs, but he could see that there was airflow, vibrating the loose web filaments and fanning the big flat webs.

Tetsuya dragged one of the fallen lockers into place below the grill, then hoisted himself up onto the other locker, where he could just crouch, bent over below the ceiling. From this position, he could reach the metal grill near the top of the wall. He grabbed it and pulled hard. It came away and clattered to the floor, bouncing off the old lockers on its way to the cold concrete floor below. The rat chorus stopped like startled crickets at the foreign sound. Tetsuya held his breath for about thirty seconds, listening for any sounds of pursuit from above. Nothing! No, there was something, but not footsteps. It sounded like water… dripping water!

He breathed again and swivelled himself around to peer through the hole in the wall. There was nothing to be seen, but much to be sensed, and he sensed an long, cavernous space. He pulled himself into the hole as far as he could and whistled into the void. The thin noise flew out into space like a smiling ghost, sending just a small shiver down Tetsuya's spine. From the sound he could tell that the space was very large. The air flowing through the hole into his lungs was fresh, but held just a hint of algae.

You couldn't see it of course, but had you been there, and had there been more light, you would have seen an uncertain smile make its way across Tetsuya Hiroko's filthy face. An idea was forming in his mind.

He needed maps of the tunnel systems. He needed to know when this area was last used. He needed to identify, track and explore these caverns. Then, if all that panned out, he would need building materials, locks, cctv, communications systems and the manpower to put it all together. If all that came together, then maybe he had found the perfect location to continue his research in total privacy.

In just nine months, Tetsuya Hiroko had found his subterranean caverns, and identified three separate ways to access them. With very little effort he had obtained the tunnel records and, with just a little more effort, had amended or destroyed any records he could find that referenced the caverns. He built everything he needed, and ensured the security and isolation of the three entrances.

When he was satisfied that all was in order... Tetsuya Hiroko went underground.

23. THE MAN IN THE DARK SUIT

The past...

Tetsuya made his way down the corridor, remembering all that had gone before, all that he had sacrificed to get to this point.

He opened the door to what he liked to call the nursery. His assistant, Grok, stood off to one side of the child, who lay on a raised bed in the centre of the room. He looked at the child, then back to Grok. Grok... always immaculately turned out in a dark suit, with a dark mind and secrets to match, was like his lieutenant. Grok did the dirty work, and ensured that the rest of the staff carried out Tetsuya's orders... to the letter. Grok's allegiance was to cold hard cash... nothing more, nothing less. As long as he was well paid he was loyal. Tetsuya had contingencies in place in case Grok or indeed, any of the staff, ceased to be loyal or even valuable for that matter. They would simply cease to exist. They would quietly follow Hideo Tanaka into the great unknown. It hadn't been hard to find them in the Tokyo underbelly, and it wouldn't be hard to lose them the same way.

Tetsuya made his way to the side of the bed and reached down to take the baby's hand. He closed his eyes as the swoon rushed through him like warm soup through his very veins. The sensation was so strong he felt himself pitching sideways. He had to steady himself with his other hand. He opened his eyes and looked directly into the eyes of the infant, then right through them and into the soul. He breathed deeply until he had regained his composure then, releasing the child's hand, blinked slowly and turned to look at Grok.

"Yes," he whispered, "It's him. I want to start work on him first thing in the morning. Be here at 7 o'clock."

It was a bright sunny morning, around 6.15, when a man in an expensive dark suit made his way through the Harajuku entrance to Yoyogi Park. He moved briskly, like a person going to work with all the other people going to work, along the gravel path in the direction of the Meiji Jingu Shrine. Drawing closer to the path leading up to the shrine, the man in the dark suit slowed and bent down. He seemed to have a pebble caught in his expensive Italian loafer.

As he fished around his shoe he observed his surroundings and then, content that nobody was watching, he stood up and walked briskly down a narrow path away from the direction of the shrine entrance. He left the path and crossed a little wooden bridge that spanned the end of a small body of water. The lazy water trickled through rocks below the bridge, but the man in the dark suit wasn't there to take in the beauty of his surroundings and, without breaking stride, he turned along the water course and climbed down into an old abandoned cistern that was well hidden beneath the thick shrubbery.

A number of large boulders had tumbled down the wall of the cistern and the man in the expensive dark suit now took a grey remote control from his pocket and pointed it at the largest of these. The boulder swung slowly and silently out on a large well oiled steel hinge, leaving the boulder above it apparently floating in mid air. The man in the expensive dark suit climbed up and through the entrance, and the boulder settled back into place as if he had never moved. Once through the small entrance, the man carefully brushed off his suit coat and trousers. He pressed another button on the grey remote, and turned his face toward the small glowing monitor mounted on the wall.

The screen showed the cistern from a small camera concealed beside the entrance. He watched patiently for five minutes. Then, happy that he was not followed, he turned and switched on the low voltage lights. He carefully moved off along the tight, narrow tunnel which ran due east. Finally he arrived at the door accessing a larger tunnel running north south under the main Shinjuku rail lines. Here he halted and, once more, took out the grey remote. The concealed camera on the other side of the door fed its image down the wires and set it glowing onto the small monitor on the wall by the door. Content that the main tunnel was empty, he opened the door with the remote and quickly stepped through. Another click on the remote, and the door swung back into place with a whisper like the rub of silk on silk.

The narrow east west tunnel, from the cistern to the main unused rail tunnel, was new. The builders had worked under Grok's direct supervision and, once their task was completed, had disappeared at his hand, They were sealed in a tomb of their own making. They had never suspected that the small horizontal alcove detailed on Grok's plan was not for ventilation gear, and so there they now slept for eternity, bricked in by Grok himself. He had done the job dressed in an immaculate pair of dark coveralls.

When the final door was closed, it was virtually undetectable in the grimy wall. As he set off along the tunnel Grok silently saluted the men who were clever enough to do such a brilliant job and yet stupid enough to miss the obvious. He travelled down the main tunnel about eight hundred metres and then, stopping midway between two dim orange lights, he pressed the remote once more. Another tribute to the recently dead swung noiselessly open and Grok stepped into another tunnel.

He repeated the previous procedure in reverse until he arrived finally at the door of his workplace. There were three ways to access the laboratories, and each way was protected by the same elaborate types of systems. Grok liked to mix up his arrival routine, but whichever way he arrived, he always enjoyed the moment when he stepped from the dank, dark and dusty tunnel systems, into the bright clean tiled environment that he had created for the professor.

At exactly 7 o'clock, Tetsuya stepped into the isolation room. Grok had the boy on the raised bed with the sides up and Tetsuya walked a full circle around the bed.

"He's had no food since he arrived right?"

"No," replied Grok. "And he's been as quiet as a mouse, not a peep out of him."

"Okay," said Tetsuya, "let's find out where he's up to."

He stepped forward and dropped one of the stainless steel sides. He picked up the child and held him at arms length. The child fixed his gaze, and Tetsuya put him down on the floor facing the wall.

On a low table against the wall were placed a feeding bottle with formula, a hard baby's biscuit, and a small plastic bowl with apple custard and a spoon in it. The child sat quietly for fully two minutes, then looked over his shoulder at Tetsuya. He rocked forward onto his knees, then crawled over to the nearest piece of furniture which was the raised bed. He pulled himself up into a standing position, then after a few seconds, stretched his arms out before him like a comic zombie, and wobbled his was across to the table against the wall. Once more he stopped and looked over his shoulder at Tetsuya, then he stretched out and grasped the plastic bowl, dragging it toward him. He grabbed the spoon in a fat little paw and began shoveling the food into his face. Some of it even made it into his mouth.

Tetsuya looked at Grok, and the man in the immaculate dark suit knew it was time to start work.

And work they did. For the next three years they progressed all five children through ever expanding phases of isolation and sensory deprivation. The first four children had arrived underground soon after their births and, knowing no different, had adapted quickly to the deprivation and darkness. They were cared for exquisitely in a mechanical environment devoid of all love and emotion. Whenever physical contact was necessary it was enacted with harsh robotic precision. These children knew no love, no nurturing and no emotion of any kind. They were slowly and inexorably untethered from their very souls. It was their souls, their esse, that would make the crossing and provide the incredible energy required to reconstruct the mortal shell on the other side of the time line.

Kioshi was already a year old when he arrived underground, and the speed with which he caught up and progressed beyond the other children, supported Tetsuya's belief that only certain people and certain souls could achieve the crossover. He gradually came to understand that Kioshi would be the only one. He would task Grok with the problem of how best to utilise the other four children in which he had invested so much time and energy. They would not be travellers. The final stages of the process involved the creation and installation of the trigger. A massive, overwhelming emotive cataclysm that wrenched the soul from the body and set the journey in motion. This trigger was identified by scanning and recording the brainwaves of the children to find an emotive deep-set subconcious memory, and then recording the child's responses to replaying or simulating that memory. Tetsuya was unable to know what the memory was; whether it was a good memory or a bad memory.

It just showed up as activity on an electroencephalograph, or EEG machine. From that point it became possible to recreate that memory at will by feeding it back into the subject's brain, using essentially the same equipment and electrodes that had been used to find and record it in the first place. Most importantly, it was possible to multiply and magnify the singular emotive memory to the point of saturation. In layman's terms the subject was maintained in a state of emotional and sensory deprivation, fed intravenously, exercised by electrical stimulation of the muscle and nervous system, with waste evacuated by drain and catheter. The subject was clinically maintained in a comatose state and suddenly, whilst in this state of virtual 'non existence', the subject was bombarded with an entirely overwhelming emotive shock. It was like being hit by a freight train. In an act of self preservation, the soul separated itself from the body.

24. KIOSHI

The past…

Kioshi was four years of age, but there was nothing, not even existence.

Suddenly he opened his eyes and through a film of mucus, saw himself as a plump, reddish blue little lump balanced on a woman's stomach. There was a slight tugging at his waist. A man in a green mask reached down and tried to place him in the woman's arms. She swatted at him, screaming…

"Get them away from me. Get them away from me."

There was a great flash of blinding light which moved in sync with the echo of the woman's screams. Growing ever louder the light and sound coalesced into one living piercing pain that set him vibrating like a guitar string. The sound split itself off again, then stopped as suddenly as it had begun. Then there was just the light, strobing, strobing. Kioshi's head expanded out to twice its normal size in time with the strobing. He felt himself lying flat, and sensed that he was not alone in that darkened space, now invaded, that he called home. Or what he might have called home if he had known what that meant. Now he felt a strap across his forehead, and only now, because the sheen of sweat across his brow had allowed his head some movement. He could feel that it would slide back and forward under the strap. On some instinct he snapped his head to the left and, there in one brief flash of light, he saw that his black space had a beginning and an end. He saw a wall and in that wall a window and in that window, the face of the creator stared back frozen, straight into his eyes.

Just as suddenly, the black became a white blinding, painful light. He snapped his eyes shut and felt the spin of the planet force his brain up against the back of his skull. He felt the blood course through his veins and rush up into his fingertips. He felt himself tilt upward and sway backwards and forwards. He felt a slimy hand reach down his throat and take a grip on his bowels and start dragging them up through his mouth, turning him inside out... then he felt nothing. His eyes looked backwards into his empty skull and all he saw was a green mist.

He heard a noise. A real noise. He opened his eyes and saw a young boy sitting opposite him. His eyes were drawn to something behind the boy's head. It was a big piece of red material with blue, white and red crosses, and things in one top corner. He looked down at his feet and saw that he was standing on a bed. It was unstable. He could feel it moving under him. Suddenly the boy opposite him threw himself down on his knees and touched himself on the head and shoulders. Of course Kioshi didn't know what any of these body bits were called, but as he touched at them he was aware of the same parts on his own body. He couldn't move, he didn't know how. He just stood on the bed looking down at him, his legs weakening.

The boy jumped up and ran from the room, then quickly reappeared with a little black box which he held up to his face. He saw the boy's finger move and his eyes opened wide. There was a tiny click-clunking sound that echoed off into space. He felt his body explode into millions of tiny fragments, as he was sucked into the little box. He felt himself bounce off the back of the box. Then his little body began expanding until it swallowed his space, then the world, then the universe itself.

Then there was nothing... not even existence.

25. TETSUYA

The past...

Tetsuya was bent over the EEG. The boy's brainwaves matched his physical reaction as recorded on the infrared camera.

He took the paper scroll and spent a minute or two matching the single frame rate on the videotape with the grid on the printout. He now knew that the trigger had worked. The boy had clearly been somewhere, done something. With the total absence of any memory other than the trigger, and the total absence of any other stimuli, he had to have been somewhere else... some *when* else!

Tetsuya had no doubt that given time he would be able to view the brainwave patterns as a basic picture; the way a television picture travels from a signal source, through a cable, and arrives on a television screen just like the one he was watching.

As he pumped the control to move the tape forward one frame at a time, he could see the umbilical cables and tubes that ran off behind the boy's head and passed through the rear wall. Frame by frame, he could see the boy's head start to move fractionally back and forth under the head restraint. The reaction to the massive stimulus had been shocking and extreme to see, and had brought out a sheen of sweat on the boy's forehead. While he watched through the window, he was concerned that the movement might dislodge one of the electrodes placed on the boy's head, but they held fast. In fact, what had actually happened now seemed far more ominous. He had been staring intently at the boy's eyes. They had opened wide at the very beginning of the stimulus, then closed. But while he watched, the boy's head had snapped sideways and Tetsuya had found himself looking straight into the boy's eyes. Watching now, frame by frame, he was convinced that the boy had seen him, that there was some form of recognition. But how? The strobe was not real but induced, and both the nursery and the observation room were in total and absolute darkness. He chose to believe that he was wrong. That the boy had seen nothing. It was easier that way. The problem was the unmistakable spike on the EEG right out there in the open space between the stimulus and the reaction to the stimulus. It stood there like a spear driven into an empty dance floor. And it lined up exactly with that point on the video tape where the boy's eyes met his.

Tetsuya shook off the uncomfortable feeling, and hit the play button on the remote. He watched intrigued as Kioshi's eyes jerked open for the third time. This time they stayed wide open for over thirty five seconds. The pupils rushing backwards and forwards like pachinko balls... this way, that way... watching, watching.

"What the hell are you seeing?" Tetsuya said aloud.

He switched off all his equipment and looked at his watch. The boy should be rested enough by now. He went and collected Grok from his office and together they went to the boy's room. Kioshi was lying awake on his side, and a white coated technician sat in an easy chair leafing through a magazine. He looked up when he saw Grok and the Professor enter.

"You can go now," said Tetsuya to the technician. "Oh and get rid of that magazine. You know you are not supposed to have any material here that's not approved by me or Mr. Grok."

The man scampered out the door and Grok closed it behind him.

Tetsuya went to the boy's bedside.

"How are you feeling Kioshi?" he said, taking the boy's hand.

Kioshi rolled onto his back and nodded.

"Okay then," said Tetsuya, "let's try and work out what happened during our experiment then shall we?"

The boy nodded again... wary.

"What can you tell us Kioshi? What did you see? You should tell us everything you remember."

Kioshi nodded one more time, then haltingly described how he had been in a room somewhere. There was a man holding him... a man in a green mask, and there was a woman; and the woman was saying, '*get them away from me*'. This he remembered clearly. He started to get agitated as he went on to describe the tunnel and the green mist, how scared and sick he had felt. Tetsuya squeezed his hand to comfort him.

"It's alright," he said soothingly, "nothing can hurt you. As we explained yesterday, it was not real, it was just an experiment, just a dream. There is nothing to be afraid of."

The boy looked from Tetsuya to Grok, then went on to describe the strange looking boy with the strange clothes, that he had seen in his *dream*.

"Now then Kioshi... I want you to think very carefully. Can you describe this boy and his strange clothes and anything else about where you were.

Gradually, over the hour, by asking lots of basic questions, and drawing lots of basic pictures, Tetsuya was able to determine that the *boy* Kioshi had seen was more than likely a girl. Kioshi described how the boy or girl had run from the room and returned with a little black box which he or she had pointed at Kioshi. He described a loud click. This was most likely a camera, and more detailed questioning and drawings by Tetsuya, indicated it was probably a Box Brownie. When Kioshi came to describe the surroundings he could only tell them that it was a room, and that there was a large red piece of material on the wall. Tetsuya became more alert.

"Kioshi, I need you to concentrate on that red sheet on the wall. Do you remember if there were any words on it or pictures?"

Kioshi screwed up his eyes for a minute, then opened them slowly and said.

"It was mainly red, except for a little patch on the right side. In the other corner there was a blue bit with red and white crosses and lines on it. It was very pretty."

"A flag," interrupted Grok. That sounds like a flag."

Four hours later, Tetsuya was forced to admit that the description of the girl and the object behind her, which might or might not have been a flag, was all he could get from the boy.

The following morning, Tetsuya arrived early with a number of reference books for the flags of the world. At about 11.00am Kioshi had identified a number of versions of the British red ensign, as close to what he had seen. After spending the next two hours checking all the flags based on the British ensign, they had found four or five that Kioshi insisted were very close. But the little colour patch on the right, in the shape of a shield, was different. For someone his age, he displayed amazing attention to detail. Finally at about 2.30pm Kioshi found two flags, both for Canada. They were almost identical, with just the colour of the maple leaves in the royal arms being different. The one with green maple leaves was the de facto national flag from 1922 to 1957, and the one with the red maple leaves, from 1957 to 1965. In 1965 the current red and white maple leaf flag was adopted.

So Tetsuya, with the same unscientific logic that he applied to testing, decided that Kioshi had been somewhere in Canada, and that the flags seemed to support a 36 year jump. Now all he needed to do was figure out where in Canada.

"Right Mr. Grok, call that technician in here and take Kioshi to the lab."

He turned to Kioshi.

"Don't worry Kioshi, this medicine will make you feel better and help you sleep."

According to plan, Kioshi woke seven hours later with absolutely no recollection of what had occurred earlier.

26. IN WHICH KIOSHI HATCHES A MEMORY

The past...

Kioshi could hear the guardians outside his door. Of course he wasn't frightened, he wasn't anything. And they were just there... every day, to take care of him, feed him, teach him. Not so long ago they had told him how his parents had died soon after his birth and that, because he had no living relatives, he had been bought here to be cared for by the guardians. There were other boys here his age and occasionally he was able to eat with them, but never to talk to them. If he had known and understood the concept of friendship, he would have known that they were not friends, they were like him, just there. The guardians had explained to him how there were guardian houses all over the world, housing hundreds of thousands of children just like him, and that often they were built underground like the one he lived in.

There was one man who seemed to be the head of the guardians. His name was Professor. Even when Kioshi couldn't see him, he knew he was always around somewhere. In Professor's presence something strange always happened to Kioshi. His heart seemed to beat faster, until he could hear it in his head. His little hands got sweaty. Had Kioshi known what emotions were he might have recognised this as a manifestation of one of the strongest emotions... fear. But he didn't!

One thing Kioshi did know, was that he was seven years old. Yesterday some changes had been made. First there had been what Professor called a birthday party. This apparently was a celebration of how many years you had been alive, conducted on the day that you had been born. It was celebrated with strange soft, sweet food called cake, and there were two other boys present, along with Professor and three of the guardians. Of course, Kioshi had had a birthday celebration exactly like this for the previous two years, but that information had been removed from his memory bank, along with any other selected memories that might cause unwanted stimulus or interference with the program. The boy didn't know what a memory was, and of course he didn't know that they were being systematically removed from his subconcious, but there was one strange and disturbing picture that lived in his head. It was like the little stories that he saw on the learning screen.

In that picture he saw himself lying on his back in a dark tunnel. The walls of the tunnel were cold, wet stone. Hearing a faint hissing noise, he cast his eyes along the tunnel and watched, as a wispy green luminous shape bled out from a crack in the stone wall. This 'thing' wafted along the top of the tunnel and paused above him, before flashing down through his gaping mouth and deep into his body, with an unworldly shuddering jolt. The tunnel started pulsing and changing shape. Mixed in somehow with this pulsing, Kioshi saw flashing patches of black. He realised he could see Professor there in the black flashes. Not really see him exactly but sense his presence there… know where his very eyes were… there in that eternal blackness. He knew he was looking right into those eyes.

Then he saw himself standing on a bed, just like the one here in his new nest. Opposite him was another boy, sitting on another bed. This boy had long hair and wore strange clothes and behind him was a large sheet of mainly red material pinned to the wall. Suddenly noticing him, the boy knelt down and touched himself on the shoulders, then jumped up and ran from the room. Kioshi couldn't move and almost immediately the strange boy returned carrying a small black box which he held up in front of Kioshi. Kioshi could feel his heart about to burst through a great gaping hole in his body, when suddenly there was a deafening click and Kioshi found himself back in the tunnel. He saw the green shape tear itself out through his gaping mouth, and stream off along the tunnel roof. Then, with a sucking noise like the last foul breath from a crone's maw, it found a crack in the rock face and was gone. He crumpled down the wall and collapsed onto the wet ground. The pain fled his contorted face and, as he closed his eyes, he released a great sigh.

Little Kioshi shuddered at the thought.

The other change was to his quarters. After the celebration he was taken to a different room; called a nest in guardian houses. He was to live here from now on. His clothes and his learning folders had been moved to the new nest, and he could see that the bed was bigger. The pictures on the wall were different and in addition to the learning panel on the wall at his desk, there was also one mounted on the ceiling above his bed.

Kioshi climbed onto his new bed. If he had been a normal child he might have jumped up on it feet first to test it for bounce; but he just wasn't. A normal child that is. He lay on his back and pulled the headphones from the bracket on the bed head. The learning screen above him hummed into life, bathing his sad face in a soft green glow.

27. GUMSHOE SAN

The present...

It's been three days since that dinner with Nick and Yuka at Ajito. Following dinner we had put Yuka in a cab and then Nick and I had headed straight for the show. I had set out that night with the idea of telling him about the rent boy and all the strange happenings, but the rain had cleared and I was still in a mildly euphoric state at seeing Yuka again. In short, I was in a great mood, so I decided not to raise the matter at all with Nick.

The show went great, and once more I marvelled at the popularity of blues rock with a young Japanese audience. Back at the hotel we had a quick nightcap to unwind, and I went to bed around three o'clock. For the first time in days, I slept like a baby.

The last three days have passed with nothing untoward happening, other than a feeling I had that the boy was in the audience. It's pretty hard to see through those lights, but I had scanned around and seen nothing, so I put it down to nerves.

· · ·

Tonight however was notable for two reasons. Firstly I had no show to do... a night off to do what ever I wanted, and what I wanted was to see Yuka again. She's back from Sendai this afternoon and that was the second notable thing... she had said yes!

Nick is off in Hiroshima setting up next week's dates, and I am standing in front of the mirror shaving. I guess like most guys, for me shaving is pretty ritualistic. I always use the same type of razor and always the same type of blades and gel. I shave in three different directions. First down, then across, then up. But why am I telling you this? Well, the thing about shaving is that you tend to keep a pretty close eye on your hands and face in a mirror and, while I'm shaving under my jaw, I see a black scorch mark literally appear on the heel of my right hand, spread up over my wrist, and disappear just as quickly. All over in a split second. Alarmed, I drop the razor into the sink, then feel a searing pain on the end of my index finger, as I notice the angry blister is back.

The boy must be near.

I stagger back to the bedroom and flop down on the edge of the bed. I feel defeated. Why is this happening to me, and why now of all times. Just as things seem to be going well. For the first time in a while I actually had a vision of a future. Something in me wants to jump up and run out of the room to search for the boy; and throttle the last breath out of him. But something tells me searching for him would be futile. He'll find me when he's ready.

After sitting and staring at the wall for about five minutes I decide on the best course of action, and that is no action at all. Forget about it for now, go out enjoy the evening and worry about all this tomorrow.

It's a nice mild evening when I climb out of my cab at Shibuya station. Yuka's hotel is part of the complex, but I make my way into the station and up the stairs to a spot where I can see the whole mad intersection that has become known as the *Shibuya Scramble*.

Even at this hour there is a good sized crowd coming and going. I lean back and watch from my position in the shadows. While I watch I start to wonder how I could possibly pick out any individual in this mangle of humanity. It's like watching ants scurrying back and forth. Then I realise that if the boy was there I would see him... or he would see me. After five minutes I'm content that I'm not being followed and I stroll around to Yuka's hotel; but I can't shake that nagging feeling.

I arrive just as Yuka emerges from the lifts and into the grand foyer. I stop and watch as she makes her way across the lounge area and picks a seat. As I walk forward she looks up and notices me. Her face lights up and it's like watching the sun rise across a pristine white beach. I swear I can hear seagulls and shimmering strings off in the background. I'm brought back to reality pretty swiftly by having to navigate through a noisy tour group heading out to sample the city's delights. Finally the group part around me and Yuka sits, laughing now as I stand with my hands raised in surrender. As I approach she stands and leans forward to kiss me on the cheek. I am so overcome by this simple innocent gesture I have to take a deep breath before I could trust myself to speak.

"So," she says, "I fancy Okonomiyaki... do you prefer Osaka or Hiroshima style?"

"Hiroshima," I reply.

"Great! There's a pretty good place about five minutes walk away if that's what you'd like. But first I'd like you to sit down and tell me what's going on."

I'm caught off guard by this, but I can hear the earnest tone in her voice and see it in her eyes.

"I don't understand," I stammer.

"Oh I think you do," says Yuka. "I'm a very intuitive person, and when we first met I got a very positive vibe, or feeling about you. I felt it was a two way thing, but all of a sudden you are sitting right there in front of me but it's like you've left the room. Your mind is off and away somewhere else, and it's not just distraction... it's something much more than that. I don't just mean that first night. When we went to dinner the other night, I sensed you were hanging back from Nick and I on purpose. It was like you were searching for something the whole way to the restaurant."

She sits back down.

"Why don't you start by telling me who that boy was?" she says.

"What boy?"

"Please," she says. "If I don't get the whole story I'm going back upstairs to my room and you're going back to your hotel. Don't take me for a fool. I think you are in some kind of trouble, and if I don't find out here and now what that trouble is, then this relationship is over before it even gets started. So... let me ask you again. Who was that boy outside your hotel the other night?"

I guess I stand there looking foolish for more than long enough. My head feels like it is spinning, and the air rushing past my ears is deafening. I suddenly felt nauseous, dizzy. I sink down into the chair opposite her. I hear someone somewhere far off say, *"okay... just give me a minute."* Then I recognise my own voice.

"Okay," I say. "Okay well... when I tell you what is happening, this relationship may well be over before it starts anyway. So it seems my options are pretty limited. But all of a sudden, just the thought of telling you my story... of sharing it with someone, makes me feel better."

So, here I am sitting in a hotel foyer in Tokyo, playing poker for my future. If I don't talk she's gone. If I lie, she'll know. If I tell her the whole truth and nothing but the truth, she may well think I'm crazy and leave anyway; but those are the cards I am going to play.

"Alright then," I say, looking her directly in the eyes, "here goes nothing!"

Twenty minutes later I stop talking. I realise that she has not spoken once since I started. It just kind of spilled out of me like rice through a torn sack, until it lay there right out in the open waiting to be cleaned up. Silence. She turned her head away and watched a middle aged woman wrestle two suitcases across the polished floor, then she reached up and cupped her mouth in her right hand and turned towards me. She was about to speak, but turned away again. More silence. She turned back towards me and made a show of straightening the hem of her skirt before speaking.

"Wow! That's quite a story. I can understand now why you were nervous about telling anyone, particularly me. But you know, I'm the one person who can corroborate at least part of your story," she says and adds. "I saw the boy, so there's that at least."

"And there's this," I say, holding up my index finger which still sports the angry blister. "In fact while I was telling you the story it started to sort of throb, like it was reacting to the telling." I paused. "So you believe me?" I say slowly.

"Yes… yes I do," she says. "But now what? Please don't take this the wrong way, because I really do believe you; but I'd rather we don't go out for dinner tonight. I think I need some time to digest all this."

The disappointment must have spread across my face like wildfire, but seeing this Yuka laughed.

"You look like the proverbial kid who's lost his candy. Don't worry… I'm not brushing you off, I just want to think it all through. Why don't we meet for breakfast tomorrow? Pick me up at say… seven thirty?"

With the old adage of a problem shared is a problem halved lodged firmly in my head, I walk back to my hotel a happy man. I like this girl.

It is 7.45am. We are in a western style cafe in Shibuya. The walk back to my hotel and the rest of the night had passed uneventfully. I had slept well and now I was feeling a little better and a whole lot in love. Maybe it was a little early to voice these feelings of undying devotion, but that's not to say I couldn't dream a little.

Yuka is sipping hot coffee, and those big eyes appear over the rim of the coffee cup like the sun coming up. She smiles… and looks deep down into her cup as if she is watching koi play, then puts the cup down and sits up straight.

"Right," she says, all business like, "here's the thing. Like I said last night, I believe your story and, like you, I have no idea what it means or what you… or we," she said with a conspiratorial smile, "can do about it. However, I may know someone who can help. A few years ago I attended a national media and broadcasting seminar in Kyoto.

There was a big fuss one day when this old guy crashed one of the sessions that was being filmed for a local news segment. He was a very eccentric character and he brought the session to a standstill. He just kind of swept in through the doors and walked straight up to the lectern, pushing the speaker aside. He was raving about conspiracies and coverups. Within just minutes, he was hefted out the door by a couple of security guards, screaming and hollering all the way.

At the morning tea break I found out that he had been a very well known investigative journalist who was nicknamed *the hound* because of the way he used to sniff out and chase down sensational stories. He must have had a pretty understanding editor, because they would let him lead off with just an explosive headline and, then a few days later, they would follow up with the meat. The stories always seemed too far fetched to be true, but they always were… true that is. They would end with arrests, government sackings and all manner of public blood lettings. Then one day he picked on the wrong target and they buried him. He raved and ranted for a few months, but he was just too hot to handle. Whoever he had upset was clearly so powerful that nobody would publish him. He was reduced to telling his story to anybody who'd listen, and all that got him was a series of pretty severe beatings. So he had just disappeared for a few years until he turned up that day at the seminar.

A group of us were in a bar later that night and there's the old guy sitting all alone in a corner drinking. One of our group, an older woman, had worked with him and she said he was one of the finest and most intuitive investigative journalists she had ever met. She had great respect for him and asked us if we would mind if he joined us. We had all agreed it would be okay, and so she had asked.

I was quite surprised at how calm and controlled he was. He actually apologised to us for upsetting our session. It turned out that he was working as a private detective. He simply couldn't get published as a journalist and he joked that detective work was the same thing only the audience was smaller, and the pay was bigger. His name was Itsuru Oka, but I remember he laughed and told us to call him *Gumshoe-san*. Some of the cases he had solved were pretty high profile, but he had always insisted on keeping his own identity out of the news. Understandably I guess, his clients were happy to oblige him in this condition."

Yuka stopped talking and took a deep breath.

"I'm sorry," she says. "I've got off the track a bit. The point is that I spoke to him for quite a while. At first he was a little reserved when I tried to dig down deeper into what had happened to him. Once he realised I wasn't a threat and that I was genuinely interested, he relaxed a bit. He wouldn't discuss the past other than to tell me he had been wrong to try and stir it all up again. But he warmed to the subject of his current cases, and I warmed to him. I never go to Kyoto without looking him up. He's my absolute favourite gumshoe. Okay, he's the only gumshoe I know, but the fact remains. I'm sure if I called him he would talk to us. Are you up for a quick trip to Kyoto?"

28. A QUICK TRIP TO KYOTO

The present...

I've always liked Kyoto. The very first time I went there I fell in love with the ambience of the place. Sure there's a noisy downtown area, but even that seems somehow trapped in another time. On leaving the city area one quickly finds oneself in beautiful, peaceful residential areas, populated by lovely traditional homes, and sprinkled here and there with stunning temples and shrines.

It was not to one of these peaceful areas that Yuka and I now travelled. We were heading instead for Karawaramachi, an area where small apartments and attic style accommodations still exist above the tiny traditional shops and businesses. Yuka had phoned Itsuru Oka a few days before and after his initial delight at hearing from her, he had listened intently to what Yuka had told him. At first he said he wasn't interested, that I was probably just some crazy gaijin who was seeing things. But when she told him she herself had seen the boy, he got a little interested. When she told him about my phantom scorch marks and blister, he went quiet for a minute or so. Yuka said she could almost hear the gears in his head turning, as he wrestled with the decision. Then suddenly, all business like, he had told Yuka to bring me to his apartment. Based on his respect for her, he would at least listen to my story.

So now here we are, in a tiny street somewhere off Shijo Dori, dodging delivery vans and trolley boys. Yuka steps off the curb and makes her way around a pile of crates on the pavement. She heads for an old red gate beside the entrance to a shop selling all manner of commercial kitchenware, including an amazing array of rubber menu items. She holds the gate for me, and I find myself in a dim alley that runs about thirty feet down beside the kitchen store and then opens up into a small courtyard. This tiny space sports an equally tiny Zen garden with three small rocks, white pebbles and a koi pond. A stand of bamboo points upwards to a first floor landing reached by a rickety old wooden staircase.

I follow Yuka up the stairs to the landing, and she pulls gently on a rope that travels up around a small brass pulley, then disappears into the timber slat wall above the door. In the relative quiet of the landing I can hear the bell chime somewhere off in the distance. I step back to look down into the courtyard. Tiny insects land on the surface of the pond only to be snatched away by the hungry carp... a tiny slapping noise and a ripple, the only evidence the insect once even existed... the circle of life. I turn back at the sound of the door opening and see an old man framed in the doorway. It is hard to tell, but he is maybe sixty years old and a little over five feet. His long silver hair is tied back with a tattered old hachimaki. Yuka bows deeply, and the old man returns a shallow bow then steps forward and takes her hand warmly in his and leads her into his apartment.

I remain standing at the doorway, being pretty much ignored, while Itsuru Oka leads Yuka down a short hallway lined both sides with books, newspapers and magazines stacked higher than their heads. They scamper through like two crabs and disappeared around a corner. After about a minute, Itsuru returns alone, and looks me up and down like he is selecting new drapes for his bedroom. Finally he takes a deep, resigned breath and looks me in the eye. I bow under his watchful gaze and stand upright and motionless, while he just stands his ground... silent and unmoving, in the doorway. I hold out my hand in greeting... it is ignored. I'm starting to feel something like anger rising in my chest. This guy is some old hack reporter... some old *sacked* hack reporter, who has done nothing to earn my respect. So why should I stand here being subjected to this rude treatment? I maintain my dignity with a curt bow, and turn on my heel to make my way down the stairs into the courtyard.

"Do you have a story to tell me or not?" says a deep booming voice with an English public school accent.

I turn to face back up the stairs.

"Oxford?"

"Cambridge," he says breaking out into a smile, "St. John's College."

I make my way back up the stairs and across the landing. He bows just a little, then holds out his hand.

I stand and stare at it for about as long as I dare, then clasp his hand and receive a firm grip in return. He surprises me by placing his left hand over our clasped grip in an intimate fashion.

"You look confused. I am sorry but I tend to test people when I meet them for the first time. You know... if you had not reacted that way... if you had not responded to my rudeness. If you had just stood there I would have closed the door and that would have been the end of it."

"So I've passed have I?" I say, still a little annoyed.

"I don't know," he says enigmatically. "Maybe the test has only just begun."

He smiles again, then laughs loudly and turns back down the passage.

"Mind how you go," he says cackling. "Hall space is crawl space yes?"

The hall opens out into a surprisingly large studio style room with modern furniture and a state-of-the-art kitchen at one end. I note the stainless steel bench tops and the expensive Italian coffee machine. Itsuru follows my gaze around the room then in a low menacing voice he says.

"I can't help noticing your surprise musician. What were you expecting... a poor hermit living off cup noodles in a hovel?"

I look at Yuka who holds my gaze steadily. Then I notice the tiniest flicker of a smile in the corners of her eyes.

"I wasn't expecting anything, and I know nothing about you other than what Yuka has told me. That is that you were once a very successful investigative journalist and now you're some kind of private detective. I certainly don't know what happened to end your illustrious career, but I'm guessing that your being such an annoying little fucker probably means you finally pissed off the wrong person. As to the state of your finances you've just told me you went to Cambridge, so that probably means family money. Finally the only reason I was so interested in your kitchen was because I haven't had a decent cup of coffee since I got to Japan and I was just wondering if you know how to use that thing, or if it's just for decoration."

Itsuru Oka never flinches. He maintains eye contact with me without the slightest change of expression. I return his gaze, desperately trying not to be the first to blink. Then I lick the end of my right index finger and raise my hand to tick an imaginary box. The universal sign for... *score one point to me!*

Itsuru's eyes follow the movement of my hand, and about half way to the tick box he realises he's been had. His inscrutable gaze cracks into a massive grin, then he lets forth with a great bellowing laugh that belies his small stature. There comes a loud banging through the ceiling from the floor above. Itsuru raises his eyebrows and shrugs his shoulders in apparent defeat.

"Okay then musician," he chuckles. "End of test, guaranteed."

He steps forward and slaps me on the shoulder.

"Now let's find out if I know how to drive my coffee machine."

Lots of time and travel in Italy and France had taught him about coffee... real coffee and so yes, he does know how to use that machine. As I sit savouring my second double espresso we get down to the business at hand. Oka-san has an uncanny sense of knowing how to take the flimsiest of facts and starting to build on them.

"The key," he says, "is to concentrate on establishing all the known facts. Once you are certain you have all the facts to hand, whether it be just one or two or even twenty or thirty, you have to be prepared to investigate every one, no matter how seemingly insignificant. You have to be prepared for every one of them to come to a dead end. That way you will not be disappointed."

"But we have no facts," I chime in.

"Oh but we do," replies Oka-san, "you just haven't recognised them as such. So let's see. Is this boy Japanese or foreign?"

"Japanese."

"Okay so there's a fact. Now what else... how is he dressed?"

"Well," I say, "I guess you could best describe him as being dressed as a rent boy. You know, dyed hair, scruffy tee shirt, hoody, big chains, that sort of thing. I don't know... very out there I suppose."

"So," laughs Oka-san, "we have facts piling up like crazy yes? How old would you say he is?"

"Well that's not so easy," I reply. "I would guess somewhere between sixteen and twenty years of age."

"Great!" says Oka. "That's two more facts right there."

"Two more facts... how do you figure that?" I ask.

"Man... you foreigners are slow," grins Oka-san. "If he's between sixteen and twenty then he must have been born between 1990 and 1994... yes?"

We work our way through the next half hour, establishing more facts, and discounting others as mere supposition. Of paramount importance to my credibility here is the simple fact that Yuka has seen the boy. She is able to confirm his existence along with some of the other facts that I have listed.

Oka-san takes notes of everything we say. By the time we have wrung out the last of the facts he has filled about five pages of his notebook. I go to speak but, without looking up, he holds up his hand to stop me. He keeps that hand raised, while he slowly leafs back and forth through his notebook with the other. Finally, he lowers his hand, closes the notebook and looks up at me.

"Okay musician, now I want you to tell me the whole story from the very beginning... twice. Leave nothing out, no matter how insignificant you feel it may be. The first time I just want to listen and the second time I will take notes," he says.

29. A NOTE FROM KIOSHI

The present....

Underground, the boy wakes with a start. The man is close, like that first time, just a few short weeks ago. He can feel him, somewhere above. These past few weeks he has felt the man come and go through Shinjuku Station above. Sometimes he would be gone for many days and the boy would wonder if he would come back. So far he always has, but the boy has begun to feel strongly that his time is running out. If he doesn't act soon... if he doesn't approach this man soon, the man will leave Japan forever and take with him any opportunity of providing Kioshi with any kind of peace in his life. That's what Kioshi has come to believe. This man can help him. He is convinced that he has met this man before but he doesn't know where. He is just as convinced that finding out where he has met this man will help solve the riddle of his mind.

He rouses himself from his bed and sits with his bare feet, cold on the glossy tiles. His mind is spinning out of control. Tiny fragments of information seem to hang there, to circulate there. But it is difficult to know how they all fit together. With each trip into the past, his control over the situation has become more obvious to him. At the same time he has felt a strong need to hide these facts because, with each trip, he has learned more and more.

Certainly he has done what was requested of him by Grok and the Professor. But he has also made many discoveries that sometimes helped him, but more often confused him. He told nobody any of this. He didn't know what this was called, but of course it was a secret. He was also unaware that the strange feeling he experienced when hiding things from the Professor was guilt. He had learnt not just to hide certain facts from the Professor and Grok, but also how to hide these feelings from the machines.

Over the years, with the trips back in time and the more recent trips above ground, he had learnt how to mark the passage of time, and to keep a basic record of events. On his very first trips above ground he had seen people with things like paper and pencils, and had realised their worth. He had smuggled some things back into the nest, but it didn't seem to be a concern.

The first experiments involved the Professor connecting him to what he now knew were called electrodes. Clearly they were scanning his brain for information, but now Kioshi knew how to blank out his brain so the machines showed nothing. After each experiment he was taken to another room where the Professor and other guardians spent a long time talking to him. He didn't really know why, but he knew he had to deceive them, so he did.

He slipped off the bed, padded across the room and into the bathroom. He withdrew his little stash from behind the sink and sat down on the toilet to inspect it. Rubber bands held some money, a penknife, a small notebook and a pencil. Not much, but it's a start.

Kioshi was teaching himself words and writing, and a lot of his time aboveground in recent years was spent in a library, looking at pictures and the words attached to them. He would often ask a stranger to tell him what the thing in the picture was called, and most people were happy to help. Crude, childlike writing in the notebook now recorded six trips into the past and a very sparse outline of the events that took place. He turned the page, and here was a record of those things that ran wild in his head. Those things he was struggling to recognise as fleeting memories or just bits of memory.

Today, he was interested in one word in particular. He had written this word many different ways based on what he had heard in his head all these years, and what he had learned aboveground. The word had come from deep down in his subconscious and was now floating there only part revealed, like an iceberg. Of course the boy had no idea what an iceberg was, let alone a subconscious. He had come to understand that this sound, this... word, was actually his name. In his notebook, the word was spelt three different ways. Keeoshi, kioshee and keyoshi were scribbled childlike across the page. The boy had decided on keyoshi. Yes keyoshi... that must be how you spell it. Probably anyway... his name that is.

He went to the back of the notebook and tore out a blank page. He concentrated hard and bent to the task of writing 'I am keyoshi'. He folded the page and concealed it down the front of his pants. He carefully replaced his stash in the cavity behind the sink, flushed the toilet, ran the cold tap for a few seconds, then stepped back out into the other room.

The boy now surely known to himself as keyoshi left his nest and, after clearing his absence with a guardian, made his way purposefully up to the surface. He came out through the south entrance of Shinjuku Station and walked quickly down the south terrace, and out onto the street overpass just south of the Sunroute Plaza. From here he could watch the entrance to the hotel. He knew the man was still there. He felt it. He knew the room the man was in and he knew the man usually left at around this time each morning.

Not ten minutes later the man appeared at the entrance carrying a guitar case. The boy hunkered down a little as the man looked up to the sky and all around. Seeming content, the man checked his watch and then strode briskly up the street in the direction of the station.

Kiochi waited until the man had turned the distant corner, then he walked down off the footbridge and into the hotel lobby. He headed straight for the lifts. On the seventh floor he was a little panicked by the cleaners and trolleys in the corridor, but he found the man's room again, and dug the folded note paper from the front of his pants. He stood there, at the end of the corridor holding the note... trying to finally decide. A maid came out of a room along the corridor and paused to look at him. He smiled at her, then bent and pushed the note under the door... and was gone.

30. A HAT WITH BERRIES AND FLOWERS

The past...

Tetsuya Hiroko watched while the electrodes were attached to the boy's head. The boy was perfectly calm, and was distracted by the story on the learning screen. A guardian took his left hand and held it, while another quietly turned his right arm over exposing his soft pink forearm. The boy felt a cold wet sensation on his arm, then a sharp prick as the cannula went in. He turned from the screen to look at his arm, but was unable to see clearly what was happening. He lost interest and turned back to the screen. The guardian connected the clear plastic tube and stood back to wait for instructions from Tetsuya, who remained bent over the monitor behind the boy's head. He nodded finally to the guardian, who stepped forward to administer the anaesthetic.

Tetsuya's concentration was such that his eyes seemed to burn like death rays into the monitor screen. The anaesthetic pushed the boy quickly through the five sleep stages. He watched as the waveforms changed shape and the boy moved into the first stage. High amplitude theta waves floated across the monitor, followed by bursts of rapid pulses as the boy's heart rate slowed and his temperature dropped slightly. Then the waves slowed and deepened as the boy reached the delta or third stage. The waves slowed further and then got even larger. Tetsuya tore his eyes from the monitor and watched as the boy moved quickly now into REM, the fifth and final stage. The boy visibly relaxed, but below the closed lids there was none of the rapid eye movement common at this stage of deep sleep. Tetsuya looked back to the monitor. He noted the total absence of brain activity indicated by thin green line that remained so flat and still, as to appear painted on the monitor screen.

He looked at the two technicians off to his left. Like him, they were bent intently over monitors, but these were in turn connected to the mainframe computer. The technicians indicated

132

that they were ready. Tetsuya nodded in acknowledgement and held his breath, forcing himself to remain calm by counting to ten in his mind. The green line remained painted on the screen. All was ready.

Tetsuya Hiroko gave the order and sent the young boy called Kioshi into the tunnel. The green line on the screen proved it was not just painted on, and hummed into life. The beta waves were now twanging through at over forty cycles a second. Tetsuya looked at the boy to see his eyes moving rapidly beneath his closed lids. The green line oscillated with life and drew with it new multi coloured lines that tracked across the screen.

Kioshi opened his eyes and found he was lying flat on his back in a cold dark tunnel. The picture in his brain! It was the same as the picture in his brain. Except it wasn't. Something was different. There against the wall... a strange man was standing there in the tunnel. Then he heard a kind of hissing, sucking sound and looked between his feet along the tunnel, just in time to see that same slimy green mist pour out of a crack in the glistening wet stone wall. He was unable to move. He watched powerless as the thing hissed its way along the roof of the tunnel. As it passed the strange man, a separate green mist rose up from the man and joined with the other. It came on and paused menacingly, directly above him. He opened his mouth to scream and the thing that was his soul drove itself forwards and down into his open mouth, to consume him.

Then there was nothing. On the monitor screens all the lines went flat... dead.

Then there was something.

Kioshi opened his eyes to find himself sitting on a strange wide seat behind two people who had their backs to him, maybe guardians. The screens went wild. There was a sensation of movement heightened by the objects racing past the glass panels that surrounded him. Suddenly one of the people in front of him turned rapidly to face him. There was a hideous scream split the air, and a strange roaring noise. Then all hell broke loose with a great rending crash, as metal struck metal. In slow motion Kioshi found himself lifting off the seat and moving forwards and upwards. He travelled past a woman with long blond hair whose face was at that very moment, crashing sideways into the cold steel windscreen pillar. Suddenly the woman was gone, left behind, as Kioshi found himself still travelling forward in a great tinkling cloud of sparkling diamonds and spatters of red. Keeping pace alongside him was a strange grey shape covered with tiny berries and pretty coloured flowers. Then Kioshi saw this drop and bounce off the hood of the car as he continued onwards into eternity.

"Please... now! We must bring him back," shouted one of the technicians, almost in a panic.

"No," shouted Tetsuya, his eyes now blazing like a mad man. "Not until I say."

Kioshi felt himself land on a hard surface and slide forward. There was no pain... no sound. He opened his eyes and saw an older boy, yes... not quite a guardian, walking toward him. The boy leaned down to take his hand and there was a great spark of electricity that jumped between them. The boy jumped back in surprise then turned away. Kioshi closed his eyes.

Again Tetsuya forced himself to count to ten... to wait, to stabilise... and slowly the waves began to settle down, so he kept counting, watching the activity under the boys eyelids. Eighteen, nineteen, twenty.

Tetsuya gave the order, and the technician at the boy's right side quickly changed the feed to the cannula. When this was done, Tetsuya signalled to the technicians off to his left to stand by as he watched the waveforms settle back. Kioshi passed back and forth quickly between two or three sleep stages then settled into REM. The techs indicated all was stable, and the professor keyed in the sequence and hit 'enter', to start the boy on the homeward journey.

Kioshi opened his eyes again and found himself back in the dark tunnel. He realised he had been holding his breath for some time now, and as he opened his mouth to breath a great burning sensation welled up in his chest and his soul tore itself out through his mouth. It clung like some shapeless puddle held in place by some crazy inverse gravity, above his head. Slowly it moved off along the roof of the tunnel then, finding a crack in the rock, was sucked in with the sound of the last dregs of a giant's milkshake and was gone. Kioshi shuddered. His teeth chattered in his head and he shivered himself into a shallow sleep; there on the damp floor of the tunnel. Kioshi woke to see the strange man bending over him. This was the person who had come toward him on the roadway. He clawed out with his hand to grab the man's leg. He missed. He lay there with his face in the puddle contemplating another try, but the man turned and fled along the tunnel. The next time he opened his eyes he was looking up into the smiling face of Professor.

Tetsuya took the syringe from the guardian and injected the contents into the rubber diaphragm on the side of the cannula. The boy returned almost immediately to a dreamless, peaceful sleep. Tetsuya checked his monitor one more time, then signalled the technicians to disconnect the boy and have him returned to his room. As Kioshi was wheeled out of the room, the technician who had called out during the transfer process approached Tetsuya and bowed deeply.

"I am so sorry Professor. I know I broke protocol. I did not mean to question your judgement. The monitors were... I just thought... well I thought the boy's life may have been in real danger. You know... what with the trauma and all. I was concerned only for your work. I mean... if we lost the boy... all your work, all these years."

Tetsuya said nothing. Over the technician's shoulder he could see Grok watching through the observation window. He nodded almost imperceptibly, but the technician couldn't have seen anyway. He was still bowed in apologetic supplication.

"Look at me," said Tetsuya to the technician, who nervously straightened up. "It's okay," he said smiling now. "No harm done. I appreciate your concern."

The technician relaxed as the professor came forward and put an arm around his shoulder.

"Come... let us have a drink to the success of today's experiment," said the professor as he led the technician out through the door.

The man in the dark suit emerged from the observation room behind them.

Within two hours the technician's head and hands were at the bottom of Tokyo Bay and his body was providing protein for about two hundred rats in a disused branch tunnel.

The next day Tetsuya arrived at the labyrinth very excited, and armed with a theory. He quickly gathered Grok and the remaining technicians in his office, and got straight down to business.

"I have been going over the printouts from our last experiment and, from those of the first experiment three years back. Three years ago there was something that concerned me about what I saw in the lab during the experiment, and what I found in the printouts the next day," he said, pushing copies of the printouts toward the others.

"Take a look here at the major disturbance in the wave patterns during the trigger phase. This indicates severe trauma, *very* severe trauma. Following my discussions with our young subject Kioshi, we have been able to determine that the trigger in both experiments involves the boy being held by a man with a green mask, and a woman screaming '*get them away from me*'. So... the boy exhibits no trauma or even mild apprehension when describing this to me, and indeed, when he's awake, it doesn't seem to disturb him in the slightest.

Yesterday, the boy described, in great detail, what had happened to him in this current event. It seems he was involved in a horrific car crash and, if you look at the sections I have marked in red, you will note that the printouts indicate major trauma while the boy was having this experience. Of course, he was very shook up and sick with what presented as vertigo, but other than that he was unhurt and will recover.

But this is where it gets interesting. If we look at the printouts for the first experiment three years ago, we see an even greater level of traumatic disturbance, but we know that the boy merely stood on a bed in a perfectly normal room and maybe had his photo taken. There was no trauma apparent in that room. At the time, even the boy said everything was very calm and normal.

Remember this is no ordinary child. This kid seems old beyond his years and has amazing recall. The other strange thing you'll see there is that the *event* trauma starts about halfway through the event, and it is even more frenetic than in either the triggers or the latest event trauma. Grok and I talked to the boy back then and timed things out. Then we compared the timing with the printouts. It would seem that the traumatic event started at about the same time as the girl was taking Kioshi's photograph.

Here the Professor paused and poured a glass of water from the jug on the table. He drank deeply, then carefully put the glass back on the table.

"We have two events," he continued. "It may just be coincidence, but I think that these jumps into the past require some kind of trauma at each end, the trigger and the event.

Maybe it is these two traumatic events lining up at identical times, thirty six years apart, that opens up these, these... pathways or wormholes... call them what you will. It may also offer an explanation as to why, when the globe is about seventy percent covered in water, the boy hasn't been dropped in an ocean somewhere. Of course this might be just good luck."

He took a small magnet from each of his jacket pockets, placed them on the table and, taking a pencil, drew a line away from him on the surface of the table.

"Let's consider that trauma is energy, latent energy."

He placed one magnet on the left of the pencil line, a foot or so away from him, then the other on the right side of the pencil line, close to the edge of the table.

"The magnets represent energy, the trauma; so watch what happens when these two energy sources pass each other on a separate, parallel track."

With his fingertip, he pushed the magnet on the right away from him and, as it reached a point opposite the other magnet, the two snapped instantly together.

"So there... two separate energy sources travelling in opposite and parallel directions cross the divide."

Nobody spoke until finally Grok said...

"So Professor, what does all this mean to us in a practical sense?"

"It means Mr. Grok, that if we can find out where these traumatic events took place, we can pinpoint exactly where the boy was in terms of latitude and longitude. As I say, the boy's recall and attention to detail are sharply honed. Before we erase his memory of this last event, I am sure we can gather more data from him to assist in finding the location of that crash. There are always news reports when people die in car crashes. The other event in Canada will of course be much harder to identify, but we have theoretical dates, so I'm sure it can be found. You and the rest of your team take two days Mr. Grok. Then let me know what resources you think you need to get this done. We may have three years, but once we have this information, we will have two firm waypoints, and that's where the task really begins."

"And what task is that Professor?" said one of the technicians.

"That remains classified," replied Tetsuya Hiroko gruffly. "You can all go now and get on with it. Except you Grok."

Grok had got to his feet, and now followed Tetsuya over to his desk.

"That technician," said Tetsuya waving his finger at the door. "He has just asked the most important question of all. I think it is necessary for you to know the answer to the question he asked, so I will tell you the answer. Your job includes keeping alert to any staff members who stumble upon answers that I don't want them to have. For that you need to know those answers. The technician asked; what is the task. The task Grok, is to send the boy back in time to a specific point, and that point is a pre-determined place that shall remain known only to me for the time being. However I can tell you that it is here in Japan. If anybody out there proffers that theory you will terminate them immediately. Thank you Grok."

"Certainly Professor... that's what I'm here for."

31. A BIG YEAR FOR KIDNAPPINGS

The present...

Itsuru Oka slouched in an easy chair, his Yukata wide open, revealing expensive designer boxer shorts. Balanced on the arm of the chair is a laptop which now sits there softly humming as Itsuru leafs back through his notes. The laptop screen darkens and sleeps. Itsuru notices and is about to punch the 'return' key to wake the thing up, when he pauses with his middle finger suspended in mid air.

Computers, he thinks. I have just done in three days without even leaving the house, what would once have taken weeks of solid slog all over the place. Trouble is, the damned things come to possess you. Every lead you click throws up hundreds, maybe thousands of new ones and once you are on the scent, it's hard to stop. But he needs rest. Instead of hitting the return button to bring the demon machine back to life, he closes the lid and uses both hands to lever his stiff body out of the armchair. He stands up and after two or three steps is limber enough to move a bit easier. He pulls the obi from the back of the chair and wraps it around his waist, straightening his robe. Then he goes to the refrigerator and pulls a frosted lo-ball glass and a bottle of Stolichnaya, from the freezer drawer. He drops in a couple of ice cubes and jams in a big slug of vodka. He takes a tug on the vodka, and it travels down his gullet leaving a friendly lava trail, followed by an empty feeling that demands filling.

He hasn't ventured out for a few days, so kitchen choices are limited, but he manages to find the makings for a half reasonable omelet. By the time the omelet is ready to turn out onto a plate, his glass is empty, so he re-fills it, and takes himself back to his armchair. Itsuru Oka feeds himself with one hand, and works through his notes with the other. After three days he has about thirty pages of notes and very little else. He reasons that most of these kids ran away in their early teens, so he has gone back ten years or so and started searching through newspaper archive and police report. He has gathered every unsolved incident involving missing boys between the years 2000 and 2005. There are hundreds of them. He still has a few good contacts at his old newspaper, and one of these had been able to help him whittle down the list considerably. Now it will be just a case of going through each of the remaining unsolved cases. He has ended up with forty six boys, and he has online photos for thirty nine of them with current ages ranging from sixteen to twenty. The chances of Yuka's friend recognising one were slim to say the least, but one never knew.

He flicks up the lid of the laptop and is about to create a folder for the photos of the missing boys, when the telephone rings. He hoists himself out of the seat again, grabs the handset off the table and flops back down into his chair.

"Yes, hello," he says.

"Oka-san," says an excited voice. It's his friend Noburo, at the newspaper. "I have something weird here I thought you should know about," he says. "You told me you were looking for a boy maybe sixteen to twenty years old. Well listen to this. I have a boy born in 1991, and that would make him eighteen now, who was kidnapped from a hospital in Kyoto, just days after he was born."

"I don't know Nobu," says Itsuru, "that sounds more like a case of child stealing. You'll probably find the kid was raised in a happy, but unscrupulous family, and is now majoring in Engineering at university."

"Maybe," says Noburo, "but the weird thing is that I have three more abductions, all in the same year, all from Kyoto hospitals, all unsolved... and all boys."

Itsuru feels his brain shift up a gear. He is no longer tired or hungry. He is hooked. He feels a scent has opened up. He looks at his glass. The ice has gone and what is left is just watery vodka. He pours it down his throat and sits up straight in his chair.

His mind ticks over. Long seconds pass and finally he is roused by the tinny voice coming out of the phone in his hand.

"Sorry," he says. "Okay, so what was the result of the investigation?"

"Well," says his friend, "that's the strange thing. There were four separate investigations. Nobody... and this is hard to believe... nobody connected the dots here. Each case was investigated separately. Nobody investigated all four cases as one."

"No!"

"Yes!"

"Alright," says Itsuru. "I'm not sure any of this relates to my case, but you may have opened a hornet's nest here my friend. How could this have happened?" He feels his pulse quicken.

"Okay, send me everything you have. I think when I get through with this current case, you and I may have a big story here."

32. LET LOOSE THE HOUND

The present...

Itsuru has spent two days reviewing everything his friend Noburo had sent him. Making phone calls and searching the web for additional information. At the end of it all he is even more convinced that none of this has anything to do with his case. It is however, the sort of thing that he liked to get his teeth into. Four newborn babies abducted from Kyoto hospitals around the same time, and each one treated as a separate case. It's hard to believe that there had not been one investigation covering all four abductions. Itsuru knew that there was a certain percentage of mistakes made in hospitals where newborn babies were concerned. There had been one or two high profile cases not that long ago, where parents were found to be raising the wrong child due to a mix up at the hospital. DNA testing was, it seems, opening more than the odd can of worms. But these babies had just disappeared, and surely these four babies had parents who would have driven the investigations forward. Losing a baby at birth was a traumatic thing. In fact it was hard to imagine anything more traumatic for a woman to undergo, after carrying a child for nine months.

Itsuru had become so fascinated with this case that he had decided to continue to investigate it alongside his other case. This was big and should be pursued. And of course there was still that issue, however tenuous, of these children roughly matching up age-wise, with the Tokyo rent boy.

So Itsuru had started with the last known abduction. Even though many years had elapsed, it was always good practice to start with the hottest trail; well okay, warmest trail. So he concentrated firstly on the last child born, and right there the case got even more interesting. On the day of her release from the maternity ward this poor distraught woman and her husband, had returned to their tiny apartment and there they had apparently ended their own lives. Their's was an open and shut case, with suicide ruled as a direct result of losing their baby. There was a small extended family, but it seems nobody had the heart to endure any further disruption or grief, and so the investigation seemed to just grind to a halt. Itsuru noticed the investigating officer's name. He had known this detective for a while, and was not a fan. Itsuru thought he could recall hearing that the guy had suffered a heart attack or something. He was slovenly, uncommitted and lived on a diet of fried food and beer, so there were no real surprises there.

Viewed now from a distance, there was one nagging issue that stood out to Itsuru. Why had these parents committed suicide just five days after the baby's disappearance? This was not right. It was only five days, and there was an investigation just getting started. To abandon all hope at five days... hmmm. Itsuru took up his notebook and circled the parent's names in red ink, then in big bold characters he wrote '*possible foul play?*'.

Before digging any deeper on the first case, Itsuru decides to have a quick look at the next case. This one involved an eighteen year old single mother. The infant had disappeared from the maternity wing nursery, sometime between the hours of ten thirty and eleven forty five in the evening, and the mother was found to be missing in the morning. Neither her nor the baby had ever been seen again. This case was marked as all but solved and downgraded from kidnapping to missing persons, with the young mother named as the prime suspect. It was considered that she had absconded to parts unknown with her new born baby. Itsuru was about to close the file when something made him dig a little deeper. And right there, amongst the witness reports, was that one page that could set a bloodhound's nose twitching.

One of the nursing staff who came on shift at seven thirty the next morning, claimed the young mother was still in her bed on the ward at that time. It was concluded that the nurse had been mistaken, or that the girl had taken the baby from the nursery the night before, hidden it before returning to her own bed, and smuggled it out in the morning. Itsuru Oka scratches his stubbly chin and shakes his head. Another outstanding example of sloppy police work. Here we have a mother who abducts her own child. Why, when she could legally walk out of the hospital with it in a few days anyway. And furthermore, why would she steal her own baby and hide it away somewhere in the middle of the night, under cover of darkness and with very few staff about, only to abscond with it in broad daylight... in full view of the dayshift? Pigs may fly thinks Itsuru, but this sure doesn't!

It hardly came as a surprise to Itsuru when the final two files revealed a similar story. Missing babies, missing or dead parents.

Itsuru has the scent. He calls his friend in the department and finds out that the detective who investigated the final case is actually still working for the police department. He's been moved to a desk in Central Filing. About five minutes later, Itsuru has his extension number and is sitting in his armchair staring at his telephone. It is difficult to know how to handle this. He'd never hit it off with this guy and didn't expect him to be exactly helpful now. Finally he snatches up the phone and punches in the numbers.

"Tanaka... Central Filing."

"Hello Tanaka-san... this is Itsuru Oka. Do you remember me?"

There is a pause. Itsuru hears paper rustling, and he could swear Tanaka was hurrying to swallow something. Suddenly he feels more confident. What... had he thought this guy was going to get any brighter with the passing of time?

Finally he speaks.

"Well, well, well. Yes, I remember you. Sorry I wasn't at your retirement drinks," chuckles Tanaka sarcastically. "What do you want?"

"Oh, not too much," replies Itsuru. "And yes, I guess I did kind of depart the scene in disgrace," he says, purposefully giving Tanaka the upper hand. "But I see you are still going strong, so I suppose at least one of us survived." Push the right buttons, play the old enemies nostalgia card thinks Itsuru. Works every time.

And it did this time as well.

"Yeah well, that's all water under the bridge I guess" says Tanaka. "Okay... what can I do for you? I'm busy."

"Well," says Itsuru, "you probably know I do a bit of investigative work these days. Nothing much, just insurance claims stuff mainly."

"Yeah, so what's that got to do with me?"

"My client," continues Itsuru. "Is an insurance company and I'm just wrapping up some loose ends on an old claim. The file they've given me shows you as the officer in charge." *In charge of catering, thought Itsuru.* "I just wanted to ask you one or two quick questions, so we can close the file. The case involved the kidnapping of a baby in Kyoto about nineteen years back. I was…"

"Which one?" interrupts Tanaka. "One from the hospital or the one from the doctor's surgery?"

"I'm sorry," says Itsuru, caught off balance. "You say there were two kidnappings?"

"That's right," answers Tanaka. "Some investigator you turned out to be."

Think, think, think…

"Oh… okay," says Itsuru. "I think that's the problem. There's a mix up in the files. I guess I'm looking for the one from the doctor's surgery, but I don't have any details. When was that exactly?"

"Jeez," grumbles Tanaka, "let me think. The hospital one was 1991 I think. A new born baby. I remember the parents suicided."

Itsuru bit his lip.

"And the other one must have been the year after. That kid was a year old. That the one you're looking for?"

"That's the one," says Itsuru, recovering quickly. "I see the problem now, the file only shows the one year old, and it shows Kyoto Hospital. So you say it was a doctor's surgery. I don't suppose you remember the name of the doctor or the address of the surgery?"

"The doctors name was Ohno, I remember because it was the same name as an instructor we had at the academy... looked a bit like him too. Anyway, his surgery was in a little private hospital in the city. That's probably why the files got it wrong. But the kid was a year old… I remember it like it was yesterday okay."

"Wow!" says Itsuru. "Two newborn baby abductions within a year of each other."

"Two! Make that five," answers Tanaka.

"Five?" says Itsuru, feigning surprise. "You're kidding… that sounds like some sort of organised crime. Why wasn't there a major investigation?"

"Don't even ask!" says Tanaka… and hangs up.

33. I'VE GOT MAIL

The present...

It's around 4.30 and I'm back at the hotel after a full day of rehearsal. The rehearsal rooms are out at Asakusa and I have been trying out a few bass players. I drop my guitar near the door to the bar, and settle myself onto a bar stool. I've got the night off tonight and I'm looking forward to dinner with Yuka. The barman is a fast learner and as I look up he stands there grinning with a bottle of Laphroiag poised above a crisp glass weighed down by a single gleaming ice cube. Smooth... intravenous, intramuscular... and the body relaxes into a groove of contentment. Ten minutes later, he barman steps up again, but I surprise myself by waving him away.

Upstairs I unlock my door and step over a folded paper on the floor. Damn... I hope that's not a note from Yuka canceling tonight. I drop my guitar in the corner and, picking up the paper, make my way to the lounge chair.

As I drop into the chair, I am overcome with what I like to call HRB, or Hotel Room Blues. One of these days I'll get around to writing a song about it, but for now I'll just wallow in it. If you are a very frequent traveller like I am, you'll know there is something 'other worldly' about hotel rooms. Lots of people I know envy my lifestyle. They travel occasionally on holidays, but that's a whole different ball game. When you travel for business your hotel room becomes a sort of spacecraft, where you sit just outside the real world. I have this feeling of entering a hotel room, and the whole room being fired off into space, where it just hangs while the world turns inexorably beyond your reach. Your life is going on down there without you in it. Your kids are growing up, your wife or girlfriend is tracking on without you, your father is dying in a hospital somewhere back on earth... and its all beyond your reach. Then there's the whole 'where the hell am I?' question.

I will frequently wake up in the early hours of the morning in some hotel room, and spend five or ten minutes peering around in the gloom, trying to figure out where I am. To me, Hiltons seem the same nearly everywhere in the world. Same travertine marble, same type of art (if you could call it that) on the wall, same type of furnishings. Sheraton is the same. I swear sometimes I have come fully awake, identified that I'm in a Sheraton, but the country remains a mystery until I actually drag my bones to a window and look out over the city. This is still a problem sometimes in Asia. If I can't crack a window for air, I'll turn the air con down to near freezing so I can sleep. With oppressive humidity outside, the resulting condensation on the windows can still mask my location when I wake in the morning.

But I digress. The possibility that the note is from Yuka has just flattened me out a bit, that's all. As I turn the paper over in my hand, I realise that it is not normal hotel stationary, and besides, their notes are always in a hotel envelope.

I unfold it and stare for some time at the three words scrawled across the paper in a childish hand.

'I am keyoshi'. It makes no sense to me, who or what is a keyoshi and what has this got to do with me. *'I am keyoshi, I am keyoshi... keyoshi'*. Nope, nothing. I guess it's just been pushed under the wrong door. So that's good news, I'm still out with Yuka tonight, and that simple fact lands me back on earth and clears my HRB in an instant. Cool!

I've got a few hours to kill before meeting Yuka, so I set the alarm on my phone and swap the chair for the bed. I stretch out into relax mode.

Something wakes me... a sound... a thought. I struggle back to the surface and claw the molasses from my eyes with tingling fingers. In the next twenty seconds I go through the many stages of a sick headache, then finally get myself sitting upright. With shaky hands, I reach out to grab my phone from the side table.

It's only 5.35. I must have only been asleep... deep asleep though, for about ten minutes. I know what woke me... a dream. A dream I now remember... vividly.

A dream where a rent boy makes his way uncertainly along a hotel corridor. He's wearing a black hoody with white lining and black formal pants. He's got on a blue t-shirt with the number twenty six printed on a torn, winged heart, and a large silver padlock on heavy chain around his neck. He pauses by a door. His right hand reaches out tentatively... probing, caressing, stroking the door as if it is some living breathing thing. He moves forward and places his left cheek against the door, and then rests both hands flat against the surface beside his head. There is a tear travelling downward across his right cheek. His right hand moves in to arrest its slow journey. He raises his dampened fingertips to his face and stares, as if puzzled at this new sensation. He looks straight into my own eyes with all the sadness of an old and dying race. It jolts me awake!

I grab the note. '*I am keyoshi... I am keyoshi*'... and I know with unreasonable certainty that this is a note from the rent boy. It was not a dream but a vision. His name is Keyoshi.

I drop my feet off the bed onto the floor, and sit for a second or two as waves of nausea pass over me. No big deal... just woke too quickly. With shaking hands I grab my cell phone and search through for Itsuru Oka's number. Two more strikes from a shaky thumb and the bells are ringing in Kyoto. It takes a while and, while I wait, I can picture Oka san searching for his phone.

"What!"

"Is that Itsuru Oka?" I ask, a bit taken aback by the telephone etiquette.

"Ah... the musician. This had better be important, I was busy... busy sleeping. I've been burning the midnight oil as they say, on this problem of yours. So what do you want?"

"Well," I answer smugly, "seeing as how you are so big on facts I thought you might like a nice juicy one. But I can call back later if I'm disturbing you."

"Okay, stop being a martyr. What have you got for me?"

"I think I know the boy's name. I came home to the hotel and found a note under the door. It just says '*I am keyoshi*'.

"And?" says Oka-san. I can picture his raised eyebrows and pursed lips.

"And nothing, that's it."

"That's it?"

"Is there an echo on this line?" I say, baiting him.

"Yeah, yeah okay. So how do you know this is his name?"

"Well, I had a vision that the boy came down the corridor and poked the note under my door."

"So... let me ask then. Were you lying down on your bed when you had this vision?"

"Well I..."

"Were you maybe even asleep when you had this vision?"

"Yes but..."

"Well, I only ask because we have a technical name for that kind of vision. We call it a dream." chuckled Oka.

I start to try and explain when he cuts me off.

"It's okay musician, I think you are probably right. Everything about this business is so odd I wouldn't be surprised if you told me you were visited by a ten foot tall pink rabbit."

"Okay... so what now?" I ask.

"Read me the note. Spell out the name"

I do that, and through the ensuing silence I can sense the wheels turning and the gears meshing in his head, gumshoe style.

"So," he finally says, "Keyoshi is not a Japanese name. At least not that I've ever heard. However Kiyochi is what you might call a Japanese surname and both Kyoshi and Kioshi are, for the sake of a better description, first names. I think there is also a Kiochi."

There is a longish pause.

"And I suppose I had better come clean," says Oka-san. "The real reason I believe your vision is because my research has already turned up a few possible names... and one of them is Kioshi... K.I.O.S.H.I... Kioshi Matsumoto."

34. HOME FROM HIROSHIMA

The present...

I am lying stretched out on the grass. From the pavilion behind my head, the beautiful, otherworldly notes from a single koto drift outward across the water. I tilt my head to the side and see, at my feet, a languid turtle peering up at me. He is joined by another, perhaps drawn in by the sadness of the koto's call. I am in Shukkeien Garden. In the heart of Hiroshima, Shukkeien Garden is a place of great peace in this city already marked with a memorial peace park. Away from that place of gawking tourists, millions of paper cranes and rent tears in the fabric of the universe, I still find no answers, but at least find more peace. Before the end of each trip to Hiroshima I come here to find a balance. To find a balance in this city that, like a nostalgic, strives to remember, and like a lunatic, begs the bliss of ignorance. One of two blinding cataclysms that shook the world, but even so, failed to change its course.

I sit up and turn to the pavilion. The koto player is a schoolgirl. Perhaps thirteen or fourteen, but to me she seems older... maybe a thousand years old. She kneels alone amongst a number of kotos that are arranged on low tables across the floor. She wears a traditional autumn yellow kimono with a deep red obi, and her downcast eyes appear closed. Her right hand floats deftly above the thirteen strings, alighting each time at the perfect note. Her left hand subtly alters pitch below the bridges. I close my eyes and take stock.

The past three days in Hiroshima have been good. The shows went well, and the relative calm of this city, and of Shukkeien in particular, seem to have replaced a fear of the unknown with a sense of resolve. I no longer feel that the rent boy, known now as Kioshi, means me harm. I have begun to feel some connection with this mysterious creature. What that connection is I have no idea. I know that this thing is important. Its resolution is one of the stepping stones of my life, and to move forward with my life I need to fill that gap. I cannot avoid it.

A change in the pitch of the koto brings me out of me reverie. The girl has tilted her head slightly, and now looks directly at me with just the tiniest wisp of a smile playing around her beautiful eyes. Then like a butterfly she floats upwards and is gone. The last note of her refrain echoes around Shukkeien and as it finally dissolves into the garden, I too take my leave of Shukkeien.

I rendezvous with Nick back at the hotel, where we gather up my guitars and our luggage and check out. We grab a cab over to Hiroshima Station, and are soon comfortably seated in a plush 'green car' on the Shinkansen bound for Tokyo.

35. YUKA VERSUS THE WORLD

The past...

At the very same time as Nick and I boarded the Shinkansen for Tokyo, Yuka Sasaki sat staring out the window of her office in Sendai. She too sensed a change in the path her life was taking. Recently she had felt increasingly that her life is on standby. Sure, she likes her job, but it holds no special challenge for her. Yuka was born into a very well to do family. The money had come from her mother's side of the family, and that fortune was founded on post-war opportunism. Her mother was a social butterfly who offered no love or warmth to either Yuka, or her elder brother Hiro. While their mother partied away on a diet of gin and American cigarettes, the bewildered Sasaki children were largely raised by their father, with help from domestic servants. She who lives by the bottle may very well die by the bottle, and so it was that Yuka's mother succumbed to cirrhosis of the liver.

Yuka's earliest memory was of her mother half naked in the arms of a much younger man. She had been maybe four years old when she had wandered into her mother's bedroom and witnessed her mother astride the man on the bed, a glass in one hand and a cigarette in the other. Her mother had delivered her a withering look of scorn, had climbed off the young man, staggered across the bedroom and pushed Yuka out with her hip... swinging the door shut with her right elbow. Whenever her father was away, this sort of thing became a regular occurrence until eventually, the young Yuka closed her own metaphorical door between her and her mother.

By the age of eight or nine, she had exorcised all feelings toward her mother, and with them any earlier feelings of guilt. Her brother Hiro was eight years her senior, and bore absolutely no resemblance to herself or her father. Their features were soft and generous, whilst Hiro's features were sharp and cruel, as was his demeanor. Like his mother in many ways, Hiro was a rake. His mother fed his habits with a seemingly never ending supply of cash and fancy cars. No less than seven months after his mother's death, Hiro turned his Dino Ferrari into his own personal coffin. At the speed he had been travelling, it was hard to determine which bits were human and which bits were machine. And so, for the second time in less than a year, thirteen year old Yuka Sasaki stood hand in hand with her father at the family grave, staring without emotion at the newly engraved name of her brother; her mother's name, barely weathered in the hard stone beside it. She felt her father squeeze her hand ever so slightly, and she turned to look into his eyes. Dry eyes that now seemed younger than she had ever remembered. He smiled down at her. It was time for them both to start a new life.

Yuka idolised her father, and had spent many years wondering how such a kind and gentle, well educated man had married such a woman as her mother. She was to discover many years later that her father had been forced to marry her after she became pregnant. He had known her only a few short weeks and was already in the process of trying to avoid her when she delivered the news of her pregnancy. Her father had of course known that the child was not his, but confronted with the issue, had felt the only honourable thing to do was to marry the girl and raise the child as his own. Very quickly he had realised that he was shackled on a ship of doom, and part of his survival technique had been to develop a non-confrontational attitude to his wife's behaviour and to immerse himself in his work as a biologist. He travelled the world teaching and lecturing. He was highly regarded in his field, and was responsible for a great many achievements in macro-biology. However, in his heart, he knew that his greatest ever achievement was to produce an astoundingly beautiful daughter from an otherwise loveless union.

Of course at first he had worried about Yuka's well being in his absence. He knew she was ignored by her mother and bullied by her brother. But he watched her resilience and strength grow, and he spent as much time with her as he could. Together they took trips into the country, visited zoos and beautiful gardens. When they had the house to themselves, they cooked together, and Yuka's father described in detail, his journeys throughout the world. With a keen attention to detail, he recounted trips on the harbour ferries in Sydney Australia, and the beautiful wildernesses of Tasmania. He painted a picture in her mind's eye of the fabulous cities of London, Paris, Rome, Venice and his favourite, Florence. He told her how he had visited the Great Wall in China, and witnessed a Hindu ceremony at the Batu Caves in Malaysia. They laughed together at his stories of the brashness and excesses of America and via these stories, he recounted the absolute and unreserved love he held for Japan.

Not long after the death of Hiro, Yuka's father sat her down and discussed her senior schooling options. He told her that it was his intention to retire from academia and research, and to concentrate on writing.

"I think it is time for you to expand your horizons beyond this house. I think together we should select a suitable college where you can complete your schooling. In addition, for me you are the only happy memory in this house. I think it would be best for both of us to leave here." He paused to let this thought sink in.

Yuka sat motionless, awaiting her fathers next words. To compose himself he looked at each of his hands in turn then flexed them in a fist and placed them on his thighs.

"Now you must listen carefully Yuka. You must understand that what I am going to say next is not to be thought of as punishment, but as a reward. Under difficult family circumstances you have shown wisdom, strength and judgement beyond your years. I think there is a chance that it is too easy now for you to rely too much upon me, and to shut out the rest of the world. It is important that you mix with young people.

People your own age. It is important that you form independent views."

Yuka had not moved. Her expression remained impassive. Her father continued.

"As you know, my family came from Mitake. When I was a child it was a long journey from there into Tokyo, but these days it is only about ninety minutes from here on the Ome line. I have purchased a beautiful, traditional Japanese house in the hills there, and once we have found you a suitable college, I wish to move there. It is peaceful and private, but still close enough to everything I need to live a good life. Of course it is too far for you to commute to a college in the city, so you will live in a dormitory at college and come home on weekends."

He saw her resolve crack just a little around the edges. He reached out and placed his hand on hers, which were clasped tightly together in her lap.

"Believe me when I tell you Yuka, that this is exactly what I did. I was some years younger than you are now, and I thought it was the end of the world. It was the opposite... it was the beginning."

Yuka fought in vain to stop the slow progress of a lone tear down her right cheek. She finally looked up at her father.

"If this is your wish father, and if you think it is best for me, then it will be so," she whispered.

"It is the best thing Yuka, and I give you my solemn promise that if you are unhappy after three months, then you can return to live with me at Mitake, and we will make other arrangements. But you must make me a solemn promise as well."

He paused for effect and smiled as he said.

"You must promise to make the most of it, and not to forget to come home on weekends. The house in Mitake is our home Yuka... yours and mine."

Finally her resolve collapsed, and she dived forward and flung her arms around her father's neck. Half happy, half sad, but wholly determined to make him proud.

. . .

Now as she stared out of the office window in Sendai, Yuka realised she had reached another crossroad in her life. She had indeed enjoyed college in Tokyo, and she still had a number of close friends from those days. She had produced good results and had enjoyed softball and debating as extra activity. For the first few months she had returned home every weekend, and had regaled her father with news of her week. She came to love the Mitake house, and to understand her father's love for the area. They took long hikes in the hills and discussed every known subject including politics, art, religion, defence, the ecology and world peace. Her father had watched proudly as she had blossomed into a beautiful, educated and informed young woman.

Yuka had enjoyed languages and the arts and, when it came time to enter university, she had pursued a degree in Journalism. She had been snatched up pretty quickly by her current employer but, as she watched life passing her by on the streets of Sendai, she realised that covering entertainment for a regional radio station was not where she wanted to be.

She turned from the window with a little shudder, stood and gathered her resolve, then marched down the hallway from her office, to the office of her Editor-in-Chief.

36. FAILURE TO LAUNCH... APPARENTLY

The past...

Tetsuya Hiroko left the university early, and took a train to Harajuku station. He looked as much like a university Professor as any other might. He wore an old tweed sports coat of a style he imagined would not look out of place in Cambridge or Oxford. He headed up into Yoyogi Park. He paused at the entrance, both to check carefully that he wasn't being followed or observed, and to try and relax his beating heart. Today was a big day. Today was three years since Kioshi's last 'launch'. The boy was now ten years of age, and Tetsuya's life's work would take another big step today. As he walked he had reflected on the past three years.

. . .

A matter of days after the last experiment with Kioshi, he had been sitting in a coffee shop in Asakusa. He had long ago made it a point to avoid any parts of the city where he might be recognised. Tokyo was a big place and it was easy to hide.

"Tetsu-chan."

Tetsuya froze. He kept his head down and ignored the voice, and the familiar use of his name. From the corner of his eye he saw an old brown pair of leather loafers step up and park themselves beside him. A hand touched him on the shoulder.

"Tetsu-chan, I thought that was you. Good heavens, it must be what, fifteen years? But I'd recognise you anywhere."

Tetsuya looked up. The voice belonged to his old mathematics tutor from university. He decided there was no option but to tough it out. He stood up and faced his old Professor.

"Professor Watanabe... what a pleasure it is to see you. I'm sorry I was engrossed in my thoughts."

"So you've not changed much," chuckled Watanabe. "It always was Tetsuya Hiroko versus the world as I recall."

Old Watanabe ordered himself a coffee and sat himself down at Tetsuya's table... uninvited. However, this chance meeting would turn to Tetsuya's advantage. Watanabe touched briefly on Tetsuya's past woes, then questioned Tetsu on what he'd been up to since his spectacular rise and fall. Tetsuya got more and more uncomfortable, but gradually he came to understand that Professor Watanabe was not remotely concerned with the events of his past. Tetsuya told him that he had continued to work privately on his theories, but that his funds were drying up. Of course, nothing could have been further from the truth. Grok had moulded the other four stolen boys into one of the city's most impressive criminal cells. Money was simply not a problem.

"You know Tetsu-chan, you always were a bit of a loner. Maybe that's why you were one of my favourites. What most people thought rude and belligerent, I recognised as commitment and focus. It wasn't that you scorned the world... it's just that you thought the world couldn't keep up with you. You know, the academic world is perhaps a more forgiving place than the corporate world. There's been a lot of time passed and, I'm sure if you were interested, we could organise a teaching position for you. Of course tenure would be out of the question."

The Professor had given Tetsuya his phone number, and this had ultimately led to Tetsuya accepting a teaching post at the university. The position had given Tetsuya a greater degree of freedom. It had allowed him, as it were, to come up from the underground.

. . .

Anybody now watching him walk along the path would have noted a happy man, humming a tune in time with the crunch of his brogues on the gravel path. In the past three years they had established that the first experiment had landed Kioshi in North

161

Vancouver, Canada. Tetsuya Hiroko knew the Canadian flag that Kioshi had seen could have been hanging in a bedroom anywhere in the world, but it was all they had, and it had paid off. They had turned up a case in Vancouver where four children had eaten rat poison. Two of them had died. Grok had got hold of the police interview records, and the dates times and circumstances were a positive match, that further enhanced Tetsuya's trauma theory.

Just before the branching path up to the Meiji Jingu Shrine, Tetsuya peeled off to the right and made his way unobserved into the garden, over the little wooden bridge and down into the abandoned cistern. Twenty minutes later he emerged, still humming, at the door of his laboratory.

Grok had organised the boy's preparation, and they now awaited him. The equipment was considerably more refined now, and stimuli and response were both more accurately measurable.

The boy lay on the bed staring straight up as Tetsuya stepped forward and placed a gentle hand on his forearm. There was that feeling again. There was something about this boy. Beyond all of this, there was something else.

"So Kioshi, it's time for your tests. Nothing to worry about. Are you comfortable?"

The boy continued to stare straight up. Of course he could not answer should he want to. He had been in an induced, near comatose state, for the past three hours in readiness for the day's procedure. Tetsuya felt the length of the comatose state could be reduced and ultimately dispensed with, but that required a certain willingness on the part of the boy to want to react to the stimulus. He had not yet reached that stage.

"Well okay then," said Tetsuya. "It will all be over in no time."

Tetsuya returned to the monitors, checked and rechecked the time, and then gave the signal to stand by. The green line remained steady on the screen.

Tetsuya gave the order and sent Kioshi into the tunnel. The green line hummed into life. The shock of the stimulus flared across the monitor screen. Everything was happening the way it should. The beta waves bounced across the screen. Kioshi's eyes moved rapidly beneath his closed lids. The green line oscillated with life, and drew with it new multi coloured lines that tracked across the screen.

In the laboratory the wave patterns remained steady on the monitor screen.

Kioshi opened his eyes and found he was lying flat on his back in a cold dark tunnel. He remembered this place and he waited calmly until he heard the hissing and sucking, and saw the green mist approach along the tunnel. Once more he was powerless, as the thing crawled along the roof and stopped directly above him. This time he knew. He didn't understand, but at least he knew, and so he opened his mouth and the thing that was his soul drove itself forwards and downwards to consume him.

Still the wave patterns remained steady on the monitor screen.

Kioshi opened his eyes to find himself standing on a street in what appeared to be a small village. He was facing a window protected by white steel bars. He looked left and right, but the narrow street was empty. A street sign to his left read 'Rue de la Poste', and a sign over the window read 'La Poste' and three other strange words. There were noises coming from the inside. Kioshi peered in, but could see nothing but a wooden counter. He pushed tentatively on the old brown door next to the window and, as it opened, he heard then saw, the small bell attached inside the door jamb. He followed the strange noises behind the counter and there, spread out in an old chair with his feet up on a desk, was a man who thrashed about, moaning and gasping for breath. Suddenly the man's feet dropped to the floor and his eyes opened. He spun his head to face Kioshi, then reached out and grabbed him by the elbow, screaming something that Kioshi could not understand.

And still the wave patterns remained steady on the monitor screen.

Kioshi just stood there looking into the man's pleading eyes. The man let go of his elbow and grabbed him by the hand. There was a great sparking sound and the man let go and screamed, screwing up his eyes in pain.

The wave pattern altered momentarily but almost imperceptibly.

Kioshi turned and left the way he had come, hearing the tinkling of the old doorbell as he went.

"Anything?" Tetsuya asked the technicians. "Anything at all?"

"Nothing.   I'm sorry professor, but it seems he hasn't responded to the stimulus."

Kioshi watched the street fade around him.

Tetsuya went to the bed and stood over the boy. He was completely still.

After a minute or so he turned and gave the order to the technician to change the feed to the cannula. When this was done, the technician indicated all was stable, and the Professor keyed in the sequence and hit 'enter' to start the boy on the homeward journey.

Kioshi felt his body being stretched in all directions at once. Had he known what plasticine was, he might have said he felt like he was made of the stuff. He was back in the tunnel, and as he opened his mouth to breath, his soul tore itself out and attached itself to the wet wall, beside his head. Now, slowly it slithered off along the roof of the tunnel and was gone. Kioshi felt sick dizzy and disorientated, but he felt strong. This time he had mastered his fear. His body was that of a ten year old boy, but his soul was already thousands of years old. He stretched out on the damp floor of the tunnel and succumbed to his exhaustion. Just like the previous times, when he woke he was looking up into the face of the head guardian, the Professor. But this time the Professor was not smiling.

Tetsuya checked his monitor one more time then signalled the technicians to disconnect the boy and return him to his room.

"Grok."

The man in the dark suit stood up from his position behind a bank of monitors.

"Yes Professor."

"What did you see Grok... anything?"

Grok wouldn't be cowered, but he would always be respectful.

"Nothing sir. Barely any noticeable alteration in the wave patterns. It seems he went into REM sleep stage and just stayed there."

The silence hung in the room like the steamy fat from an indoor barbecue. Grok felt an itch under his left eye and struggled to keep his hands off it. After fully thirty seconds, Tetsuya Hiroko walked to the wall and ripped a small screen monitor out of one of the racks. He lifted it over his head, and flung it full force through the observation room window.

"Three years... three goddamned years!"

He took a deep breath and turned to face Grok... now calmer.

"Okay, just in case there is some kind of time or date aberration, we'll do this again tomorrow, and the day after if necessary."

And they did exactly that, but both attempts failed. Sure, Kioshi went to sleep, soundly to sleep, then woke a little while later on the bed in the lab. Just like he knew he would.

37. TOKYO CALLING

The present…

Nick and I arrived back in Tokyo at about 4.30 in the afternoon and made straight for the hotel.

On the Shinkansen, I had finally filled him in on the whole rent boy mystery. I figured he'd known me for a lot longer than Yuka and Itsuru Oka, so surely I could convince him. Of course at first his natural, healthy skepticism shone through, and he got off a series of spook jokes that had him laughing a lot harder than me. I let him have his fun, but when he came back down the corridor from the toilet dragging his right foot behind him and yelling… the bells, the bells… I had to reign him in. Finally he settled down, and I outlined all the strange events from start to finish. By the time we made it into Shinjuku he was hooked.

At the front desk there was a note waiting for me. It was from Yuka. My spirits soared. I hadn't been expecting to see her until I came back to Japan for the Osaka show in three weeks time. The note said she had some exciting news for me. There was a PS which told me to turn on my cell phone and she would try to call me. I had turned it off when I went to the Shukkeien Gardens, and had completely forgotten to turn it back on. I arranged to meet Nick back in the bar in an hour, then went up to my room for a shower. I sat on the bed and switched on my phone. There were about five missed calls and two text messages, one from Oka-san and one from Yuka. Oka-san went to the back of the queue while I read Yuka's text. It was pretty much the same as the note at the desk, but I looked up and saw myself smiling foolishly in the mirror. Next I checked Oka's message. It read *'Where are you musician? I have been trying to reach you all day. I have some very interesting news. Please phone when you get this message, urgent.'*

Itsuru Oka didn't seem like the type of person who would loosely bandy about words like *'urgent',* so I called him immediately.

"Ah musician... there you are. Or rather; where are you?"

"Oh hello Oka-san, I'm fine thanks. How are you?"

"Yeah, yeah... hello and all that stuff. Look things are moving pretty quick. In fact, in detective parlance I think I could say things have escalated." He sounded positively excited. "I'm coming to Tokyo tomorrow, so it's time for you to dig into your expense account. Can you book me a room in your hotel for say... oh a week? By the way, which hotel are you in?"

I told him which hotel and how to find it.

"Okay then, can you tell me anything?' I asked.

"No no, let's do all that tomorrow, I should be there late in the afternoon. Oh and by the way, is Yuka-chan with you?"

"No, she's gone back to Sendai, but I have a message to call her, why?"

"No real reason musician. It's just that being a detective, I detect love in the air."

"You know Oka-san, you probably don't have to be much of a detective to figure that one out. I've only known her a few weeks and I'm head over heels in love with her."

"Well, she's a hell of a catch musician. Don't hang about, you need to tell her how you feel."

"Okay, well if you'd hang up I could do just that. Call me when you get to the hotel."

I hung up and used the house phone to book a room for a week in the name of Itsuru Oka, charged to my account. As an afterthought I asked if there were any one bedroom suites available in the hotel. It seemed we would need a bit more space for meeting and planning. Then it occurred to me that the boy Kioshi had contacted me in the room I currently occupied. Within half an hour I was ensconced in a spacious suite on the top floor and my old room would be made up for Itsuru Oka. That way, if the boy came again or delivered another note, we would know about it.

Twenty minutes later I sat down on the couch in my new, spacious lounge and called Yuka.

Her voice on the line was… well was fantastic. I took a bit of a plunge immediately.

"Before we say anything else, I need to tell you how much I have missed you. I'm sorry, but I feel like a school kid with his first girlfriend. I know I told you I was going back home, but now I have decided to stay and I want to see you. Can I come to Sendai?"

I could hear her sweet breath on the end of the line. When she spoke she seemed happy, but somehow still hesitant.

"Well," she said, so softly I have to strain to hear, "I really wanted to see you face to face and tell you my news but I guess I should tell you now. You don't have to come to Sendai… I'm coming to Tokyo, tomorrow. Since we met I have felt a bit rudderless. Coming back here I realised that I am just marking time in this job. You know, kind of waiting for my life to get properly started. I seem to have strong feelings for you and…"

My heart was swelling in my chest. It was all I could do not to get up and dance around the room high stepping and hand pumping like some over-excited gridiron player.

"…And I would like to spend some time with you."

To calm myself down I told her all about Oka-san, and how Nick now knew the story.

"Great," she says. "We need to get this thing figured out and see an end to it. Mind you, if it hadn't been happening I might have just interviewed you and gone off back to Sendai without us ever seeing each other again."

"When we find out who this boy is, remind me to thank him," I say jokingly.

We chat a while longer and she says she'll call me when she gets to her hotel.

By the time I get down to the bar, Nick is on his second Bacardi.

"Thought you'd stood me up and gone to bed or something," he says chewing on an ice cube. He's always been a class act.

I ignore him and order a Laphroaig. I savour the peat fire and seaweed nose, before pouring a trickle down my throat. Then I turn to Nick and fill him in on the events of the last hour and a half.

"Do you know," I say, "I feel like a good old steak tonight. Nothing fancy, just a good honest chunk of beef... and I know just the place."

We leave the hotel and head for a basement beer hall that I know of, around on the north east side of Shinjuku station. As we pass the front of the south entrance to the station and cross Koshu Kaido, I feel a burning sensation in my index finger. I grab Nick by the arm and together we watch as an angry red blister forms on my index finger. Nick's eyes are out on stalks. He looks up at me then back at my finger.

"That's just bullshit man..." The last of his words are snatched away by a passing siren.

I knew the boy was there… shadowing me. I tell Nick to stay where he is, and I go out onto Koshu Kaido. I stop in the middle. There's a throng of people crossing, but I know he is close… watching me. I raise my arms and turn full circle.

"KIOSHI… I KNOW YOU!" I yell as I turn in a circle.

Everybody on the bridge seems to stop moving as one. A quick heartbeat to identify the mad man, and they all go hurrying off to wherever they are hurrying off to. About twenty metres away, on a bulwark that is mainly obscured from my view behind an advertising sign, stands a rent boy.

His hair is three colours; blond on the tips, green in the middle and native Japanese black at the roots. It is teased high on his head but, spills spear like down his face, almost covering his eyes. There's a large metal stud to the right side of his bottom lip, and his eyebrows have been shaved off and replaced by two sharp pencil lines peaking at the centre like a child's drawing of Mount Fuji. He's wearing a black hoody with white lining and black formal pants. He's got on a blue t-shirt with the number 26 printed on a torn, winged heart, and a large silver padlock on heavy chain around his neck. He reaches up and with his thumb, wipes away a tear from his right eye. He looks down at his damp thumb. This is the second time that has happened. He climbs down off the bulwark and disappears in the south entrance of the station.

38. FAILURE TO LAUNCH... AGAIN

The past...

It was two and a half years since the last attempt to send Kioshi back, and in that time Tetsuya had undergone some changes.

Now approaching fifty years of age, he had become somewhat maudlin. Since the failure with the last set of experiments, he had lost some of the steely resolve that drove him on like a juggernaut against all the odds. By the age of thirty, he had expected his great intellect to have been 'on-show' to the world. He was to be a savior. His eccentricities would be excused when balanced against his achievements. But here he was, forty nine years old and working as a lecturer in a two-bit post at the university.

Immediately following the last set of experiments he had to rationalise both scientifically and economically. Including Grok, there were nine staff underground. The two historians used to assist in searching archives for the traumatic events, had been despatched the previous year. Three of those remaining were technicians and these were 'recycled' at the end of each experimental period, and re-sourced about eight or nine weeks out from the next scheduled set of experiments. On each occasion they were ostensibly hired by the government to engage in vital, secret experimentation. Their contract called for them to live in the 'government funded' secret facility without leaving, for six months. Everything was provided to them, food, lodging, top research facilities and equipment, everything they needed.

Every fortnight they each received a bogus pay slip detailing an almost obscene amount of money that had been transferred to their nominated account as compensation for their hardship and isolation. Of course they were carefully chosen. Generally loners with little or no family connections, they were replaceable; and given their existing level of expertise, were relatively easy to train. Each one in turn was given a well thought out cover story, and pre-prepared forged documents led their trail somewhere overseas at the completion of their 'contract', where of course the trail went cold. If Grok had done his job properly, there was most likely nobody to even wonder what had happened to them, let alone try to find them.

Two chefs were rotated on a similar basis, and a full time housekeeper was simply little more than a prisoner. Grok's methods of staff disposal were of no concern to Tetsuya, but they were undeniably creative. Barrels of quick lime and dry ice ensured a nice balance of fast and slow disposal, and the fishes in Tokyo Bay, particularly around the Minato drainage outfalls, received regular meal supplements.

In addition to 'human resourcing', Grok's duties included provisioning and control over the activities of the five boys kept underground. Tetsuya Hiroko had quickly lost interest in the first four children, but had agreed that their unique skills and geographical situation provided an outstanding opportunity. Again he entrusted the care of this operation entirely to Grok. Provided there was no problem and the money kept coming, he was content. For Grok's part, he outwardly exhibited total subjugation and dedication to the Professor, but his motivation was all greed. Grok was himself a graduate of the streets. He was cunning like a snake. Aside from the potential to distort time, Tetsuya Hiroko's other great achievement in life was finding and recruiting Grok. But to quote a great Tom Waits lyric... 'a rat always knows, when he's in with weasels', in fact it was really Grok who had recruited the Professor.

Grok had already salted away a substantial fortune, and could live like a king for the rest of his life. However the greed that got him started in the first place, was the same greed that kept him at it now. He was under no illusions that the Professor was clearly as dangerous and cunning as he himself was, and that his subterfuge could be discovered at any time. Grok was aware that a detailed audit of his own expenses (drawn from the Professor's private funds), and close questioning of the boys and their activities over even one month, would highlight a large discrepancy in the budget. Multiply this over the whole term of the operation and we are talking many hundreds of million yen. However, from the very beginning, Grok had discreetly established his own means of escape. At the first smell of trouble from either the authorities or the Professor, Grok would be on the first secret conduit out of town.

Grok kept an apartment just off Okubo Dori in Shin-Okubo, a few short stops on the Yamanote Line from Harajuku. From here he would range about the city, using his well honed criminal instincts to identify larger heist opportunities to supplement the daily routine of pick-pocketing and snatch and grab. The four boys had been trained from about the age of seven, and were sent out generally as two teams. The income from this activity had steadily risen (allowing Grok to skim even more for himself), but once the boys had reached the age of ten or eleven, revenue had started to fall off. As well presented seven or eight year olds, they attracted little or no attention. As they neared their teens this situation changed, and their presence was often treated with suspicion, if not a certain wariness.

In the past twelve months, Grok had often taken Kioshi out with him, to train him and to ultimately put him to work. Kioshi had a natural ability for this type of thing and his resourcefulness amazed even Grok. By the end of that first twelve months, Kioshi was working on his own, and his skill in identifying lucrative targets was supplementing the loss of income from the other two teams combined. Sometimes he came back empty handed, but not often. Grok thought Kioshi's intellect might even be a match for the Professor himself. In fact Grok could sense many similar traits in the two of them.

At first Tetsuya had been unhappy about involving Kioshi, but something drove him on towards his elusive goal albeit with less vigour, and he finally relented. While Grok started rebuilding the team and readying the lab areas, Tetsuya had started trawling the entertainment areas. He was an unhappy man. A cloud of doom hung over him, and thoughts crowded his mind like ants in a nest; rushing this way and that, but never aligning, always uncontrollable. He forced these thoughts out of his head with the liberal application of whisky, saké, beer... in fact anything alcoholic. He somehow managed to turn up for his work at the university reasonably presented and apparently sober. He was able to hold the contempt which he felt for his students and fellow faculty (including Watanabe), in check. He even managed to target two promising undergrads as technicians for his project. They were, even now, underground the signing of secret contracts and other documents, brought to them by a man from a government research project. That man was immaculately dressed in an expensive dark blue suit.

While Tetsuya was wobbling around like a bendy man in a bar in Roppongi, Kioshi was stretched out on the bed in his room. All pretense of 'nests' and 'guardians' had gone by the wayside. The four original boys simply thought of themselves as fortunate street kids under the protection of an organised crime syndicate. Kioshi on the other hand, now knew differently. Ever since the last set of experiments (as the Professor called them), Kioshi had realised he could control whatever this thing was they had awakened inside him. That's how he felt... that it had always been there and they had triggered it off. The first few times they were clearly very excited, the Professor, Grok and the technicians, by the results. On the last occasion, they were very disappointed. They thought they had failed. Kioshi had been able to use his mind to control the experiment, or his reaction to it. He knew that while he slept they were sending him back in time. He also knew that the monitors and machines that he was connected to in that room, told them what was happening, and that now he could sink even deeper and transcend their monitoring systems.

Kioshi, now almost thirteen, knew more than anyone could have imagined. Lying in his room after the second experiment, he had realised that both times he had seen the same image just prior to his world exploding. Then he would wake in the tunnel and his journey would begin. After a set period of time, he would find himself back in the tunnel, sick, drained and exhausted. These parts were always the same. The bit in the middle however, was always different. He now knew that the first ever journey took him out of Japan, as well as out of his time. Bit by bit his memory of these events was returning. On that first occasion he was not at all sure where he was, because he had never left that one room. He now understood, because of the flag he had identified, that he had been in a place called Canada. He also knew that the boy he had seen was actually a girl, and that she was not Japanese. With the second journey, he could not be certain exactly where he was either, but they spoke English, and the car in his memory had the steering wheel on the right hand side. He had taken to visiting the Tokyo Metropolitan Library in the Minami-Azabu section of Minato to research these things and, as a result, was now reasonably sure he had been somewhere in Australia. What he didn't understand was why his memory of these events was so strong when he first returned, then the next day he could remember nothing. It took a long time to knit these little fragments of memory back together.

The third journey was easiest. He was able to quickly determine that he had been somewhere in France, in a post office. He even knew the name of the village he had been in. Of course the third 'experiment' started with the same jolting image, but as he had been expecting it this time, there was no element of surprise… no violent reaction. He simply observed and passed through to the next stage. They tried for three days to send him back, and each time they did so without ever being aware of having been successful. His fourth journey took him to a field somewhere in Japan. There was lots of snow, and a sign pointing to the Tohoku Expressway and a place called Morioka. Back in real time, a trip to the library identified this as a town in Iwate Prefecture in Northern Honshu. The fifth journey taught him even more. This one landed him in a kind of newsagent in Greece. He had frightened the daylights out of a customer but there was a pile of newspapers with the masthead 'Athens News', right in front of him. He clearly saw that the date was exactly thirty six years to the day behind his real time.

He was aware from overhearing conversations between the technicians, Grok and the Professor, that they believed the opportunity to connect with the past was limited to set periods every three years. But of course, the biggest discovery of all was that he could simply lie on his bed at any time and conjure up that trigger image of the hospital ward. In other words, within the confines of that 36 year cycle, and with deference to never knowing where he would end up geographically, he could cross the time divide at any time completely unassisted. Of course he also ended up feeling very ill for an hour or so after each journey.

And now as he neared his thirteenth year, he knew he would soon be taken to the laboratory. He had learnt much in the past three years or so. Particularly since Grok had started allowing him to travel above ground alone. He had a sharp mind, and had realised very quickly that so much had been kept from him. That so much of what he was taught had been wrong. During meal times he was kept separate from the other boys… he didn't know why. He presumed they all lived the same way, that they all went to the laboratory and travelled the time divide. On very rare occasions he could speak to one or the other of the boys unobserved. On one occasion he had heard them talking about doing a job at some place called the Metropolitan Library. One had commented that he thought every book in the world was kept there, and that you could learn everything you wanted from books. This had led to some banter about manga. Kioshi knew what manga was, but he was much more interested in hearing about this metropolitan library place, and all the books in the world.

As usual, Grok had taken Kioshi to the surface via the old green door on the lowest platform. There were cameras there now, monitoring the platform, but the green door was obscured from camera view in a recessed section of the wall. Grok had explained that it was now critical only to come and go from that door when there were lots of people on the platform. A person arriving at the far end of the platform as if from nowhere or, disappearing as if into thin air, would attract mighty suspicion. Coming and going from a crowded platform should attract less interest. Pushing aside the false cupboard, Grok had shown him how to listen for the rush of air around the door jamb, which signified the arrival of a train. He would then crack the door just a tiny fraction and wait for the right moment to slip out unobserved and join the throng on the platform. Similarly on returning, he lounged close to the door, out of sight of the cameras, and waited till the throng were loading before slipping through.

The method of entry and exit meant that it was really only safe to come and go during peak travel times. The system relied on lots of people milling around on the platform. Kioshi had secretly followed Grok on a few occasions, and so he knew that there were at least two other ways in and out of the labyrinth; but he needed to investigate these further. Grok had also given him a safe location to go to if he was delayed or otherwise unable to return underground during peak travel times. He would wait at the front gate entrance of the Yoyogi National Stadium near Harajuku Station and Grok would come to collect him from there.

On his last trip above ground, Kioshi had discovered a small settlement of homeless people camped in the wooded area at the southern end of Yoyogi Park. Today he wanted to make the long trip to the library and on the way back, make a closer inspection of the settlement in the park. It took him forty minutes to get to the library, but once there he made straight for the reference section and got to work. He left the library at 1.30, a little more educated, a little more worldly. He didn't know why this was important, he just knew it was. He also understood that almost everything he had been told by the guardians was untrue, or at least altered factually. He also knew that the Professor was called Tetsuya Hiroko, and that he had at one time been considered famous; before very quickly disappearing from the public view. At the library he had followed a side note and discovered that Tetsuya Hiroko taught physics at the Kagurazaka Campus of The Tokyo University of Science. He had the address for the campus, and a strong inclination to go there, but he resisted the impulse and, instead, made his way quickly back to Yoyogi.

As he approached the homeless camp, Kioshi noticed it was quite a bit bigger than he had originally thought. He could make out blue tents stretching through the shrubbery all the way down the gradual slope towards the fence and the road beyond. Many of the tents were made from blue plastic tarpaulins, but there was the occasional white tent scattered around. There were some people gathered around in small groups, but it seemed as if most of the residents were 'out' for the day. As Kioshi observed all this, he realised that he himself was being observed by more than one of the residents or 'homuresu'. He selected one old man in particular, and held his gaze. The man was maybe sixty years old. He was quite plump or well fed, and he was brewing tea on a small fire. Neatly stacked by his tent were a couple of plastic crates and a bicycle. It gave the impression of being very permanent. After three or four minutes, Kioshi turned and made

179

his way slowly back to the main pathway. He sat himself down on a cast iron and wooden seat under some large trees.

He waited patiently for about five minutes, then off to his left he noticed the old man emerge from the bushes onto the path. The old man seemed short and round. He was neatly dressed in a long dark overcoat with the hood of a black parka at his fat neck. Pale grey trousers, brown rubber soled brogues and a grey felt cap finished the ensemble. As the old man drew closer, Kioshi could see that all the clothing was a little worse for wear. The old man carried a black umbrella in his right hand. It was held closed with a thick, red rubber band, and he used it to poke at the leaves and anything else that attracted his attention, on his painfully slow walk toward Kioshi. In his left hand he carried a long folded cardboard box, which maybe at one time had been packaging for a child's toy. Peeking out from under the cuff of his overcoat was an expensive gold watch.

Eventually he reached the bench upon which Kioshi sat. Kioshi had no fear. He could clearly outrun this little round man, but also he felt this little round man meant him no harm.

The old man stood looking down at Kioshi, then used the tip of his umbrella to swipe a leaf off the seat. He sat down silently and remained staring ahead for an age. Kioshi could hear his breathing… through the nose. It reminded Kioshi of the sound that burst round the green door when a train rushed into the platform at Shinjuku Station. The silence hung in the air like sea mist for a long time, and Kioshi had involuntarily matched his breathing to that of the old man. When the old man finally spoke, it came from so far away as to startle Kioshi.

The old man's voice was high pitched.

"What is your name boy?"

Kioshi recovered his composure and turned to face the old man, who still stared resolutely ahead.

"My name is Kioshi," he said directly and confidently.

"You are not afraid of me boy." It was not a question.

"No… I am not," said Kioshi. "I am Kioshi and I have no reason to fear an old man."

The old man chuckled. He finally turned to Kioshi.

"What do you want boy?"

"I want to know about this place where you live. I am looking for somewhere safe, where I will not be found. I need to know I will not be harmed," said Kioshi.

"I will not ask you why you wish to live here boy. That is an unspoken rule here. You respect other people's privacy and space. The people that live here end up here for many different reasons. Sometimes there are hundreds of us, like now. At other times, as few as forty or fifty. Sometimes we have young people, even foreigners, but they are like tourists, and they come and go. I have been here a long time. I am simply called Ojiisan."

The old man paused and raised his chubby little hands to his cheeks. There was a far off distant rasping sound as he drew his hands downward across his stubbly chin. He seemed now to be staring up into the treetops.

"There are park guards who come once in a while, but they mainly leave us alone. The police do not come into the park, so if it is them you are hiding from, you are safe here at least."

He stopped talking to prod at a big piece of paper that blew along the path and under his feet. He deftly stabbed it with his umbrella, took it off the point, folded it and tucked it into the folds of the cardboard box.

"If you stayed here," he continued. "There are one or two people here you should avoid, but otherwise it is just like any other small village. A lot of the people here go out and find work in places like the markets or cleaning. The pay is bad but our needs are few. If you beg in the park, the park guards will come for you."

The silence returned around them like the sea mist and they sat in silence for a time. Finally Kioshi spoke.

"I may see you again Ojiisan," he said quietly.

"I have enjoyed talking to you young Kioshi, so I shall look forward to it."

Back in the station, Kioshi waited by the manual ticket entrance for an opportunity to slip through with a group of other people. Once in he made his way to the lower platform. He moved to the end of the platform and leaned against the wall. Three minutes later a train arrived at the platform, and in twenty more seconds, Kioshi was through the green door.

39. KIOSHI TAKES A HOLIDAY

The past...

For the next two days Kioshi took every opportunity to familiarise himself even more with the labyrinth. He took great care to avoid the cameras that were mounted around the concealed entrances, and the passages that led to them. During the day when there was important work happening, Grok generally observed all from his monitor station. At night the boys, and all the staff, were locked into their rooms before Grok left... if he left. Then the cameras were turned off. Kioshi had heard the metallic clunk of the lock nearly every night since he could remember. One night some time back he had become curious and jammed his door open with a shoe. At around seven thirty a snapping sound signalled the action of the door locks. Kioshi had waited nervously, feigning sleep in case somebody came to his room. But apparently there was no way for anyone to know if the door was closed or not when the bolt slid home. After waiting for what seemed an interminable time, Kioshi made another interesting discovery.

The steel bolt was still seated in the door. It was held there by a light spring. He discovered he could grab at it with his fingernail, pull it out and slide it back and forth without any effort. When he let it go it pulled itself back into the door. The electro magnet was located in the door jamb, and drew the bolt into the jamb, holding it there until the current was switched off in the morning, or overridden by the fire alarm systems. Then he realised he could close the door on the ordinary day latch, and insert something into the gap that prevented the magnetic bolt from sliding home. When he returned to his room it was a simple matter of removing the blocking device, and the door would automatically lock. On a subsequent trip above ground he had gone into an electronics store in Akihabara, and lifted a roll of duct tape and some hard, grey plastic modelling sheets. Snapped in half and taped over the bolt hole, these worked perfectly.

Kioshi also needed money. He could readily steal food and drinks from convenience stores or the food basements under the large departments stores, but the supplies he would need for Yoyogi village were a different matter. He knew there would be money somewhere in the labyrinth, but the private staff rooms and offices also had cameras installed. One possibility was the room where all the security cameras terminated… Grok's office. He had not been in there before. He could think of no reason why there would be a camera there, so that the person sitting there watching could watch themselves. There was a small kitchen beside the dining room. It was just big enough to house a sink, a microwave, a refrigerator and a small table with a few chairs. It was intended for the boys and the staff to use for snacking. Kioshi lodged himself in the chair beside the passage door, and from here he could lean back and see the door to the Grok's office without being observed by the cameras or, by anyone in the passage.

He knew that Grok's visits to the toilets were almost ritualistic. When he entered the washroom, he always removed his dark blue suit coat and put it on a special hanger placed there specifically for that reason. Then he rolled up his shirt sleeves and washed his hands. Finally he made his way into the cubicle before re-emerging, washing again quite thoroughly, combing his hair, rolling down his sleeves, straightening his tie, and putting on his immaculate dark blue suit coat.

Grok was nothing if not a creature of habit. Kioshi waited patiently for almost an hour before he saw Grok step out into the corridor and turn to head for the washroom. He knew he had at least five minutes, but he would not need nearly that long. Grok had barely disappeared around the corner, before Kioshi was along the passage and had the office door closed behind him. He started counting the seconds in his mind. Once inside he checked for a camera on the walls or ceiling, but his logic had proven correct. Next he checked the four drawers along the front of the white melamine desk. Grok's drawers were as clean as his suit.

One held a menacing grey metal pistol and a fully loaded magazine. Apart from a log book and some pencils, biros and writing pads, the rest were clean. Twenty seconds elapsed. The desktop was likewise clear. There were two keyboards, two little boxes with joysticks on them, and a copy of a book called '*Breakfast of Champions*', by somebody called Kurt Vonnegut, opened and upside down on the desk.

Thirty seconds elapsed. Kioshi was about to turn and leave, when he noticed the images on the monitor screens changed. There were six monitors in all. Four in one cluster, and two more to one side. The cluster of four seemed to cover the corridors and important rooms in the labyrinth. Kioshi forced himself to stand there and watch, as each screen cycled through. He was able to understand that there was a total of sixteen cameras covered by this bank of monitors.

One hundred and eighty seconds elapsed. He forced himself to remain calm, and switched his attention to the separate bank of two screens. Each of these also covered four cameras each, and here Kioshi made a valuable discovery. He was able to identify the route to the three exits that he knew about. There were cameras in the approach tunnels and cameras at the actual exits. That's two cameras for each exit. Then there was another tunnel camera, the location of which Kioshi was sure he recognised from his little discovery tours. The exit was a mystery to him, but he was confident he could find it now that he knew where to start the journey. A bigger mystery was that one of the exits that he had followed Grok to, and seen him use, was not on the camera grid... curious.

Two hundred and forty five seconds elapsed. Kioshi cast around the room to make sure all was as he had found it, then he opened the door a crack to check the corridor was clear and, finding it so, he was gone. Grok was back a mere twelve seconds after Kioshi had closed the left the room. He opened the door and stepped in. Halfway to his chair he stopped dead in the middle of the room. He raised his big nose and sniffed the air. He turned ninety degrees and sniffed the air again. He looked for all the world like a wolf. Then he decided he was mistaken. He sat down and using the keyboards and joystick, he did a full cycle through all the cameras. All was as it should be. He reached for his book.

Back in his room, Kioshi reviewed the location of all the cameras in his mind. When he was sure he knew of all the locations, he lay on his bed and switched on the learning screen above his head. If Grok left this evening, he would confirm all the camera locations, and try and find the final exit. He now knew with reasonable certainty, that he could come and go overnight without being observed, provided he used Grok's secret exit... the one with no cameras. The one nobody else knew about... maybe not even the Professor.

Later that evening, Kioshi was on his way to the dining room, when he passed Grok locking the door to his office. After he had passed, Grok raised his head and sniffed the air. He watched Kioshi go into the dining room. Later, when the dining room was closing for the night, Kioshi returned to his room and immediately taped a piece of hard plastic over the bolt hole in the door jamb. Then lay on his bed. Fifteen minutes later he heard the snap of the bolt. He went to the door and opened it just a crack. The corridor ended about twenty metres to the left beyond his door, and the three doors in that section were all closed. He waited patiently until he heard the sound of a door closing off in the distance. This was the riskiest part of the whole plan. There was a camera about ten metres to his right. It was placed at the junction to his corridor and the corridor that led to the dining room, then on to Grok's office and the rooms and laboratories beyond. The camera moved through ninety degrees, and could be facing down either corridor. There was a tiny red light below the lens that indicated if the system was on and working. He would not know which way the camera was facing, or whether the light was on, until he stuck his head out of his doorway recess.

Kioshi remained motionless, hidden in the doorway. He was apprehensive certainly, but the odds were in his favour. For it to go wrong, first the monitoring system had to be turned on. Then the camera had to be facing down his corridor and finally, Grok had to be in his office and see that very camera feed on that very cycle at that exact time. Kioshi took a deep breath and stepped squarely out into the corridor. The camera was facing away down the other corridor. He made his way to the corner and came up under the camera, while remaining outside its field if vision. The light was off. He heard a door opening, and suddenly light flooded into the gloom at the other end of the corridor. Grok!

Kioshi ducked back around the corner and pressed himself against the wall. His heart was trying to punch its way out of his chest. Keys rattled. He risked a peek around the corner. In the gloom of the corridor he saw Grok drop the keys into his suit coat pocket. He brushed a speck of dust or lint off his coat sleeve, then he picked up a small blue canvas bag from the floor at his feet, and strode off down the corridor.

Kioshi followed as closely as he was able. He trailed Grok through the laboratory area, which was now lit only by soft green night lights. Off the end of the final lab, there was a large storeroom. Kioshi melted into the shadows and froze. Grok paused at the storeroom door and looked around, peering into the surrounding gloom, and sniffing the air. Apparently satisfied, he took a grey dust coat and a small torch from the canvas bag. He shrugged himself into the dust coat then pausing once more to check around him, he switched on the torch and stepped through the door. In the darkness, Kioshi started breathing again.

This was the exit not covered by the security cameras. This was the exit that Kioshi had observed Grok using a few weeks back. On that occasion Grok also had the canvas carry bag. From his hiding place, Kioshi heard the scraping sound of a large metal sounding object. Then a muffled thud... then nothing. He waited there in the dark, listening to the rise and fall of his own breathing. After more than ten minutes had passed, he stepped out of his hiding place and made for the storeroom door. It opened easily, and Kioshi stepped through into pitch darkness, closing the door behind him. He waited for a minute or two for any sounds, and then started feeling around on the wall either side of the doorway for a light switch. Finally he gave up and opened the door back into the lab. He remained inside the storeroom and used the small amount of green light from the laboratory, to adjust his eyes in the storeroom. Slowly a metal conduit appeared about an arms length to the right of the door and there, at its end, was a light switch. He placed his right hand on the switch, his left hand on the door, and closed it gently. Once closed he flicked the switch.

The banks of fluorescent lights along the ceiling twanged into life like bubbling lava, and Kioshi shielded his eyes from the shock of the sudden glare. The storeroom was six by four metres square, with shelves and cabinets around the walls, and a row of metal free standing shelves running down the middle. He searched around the walls, carefully moving shelves and cabinets just enough to see behind them. Nothing but brick or solid concrete walls. Grok seemed to have simply disappeared into thin air. There was nothing for it, but to note the location of the last exit covered by the camera system, and then return to his room. He wandered up and down the storage shelves looking for anything that might prove useful in the future. In one box he found matches and candles. He would have to steal a torch on his next trip above ground, but until he did the candles would come in handy. He took two boxes of matches and four candles, stuffing three in his pocket. He lit the remaining candle and walked to the doorway. He switched off the light and quietly opened the door. As he did so there was a weird but faint guttering noise, and the candle flame bent voraciously back into the storeroom, threatening to extinguish itself. Kioshi quickly closed the door and turned the light back on. The candle flame settled down with a slight but steady lean to the left. He checked the room again. As he passed down the space between the shelves, the flame almost imperceptibly changed direction. Kioshi looked up. There, above one of the centre shelves was a vent of some kind. And another one the same at the other end of the shelves. *How did I miss them?* he thought.

He climbed carefully up onto the face of the shelf. The candle danced towards the vent. He climbed down and repeated the process at the other vent, but the candle still bent slightly towards the first vent. He climbed even higher, until he could get his elbows on the top of the shelves. The candle still failed to react to the nearest vent. *The other one must be the way out* he thought to himself and was about to climb back down when he noticed a mess of scuff marks and footprints in the dust on top of the shelf in front of him. Kioshi hung there thinking, this is the way out! It sucked no air, so Kioshi presumed it was a fake intended to look like the other 'real' air vent. So Grok had a secret exit he could use when he wanted to take things out of the labyrinth without anyone knowing.

Kioshi made a decision. He climbed up onto the shelf, taking as much care as possible not to leave any marks that were obvious stand outs. He tried to push up the vent, but it was heavier than he had expected. He rested his shoulder under it and pushed a little harder. The vent rose out of its seat, and Kioshi was able to lean forward and slide the vent on his shoulder. Once there was a large enough space to climb through, he stood upright. His head and shoulders were now inside the cavity. He held up the candle. It was a smooth but narrow concrete tunnel, big enough for a man to make his way through without stooping. There was only one way to go… so he hoisted himself up and went. He soon realised that he was making his way in the opposite direction he had come from his room. In other words, he was travelling right across the top of the labyrinth. The tunnel was perfectly straight, and very soon Kioshi heard faint noises ahead. Proceeding now with more caution, he came to the end of the tunnel barely two minutes after setting out from the storeroom end.

Holding up the candle, he found a sheet metal panel beside him at waist height. There was a thin steel handle welded in the centre of it. He took the handle and pulled. Nothing. He pushed the handle and the panel gave outwards into a narrow duct. Faint light shone from somewhere above and to the left, and now the faint noises he could hear became voices and distant traffic sound. He carefully placed the panel against the wall of the duct, blew out his candle and climbed through. The duct ran either way, but just off to his left there was a metal grate in the top of the duct. He shuffled along and pushed upwards on the grate. It hinged up, allowing Kioshi to peer out. The grate was part concealed behind a large white tiled pillar, but on either side of the pillar, a well lit tunnel, clad in white tiles, reached off in either direction. About seventy metres away, a homeless man with a pile of coloured shopping bags was shuffling towards him. Kioshi knew this place. It was the pedestrian subway underpass from the south entrance of Shinjuku Station. He quickly lowered himself down into the duct, pulling the grate shut behind him. He shuffled back to the tunnel entrance and sat there catching his breath. He suddenly realised that there was no handle on the inside of the metal panel. This meant that once it was back in its tight seal, there was no way to open it from the duct side without some kind of thin, sharp tool to grip the edge. Once you pushed the panel into place and climbed out into the subway via the grate, there would be no getting back into the labyrinth this way, without such a tool.

Kioshi climbed back through into the tunnel, reached back into the duct and took hold of the sheet metal panel by the handle. He lined up the panel with the opening and pulled gently but firmly. The panel sucked back into its seat with a satisfying ping. Kioshi lit his candle and retraced his steps back to his room in the labyrinth, careful to leave no evidence of his presence. All was quiet.

The following day Kioshi sought permission from Grok to go above ground. As he stood before him, the wolf's nose twitched and his head seemed to range about almost automatically.

"I need to make up for the last time, when I came back empty handed," he said.

He could see the faint look of uncertainty in Grok's eyes; maybe even a hint of suspicion. Grok stood up from his chair and flexed his arms, swiveling his fists back and forth on the end of his forearms. Kioshi could see the dark, wiry hair on the back of Grok's hands, and he could see where it thickened as it disappeared under his cuff. He is like a wolf, thought Kioshi, struggling to remain impassive. Suddenly Grok reached out and laid his great hairy wolf's paws on Kioshi's shoulders.

"This will be your last trip," he said. "The Professor is not happy about your going out, and besides you are due in the lab the day after tomorrow." He squeezed hard with both hands. Kioshi wanted to cry out, but not as much as he wanted *not* to cry out.

"Be back by five o'clock," said Grok as he sat back down and turned his attention to the monitors.

"Yes sir," said Kioshi.

Kioshi returned to his room and recovered his treasures from their hiding places. Not much to speak of. Chopsticks, a butter knife, three and a half candles and two boxes of matches. He pushed the plastic cards and duct tape into the gap between the learning screen and the ceiling. He took one last look around, and strode purposefully towards the stairway access to the green door exit.

Back in his office, Grok watched him enter the white tiled room, and exit through the old machinery room door. He tapped his big long front teeth thoughtfully, before turning his attention to other things.

Once out of the station, Kioshi hurried straight over to the Tokyu Hands shop at the rear of Takashimaya Department Store. On a recent outing he had seen something here called binoculars. They allowed you to see great distances, and Kioshi thought these would be very useful. He had been about to make off with them, when a salesman had approached him. This time, when he went into the store he found they had many different sizes including a small pair that was on a display. They would fit into his pocket, so he stood back and watched the staff and customers carefully, then in one fluid movement, he was past the counter and out the rear door, before anyone even noticed his presence. Once outside he slid the binoculars into his pocket, and hurried off down the side streets. He soon came to the northern entrance to Yoyogi Park. This was a soothing place... a place of great peace in the heart of the city. In parts, the trees appeared to join across the top of the path, forming a cool green canopy. He continued on through the park to emerge at the Harajuku entrance and from there he made his way down Meiji Dori until he found a convenience store. He was like a damned phantom. He stood out on the street to determine the layout of the store as best he could, then when the store seemed to be filled with lots of shoppers, he was in and out without even being seen. He went straight into a side street and doubled back for the Harajuku entrance to Yoyogi.

Once back in the park, he wandered down to sit by the water in between two ponds. Here he unbuttoned his shirt and pulled out three drinks, four packets of rice balls with bean paste, and two packets of hotcakes... not too bad. He ripped open a pack of hotcakes and pulled one out. Then he carefully rewrapped the package and placed it with the other food. While he chomped on the hotcake he took out the binoculars and figured out how they worked. Soon, he was able to focus in on people walking on a path well beyond the larger pond. Without the glasses he was unable to make out their facial features. With the glasses he could.

Kioshi's plan was a simple one. He assumed that when he did not return in the afternoon, Grok would come looking for him at the entrance to the National Stadium, as per the procedure he had been taught. He would conceal himself there and follow Grok to wherever Grok went of an evening. It might not be much of a plan, but it was all he had, and instinct told him it was the right thing to do. Once he had some money, he could get far away from this city or at the very least, well away from the labyrinth. The noon sun broke through the trees and touched his head. He stretched out on the grass and closed his eyes.

40. THE TEAM ASSEMBLES

The present...

Itsuru Oka has arrived at the hotel like visiting royalty at around five thirty. He is finally back working on something important and his energy levels are high. He calls me from the front desk, and I step out of the lift to see him attempting to charm one of the young ladies at the front counter.

"Oka-san," I call as I approach, "you seem very happy. Why is that?"

"Happy... of course I'm happy," he says beaming at me. "I've got full expenses and a week in a nice hotel. Why wouldn't I be happy?"

He took his key and, with a final wink at the young lady behind the counter, picked up the most dilapidated suitcase I have ever seen. At the elevators he turns to me and says...

"In all seriousness musician, I have so much to tell you."

We arrange to meet in the bar in half an hour's time.

Yuka has also just called to say she has arrived at her hotel in Shibuya. She has suggested that Oka, Nick and I meet her at her hotel at 7 o'clock for dinner. I try thinking of all sorts of good reasons why I should meet her alone first, but she is adamant that her news should wait until we have heard what Oka has to say. Well... a little bit of something great is better than nothing at all.

I head for the bar, order a Laphroaig and call Nick. He comes straight down, and we compare notes on our day off. I've been out at Ochanomizu half the day looking at guitars and amps, and Nick says he's been in Akihabara checking out all the latest gizmos. I fill him in on Oka's arrival, and tell him we're all meeting Yuka for dinner in Shibuya.

"Ah… musician!"

Oka drifts across the floor like the prince of the gumshoes. I start to introduce him to Nick, but he holds up a hand to stop me.

He looks at my drink on the bar.

"I'll have what he's having," he says to the barman.

"Get him a whisky please," I say.

"No no… I said I'll have what you're having," says Itsuru Oka.

He wafts a hand over my drink, sniffs and smiles. He turns to the barman.

"Laphroaig," he says with a grin.

Somewhere in my head I hear a loud *'ka-ching!'*, and I don't think it will be the last. The barman looks at me and shrugs, palms up.

"Okay," I say, "if he can pick it from that distance I guess he wins the lucky door prize."

"Right," says Oka, turning finally to Nick who is leaning on the bar with a big smile on his face. "So who do we have here?"

I introduce them and then sit back in amazement as they become the best of friends in the shortest possible time. Nick had started life as a cadet journalist on some two-bit regional paper. He'd enjoyed a pretty good reputation before he followed that well worn path, furrowed by so many journalists before him, into public relations work. It didn't take long for him to set up his own PR practice which included an entertainment management and publicity division. As a long term friend, I was destined to become his first client. I'm not sure I was worth the effort that he made on my behalf, but he was totally committed and almost always travelled with me when I toured. I think I was really just his pet project, although finally his investment seemed to be paying off.

Nick and Oka have really hit it off. At some point in their journalistic careers they had both filed for Reuters, so I stand to one side as they compare notes, reminisce about various evil editors, and generally knock a hole in my bar account.

It's six forty, so I drag them out of the bar and up to Shinjuku Station, where we jump on a train to Shibuya. As we walk into Yuka's hotel, my heart is pounding in my chest. There she is, seated on a low, white leather couch on the other side of the expansive foyer. If I was in any doubt (and I'm not), then right there it all washes away, as I realise that this is the woman I want to spend my life with.

We take ourselves off to an izakaya style restaurant close to the hotel, and seek out a private room with solid walls and doors rather than shoji screen doors. I feel we need to keep this discussion private. With the drinks in and the order placed, Oka takes the floor. To begin with I'm struggling to stay focused, but I know I need to settle down. Business first, pleasure later.

"So," says Oka. "My enquiries over the past two weeks have provided the following solid facts. In 1991, in a period of just under two months, four newborn male babies went missing from Kyoto hospitals. They just disappeared off the face of the earth; a couple of them within hours of being born. This is undeniably tragic, and the consequences for the families were extreme. However to someone like me, the curiosity value is irresistible. Now I'm sorry if that sounds unsympathetic, but stick with me. For instance, it is almost impossible to comprehend, but each case was treated as separate. The police never investigated the disappearances as one interconnected case.

To this day, official police records show one case as a probable but unsolved kidnapping, one case as child stealing involving the young unmarried mother who, by the way, has also never been seen since. The other two cases still remain unsolved, with absolutely no leads whatsoever. Another very salient fact surrounding these cases is the high incidence of disappearance, or apparent suicide of, the parents. When I take a long hard look at each of these families with the benefit of hindsight, I can only conclude that nobody went missing or suicided. I believe that anybody who would push the police investigations harder just simply got dead, and the police from various offices never connected the dots."

"Do you think there was any cover-up or complicity involving the police?" chimes in Nick while Oka-san takes a breath and a pull on his Asahi.

"No, I don't believe there was. I believe it was just the sad result of geographical police divisions, and a pretty liberal dose of stupid in some of those divisions." Oka pauses as the door opens and plates of edamame and pickles arrive.

As the door slides closed, Oka takes four salted soybean pods off a plate and theatrically lays them down in front of him on the table.

"One baby, two babies, three babies, four babies," he says, pausing for dramatic effect.

Then he reaches back into the edamame and takes another bean pod. He holds it up for us all to see, then lays it on the table just a short distance from, but separate to, the other four.

"Five babies," he says. "Only this last one disappeared almost exactly a year after the others. And guess what? This one was not a newborn, but almost exactly one year old. I just can't help thinking that whoever took these kids missed him the first time around, but got him later. This last child's name was Kioshi Matsumoto, and the circumstances surrounding both his birth and his disappearance are particularly odd. We'll come back to that in a moment, but I am now almost one hundred percent certain that this is the musician's rent boy."

"*Our* rent boy," whispers Yuka. "Remember I have seen him too."

"Well, we know that our friend here received a note under his door saying *'I am keyoshi'*. We know the boy is Japanese and we know that there is no such name in Japanese: at least none that we have been able to turn up. However, we know that Kioshi *is* a Japanese name, and that one of the missing boys was called Kioshi. Now... since welding these two facts together, I have concentrated my energies only on this boy. In the mean time I have called in all my old favours in the newspaper business, and these in turn have led to some very interesting information."

He pauses again as the door slides open and a selection of dishes arrives on the table. He takes another pull on his beer, then as the door closes he takes up his chopsticks and selects two gyoza and drops them into the bowl of soy sauce in front of him. He turns one over, stuffs it in his mouth, then proceeds to try and talk around it.

"Sssho... Oh sorry," he says chewing faster. "So... here's what my contacts have found that seems relevant. For about seven or eight years, there have been a couple of well organised child criminal gangs working the city. Even before the widespread use of security cameras, we have reports of two separate pairs of children working rackets like pickpocketing and smash and grabs around the city. The first reports are interesting. Early in the year 2000 for instance... and I quote... 'The two boys appeared to be about eight or nine years old, but they were clearly well trained and organised'. In 2001 we have many similar reports of child criminals, but two pairs stand out; firstly from the early descriptions, and later from video surveillance footage."

He scoffs another Gyoza, waving his chopsticks around like a baton, signifying that we should remain silent and not interrupt. He digs into a beat up old briefcase he has beside him, and pulls out a large manilla envelope.

"Now… in 2003 it gets very interesting. Up until then, there was nothing connecting these two pairs. Then security cameras in the Isetan department store caught both of these pairs pulling grabs on different floors at the same time. Then about nine or ten minutes later, it caught them stealing food from the food court; this time… all together. Of course they got away clean. From the shots we have it is clear that they know each other, and in fact, may all be part of one unit. But what unit?"

Oka looked a little coy here, but pushed on anyway.

"There's no need for me to go into too much detail here, but these kids were very active in the city for three or four years, so straightaway I thought Yakuza. But… I still have one or two contacts in that department, and I have been told point blank that these particular gangs of children are not controlled by them. If they are not controlled by the Yakuza then they must at the very least be paying them some kind of protection money. I've seen it before."

He dropped a still photo on the table. It showed four boys who appeared to be aged eleven or twelve, in what looked like the imported food section.

"If you look closely, you can see that two of them are pretending to be with this woman in the yellow dress. They created a disturbance, while this young fellow here kept watch and gave the all clear. The fourth kid can be seen loading about six cans of Caspian Sevruga, Russian Black Caviar, into his pockets. Expensive tastes. Each of those little red cans is worth about 8000¥, so that's more than 60000¥ right there. But now it gets even more interesting. The store has cameras mounted at various points around the perimeter, and through a contact we were able to get at old file discs for the same day. We hoped there might be something to confirm they were indeed all acting together. The camera on the north east corner of the store, the Meiji Dori side, turned up a real unexpected jackpot.... Taadaaa!"

And with a flourish our gumshoe dropped another A4 photo onto the table. It was rather grainy, being a video lift, and having been blown up about two hundred percent. It showed the four boys all gathered around a tall, dark haired foreigner dressed in a dark blue suit. One of his hands was depositing a small red can into his left hand suit coat pocket, and the other was ruffling the hair of the boy who had actually pulled the lift. The man had a big nose, like a wolf.

There was a longish pause which I finally broke.

"So who is this guy?"

"Damn but I was hoping someone would ask that question. I mean it's so much more dramatic with audience participation. I remember once I..."

I cut him short.

"Okay," I say, holding up my hand in a reasonable impression of a traffic cop. "Like I said, who is this guy? Or how do we find out?"

I looked up from the photo to see Oka beaming brighter than the early morning sun.

"I already know that. At least I'm about ninety nine percent sure. Turns out that I'm not only a brilliant journalist, but a pretty mean private detective as well. If I'm right, his name is Bronislaw Jasinski. A polish national, who disappeared from Warsaw in 1987, after a bungled gold heist. He was just a bit player, but prior to that he had insignificant form. Seems he tried to graduate to the big time and failed. He was twenty three then and that makes him about forty five or forty six years old now."

The door slides open again and more food arrives. More drink orders are placed, and more saké is consumed as we wait for the door to slide closed again.

"Now… and I guess this is particularly for the benefit of Yuka and our musician here."

"I have a name you know," I say to him.

"Yes I know, but to me you will always be the musician."

"Have you actually heard him perform?" laughs Nick, around a mouthful of noodles.

"Okay settle down class. You were saying Oka-san?"

"I was saying that these next photos are for you and Yuka to check carefully. They are the most recent photos and video lifts we have been able to turn up. They only take us up to the year 2004, so you will need to try and imagine these boys at least five years older."

"So why are there no photos after 2004?" asks Yuka.

"Don't know the answer to that one. All we know is they seemed to cease activities in 2004. There have been no reports of this particular group since. Who knows? Maybe the Yakuza finally did shut them down. Anyway, look carefully."

He laid out a total of seven photos. Both Yuka and myself studied them with great care. I looked across at Yuka and she shook her head slightly.

"No," I said to Oka, "he is not here."

"How can you be so sure? Remember the boys in these photos would be at least five years older."

"I can be sure because these boys look alive. The rent boy I am seeing looks dead, especially his eyes. He is like a zombie or something."

Yuka nods in agreement.

"He is not here," she says.

"Right, good. Now I have eleven more photos." He pulls them from the envelope.

"These photos are of boys the same age, involved in the same kind of activities as this other group but, they seem to have acted alone, and they don't resemble any of the boys in the other group."

He deals the photos out like playing cards, carefully watching me for any sign of recognition. One, two, three, four, five, six. He pauses to take a bite of katsu don and a swig of his beer. Nothing. Seven, eight...

"Wait!" I yell, altogether too loudly. At the same time I hear a sharp intake of breath from Yuka. There in the photo, looking almost straight into the lens is my... our rent boy. His arms are blurred from rapid movement, but you can make out two boxes in his hands. One seems to be branded Panerai, the other is clearly IWC.

"That's him... that's Kioshi," I say softly into the silence that has fallen over the group. The boy's cold, dead eyes stare out at us, just focused slightly left of the lens, but there can be no mistake. This is Kioshi.

Oka-san reaches out and lays a hand softly on Yuka's shoulder. He lifts his eyebrows to ask the question.

Yuka nods silently.

"So we have our boy!"

Oka sits back down, pushes his empty beer glass aside and takes up a saké cup. Gripping the sides with his right hand, he holds it in his cupped left hand. He proffers the cup to Yuka, who takes up a flask and fills his cup.

He proceeds to tell us the strange story of Kioshi's birth, his mother, Sato's suicide, and his father Akira's decline into darkness.

"Little is known about the boy for the next year," said Oka. "He was taken to be raised by Sato's mother. Then the most amazing coincidence seems to have ignited a whole new and strange series of events. The first of these was when Akira's cousin Miyuki was having a weekend with friends in Osaka. She was walking back to her hotel late one night, when she happened upon Akira, sleeping rough in Shinsaibashi. What are the odds? Over two million people in a city and their paths cross just like that. Now I can't determine this with absolute certainty, but it seems as soon as Miyuki stumbled upon Akira in Osaka, there was a very definite change of behaviour in the infant Kioshi, back in Kyoto."

I spoke with Sato's mother just a week ago. She is about seventy years old now, but she remembers all of this like it happened yesterday. She explained to me that the child had been named 'Kioshi' or 'quiet one' because there was never a peep out of him… literally. He never cried or whimpered… nothing. She had never heard from his father Akira, since he had left the child in her care not long after his birth. She said the infant was deep, but alert. She felt there was something very odd about him, apart from his never making a noise. Then suddenly, the very day after Miyuki had found Akira, and in fact the day she had got him to board a train to Kyoto, the child started screaming… right out of the blue. A whole year nothing then, according to this poor woman, the child's screams were like the rush of banshees from the very depths of hell. The child was thrashing about madly, and when she picked him up she said he fixed her with what she called a *death stare*. She was petrified.

Even talking about it all these years later, you could see the fear in her eyes. When she had calmed down she had taken the baby to her doctor, and that was the last she ever saw of him. She said that when she arrived at the doctor's surgery, a nurse came and took the infant for tests on the doctor's orders. When she got into the doctor's office, it was discovered that the doctor had ordered no tests on the child, and in fact had no nurse matching that description. But it was too late. The child was gone. The police were called, but the case remained an unsolved kidnapping. It was the only one of the five cases that was actually allocated 'kidnapping' status. There never was any ransom note or demands of any kind, and the case file eventually sank to the bottom of the pile like a broken bottle to the sea bed. And there it stayed."

"So that's it; there's been nothing until now?" says Nick.

"That's right... oh wait, there was one other thing. Sato's mother said the strangest thing. She said when the nurse took the child off her in the waiting room, it was like Kioshi knew the nurse or was even expecting her."

We all sit and digest this information, and decide to meet in my hotel room at ten o'clock in the morning to work out a plan. I explain that I have moved rooms to provide us with a larger space and that Oka-san is now in my old room just in case any more notes from the boy should appear.

When we finish dinner, Nick and Oka head off back to our hotel and Yuka asks me to go with her to her hotel lobby bar. She says she wants to talk.

41. TRAIN RIDE TO SHIN OKUBO

The past...

The first thick raindrops splashed onto his face and into his open mouth. Kioshi woke and sat bolt upright. The sun was hiding behind a grey sky and the rain was getting heavier. Kioshi gathered up his belongings and trotted off down the path. A short distance away was a bank of vending machines, and behind that, some kind of small hut. The roof overhang afforded a small amount of cover, so he huddled there with his back to the wall. A disposable plastic shopping bag was tangled in the leaves near his feet, so he picked it up and gave it a shake. He took all his possessions, except the binoculars a packet of rice balls and a drink, and wrapped them in the plastic bag; which he then stuffed under the edge of the hut. He must have been asleep on the grass for some hours, but he figured he might as well stay as dry as possible for as long as he could. He settled down for another wait.

A few hours later he set off through a light rain to the south eastern corner of the park, and made his way into a small garden bed overlooking the road. Opposite him was the Yoyogi National Stadium. He took out his binoculars and scanned around the forecourt of the stadium until he found what he was searching for. A backlit four sided clock mounted on a high pole told him it was 5.27. He looked at the binoculars in his hands and smiled... wow! He lifted them back up to his eyes, and carefully searched for any sign of Grok in the nominated location. One or two people walking along the footpath on the other side of the park fence, gave him strange looks. Most were hidden under their umbrellas, but nevertheless he decided to reposition himself where he was less visible but, still had a good view of the stadium entrance opposite. And he waited. But waiting was not a problem for Kioshi. In fact one could say he had almost thirteen years experience at it. At least the rain had stopped.

It was seven fifteen before Grok made an appearance. Kioshi first spotted him on the overpass near the stadium entrance. There he was, as still as a statue, staring straight down towards the stadium. He stood stock still for at least another five minutes, taking in his surrounds, sniffing at the universe for any scent of trouble. Through the binoculars, Kioshi could see his big nose, slightly raised. His receding hairline was underscored by large bushy eyebrows that shielded dead, deep set eyes. His high, prominent cheek bones led down to a cruel mouth, accented by a weak chin. *On reflection,* thought Kioshi, *he looks as much like a shark as a wolf.* Finally he turned and walked off to his left. Kioshi lost sight of him for fully forty five seconds, and was beginning to feel a little spooked, when Grok finally reappeared on the footpath outside the stadium.

The man in the dark suit strolled along like a sightseer; someone with time on his hands. Through the binoculars Kioshi could see that he carried the same blue canvas bag. He could see the slight tilt of his head to the left. The eyes snapped around like machines and every so often the big nose twitched. Grok carried on past the entrance and continued strolling until he was almost opposite Kioshi's position. The sound of Kioshi's own heartbeat thudded in his ears, but he breathed more deeply and was soon calmer. There was a hedgerow along the dividing strip, and another along the edge of the footpath on Grok's side. The hedge was broken every five metres or so by mature trees that lined the avenue, and it was by one of these that Grok took up his position and waited. He waited an hour, then made another pass of the stadium entrance. Finally he looked at his watch, then pulled out a mobile phone and made a call.

Suddenly, Kioshi knew what to do next. As Grok moved off in the direction of Harajuku Station, Kioshi slunk out of the garden bed and shadowed him from the opposite side of the road. For a moment or two he lost track of him. But after a short breathless minute, where he half expected to feel Grok's hand on his shoulder, he spotted him up ahead beside the pylon for the pedestrian overpass. Grok had taken out his phone and was arguing with someone. He was clearly unhappy. While Kioshi watched from the other side of the pedestrian crossing, Grok hung up and stuffed the phone back in his pocket. He strode off with a purpose toward the station. Kioshi hung back until Grok cut behind the bank of vending machines to make for the station entrance. As he positioned himself behind the vending machines, he realised that following Grok into the station would call for all the skills the man he was following had taught him. How to stay invisible, how to blend if you couldn't, how to get through the turnstiles without tickets. Generally not too difficult for Kioshi... but this was Grok he was stalking... the wolf, the shark.

Grok went to the ticket machines without pausing or looking back. There were enough people in the station to afford Kioshi good cover. Kioshi waited until Grok was through to the platform for the Yamanote line. He slipped through and was able to position himself about sixty feet from Grok, close in behind a group of commuters. The train was at the platform before he had time to think, and there was a mere twenty or thirty people separating him from Grok, as he boarded the same carriage through different doors. Grok stepped straight into the carriage and took hold of a centre pole, never letting go of the bag. Kioshi grabbed a space at another pole, and was able to keep an eye on him via his reflection and surreptitious glances. Kioshi memorised the stations they passed through. There were just two stops, Yoyogi and Shinjuku, before Grok made a move toward the door as the train slowed for the next station. Kioshi hung back as the doors opened at Shin-Okubo. Then, as the doors began to close, he slipped through them and took up position behind a couple of students who made their way along the platform. Grok made his way downstairs to street level and once outside the station, he turned right and walked under the train line, and east along Okubo Dori.

Kioshi hid behind one of the silver pillars at the station entrance, then bounded across the wide pedestrian crossing and made his way cautiously under the tracks. He kept a steady eye on Grok, who was about fifty metres ahead on the other side of the street. Grok continued on with a brisk stride, and suddenly he switched the canvas bag from his right to his left hand and veered off into a Seven Eleven convenience store. Kioshi ducked into a small gift shop opposite and pretended to look through a stack of music CDs in a bin by the door. Five minutes later, Grok emerged with the canvas bag in his right hand, and a white plastic bag in his left. He made his way straight across the road on a pedestrian crossing in front of the convenience store. Kioshi froze as Grok crossed. *Which way would he turn?* But Grok peeled off up Okubo Dori and disappeared around the corner just a short way ahead. In case Grok had seen him and was waiting around the corner, Kioshi ran across to the other side of Okubo Dori and hid behind a large green metal box of some kind, that was installed on the edge of the footpath.

From here he could see Grok striding away up a narrow street. Kioshi raced across the road and stopped behind a small delivery van. He watched Grok pass between two neat brown apartment buildings, then continue on about another hundred metres before entering a small building. Kioshi advanced carefully up the street and into a car parking area almost opposite. He concealed himself behind the wall of the car park, and peered carefully around the corner. The building that Grok had entered was a neat off white colour. It had some kind of small shop with a large glass window and door on the ground floor, and two floors above, each with a good sized balcony facing over the street. On the left of the store window was a low brick garden bed with some shrubs and a large tree. A six foot brick wall backed the garden bed and filled the space between the footpath and the corner of the building. On the right of the storefront was another door which was the entrance for the apartments above. That door was solid, except for a thin glass strip that ran from almost the top to the bottom. To the right of that was a single car space, occupied now by a small brown hatchback. Kioshi watched as a light came on in a thin window over the door, and then more light flooded out onto the first floor balcony.

Kioshi heard the sound of a sliding door, and saw a shadow cross the light on the balcony. He ducked back behind the wall as Grok's head and shoulders appeared on the balcony. From his hiding place he could hear Grok's voice. He was on the phone.

Kioshi strained to hear, but parts of the conversation were snatched away, as Grok turned this way and that while he paced the balcony.

"I don't know," Kioshi heard. "The boy wasn't there. I could... Yes but... but... Professor listen to me. I am right here outside the stadium.... Yes I have. Alright then... but how long should I wait for him?"

Kioshi risked a peek around the corner. Grok was facing away from him. He was in his shirt sleeves and was violently rubbing his left hand through his hair while his right hand held the phone to his ear... now bigger... and redder.

Kioshi ducked back under cover and heard Grok swearing. He had hung up. Kioshi heard the sliding door open, then close again. He waited... uncertain of what to do next. It was now darker and he felt safer wrapped in the invisible cloak of night. Presently the light in Grok's apartment went out. Kioshi quickly moved back deeper into the car park and hid behind a silver Toyota station wagon. Concealed in the shadows he saw Grok come out of the apartment door onto the tiled forecourt. He headed off back down the narrow street and turned right onto Okubo Dori. Kioshi followed at a safe distance and watched Grok retrace his steps back to the station. After about seven minutes, a green line train appeared on the bridge, paused, and then moved off almost silently. Grok was gone.

Alone now, Kioshi realised that he had no plan. *So why am I here? Why did I follow Grok here? Why am I not following him now?* He turned and wandered back towards the convenience store. He was hungry. *Wait…* he told himself, *think. What do I know?* he asked himself. The biggest question of all seemed to be why he had left the labyrinth at all. Why he had wanted to escape?He felt that the answer to this question was a simple one. Why do I live in the labyrinth, when there is another whole world up here with light and sun and sound and people? All his life his guardians had taught him that his was a better world, his was a bigger purpose. It was simple. He had left the labyrinth because he wanted to find out for himself. And now he had discovered that Grok had a separate agenda.

He stopped and leaned on the low green railing that separated the footpath from the road.

He tallied up all his new information. Things had changed in the labyrinth. Where he used to feel at least safe, secure and protected, he now felt vulnerable. He felt some kind of strange bond with the Professor, which seemed to be growing within him. The more it grew, the further he wanted to separate himself from the man. His trips to the library had provided the information that Tetsuya Hiroko's research involved travelling backwards in time, and this information had led to Kioshi understanding that what went on in the labyrinth, was probably an extension of that research. He also knew that Tetsuya had actually succeeded in distorting time, but with very little control. He also understood that this last and very important fact, seemed to have eluded Professor Hiroko.

Then he came to Grok. Where Grok was concerned he knew that he was keeping information from, or even lying to, the Professor. He had a secret exit from the labyrinth that nobody, especially the Professor, seemed to know existed. On the two occasions that Kioshi had observed Grok leave the labyrinth by this exit, he was carrying the same blue canvas bag full of something unknown. He had seen him leave hundreds of times from other exits, but never with any kind of bag. He had also heard Grok talk many times with the Professor about his home. Kioshi remembered well that he had said it was a small room over a hair salon in a street call Meiji Dori (Kioshi remembered that because of the name of the shrine in Yoyogi Park), right by the... now where was that? Ikebukuro... yes, Ikebukuro Station. But now Grok seemed to have a large expensive apartment in Shin-Okubo. Not the same place at all. While he hid behind the wall in the car park, Kioshi had heard Grok tell the Professor that he was still standing outside Yoyogi Stadium looking for Kioshi, when in fact he was on a balcony in Shin-Okubo.

Kioshi pushed off the green railing, hurried along the street and back to the car park opposite Grok's apartment. It was now quite dark, but directly opposite him and about twenty feet from Grok's apartment building, was a big concrete power pole with a street light. The light faced over the road but spilled some light onto the side of the building. Kioshi made a decision. He would climb onto Grok's balcony and after that... well, who knows. The low brick wall around the flowerbed was a little more than knee high and the wall beside it was about six feet. Kioshi felt that he could quickly scale up the low wall, onto the high wall and be reasonably well hidden amongst the branches of the tree that grew against the wall. He would pause here to make sure he was not observed, then it was an easy climb a few feet into the tree and onto Grok's balcony.

Without further thought, and with a quick glance up and down the street, Kioshi was over the road, onto the low wall, and had hoisted himself onto the higher wall in less than six seconds. A quick crab shuffle into the lower branches of the tree, then absolute stillness. Somewhere far away a dog barked. Kioshi waited a full minute, then took hold of a sturdy branch and climbed upwards until he was chest height with the silver rail that ran along the top of the concrete balcony wall. He looked around again then, happy his climb had gone unnoticed, he hauled himself over, and dropped down out of sight behind the wall. With his back to the wall he was facing a double sliding glass door. He slid over to the door and peered in through the glass. There was a thin mesh curtain which was half open, and he found himself looking into a large room with what appeared to be very expensive furniture and fittings. He put his right ear to the glass and plugged his left index finger into his other ear. All he could hear was the soft muted drone of the building's equipment. Air conditioning or ventilation fans maybe.

He knelt up and took hold of the door handle, pulling it to the left. Nothing. It was hard to get a purchase from the angle he was on. He stood up in a crouch, and peered over the balcony wall. There was a small white, two storey building opposite whose top floor window faced directly at the balcony. On the left hand side of that, a five story apartment block with the stairs running up the outside right hand corner of the building. The window was in darkness and the stairs were empty. He turned, stood up and gave the handle a sharp tug to the left. Once it broke the seal of the draft extruders, it slid quietly open. Kioshi pulled off his shoes, stepped through and pulled the door shut behind him. He crouched down and peered back out through the door. Still nothing.

Kioshi waited a few seconds more, then turned to examine the room. With the glow from the street light beside the building, his eyes quickly grew accustomed to the gloom. The front section of the room was a lounge area with beautiful leather seats like nothing Kioshi had ever seen before. There was a large low coffee table and a matching side table with a white, frosted glass lamp. The carpet was long nap and luxurious beneath his feet as he moved further into the room. There was a stone dining table with four white leather chairs, and beyond that a wide granite topped bench that gave onto a modern kitchen. On the kitchen bench beside the sink was an electric kettle, but apart from that, the whole area was pretty bare. There were no plants, pictures, magazines... nothing. Kioshi opened some of the kitchen cupboards. There were two or three coffee cups and a few small plates. Another cupboard held a few cans of something called

Black Russian Caviar, some packets of dry crackers, two bottles of French wine, and a bottle marked Armagnac. Another held some teabags, and some American brand instant coffee. Below the sink he found basic dishwashing and cleaning gear. He pulled open the last drawer and found only a stack of red and white check tea towels. He went to push the drawer closed and paused on instinct.

He leafed through the towels, and uncovered a pistol almost the same as the one in Grok's office. Cradling it in the cloths he picked it up and carefully turned it over, reading the name engraved on it and committing details to memory. He didn't know why but it seemed important. Then he carefully put it back how he had found it, and resumed his search. There was no food, and nothing to cook it in anyway. In a drawer below the microwave, he found a smattering of cutlery and a few pairs of chopsticks. In the refrigerator he found a white plastic bag like the one that Grok had emerged with from the Seven Eleven. Alongside that, some long life milk, two cans of beer and a bottle of vodka. He opened the bag and discovered a curry roll and an apple. Hunger rushed in on him like a pack of dogs, and he had to fight off a slightly nauseous sensation, as he realised he could not disturb the contents of the bag. Grok must never know he was here.

He closed the refrigerator door and made his way out of the kitchen and into a short hall. Here was the entrance, and the carpeted hallway skirted a small, polished wooden floor area that stepped down to the front door. There were two pairs of slippers on the edge of the step. Kioshi crept down the hallway, past the front door. Immediately to his left was a bathroom and laundry space. He went in, checked the cupboards and found nothing but the very minimal requirements. A blade razor, shaving gel, one toothbrush, toothpaste and a wooden hairbrush. One side of a larger cupboard housed clean towels and spare soap. The other side housed a vacuum cleaner, a broom and a small set of folding steps. He closed the cupboard door and made his way further down the hall to the only other room, which was a bedroom. Kioshi stepped through the door and let the light from the window gradually illuminate his surroundings. There was a large bed, neatly made and flanked on both sides by a small table with a frosted glass lamp. On the left hand bedside table were two books. Kioshi memorised their position and picked them up. The large book on top was called, *For Whom the Bell Tolls* by someone called Ernest Hemingway. The smaller bottom book was called *Slaughterhouse Five* by Kurt Vonnegut. Kioshi remembered he had seen this name on the book in Grok's office at the labyrinth. He put the books back exactly as he had found them. This seemed to indicate that this was indeed Grok's apartment, but if he needed further proof, he found it almost immediately as he turned his attention to the wardrobes opposite the foot of the bed.

He slid the doors apart and was staring at four immaculate dark blue suits, three of which were shrouded in thin plastic. Beside them hung at least a dozen identical white shirts and two grey dust coats. In the left hand side of the cupboard was a set of cube like storage shelves. There were three cubes on each row, housing underwear, vests and socks. One cube held neatly pressed and folded running or exercise gear, and a folded red track suit. He reached into another cube and pulled out a pile of magazines that had been pushed to the back. The magazines were all foreign travel and real estate publications. He placed them back in the cube, and pushed them up against the back wall as he had found them. The cubes below that held three identical pairs of Julius Marlowe leather shoes alongside a pair of Adidas trainers. Looking up, Kioshi could just make out the handle of a bag in one of the upper most cubes. Again, he noted the position of the handle, and stretched up to take hold of it. It tumbled down on him... much heavier than he had realised, and bounced off his shoulder. The blow and the noise startled him and he gave a muffled cry. Again he had to wait and listen for any reaction, but after a few minutes he resumed breathing normally and knelt beside the bag to open it. As the zip slid away, Kioshi discovered a number of stacks of banknotes held by rubber bands. Pulling these out he found wallets, credit cards, jewellery and a large number of men's and women's wristwatches including a new IWC Pilot's Chronograph, still sealed in its packaging. He recognised this as one of the watches he himself had stolen from a luxury watch store on the Ginza just weeks before.

Kioshi needed money, so he decided to carefully remove a selection of notes from some of the bundles. He had no real idea of the value of the money, nor how long it would last. He was concerned that Grok might notice the money missing if he took too much. He closed the bag, and on tip toes pushed it back up onto the high shelf. Something seemed to be blocking it, so he pulled it down and put it on the bed, while he went into the laundry to get the folding steps from the cupboard. Working quickly he opened the stairs, then grabbed the bag and climbed up. At eye level with the shelf, he could see that all three top cubes were only about half as deep as the lower ones. He looked at the cubes underneath. They reached back a lot further. He looked at the top cubes again, then out of the corner of his eye noticed a small wire tab protruding from the bottom right hand corner of the back section. He stretched across to look at the two other top cubes. Both had the same small, almost invisible wire. He stuffed the bag in the centre cube, and reached in and took hold of the wire loop in the right hand cube.

As he pulled gently, the paned lifted out. He lay it down flat in the cube and noted that it was held in place with magnets. There in front of him was a pile of money that, to Kioshi, looked like all the money in the world. There were two layers of high denomination notes stacked end to end, completely filling the hidden space. He went down the steps and moved the ladder to the left then climbed up and opened the left hand cube. This space held lots of files and paperwork. Kioshi knew these must have great importance to Grok, otherwise why were they hidden like this.

Beside the paperwork he noticed a thick envelope. It was full of photographs of all parts of the labyrinth as he flicked through the photos he came to pictures of the boys and finally four or five pictures of himself, and a number of very small babies. He shifted the bag out of the middle cube and in the cavity found six big stacks of banknotes that were not bound or contained in any way. Next to them were three stacks of documents, each including a passport. He opened each passport in turn. The first was from the United States, and Grok's head stared up at him from the small photo. The name on the passport was Kevin Myles. Grok also featured in a British Passport as Charles Brock, and a Polish passport as Dariusz Kaminski. Under each passport was a pile of official documents like driver's licenses and so on.

Kioshi made another decision. He reached in and fanned up each of the six stacks of banknotes and, from about halfway down each pile, he removed a wad about a centimetre thick. He stuffed the money into his trouser pockets, then he stared at the pile, shuffling it around a bit until all seemed in order. He replaced the panels concealing the centre and left hand hiding spaces, then hefted the bag into the centre cube before climbing down and shifting the steps back to the right. Back on the steps he closed the rear panel of the right hand cube, grabbed the canvas bag, and placed it back how he had found it. He climbed down and checked from below, stretching up like a stage manager to make a tiny adjustment to the position of the handle.

He folded the steps up, scrubbing at the carpet with his foot to remove any sign of them, then carried them to the door where he turned back and carefully checked the room. All was in order. He made his way to the bathroom and placed the folded steps exactly as he had found them in the cupboard, then made a quick circuit of the kitchen and lounge area. Back at the front of the lounge room, he dropped to his knees and pulled open the sliding door just enough to slip quickly through. Once on the balcony he pulled his shoes on, then crawled over to the wall and peered down into the street. The coast was clear. Thirty seconds later he was over the balcony rail, through the branches, off the wall, and heading down the street toward Okubo Dori.

In the Seven Eleven, Kioshi gathered up some food and drinks and, for the first time in his life, went to the checkout. He dropped his purchases on the counter and reached in and pulled a single note from his pocket. It was 10000¥. The clerk scowled when he saw the size of the note, but took it and gave Kioshi change consisting of smaller notes and coins. While the clerk loaded his food and drinks into a bag, Kioshi put his change in his pocket. He noted the amount on the cash register and resolved to work out the costs later, so he could figure out the real worth of the money he had. Taking his supplies, he headed back towards Shin-okubo station, but paused at the little cross street just before the bridge. He could not afford to run into Grok anywhere, so he headed off down the street to his left knowing this was the direction the train had come, and hoping to stay in sight of the railway line.

He was in luck. On his left were houses and yards. An unseen dog growled lazily at him. On his right was the elevated railway lines. The rain had stopped, but as he trudged along he began to feel incredible tiredness. It had been a long day and Kioshi was almost out on his feet. Presently he came to a spot where an access tunnel for cars and pedestrians ran under the railway lines. He looked up at the diagonal yellow and black stripes across the head of the tunnel and the image swam before his eyes. A little further on, the embankment holding up the railway track was surrounded by a low wooden rail fence, and completely overgrown with high, thick green weeds. Kioshi dragged himself forward and hoisted his exhausted body over the fence and down into the weeds. By chance he was well hidden. The ground and weeds were damp, but it didn't matter. He rolled on his side and reached into his shopping bag for something to eat. He fell soundly and rapidly asleep, with his hand wrapped around a tuna and mayo onigiri.

42. WAITING TO EXHALE

The present...

The lobby bar is pretty quiet, and the dozen or so people there are seated at or near the bar itself. Yuka and I make our way to a cosy little spot further away from the bar, with a low table and a pair of comfortable lounge chairs. As we make our way through the furniture, I can see a drink waiter in black pants, white shirt and burgundy vest, shadowing us on a parallel course. Yuka fancies something light and refreshing so we order two long gin and tonics.

"So... your news?" I say with a question mark.

"Yes, my news," Yuka replies, straightening the hem of her skirt but not making eye contact.

Suddenly she slaps her palms on her knees. It startles me a bit, and one or two people at the bar look over in our direction. *Nothing to see here,* I think to myself.

Yuka sits forward and perches on the edge of her seat.

"I'm not really sure where to start," she says haltingly.

I watch those big beautiful eyes and for just a moment I thought I may have misread the situation. This might just as easily be bad news.

"I have resigned from my job in Sendai," she commenced. "I kept a very small apartment there and I have already packed up everything I had and arranged for it to be shipped to my father's house in Mitake."

She went on to tell me a little more about her father and his wonderful house in the mountains west of Tokyo.

"So... two things have happened to me recently and these things have made me realise that, up until now, my life has been sort of… lacking in direction. I have just taken the easy road, gone with the flow. Until now I have never really taken any risks or stepped out of my comfort zone. Just before we met I visited my father. I came down to Tokyo a couple of days early because I had not seen him for almost four months, and I was missing him. When I arrived home I was shocked to see how much older he looked. He had been unwell. It was his back. He sits and writes all day and he must have aggravated an old complaint. He was on the mend, but for all that he was looking pretty haggard. It was then I realised that he will not be here forever, and I do not wish to live so far away from him. My life and work in Sendai had stretched out the gaps between my visits home with my barely noticing it."

She pauses as the waiter returns with our drinks, and places them on napkins on the table. He sets down a small bowl of nuts, then bows shyly and leaves.

Yuka takes a long slow breath as if steeling herself for an unpleasant task. I have stopped breathing and every muscle in my body, every nerve, every cell is just hanging there waiting for her to exhale. Only when she has exhaled can I do so, and restart my body.

"And then I met you."

I am so focused that I actually missed what she said.

"I'm sorry?" I mumble in a voice that belongs in a Disney cartoon. I clear my throat.

"I'm sorry?" I repeat. This time more legibly.

"I said, and then I met you. At the very same time as I am questioning my life, I meet you and well, I may as well jump right in here. I think in the short space of a couple of weeks that I may have fallen in love with you."

And right there I stop breathing again. In fact I think the whole world may have stopped breathing. It seems it had been doing that a lot lately. It is probably only four or five seconds, but it feels like an eternity later, that I hear a thumping noise start up somewhere in the room. Gradually it grows louder and louder until I finally realise that it is my heart. She just said *'I may have fallen in love with you'*... I'm sure she did.

Yuka went to speak again, but I held up my right index finger to stop her, before picking up my drink and giving it a solid beating. I put down my glass.

"Are you okay... you look... I don't know... strange."

My thoughts are jumbled like scrabble tiles in a blender. I struggle to compose myself. When I open my mouth I want the words to come from my heart, not like something from a Disney cartoon. Then suddenly, I feel a mood of perfect contentment wash over me, and I relax.

"Yes, I'm fine now. I have to admit that I had built my hopes up so high, that I was petrified all this would go wrong."

"All *what* would go wrong?"

"Well, ever since I last saw you, I've been missing you like hell. I had decided that I was coming to Sendai to tell you that... well, that I think I may have fallen in love with you too. I've had many relationships, but until now I've never met that one person I wanted to spend my whole life with. I thought I had once, but I was wrong, and even then I never felt like this. I have been scared that you would brush me off or worse, laugh at me. I mean, as you say, it has been such a short time since we met."

I stand up and reach out my hands. She wafts upwards into my arms and we kiss. That first heavenly kiss upon which we will build the foundations of our life.

"Pay the bill and meet me by the lifts," she says, her voice somehow deeper and huskier.

Our second kiss takes us five floors skyward, and would take us higher if not for the sound of the bell and the doors opening. Now we are in her room, Yuka takes both my hands in hers and steps backwards, away from me.

"Like you, I have had one or two relationships that I thought maybe would develop, but it quickly became apparent that they held no future. This feeling I have for you is very different. If we need feel any guilt about the speed at which this is all happening, then we will wear this guilt equally, together. I have never felt that anything was so right."

And with that she unbuttons her white silk blouse and peels it off. Then she unfastens her skirt and slides it down over her hips.

. . .

It is early morning. We have made love three times and in between, slept in each others arms.

We decide to get up and shower, then go look for a nice cafe for breakfast. It is so early that we have walked almost to Harajuku Station before we find a little coffee shop that lures us in with the irresistible scent of fresh croissants and good espresso. Mind you, the way I'm feeling, I could eat horse if it was well cooked and properly garnished. Everything smells great, the rising sun heralds a great day, and even the early traffic seems to flow in harmony like a well timed waltz. So this is what it's like to be in love.

After breakfast, we decide to carry on walking to my hotel. As we make our way into the Harajuku entrance to Yoyogi Park, my forefinger gets itchy, then sore.

I speak to Yuka without turning towards her.

221

"Don't look around. Just keep smiling and walking, but the boy is close. I think he may be watching us right now."

"Do you think we should stop and try and communicate with him? Do you think he means us any harm? He's had plenty of opportunities to harm you, but has never done so."

"I don't think the time is right. I think we need to know more about all this."

My finger is throbbing as we near the path up to the shrine entrance. I think I sense movement in the bushes about thirty metres off to my right. I stop walking and look down at my right hand. Yuka does likewise, and we watch as the black carbon stain spreads across the heel of my hand and up under my shirt cuff like a swarm of bees.

I note the look of concern on Yuka's face, and reach out with my left hand and pull her towards me. I kiss her forehead.

"Don't worry," I whisper. "Don't ask me how I know, but I'm sure the boy means us no harm. It's weird, but I feel I have met him somewhere before. I think he is… I think he is…. I need to sit down."

I step over to the side of the gravel path and sit down on a large rock near the edge of the garden. I feel weak.

In the shrubs near the cistern, Kioshi peers out at us. We can't see him, we just know he's there. If we could see him, we would notice him squat down, clench his fists and screw up his eyes. We would see him rocking back and forth on his heels, and we would see him collapse sideways onto the ground at the same time as I fall sideways off the boulder. In the distance I hear Yuka's scream… far away… far, far away.

The blood rushes through my head like a deafening torrent, and there is a great rending sound of metal on metal. Then there is nothing. Just the silent whooshing sound of the air passing my ears as the planet turns. All life goes on... but silently. I watch behind closed lids as a policeman drapes his uniform jacket over the head and shoulders of a dead woman.

I see a silent ambulance arrive on silent, screeching tyres.

Suddenly the sound comes crashing back, and I clutch my ears against the clamour of sirens, the screaming of instructions. Then one horrific other worldly sound tears through the atmosphere with all the horror of the apocalypse pushing it out into space and beyond.

Viiiiiiiince!

Then nothing.

I open my eyes to see Yuka staring down at me with a horrified look on her face. Her great big beautiful eyes seem twice as big with surprise. Mustering as much bravado as I can, I smile weakly up at her and she collapses sobbing on my chest. I struggle into a sitting position to catch my breath, then hoist myself up onto the rock. A small group of concerned people, or sticky beaks, are hanging around. A little short man dressed in a long grey overcoat and a grey felt cap pushes his way through the gathering, waving his umbrella like a sword.

"Move along you lot. There's nothing to see here."

He smiles at me and says...

"I always wanted to say that." Then chuckles to himself and shuffles off down the path.

I slide over and make room for Yuka beside me on the rock. She seems smaller... scared.

"What just happened? It was so frightening. I thought you were dying."

I took her hand in mine and noticed that the black mark and the blister were both gone. I held it up to show her.

"Well," I started, "I don't know what you saw happening, but I have just had a vision or something. I had a major flashback to an event that happened when I was a teenager. Something I have completely forgotten about until now. It was like I was watching a replay or something; and what I just saw reminds me of a lot more besides. I think the boy did it, or caused it... or something like that. I had just got through saying I had a strong feeling that I had met him somewhere before, and I think I was right. It makes no sense at all, but I have met this boy before."

I stood up from the rock, and pulled Yuka up into my arms.

"I'd like to think all this through before I try and tell you what I think just happened, but I don't believe there is any need to be frightened by the boy. If it's okay with you, I'd like to go to my room, have a shower and some more strong coffee. Then I can try and get my head around this."

We start walking hand in hand in silence toward the Northern Torii Gate, and suddenly my nose is bleeding. I'm holding my hand up trying to pinch my nose and stem the flow, but the blood is literally pouring out of me; coursing down my hand and up my sleeve... soaking my shirt and the cuff of my jacket. Outside the gate we stop, and I sit on the ground with my back against a tree. If I lean my head back, my mouth fills with that strong metallic taste. I close my eyes and wait. I've been bleeding for about ten or fifteen minutes when, as suddenly as it started, it stops. I'm on my feet now, but feeling a little lightheaded. We continue on to my hotel in Shinjuku. In my room, I hit the shower and hang under the steaming water as I gather my thoughts. Yuka orders up coffee and a couple of brandies. She must have been a girl guide as well as a mind reader! I come out of the bathroom toweling my hair to find her naked in my bed, sipping a brandy.

"It's for my nerves you know." She says smiling.

"Maybe you should have ordered champagne," I say.

"Why champagne?"

"Well, then I might have asked you to marry me."

Her eyebrows shot up in surprise. There's those great big unbelievable eyes again.

"Did you just ask me to marry you?"

"No, I said I might have asked you, if you had ordered champagne."

"Damn," she laughed. "Well, we have an hour before the crew arrives, so what are you doing standing out there."

And with that she flings back the sheet to reveal her perfect naked body. My eyes travel down her long, slender neck to stop and gaze on her small but firm and perfect breasts, I continue on across her taught, flat stomach and down into a thin strip of dark pubic hair marking the start of two of my favourite legs in the world. Her feet are perfect and delicate.

"I'm weak... weak I say," jumping in beside her.

The coffee goes cold as we continue our exploration of each other's bodies. Afterwards, we talk about anything but the boy, making the moment last, refusing to let anything spoil the moment. But soon it is 9.45am, and we drag ourselves out of bed and dress ready for Nick and Oka to arrive. I pour myself a cup of cold coffee and order down for another large coffee pot, tea, cookies and a flask of ice water. We're sitting in the small lounge area when the bell sounds. I open the door to find Nick and Oka standing in the hall. Oka looks pretty perky as always, but Nick looks kind of worse for wear.

I swing a couple of dining chairs around for Nick and I, and Yuka and Oka take the small couch. Once we are all sitting down, Oka regales us with tales of Nick's behaviour last night.

"Drank half of Tokyo," he laughs.

"Yeah and you drank the other half, so why do I feel like death and you look set to start all over?" groans Nick.

The bell rings, and in comes a trolley with a steaming jug of black coffee, boiling water, teabags, iced water, milk, lemon and sugar. Nick makes a very ungentlemanly lunge for the coffee pot, and pours two steaming cups down his throat before he realises we are all watching him. He sheepishly pours tea and coffee for the rest of us, then places the ice water jug and four glasses on the coffee table.

"Right," he says, "almost human again."

"Well," says Oka, pulling his notepad from his beat up briefcase.

"Sorry Oka-san, but I'd like to stop you right there. There's been a major development which I need to tell you all about before we proceed. I think it will affect what we do next. Something happened to Yuka and I this morning while we were walking in Yoyogi Park. Well, something happened to me that Yuka witnessed. She only knows what she saw, but there's a lot more to it, and I've been saving that for when we were all together. So here goes."

I settle myself a bit more comfortably on the seat and begin.

"Okay… as I say, Yuka and I were walking through Yoyogi Park early this morning. As you know I can tell when the boy is near by the mysterious appearance of the blister on my right index finger and sometimes the appearance of a black kind of scorch mark that runs up my hand to my wrist. You haven't seen this strange phenomenon yet Oka-san, but both Nick and Yuka

226

have. When the boy is near, the injury flares up and when he departs the damage simply disappears. So… this morning in the park, I felt the pain starting in my hand and finger. It got stronger and stronger and then I started to feel very dizzy and nauseous. I was pretty disorientated, and I sat down on a rock. I felt as weak as a kitten. The blood rushed to my head, and I felt myself toppling sideways. The next thing I knew I was waking up in the middle of a scene from my teenage years. When I say a scene, I mean a real event, something that really happened. I saw quick glimpses of something that really happened to me, but that I had forgotten about. When I came to, Yuka was leaning over me. Well, to cut a long story short, a few minutes later, as we were making our way out of the park, my nose started to bleed. And I don't just mean bleed… I mean seriously bleeeed!"

I look at Nick and Oka. Nick is leaning on the table with his hands under his chin, looking perplexed. Oka is slouched down into the couch cushion with a scowl on his face. I look at Yuka. She reaches across and touches my hand.

"To me it looked like he had just fainted," she said, "but the nosebleed was awful. I didn't even know we had that much blood in us," she says with a grimace. "Sorry… go on," she says to me.

"Right, so the glimpses I had were all tangled up, but they were enough to remind me of the event itself. I was at the scene of a car accident, I saw the two cars involved, and a policeman. There was a dead woman on the pavement, and I saw an ambulance arriving. Another strange thing is that it is like… I'm not sure how to describe this, but it's like I was in a glass box watching all this happen, then at some point somebody put a lid on the box and it became perfectly quiet… totally silent. Then after a little while it was like they had pulled the lid off again and the sound came crashing back… deafeningly loud. As the sound returned I hear a man screaming. He was screaming a name and that name was… Vince."

I looked around at our little group once more, to find no discernible change in the expressions of Nick and Oka.

Yuka was on the edge of her seat, staring intensely at me.

"So, I can see you are completely underwhelmed by this information, but now if you'll let me tell you another little story, I think you'll begin to understand.

When I was a teenager; I don't know, I must have been around sixteen or seventeen years old, I had a very vivid dream. What I saw this morning were glimpses of that very same dream. When I had the dream, the buildings and the cars in the street were all very old. Not vintage cars or anything, just like... you know, cars from the fifties or sixties. It was like watching an old episode of 'Sunset Strip' or something. Now, the thing is, that I have an unshakeable feeling that this boy Kioshi, caused what happened to me this morning. He made me remember that dream, and that's not all. I think he was the cause of the first dream, the one I had when I was seventeen. That's if it really was a dream."

"Wait, wait," says Nick, "you're losing me. If it wasn't a dream, what was it? And how could the boy control it?"

"I didn't say he controlled it. I said he probably *caused* it."

Oka-san was staring at me with a strange expression on his face.

"Go on," he said. "Let's see where this takes us."

43. A DAY IN THE PARK

The past...

"What the hell do you mean you can't find him? What is that, has he run off... what?"

Tetsuya Hiroko's blood pressure had pushed up into dangerous levels. He felt like the top of his head about to blow off. Of course that could have something to do with all the drinking he had been doing lately.

Grok turned away and poured himself a cup of coffee from the filter pot on the bench. With his back to Tetsuya he felt his top lip curl into a snarl. He had taken a lot of crap from this guy, but he figured the returns made it all worthwhile. Better to play the humble servant. He composed himself and turned back to face the Professor.

"I don't think he could have gone far. I waited hours at the appointed spot. Maybe he's simply lost," he said, with just the right amount of subjugation. "I'll go straight back there early in the morning. I'm sure he'll turn up. There will be a simple explanation."

"There had better be," hissed Tetsuya. "We are just two days from our deadline. I haven't waited around for the past three years to have him go missing at this critical stage."

"I'll find him," said Grok. "He'll be here."

But he didn't find him... and he wasn't there.

The deadline came and went with no sign of the boy.

. . .

Kioshi woke early. This was the hottest time of the year and it tended to rain a lot, so even at an early hour it was steamy down there in the shrubbery. For a minute he was unable to figure out where he was. Was he somewhere back in time? He rubbed at his eyes and sat up. A head was passing by. He craned up a bit further. The head was attached to a perfectly normal person walking a dog, and as they passed he saw that they both had nice healthy shadows. *That's something anyway,* he thought. Slowly it all came back to him, and he realised where he was. As he did, a major hollow seemed to form in his stomach and claw at him for attention. As the previous night's events formed in his mind, he remembered the bag of supplies from the convenience store. It was right beside him, and he wasted no time tucking into a makeshift breakfast from what was intended as last night's dinner.

When he looked up he could see that the sun had made an appearance on the top of a big white building opposite his weed patch. He could hear more talking as the city came to life and, people crossed backwards and forward under the railway bridge beside him. He felt in all his pockets to make sure the money was still there… good, not a dream. He quickly grabbed his shopping bag and climbed over the low wooden fence and back down onto the road. Nobody had taken any notice of him and if they had, they had bigger problems to worry about than some scruffy looking urchin sleeping in a weed patch by the railway tracks. He resumed last night's journey south along the road beside the tracks. Presently he came to a very large intersection with three lanes flowing east and three lanes flowing west under the railway tracks. Even at this early hour the traffic was building, so he found a safe place to cross. On the other side of the intersection, he continued along beside the railway tracks until he came to Seibu Shinjuku Station with lots of shops on his right. He passed a large, modern hotel and then the little street opened up into a large, busy intersection. The signs told him he was at the corner of Yasukuni Dori and Shinjuku Dori, but he already knew where he was. This was familiar territory. He was on the northern side of Shinjuku Railway Station. He was somewhere above the labyrinth.

He realised that he would need to be careful from here on. He needed to change his clothes. He could easily be spotted in his current outfit. He crossed over into Shinjuku Dori and took the first small street on the left. Here there were shoe shops and clothing shops, but they were all still closed at this early hour. He stopped a passerby and politely asked the time… 9.15. Then he asked a street sweeper what time the shops opened… 10 o'clock. He wandered up the road to the east side of Shinjuku Station and sat down, well hidden on the edge of a small garden bed, to wait.

At 10 o'clock Kioshi made his way back to the shops. Thirty minutes later he emerged, having swapped his grey wool shorts for a pair of faded Levis, his blue sweater for a black hooded top, and his black leather shoes for red and white trainers. Now he looked like a different person. He looked like all the other kids his age on the street. Topped off with a wool hat and a cheap pair of sunglasses, he not only looked different, he looked about three years older. He stopped and checked his reflection in a shop window and was pleased with the transformation.

He set off once more up the road beside the huge station, and continued under the road bridge. On his left was a store with a camping display out front. Inside there was all sorts of clothing and sports equipment, but he wandered around until he came to the camping area. He left the store about a half hour later, weighed down with a small tent, a blue plastic tarpaulin, a cheap hunting knife, a sleeping bag, a small spirit stove and some fuel, some camping cutlery and crockery and a small canvas folding stool. He stomped off towards the Yoyogi camp sight.

On his arrival at the southern end of the park, Kioshi had wandered down to the edge of the camp, dumped his gear on the ground and looked for Ojiisan. After some time he located him and was able to attract his attention. The little round man made his way slowly up to where Kioshi stood and without a word, picked up one of Kioshi's bundles and signalled for Kioshi to follow. All of this was new to Kioshi, and the old man sat on Kioshi's new folding stool giving instructions on how it all went together and often laughing hysterically. Kioshi struggled with his new gear, but his tent was finally erected close alongside the old man's and facing away from prying eyes. That night, Kioshi and Ojiisan shared a simple meal from Kioshi's supplies. The old man made hot tea. They barely spoke. As night drew in, Kioshi could hear the sound of other camp inhabitants, laughing, arguing, drinking. For the first time he could remember, Kioshi went to bed with fear in his heart. Fear of the unknown. In the labyrinth all was taken care of. His future was mapped out. Out here everything was up to him. As he closed his eyes to sleep, all he could see behind his eyelids was the Professor's face.

Kioshi slept for thirteen hours solid. He woke to the second or third drop of water to hit him on the forehead. When he first opened his eyes he struggled to figure where he was. He was on his back looking up at a green translucent ceiling. As he watched another big drip form above his head, it slowly dawned on him where he was. He was in a tent in the Yoyogi homeless village. Ojiisan had told him to put the blue plastic tarpaulin across the top of the tent, but Kioshi had been just too tired. Now he paid the price.

He rolled on his side and tried to go back to sleep, but the next drop scored a direct hit in his exposed ear. Finally, he came fully awake. He sat up in the tent and wriggled himself out of the way of the drip, which was growing more insistent. He fumbled around in his parcels, and dug out a metal bowl that he had bought with his camping gear. He placed it under the drip, then like a butterfly escaping from a cocoon, he slowly peeled himself out of his sleeping bag. He sat listening to the rain, then crawled to the tent flap and peered out at a miserable rainy day. There seemed nobody about. Ojiisan's little tent and box house was neatly shut up, so he pulled the flap back down and rummaged around for breakfast.

While he ate, Kioshi emptied all of his bags and his pockets. He sat there surrounded on one side by his meagre provisions, and on the other by a pile of money. He sorted the money into denominations then started methodically counting. When he finished, he closed his eyes tightly and his lips moved soundlessly as he repeated the amount over and over to himself. Then he began counting again. At last he pushed the pile of notes to one side and reached for a can of soda. Thirsty work this counting. He pulled the top off the soda and took a big swallow. Then he rested the can between his legs and stared straight ahead. Just under three and a half million yen. Kioshi didn't really understand how much it was, but he did know that it was a lot; an awful lot for a thirteen year old runaway to have lying around in a homeless camp! He took a handful of notes from the stack and stuffed them back in his pocket, then he unpacked the last of the camping gear he had bought, and used the plastic wrap to bind up the pile of money. He dropped the parcel into one of the plastic shopping bags and forcing the air out, tied a knot in the top. He repeated this with the second shopping bag then put it into his sleeping bag cover and pushed it down into his sleeping bag. Then he pushed himself down into the sleeping bag and, well fed and a little more organised, was sound asleep again within minutes. The rain fell steadily and now invaded the tent on many different fronts, but the boy Kioshi slept on.

When he woke, he came alert instantly. The rain had stopped and there were voices close by. He felt about for the parcel of money and finding it, tucked it against his thigh. Staying in the bag, he squirmed like a bug towards the tent flap. Carefully he unzipped it and lifting it slightly took stock of what was happening around him. Ojiisan was at a site about thirty metres away talking to another man. This man looked pretty much like a bundle of rags and wore a wide scowl on his filthy face. From what Kioshi could make out, they were arguing about him, Kioshi. The rag man yelled something and pointed towards Kioshi's tent, then seeing Kioshi peering out, started yelling even louder. Ojiisan turned just in time to see Kioshi's tent flap drop down. Kioshi stayed quite still and heard the quiet shuffle as Ojiisan made his way back to his own tent.

"I can see you there boy. You need to come out from there and get your tarpaulin up while it's not raining."

Kioshi kicked his way out of his sleeping bag, unzipped his tent flap, and slowly emerged onto the wet grass and slippery leaves. Ojiisan was digging around in a plastic crate then slowly straightened up and shuffled towards Kioshi with his umbrella in one hand and a coil of yellow nylon rope in the other. He held out the coil of rope to Kioshi.

"Here boy, take this and tie it off in that tree behind your tent. As high as you can. Then bring the other end across here to this pole of mine and tie it off tight here."

Kioshi did as he was told, then pulled his brand new blue plastic tarpaulin out of his tent, and spent the next half hour battling to carry out Ojiisan's instructions on how to fix it in the right place and peg it to the ground. Occasionally the old man would prod him with his umbrella and swear and growl, but eventually the job was done. Kioshi would at least stay dry tonight.

"You've never been camping have you boy?" said Ojiisan.

"I've never been anywhere," said Kioshi.

"Tea then!" said the old man after a long pause.

44. I LOOKED AROUND AND I WASN'T THERE

The present...

"Alright, so I'll explain what happened in the dream or whatever it was.

I was walking in the city. It was a quiet Sunday morning. I don't know how I knew it was Sunday morning, I only know it was. Suddenly two cars collided right behind me on an intersection. There was a great crashing noise followed by the sound of a car engine revving. One of the cars ended up flying above me, and I had to dive out of the way to avoid being hit. That car was an old red Ford, and it ended up jammed in the doorway of the brick house on the corner. I distinctly remember now that everybody in the dream was wearing what I thought were old-fashioned looking clothes. I realised that the clothes were from the sixties. I had seen photos of my own parents dressed that way. One of the cars was also from the early sixties. It was a pale blue Ford. As I said, the other car, the red one that just missed me, seemed older.

When the blue Ford finally came to a halt I could see two people in the front seat, but on the road in front of the car, I saw the body of a young boy. I went over to him and saw that he was Japanese. He opened his eyes and looked right at me. I went to try and help him, but a great spark of electricity leapt between his hand and mine. I jumped back startled. Right then I was distracted by a blood curdling scream from behind me. A guy was screaming... *Vince*, but Vince was dead... well he looked dead to me. Then an ambulance arrived, and when I turned back to the boy, he was gone. Like he was never there. An ambulance person came over to me thinking I had been involved in the accident. I didn't understand until he pointed out that I was clutching my right hand. There was a burn on my index finger and a fierce scorch mark up my hand."

There was a mass intake of breath as I stopped talking. Everybody started breathing again at the same time.

Oka spoke first.

"And then you woke up, and you remembered all this incredible detail. You know that's not normal. You know dreams don't normally happen with such a logical timeframe. The only dream-like thing you describe in your story is the boy. Now you see him now you don't!"

"Well actually Oka-san, I remembered a whole lot more detail than that. I remembered every single minute, every fine detail. It wasn't anything like a dream. It was too real. It was like I was there. I've never had a dream that conducted itself as logically as this one, either before or since. But there's a few other things that are really important. In the middle of all this, everything went deathly quiet. I could see it all happening, but I could hear nothing… just like this morning. And then as I left the scene of the crash, my nose started bleeding and it just poured out of me for about fifteen minutes then stopped dead… again, just like this morning. There was one other thing. I remember the light was odd, really odd and at some point I noticed I had no shadow. I thought it was just a trick of the light."

Oka went to speak, but I cut him off.

"There's more… within an hour of waking up I had completely forgotten the whole episode… until this morning in Yoyogi, when this boy Kioshi did whatever it was that he did to remind me. And Oka-san, your comment about the boy… now you see him now you don't. You're right. I did see him. He was there and I was there… in the sixties… and then he wasn't… and then I wasn't."

"So what are you saying?"

"I'm saying that somehow I was there. I don't know how, but I was. I recognised the city. Hell I recognised the intersection. I knew where I was. It was Hobart, in Australia, where I grew up. Of course it was about twenty years before I was even born, but that's where it was. That means we can search the records and find out if this accident happened. I mean we've got all the details."

"Okay then," says Oka. "I think what you are saying then is that the Japanese boy on the roadway was Kioshi, but he's only eighteen now. If what you are saying is true, this all happened about thirty years before the boy was born. How could he possibly be there?"

"How could I possibly be there? How could I possibly describe all this if I wasn't? I think we need to start with this accident and see if we can find a match. Another very salient point is this blister and burn thing. Blisters and burns don't just come and go in an instant. After that first time on the streets of Hobart, which I thought was a dream anyway, I completely forgot about. It never happened again until a couple of weeks ago when I first saw the boy outside Shinjuku Station and he pointed up at me and called '*I know you*!' I think the burn comes from that big electrical spark when I went to touch the boy lying in the road."

I pause to let all of this sink in. Somewhere way off in the distance, perhaps in another world, a long low wailing siren chases the blood trail.

"So then... because we are talking about things that until now I have believed were just bizarre dreams, we need to fast forward to a few weeks back, when all this started. I have told you all that I first saw this boy Kioshi, as we now know him to be called, outside of the south entrance of Shinjuku Station. But what I haven't told you before, for fear you'd have me committed, is that the first time I came upon this boy was in a dream, or what I thought was a dream, just before I encountered him outside the station."

I recounted the whole episode for them in detail, the tunnel, the green mist and my flight in fear, which had caused me to graze my head on the rock. I told them how I had made my way upwards from below Shinjuku and burst through that final door which I knew would open out onto the lowest platform of the station.

"Don't ask me how I knew that... I just did. But when I pushed the door open it was the door to my hotel room. Classic dream sequence right. Wrong! In the morning I find blood on my pillow and a small wound on my forehead... exactly where I scraped myself in the tunnel."

"You should have told me this before," says Oka.

"I don't think it's any big deal," I retorted.

"No?" yells Oka. "What about the scrape on your head and the blood on your pillow."

"Well, yes but as you can imagine I was starting to doubt my own sanity."

"Well, facts are facts, and now we have another one and, I have a gut feeling that it is important," says Oka as much to himself as anyone.

"Okay, I give in," says Nick. "What fact? If we assume it wasn't a dream, then I say again... what fact?"

Oka leans forward and playfully slaps Nick on the forehead with the palm of his hand.

"Think boy... think! Our friend here says he came through a door that he knew somehow, was on the lowest platform of

Shinjuku Station. Let's call that a fact shall we?" Oka turns to me.

"I think we should go find out if this door exists," he says.

I lean back in my seat and clasp my hands together behind my head.

"Well, we have a decent number of facts, but still far too many questions. I think we can find a lot of the answers with a bit of hard work, and we can only hope those answers help us with the big question. And that is... what this boy wants with me? So Oka-san, you're the famous gumshoe, do you think you can find out what we need to know about that car accident? Of course there were no computer records back then, but presumably all the newspaper records have been kept somehow."

Oka just curls his lip in a mock sneer and shakes his head.

45. RISING DAMP

The past...

Life in the park was hard for Kioshi. His presence was viewed with suspicion, and he had only Ojiisan to protect him. There were one or two people in the close vicinity who were openly hostile towards him. He had stayed either in, or very close by his tent for the first two days. On the third day, whilst Ojiisan was not present, the man who looked like a bundle of rags, had tried to enter his tent. Kioshi had been sitting on his little folding stool and the rag man had simply rushed up, bowled Kioshi backwards off his stool, and tried to get in his tent. Kioshi had jumped up screaming and grabbed the rag man by the arm. All the noise attracted the attention of other camp dwellers, and the rag man backed away, unwilling to break the unwritten law of the camp in front of witnesses. He had slunk off back to his own tent, but Kioshi knew that he had probably not seen the last of the rag man. He would not give up so easily, and Kioshi knew that Ojiisan could not protect him forever.

That same evening, Kioshi had sat awake in his tent until well after midnight. He waited... and if there was one thing that Kioshi was good at it was waiting. Then... when the camp had been completely quiet for at least an hour, he stuffed his bundle of cash and his hunting knife down the front of his jacket and unzipped the flap of his tent so that he could peer out carefully. He put his whole head out and sat stock still for another three or four minutes then, when he was certain it was safe, he climbed out and zipped his tent behind him. With all the stealth he could muster, he left the camp and headed west around the park's man made lake. There was a light misty rain, and a sliver of moonlight hung in the sky like a pale slice of melon. There was just enough light for his needs. After five or six minutes he had skirted partway around the lake, and looking quickly all around him, he left the main path and faded phantom-like into the darkness. Again he waited, this time for ten minutes until he was certain he was neither observed nor followed. Staying off the pathways and well back in the shadows, he made his way to the back of the small hut where he had concealed some food and belongings a few days earlier.

Once more he sat, like a statue for a good ten minutes, then he reached under the hut, scratched around and located the parcel. He pulled it out, placed it on the ground beside him. He then commenced digging with his hunting knife, as far as he could reach in under the floor of the little building. He had to be as quiet as possible, so it was slow work. In twenty or thirty minutes he had a hole about a foot and a half deep, and wide enough to stuff his money package down into. He packed as much soil as he could back in to fill the hole, and took handfuls of the rest and threw it around the ground behind him. Then he took the parcel with his belongings, stuffed it inside his jacket and backed away on all fours, leveling the ground and spreading leaves and waste about to cover any sign of his activities. He kept crawling backwards like this for about a hundred feet, then he carefully stood and made his way to a spot where he could watch the back of the hut unobserved. Here he waited again, this time for more than an hour. Finally content that he had not been seen or followed, he set off via the lake, where he scrubbed his hands then, carefully avoiding the main pathways and any pools of light dropped here and there by careless lamp posts, he made his way back to the camp.

By the time he was back in his tent, he was soaked through. The rain had gradually increased in intensity and, as he removed his jacket and jeans, it occurred to Kioshi that along with some new clothes he was planning to buy, he could use a good raincoat. The rain beat an ever increasing tattoo on the blue tarpaulins of the Yoyogi hobo village, and the young Kioshi finally drifted off to sleep.

For the next six days straight it had rained heavily. The ground outside Kioshi's tent was a quagmire. It was not cold, at least not unless you got too wet; but so far, he had gotten soaked every day at least once. On one occasion a falling branch had crashed onto his tarpaulin, tearing a large hole and dropping gallons of water onto his nylon tent roof and beyond. His belongings and bedding were one big soggy mess and with the rain refusing to let up, there was no way he could get things dry. In the finish he had to go and buy some dry clothes, a new sleeping bag, and a new tarpaulin.

Kioshi's other problem was food. In the labyrinth the food might not have been exactly gourmet, but it was a damned sight better than what he had survived on for the past week or so. Some of the camp inhabitants had little spirit or gas stoves. When it rained, they risked using them inside, or under the edge of a tarpaulin, but since his first attempt, where he'd nearly burnt his tent down, Kioshi was too scared to use his stove inside. He was surviving on convenience store food. He'd had a rotten belly ache for the past three days and that was another huge problem given the lack of toilet facilities. All of a sudden life in the labyrinth was starting to look like the preferred option. Kioshi was sitting outside his tent under the overhang from his tarp. Drops of water were racing down the blue plastic and launching themselves into mid air to drop onto the edge of the soggy cardboard that Kioshi sat on. He tugged his ankles in tighter to avoid the raindrops and sank his chin onto his knees. He stared ahead listlessly, but the unseen gears in his head were whirring around, seeking a course of action.

He was convinced he could not stay in the camp. Even Ojiisan had told him as much. He liked Ojiisan, and now he knew what it felt like to have a friend, even if he was a funny little round man with an umbrella. The previous day, Ojiisan had actually said that it was getting harder and harder for him to protect Kioshi, and that he had always thought the boy would get over this *fad* and return to wherever he had run away from. So... thought Kioshi, his young mind growing older and wiser each day... I can stay in the camp, but I will undoubtedly come to harm. He discovered he was really less concerned about that than the possibility that his friend Ojiisan might also come to harm because of him. So he had decided finally that he must leave the camp, but to go where?

He was only thirteen and even though he had a considerable stash of money, he was unable to pay to live anywhere. Of course he could go to another park, and he had seen some smaller parks where people slept, but they looked much worse that Yoyogi Kouen. He had these major flashes and glimpses of the first year of his life. A man who might be his father, two women either of which might have been his mother... or not. But he had read in the library, that no child could have memories like this before the age of one. He was not so sure about that, but he realised that these memories could not help him to find his family even if he had one. So the more he thought about it, the more he realised that the only real option remaining was to return to the labyrinth. He knew they would be angry. He expected to be punished. He had been punished in the past, but he thought that the Professor would protect him. Whilst he feared the Professor he still felt some strange but strong bond with him.

Grok on the other hand... well Grok was another story. Kioshi now knew that he should fear Grok. Grok was acting independently of the Professor. He had secrets from the Professor, like the hidden exits and the money and other items that he was stealing and smuggling out of the labyrinth.

However, Kioshi had acquired two valuable pieces of information that gave him some comfort. Firstly he knew to be very careful of Grok. He also felt that Grok's apartment could be a source of money if he needed it.

Secondly, he knew that he could travel back in time for short periods without the Professor knowing. He could do this almost any time he wished, but it was exhausting and weakened him for many days after. He knew that the Professor had been working on these experiments almost all of his life and that he now felt the experiments were, for some reason, failing. Kioshi realised that with more trips to the library, he could learn more about almost everything including maybe where he himself had come from.

He would learn about the world at the library, and he would strengthen his body and his soul so that he might learn more about this curious path that the Professor had set him on. To simplify or even justify his decision even further, he reasoned that over the next three or four years he could live safely in the labyrinth, withhold the proceeds of his own scams and grabs, and then he could secretly visit Grok's apartment and help himself to some more of Grok's secret stash. Of course all this depended on them coming to trust him enough to let him travel above ground again. They were greedy, and he knew he was the best earner they had.

Kioshi finally set his eyes on the small round shape coming down the wet grass from the main path. He blinked a few times and the smiling face of his only friend, Ojiisan, came into focus.

It was decided then.

46. GETTING TO KNOW YOU

The present...

It's less than twenty four hours since our last meeting with Nick and Oka, and Yuka and I have spent all of that time getting to know each other better. True, we have spent a lot of time in bed exploring, but we have also dealt with the more practical issues, like checking Yuka out of her hotel and moving her in with me. It does seem like this has all happened pretty quickly, but well... when something is right, it's right. After Oka and Nick had left yesterday, each with their own list of tasks to complete, we had ordered up lunch, complete with champagne. I had gone on with my life's story such as it was and then Yuka had told me about her childhood, her disappointing mother, and the special bond she had forged with her father. We had both had what could at best be called problem childhoods, but at least we had made it through relatively unscathed.

I had no living parents, but there were a few brothers and sisters spread around the globe. Like me, they were probably restless souls, but at least a few of them had finally found their niche. Yuka was the opposite. Her only brother had died in a car accident at age twenty one, but she told me she had never felt any kind of bond with him. She had always suspected that as a matter of honour, her father had married her mother and knowingly raised someone else's child as his own. So now, she had only her father, and with deep affection, she painted a picture of a man who was wise and caring. She told me about his house in the hills near Mitake and how happy he now was that he had returned to the place where he grew up. On this occasion, she stopped short of telling me she wanted me to meet him, but it didn't matter because meeting him and asking formally for his daughter's hand, was one of my priorities.

The rest of the afternoon and evening had passed blissfully enough, with more room service and more... well anyway.

We were now facing each other across the breakfast table in the hotel restaurant, having decided that we needed to stretch our legs and recharge our batteries before the others arrived.

"I suppose we had better get back upstairs, they'll be waiting for us. And I guess we'll have to tell them... about us I mean," I say before draining my coffee cup.

"Tell them?" laughs Yuka. "I don't think you'll have to say anything. I think they will guess from that big grin on your face."

And of course they did, and they both seemed genuinely happy for us.

47. THE PRODIGAL RETURNS

The past...

Grok came at him like a wild dog, his eyes mad with rage. Kioshi held his ground; did his best to stare him down. In all the years he had known Grok, he had formed no bond at all with the man, and no opinions about him either. Now he had an opinion, and he knew Grok had a weakness.

Grok skidded to a halt about three feet from Kioshi, with his arm raised across his face ready to strike. He checked himself... stood there breathing deeply, struggling to bring himself under control. Kioshi looked up at that big nose, saw the long hairs that grew there swaying back and forth like wheat stalks in a lazy breeze. Right then he knew that he wasn't scared of Grok. While he was still of some value to Grok, the man would do him no real harm. Grok's arm fell to his side and his breathing gradually became more normal. Kioshi saw the little twitch beside his nose, as Grok's hard mouth struggled to soften into something like a smile. Now that was scary!

He reached out and grabbed Kioshi by his shirtfront.

Kioshi had re-entered the labyrinth via the green door in Shinjuku Station early that morning. Before returning underground, he had thought to change back into his old clothes; those he had on when he left. They had been balled up in a damp mess in the corner of his tent, so he looked and smelt like he had lived in them the whole time.

Grok dragged him into his office and pushed him against the wall. He closed the door and sat himself down in his chair.

"You stink boy," he said, his nose twitching again. "You need to tell me where you have been and what the hell you have been doing. You know the Professor is in a rage. He has missed out on a critical window of opportunity for his research. That window

247

only comes around every three years, which means that now we're all stuck here for another three years, waiting for the next opportunity. So start at the very beginning and make it good boy, because if you lie to me I'll know, and the Professor's rage is nothing compared to what you can expect from me. I've been stuck here now for more than fourteen years looking after you little shits. Living half underground like some bleeding mole, and frankly I've just about had it. You have no idea what I have sacrificed but…"

And here the big man in the immaculate dark blue suit stood up and stuck his big red face just inches from Kioshi's.

"You need to know boy, that if you cock up all of my hard work, all those years of sacrifice, then I will squash you like an ant without a second thought."

Grok seemed to catch himself then. He backed away from Kioshi and straightened up. His big leathery face broke into a horrifying, florid smile.

"Yes sir mister Grok."

Kioshi had decided that his planned story was still the best explanation to feed Grok and the Professor. As Grok resumed his seat, Kioshi told him how he had come to fear and hate the experiments. He explained how they made him sick, and exhausted him. He said it took him many days to recover from them (which was not entirely untrue), and that they confused him in his head somehow. He told Grok that when he realised the big experiments were due again any day, he had just panicked.

"I had not planned to go, but on that last day, when you let me out, I just decided I wasn't going to come back. Of course I had no money and nowhere to go. I had to steal food, and on that first night I slept in a garden bed right near the east entrance to the station. Then in the morning I wanted to come, back but I got scared that you and the Professor would punish me. That night I went to the front entrance of the Yoyogi Stadium and I saw you there... but you looked so angry that I panicked again, and went off and hid."

"So where have you been all this time?" said Grok, his face now impassive.

"The next two nights I slept in a park opposite the Aoyama High School, but it was cold and wet, and I was a little scared of being there. Each night since, I have found somewhere closer to here. Last night I slept under some cardboard boxes in a lane near the east entrance."

Grok said nothing, but just stared at the boy. He raised his chin an inch and sniffed the air, then checked himself and continued to stare at Kioshi.

"I'm so sorry mister Grok," continued Kioshi, being careful not to overdo it.

"I was wrong. I just got scared of the experiments. I will do everything I can to make it up to you and the Professor. I did not like living out there. I was hungry, and what food I could steal was cold. I ended up feeling sick and tired and I still do. I know now how hard it is out there, and how well I am looked after here. I missed it. It is safe and quiet, and I am taken care of."

With that, Kioshi stopped talking. He sensed he had said enough. Any more might be too much. Grok seemed more relaxed.

"Well," said Grok. "You know you will be punished, but the Professor will decide on all that. I think you should go and get showered and changed out of those filthy clothes. Throw them out. I will go and see the Professor and tell him you are back."

Five minutes later, Kioshi was standing under a shower of steaming hot water. He had scrubbed away the exploits of the last week or so and now, as he stood with his head under the hot stream, he really was happy to be back. But he reminded himself that it was temporary. In a few years he would have a place of his own. Maybe something like Grok had. He *would* go into the world above, but on his own terms.

48. AN OUTING WITH THE PROFESSOR

The past...

Kioshi was in the dining room when the Professor came in. It was mid morning and Kioshi was the only one there. The Professor had just appeared in the doorway, and stood there for what seemed an interminable time. Kioshi looked up at him, then back at his plate, and continued to shovel the rice and fish into his mouth. When his plate was clean, Kioshi took a drink from the glass of water beside him on the table. Then he pushed the glass and plate away from him, and sat with his eyes down and his hands in his lap.

Finally, the Professor stirred. He moved into the room and sat at the wooden table directly opposite Kioshi.

Kioshi sensed that strange bond. Like he was in the Professor's head. Like he knew what he was thinking. Like he knew what he was feeling. Why was this?

Sensing the Professor was waiting for him to react, he looked up. He was immediately shocked. It had only been a matter of days since he had last seen the Professor, but now the man looked years older. There were dark, puffy circles under his eyes, which were themselves bloodshot and yellowed. His jowls seemed to hang slack like a bloodhound, and his whole face seemed lined with deep wrinkles. Kioshi could see that his hands were trembling. He felt an almost overwhelming sympathy for this man.

Tetsuya Hiroko looked down at his hands and clasped them together to stop them shaking. He noted that the backs of his hands now had spots. He had heard them called *age spots*. He looked up at the boy opposite him. His emotions churned inside him like concrete in a mixer. When Grok had gone to him with the news of Kioshi's return, his emotions had passed through anger, fear, relief and, after stopping at each of these albeit briefly, had finally settled on determination. There was something about this boy. Looking at him now he sensed they had passed through some kind of watershed together. This boy was the key to some mystery... hell he could feel it, and even more strongly in his presence, but the key to what?

Tetsuya felt his emotions harden within him and, on this foundation, he felt his strength returning. He had come this far. Now he had to stop drinking, stop feeling sorry for himself, stop dragging dodgy women into love hotels, and just get back to work. *That's it,* he said to himself. *Get back to work.*

"So Kioshi," he began quietly, "you are back with us then. Mr. Grok has told me your story. Do you know how much trouble you have caused, how it has affected my work?"

Kioshi knew this was not a question and he remained silent, suitably contrite. He didn't know why, but he sensed the pain in the man opposite, and again felt some sympathy for him. In his thirteen year old mind, he understood that he was something of a captive here. He didn't know how he had come to be here, other than that his parents were both dead, and that the Professor had become his main guardian. Had the man not looked after him? Had he not fed him and provided for him? Certainly Kioshi now knew that what he and the other boys did above ground was neither right nor legal, but what might have happened to him if the Professor had not taken him in when he was a baby? Kioshi was confused about his feelings toward this man, but through this confusion, an idea starting to form in his mind. He sensed there was a way to both avoid punishment, and at the same time to help the Professor. He didn't understand why he wanted to do this, but it seemed the thing to do.

Kioshi resolved to tell the Professor that his last big experiment, now over three years ago, had worked. From his trips to the library; from studying all the clues, he had figured out where he had been. He could now even draw the words he had seen in that strange language. He would tell him everything he had seen, but he would not tell him that he was able to trigger these episodes himself... not yet. He felt this information was best kept to himself. He felt strongly that by feeding the Professor just a certain amount of information, he could become more than just an object for experimentation. Maybe he could even become a sort of collaborator, and by doing so he could protect himself from Grok. By voluntarily helping the Professor he could earn more trust.

On the other side of the table, Tetsuya Hiroko was now set in his resolve. He even felt solid for the first time in years... like a big concrete block. He was a damn scientist. He would squash these feelings he had for the boy. What had he been thinking? After all, he had possessed the resolve to brutally take Hideo Tanaka's life with his own hands, and then to order the termination of dozens of other people in pursuit of building and running the labyrinth and the laboratories. He was Tetsuya Hiroko... hell, he was smarter than this kid.

Tetsuya was snapped out of his thoughts by Kioshi speaking.

"Professor, I wish to apologise to you for all the trouble I have caused." He stood up from the table and pushed in the chair. Then he stepped back and bowed to the Professor.

"Everything I told mister Grok is true, but now I must tell you that there are some things I did not tell him. They are things that I feel I should only tell you. I did not want to tell mister Grok, because I am scared of him. You see, when I went outside and stayed away one night, I wanted to come back straight away, but I was scared of mister Grok. I saw him waiting for me at the meeting place at Yoyogi Stadium, and I could see how angry he was. I am so sorry Professor, but I was too scared to go to him. Finally, my hunger and loneliness overcame my fears, and I have returned."

"Is that what you wished to tell me... that you are scared of Mr. Grok?"

"No, that is not all. As I told mister Grok, I stayed away that night because I didn't want to do the experiments. They make me sick and they exhaust me."

Kioshi stepped forward and took hold of the back of the chair. He looked down at his hands.

"Professor, what I will now tell you may make you very angry, but please understand I just wanted the experiments to stop. I feel now that I have been outside, that I belong here. I feel I can be stronger. I think that I can help you with your experiments now."

"Why would you think that?" said Tetsuya.

"Because," said Kioshi, his knuckles whitening as he clutched the chair back more tightly. "Because last time the... the experiments worked."

Tetsuya was sure he had heard the boy correctly, but he remained blank faced.

"But the instruments told a different story. They registered nothing. And when we spoke afterwards you said nothing had happened."

"I'm sorry Professor, but once I knew that you thought it had failed, I said nothing, because I thought then you might stop the experiments."

"But," said Tetsuya, now wide eyed in spite of himself, "why didn't the instruments register anything? They should have picked something up."

"I don't know about instruments and things Professor, but I was somewhere else. Somewhere where I have no shadow. All I know is that this time I was prepared. You had done the experiment before, and the start was always the same. That time I was prepared for the start, and I was not so surprised. After that I was able to stay very calm. I felt very calm. I didn't think I had any reason to be scared of anything during the experiment. It is only afterwards when I wake up that I feel so sick and weak. I feel like I have died. That is the bit that frightens me."

"But this is astounding," said Tetsuya. "You said you were somewhere else. Where were you... and what do you mean, *somewhere where you have no shadow?*"

Kioshi carefully recounted what he had seen. He told the Professor that he could draw the words on the pole beside the road, the words on the shopfront. He said he remembered them vividly.

"When I say I have no shadow, that is how I know I am somewhere not of this world or time. I simply have no shadow, and this time again, I checked... no shadow. I don't think there is anything else that I can tell you that might help us to know where I was, but I am happy to go through it all with you. If you explain to me what is happening, what to look for, I sense that maybe I can help you with your work."

The hardness in his heart now matched the hardness of his resolve, and Tetsuya had to struggle not to show his emotions. This was astounding news, there had been no failure. He wanted to jump up and shout... yes, yes and punch the air with his fist, but he maintained his composure. This stupid boy was the key. His emotions were expendable, but cooperation would be best won with kindness.

"Don't worry Kioshi. You have nothing to fear from Mr. Grok. He will do only what I tell him to."

But now both Grok *and* Kioshi knew that wasn't true.

. . .

For the next ten weeks, Kioshi was confined to the labyrinth. During this time he decided it was safest to stay put, and not to sneak out via one of Grok's secret exits. He would have liked to have visited with Ojiisan, but that would have to wait. Each day the Professor came to see him and they spent hours trying to dissect whatever Kioshi had seen during the experiments. The Professor brought books and an atlas and, over this period, he gave Kioshi a reasonable but selective grounding in geography. Together they sounded out basic words from various languages. They were able to confirm that the language in the first two experiments was English, but each one sounded different. The third language was French. At the end of this ten weeks, the Professor had confirmed three definite data points for where the boy had been, and Kioshi had soaked up an intensive course in geo-politics.

Initially, Grok had been more wary, more wolf-like than before; but he had restrained himself. Kioshi gave him no reason to doubt his story, and eventually his interaction with Kioshi returned to normal. Apart from the noisy return of the other boys from their above ground sorties, life in the labyrinth was quiet.

One morning the Professor came to Kioshi's room, just as he had for the past weeks. But this time he told Kioshi they would be going out together.

They went out via the Yoyogi cistern entrance. Once they had cleared the tunnels and were ready to exit into the actual cistern, the Professor pushed a button on the remote, and the small monitor on the wall pinged into life. The picture grew out from infinity to reveal a wide-screen view of the inside of the old collapsed cistern. Kioshi could see rocks and bushes and long grass, but the cistern was empty. The Professor pushed another button and the boulder door swung out and they both stepped into the cistern. The cistern was a simple rock or boulder lined tank or depression, about eight feet deep and heavily overgrown with weeds. At one point it had held water used to irrigate this section of the park, but with modern poly pipe and low maintenance self priming pumps, it was no longer required. Now it just formed an interesting feature in this wild native section of the garden, where nobody ever ventured. Kioshi scampered up the rocks and peered over the rim. There was nobody around, and so the two of them climbed out onto the little wooden bridge and strolled casually up onto the main pathway.

The main pathway was about thirty feet wide, and was formed using crushed gravel. A strange crunching sound signalled the arrival of a large group of people coming from the Northern Torii Gate. There were families consisting of fathers in black suits and mothers and grandmothers in kimonos. Following behind the second group was a tiny little girl. She was maybe three years old, and was dressed in traditional costume with a white and blue kimono and wooden sandals. She struggled along behind her family, determined to deal with both the unfamiliar footwear and the uneven gravel path. Each time her father went back to her and attempted to pick her up, she shrugged him off and maintained her steadfast progress along the path.

Kioshi watched the little girl and smiled. Tetsuya observed Kioshi watching the child and decided to indulge him.

"A wedding," he said. "There is a wedding at the shrine. Would you like to have a look?"

"Would it be okay for us to do that Professor?"

"Well, I'm not sure, but why don't we go and see?"

The whole purpose of Tetsuya spending this time with the boy was what they called bonding. He was still puzzled by his feelings toward this boy but, regardless of that, he had decided that befriending the boy was better than forcing him into submission. There was an old saying... something about catching more flies with honey.

They took the pathway up to the Meiji Shrine, and when they went in through the gate, Kioshi was delighted by the colour and pageantry laid out before him. There were at least three wedding parties gathered at the Shrine and, as they watched, a Shinto priest in long white robes and a strange black hat led a procession out of one of the side buildings. Behind him came two miko, young women in white robes over red tunics. They wore golden headdresses mounted with flowers, and fine green woven tassels flowed down from the tiaras to their waists. Immediately behind them came the bride and groom. The bride was all in white, with a large hooded robe pulled up over her black wigged head. Her bright red lipstick stood out in stark contrast to her white powdered makeup. On her left, holding her hand and acting as her handmaiden, was her mother, also dressed traditionally. Her black kimono and peach patterned obi signalled authority. On her right was the groom. He wore a black haori over a black and silver striped hakama. A white robed assistant shielded the bride and groom with a giant red paper parasol. Behind the bride came her family and friends and, behind the groom, his family and friends in single file. Kioshi had passed the pathway to the shrine many times, but had never ventured up into the courtyard. He stood now transfixed by the solemn procession that passed before him. All over the courtyard, people were coming and going, laughing, taking photos and simply enjoying life.

Tetsuya watched Kioshi carefully. He saw both enjoyment and puzzlement fighting for a space in his brain.

"Kioshi... I wanted to come out with you today so that I might explain my work to you. It is good that we are here at the shrine, because this provides me with a good way to illustrate why I am so passionate. All of these people are different from you and I. They are part of a family. They know where they come from.

They know the stories of their ancestors. That young man there," Tetsuya said, indicating a large heavyset boy, dressed as a groom, standing awkwardly while his photo was taken.

"Let us assume that he is a fisherman. This is just as an example mind you. If that is the case, he may have brothers, and some of them might also be fishermen. His father and his grandfather before him may have been fishermen. The point is the boy knows his family history. He has a strong sense of belonging somewhere. He is anchored to his past, and it generally gives him great comfort."

Tetsuya took Kioshi by the shoulders and turned him so that he could look him in the eyes.

"You and I Kioshi, we have no anchor. We do not know where we come from or, who our families are."

He noted the look of surprise on Kioshi's face.

"Yes… it is true. I too am an orphan. I was raised in someone else's family. When I started my work all those years ago I did not know why I was so interested in this field. I only knew that this was the area where I would work. However over the years an idea has grown in me, and that idea is that my work was predetermined. I now believe that through my work I may come to know who I am, where I came from. I'll admit I have a big ego, and I certainly seek the glory of great discovery; but I think my first goal is finding my own past. If I succeed, and I think we are getting closer, then we may be able to find your past as well."

Kioshi said nothing. He looked behind the Professor's eyes, but all he could see was conflict. He strongly sensed that the Professor believed most of what he had said, but it was too cloudy for Kioshi to be sure.

"You see Kioshi," continued the Professor. "Most people believe that time is like a rope. They consider that each of us is like a man climbing down a very long rope. Above you is the past, below you, the future. There are knots in the rope above you, a knot that you are holding now and many more knots disappearing off into the distance below. A man can only move down. He can never go back up the rope. This is what people believe, but I do not. I do not believe that time travels in a straight line. I believe that the past, at the very least, collapses in on itself. I believe that we can manipulate it and move through it as we please, once we have figured out the mysteries. And you and I Kioshi," he said laying a hand on the boy's shoulder, "you and I have proven this. Now we must refine the process. I believe it must be possible to breach time at any point and to overcome these three year cycles we seem stuck with. We should eventually be able to cross to any place and any point in the past, from any point in the present. The answer lies within the mathematics."

Kioshi smiled inwardly. He already knew that at least some of this was possible, but he still felt that was information best kept to himself.

"But what about the future Professor?"

"Ah… the future, well Kioshi, I fear that we cannot go there other than by growing old. However, what we can learn from the past may certainly influence the future. Have you heard of Hiroshima and Nagasaki, and the bombs that were dropped there?"

"I don't really know anything, only that a bomb was dropped in Hiroshima and the war ended."

"Yes, an atomic bomb was dropped over Hiroshima, and its first blast killed over one hundred and seventy thousand people… in an instant. But the final toll was much higher. In fact, the radiation from that blast is still claiming victims today.

But imagine if you... Kioshi, crossed back and were somehow present at that meeting where it was decided to drop that bomb. You could do nothing to influence the decision, but you would know more about the reasoning that led to the decision. In that way, at some point in the future, you might bring argument or influence to bear on such a decision. Do you understand what I mean?"

"Yes Professor I think I do."

"Then why do you have such a puzzled look on your face?" said Tetsuya.

"I was just wondering about those many thousands of people who died in that bomb blast. If the war had not ended then, how many more thousands of people might have died?"

"That is a question that has occupied historians ever since. I think you have a questioning mind Kioshi... the mind of a philosopher. I think together we will solve the question of time."

The Professor and Kioshi made their way back under the Northern Torii Gate, and walked back towards Shinjuku Station. They sat together in a small bakery on the south eastern side of the station, and ate a simple lunch of curry buns and green tea. They sat on stools facing out the window, and together they watched the busy comings and goings of the station, each locked silently in his own thoughts. Kioshi's mind was firmly planted in the present. *This is how it was meant to be* he thought to himself, *this man and I.* Eventually Tetsuya broke the silence and they made their way down to the platform. Avoiding the inquisitive stare of the cameras, they entered the labyrinth through the old green door.

49. THE MICROFICHE TELLS ALL

The present...

"Computers," mumbles Oka, "are how you would say in the West, bloody marvellous. In the space of about two hours, I was able to track down the Hobart City newspaper, the Mercury, that you told me about. The records for 1962 were a little harder because that was right at the time the paper had started using microfiche to store daily editions. They were not categorised at that stage, just photographed and stored as one complete daily edition. Now, as they digitise their archives, they are breaking the editions down into sub categories. But they are working backwards. So I had no choice but to pore through each edition at around the time you estimated this happened. You were out by a couple of months, but when I finally found it, it was pretty big news."

He pulled out a piece of wrinkled paper and smoothed it out on the coffee table.

"The headline says... *City crash claims three lives.* And the text... *Three people died yesterday morning in a two car crash at the corner of Murray and Patrick Streets in the city. Police said it was difficult to determine the cause of the accident, but it was possible one of the drivers may have suffered a heart attack before colliding with the other vehicle. There were no skid marks and residents reported hearing no screeching of tyres before the crash, which left one of the cars lodged upside down in the doorway of a house on the corner of the intersection. The victims were Stanley Robinson (43) and his wife Elaine (38) in one vehicle, and a Vincent Morelli (20) in the other. All three died instantly. A second occupant of Mr. Morelli's vehicle was taken to hospital in a serious condition, but remains stable.'* So there's your Vince, but listen to this, listen to this!" he says excitedly. *"Police are appealing for a witness to the accident to come forward. A teenage boy who police believe can help with their enquiries, left the scene before he could be interviewed. He should contact police at the Traffic Branch...* The rest of the article is the usual stuff about their families and occupations and so on. But there you have it musician. Seems the police want to talk to you about leaving the scene of an accident," he chuckles.

"Unbelievable," says Nick. "You guys do realise that all of this is proven and none of it is possible!"

"That's right," says Oka. "We now seem to have proof you were at the scene of an accident that happened twenty years before you were born and, if you are right about the boy lying on the road, then he was at the scene of that accident some thirty years before *he* was born." Oka paused and looked at each of us in turn.

"Now I know that all of this evidence is what we would call circumstantial, but I'm sold. There's just too many coincidences... too many alarms going off here..."

"Could someone," interrupted Nick, "please tell me what the hell is happening here."

"Well, that's the thing," says Oka. "None of us know what the *hell* is going on, but I suspect there is someone who can tell us."

He pulled out the video surveillance photo he had shown us the day before, and threw it on the table.

"Kioshi! I think it's time we had a talk to this boy."

50. LIFE IN THE LABYRINTH

The past...

Life in the labyrinth returned to normal. That is if you could call that life normal.

The weeks blended into each other and became months, and the months became years. Throughout this time Kioshi and the Professor worked more closely together on both the experiments and Kioshi's education. Of course, there was a heavy slant towards geography and languages, and at the end of three more years, Kioshi was reasonably proficient in spoken English and French. He had a very basic knowledge of Italian, German and Spanish. He was no fool, and he lapped up the knowledge. He was able to write in one or two of these languages, but only at a very elementary level. The Professor's teaching curriculum was designed solely to enable Kioshi to identify where he was, and when he was. The Professor needed all the facts he could get. Of course he wasn't the slightest bit interested in these other countries. He was only interested in travelling back in Japan, but he had to establish evidence for random versus logic, if he was going to be able to control the geography along with the time.

Throughout these years, Kioshi and Grok remained civil, but it was clear by Grok's slightly more icy demeanour, that the Professor had warned him not to upset the boy.

Apart from being busy learning and assisting the Professor, Kioshi had advanced his own agenda. In the past three years he had spent quite a bit of time at the library supplementing the Professor's lessons. In actual fact, he was filling in the holes that the Professor was leaving out on purpose. His skills as a thief and pickpocket were developed to the stage where he could achieve a good take in just a few short hours. This left him with adequate time above ground to visit his friend Ojiisan, and to go to the library. In a small street off Meiji Dori in Shibuya he had found a perfect hiding place for the funds that he was now skimming from the proceeds of his pickpocketing endeavours. He could duck into an alleyway unobserved, and conceal his money in the plastic bag that he hid behind the storm water collection head. When the opportunity presented itself, he would transfer the money from there to the hiding place under the cabin in Yoyogi Park. He had of course passed by the cabin many times as he went to visit Ojiisan, and he always carefully observed that the area behind the cabin was undisturbed.

On four occasions, Kioshi had followed Grok onto the Yamanote Line and then, at a distance (there was no need to get up close, he knew where Grok was going), to follow him off the train at Shin-Okuba and then to his apartment. Three of these occasions were during the daytime. He had observed Grok taking the blue canvas bag into his office. He waited in the kitchen until Grok emerged from his office, then left briskly but with great caution, via the green door exit. He had then made his way to a vantage point where he could watch the stairs to the pedestrian subway. In his mind's eye, he timed Grok making his way into the storeroom, up onto the shelving, and then along the straight tunnel to emerge in the air duct in the floor of the pedestrian subway. On two occasions, Grok had appeared almost exactly as Kioshi had estimated. On the third occasion, Grok took a while longer, most probably due to the large number of people using the subway. On these occasions, Kioshi took no risk leaving the labyrinth. It was daytime, and now he was free to come and go in daylight hours. Of course all these being in the daytime, it was impossible for Kioshi to gain entry to Grok's apartment without risking detection.

The fourth occasion was different, and Kioshi did risk being caught out of the labyrinth at night. It was after dinner one evening, as he was coming out of the dining room, that he had seen Grok go into his office with the blue canvas bag. He had estimated that Grok would leave within the next fifteen or twenty minutes. He had gambled that nobody would check his room that night. It had been a long time since they had done this, and so he rushed back there to pick up his flashlight, a pencil and notepad, and to tape his little plastic lock stopper in place. Then, looking as casual as possible, he strolled off down the corridor past Grok's office and around the corner. Once out of sight of the cameras he ran to the storeroom. He ignored the lights, preferring to use his flashlight and, going to the far side of the middle shelves, pulled himself up to the top. He slid the heavy fake vent aside with his shoulder and scrambled through. Before he moved away he hung his head down, and inspected the area below with his flashlight.

He could see nothing that would indicate anyone had been there. He slid the vent back into place, and quickly made his way along the narrow concrete tunnel. In no time at all he was at the end. He put his torch in his mouth, took hold of the thin steel handle on the metal sheet near the end of the tunnel, and pushed. The panel popped out easily and silently and Kioshi started to climb through. With half of his body in the tunnel and the other in the metal duct beyond, Kioshi froze. Off in the distance there was a muffled thud, and then the sound of metal scraping on concrete. Grok! He was right behind him.

Kioshi knew he had less than two minutes to get into the duct, replace the metal sheet from the other side, and get out into the pedestrian subway without being seen by anyone. More importantly, he must not be heard by Grok, who would now be moving along the tunnel. He dragged his other leg in and knelt on the floor of the duct, quickly replacing the metal sheet. As quietly as was possible, he crawled the small distance to the metal grate. It hinged upwards as he pushed. With his eyes just above the rim of the tiled subway floor, he saw a group of salarymen coming toward him. He had to wait until he was hidden from them by the tiled pillar, then he pushed upwards and out. He carefully closed the hinged grate and as he did so, saw a flicker of light appear on the duct wall below. Grok was climbing into the duct. He had made it! Now that he was out, he had little regard for who saw him, so he ran up the subway in the opposite direction to that which Grok should head. From the safety of another pillar, he watched Grok emerge and lean casually against the wall. He ducked his head back in and held his breath for a full minute before daring to peek around the pillar again. He half expected to see Grok heading toward him, but mercifully, the man in the immaculate dark blue suit was striding away in the opposite direction, without even so much as a sniff of that great big wolf nose of his.

Kioshi held well back from Grok as he emerged from the south entrance of Shinjuku Station and in a very round about way, made for Yoyogi Station. Emerging onto the platform, Grok wandered down about fifty yards while Kioshi lingered back in the gloom of the platform entrance. The train arrived about three minutes later, and Grok boarded without looking around. Kioshi dashed across the platform and boarded the carriage two back from the one Grok had boarded.

As they neared Shin-Okubo, Kioshi had to make his way forward in the train to ensure he did not exit the carriage in front of Grok. He actually emerged through the same doors as Grok, but hung well back. He stayed on the platform for five minutes before heading down through the station and emerging out onto Okubo Dori. Making his way along Okubo Dori and around the corner into Grok's street now seemed almost second nature to him, and he was soon hidden well back in the darkness of the car park opposite the small, modern apartment block. Grok's lights were on, and there was nothing for Kioshi to do but wait and see if Grok was staying put for the night.

Kioshi waited for about an hour and a half (Kioshi was good at waiting), and was just considering giving up and heading back to the station, when a small red Mitsubishi pulled up onto the footpath outside the apartment block. The occupant heaved himself out of the car. He was a short squat man dressed in golf attire. A yellow sweater matched with a pair of red tartan pants did nothing to enhance this man's appeal. He reached inside his sweater to retrieve a pack of cigarettes from his shirt pocket. He patted down his trouser pockets and pulled out a lighter. The flame lit up his mean fleshy face. The little man took a great drag on his cigarette, then reached in through the open window of the car and blew the horn three times. Kioshi sank back further into the shadows. He saw the balcony doors slide open, and then Grok appeared on the balcony and looked down at the man.

A few minutes later, Grok's apartment lights went out, and he emerged from the front door of the building. He stood in front of the little man and looked him up and down. He shook his head at the man's attire, then strode towards the car.

"Get in," he said, "I'm driving."

Grok turned in the narrow space, and the headlights of the red car transversed a wide ark across the car park. Kioshi sunk back even deeper into the shadows. As the car turned out onto Okubo Dori, Kioshi came out of hiding and checked the road and surrounding buildings. Then in what was almost one swift movement, was up the wall and over onto Grok's balcony. The balcony door opened with a little tug and he was in. This time he knew exactly what he was after.

Wasting no time, he went straight into the laundry room and retrieved the small folding steps, then on to the bedroom, where he set up the steps below the centre of the shelving. With his flashlight in his mouth, he pulled the false back out of the centre cube, then scooped up all of the passports and documents in the three piles. He sat on the floor, pulled the notepad out of his shirtfront, and began the painstaking task of copying down all the names, addresses and numbers in the passports, along with anything he thought might be important in the accompanying paperwork. The whole time he worked, he imagined the small red car returning to the apartment block, and the florid face of Grok the wolf arriving at the doorway. But he pushed these thoughts aside and pressed on with his work. Each pile had contained what he realised were real estate deeds and he skimmed these quickly, noting that the properties were in the same name as the passports. In each case, an alter ego for Grok. He closed his notepad and stuffed it back down his shirtfront.

When he was finished he climbed back up the folding steps and put the paperwork back exactly as he had found it. Before he climbed down, he reached across and pulled the false back out of the right hand cube. There were even more notes than before. He took a small slice from each of the front piles, then carefully replaced the false back. He climbed down, folded the steps and backed out the door, sweeping the torch back and forth to make sure all was as he had found it. A flash of blue. There under the bedside table was the blue canvas bag. Kioshi knelt and pulled it out. It was heavy. He undid the zip to reveal a mess of banknotes, watches and jewelry. He dug down deep into the pile and pulled out a huge handful of banknotes. As the pile settled down into the hole made by Kioshi's withdrawal, a gold Rolex slid into the depression. Kioshi knew that this watch was worth almost two million yen. It seemed Mr. Grok was becoming a very wealthy man. He stashed the blue bag back where he found it, and made his exit over the balcony almost six million yen richer.

Kioshi made his way quickly back to Shin-Okubo Station and, about twelve minutes later, he was on a train back to Harajuku. Once off the train, he hurried down Meiji Dori and into the gloomy side street. The alley beyond was so dark that he needed to pull out his flashlight. He made his way into the alley and reached up behind the storm water head to feel around for his plastic bag. He pulled it down, switched off his flashlight. He turned around to face out of the alley toward the little side street, letting his eyes grow accustomed to the gloom. He jammed the plastic package down his front, and peered both ways into the side street. There were plenty of people about, so he just stepped out and walked off toward the Harajuku entrance to Yoyogi Park.

Once in the park he made straight for the little cabin beside the vending machines. He waited in the shadow beside the cabin for a long time, to be sure there was nobody close. From the seats over by the lakes, came the sounds of a young couple laughing and giggling. Finally he slipped back into the dark and crouched behind the cabin. He knew exactly where to dig, and he soon felt the parcel in the bottom of the hole. He pulled it out. He took the other package from his shirtfront, pulled the pile of notes he had taken from Grok's stash out of his pocket, and proceeded to re-wrap the whole stash as one secure, waterproof parcel. This he jammed back into the hole. Then he repeated the previous procedure of backing out, covering his tracks as he went. Finally clear of the cabin, he took the long way round to the lake and washed his hands as best he could. Walking back past the cabin, he stopped at the vending machines and bought two cans of hot coffee, then made his way down the path toward the tent village. Standing in the darkness just outside the edge of the camp, he could just make out Ojiisan, his camp now looking considerably better, due to the gear that Kioshi had given him when he left. He approached to within about thirty feet and called out to his friend.

"Come in boy, don't stand out there."

Kioshi moved into the soft glow of Ojiisan's candle. He passed him one of the hot coffees and dropped down lotus fashion on the cardboard floor at the entrance to Ojiisan's tent. Ojiisan held the can at arms length and adjusted his wire frame glasses in and out to find focus.

"This is black boy. If I drink this I'll never get to sleep."

Kioshi could see the top of a bottle of cheap sherry sticking out of the sack at Ojiisan's feet.

"I don't think you will have any trouble sleeping old man," he said laughing. "I recall you could sleep through an earthquake."

"You know you are very cheeky boy. You need to learn to respect your elders."

Kioshi bowed his head.

"But it is good to see you my young friend," said Ojiisan, and they raised their coffee cans in salute to each other.

Kioshi spent an hour with Ojiisan at the camp, then he said his goodbyes to his friend and headed back through the park to Shinjuku Station, where he was once more swallowed up by the rusty green door.

51. THE PROFESSOR MAKES SOME BUDGET CUTS

The past...

Grok and Tetsuya Hiroko faced each other across Tetsuya's desk. Grok looked a little shaken. Not much rattled him, but it seemed the Professor had just hit a nerve.

"But Professor," spluttered Grok, "why now? I mean is this really necessary? Think of the money Professor."

"We don't need the money Mr. Grok," said the Professor quietly.

Grok knew that he was serious. Whenever the Professor got serious or angry, he called him *Mr.* Grok. It was just like when he was a kid. Normally his mother, who was a kindhearted drunk, called him Bronnie. He knew he was in trouble when she called him Bronislaw. And *Bronislaw* was normally followed by a solid smack around his ears.

Grok could feel the growth of his retirement fund coming to a rapid halt.

"We have funds for at least three more years, and if we get rid of the other boys, we could call that four years. Don't worry about your wages and your bonus Mr. Grok. Now that Kioshi is working *with* us we are making rapid headway. These last two months have been very revealing. He is helping me, but I have the distinct impression that he can let's say, manipulate time, whenever he likes, within reason of course. And if I am right about that, then I can start to zero in on geographical locations, and to extend the length of time that he spends in this other time."

"But how? I don't understand."

"Well it is basically very simple. Let's talk about this other body. We know that the boy's body remains here. Yet he says he has a body on the other side of time. He says he can tell he is on the other side of time because he has no shadow. Now… this thing that Kioshi calls his soul. This *soul,* or whatever it is, is activated by a traumatic trigger. Kioshi himself has now told me that he can now just visualise this trigger and start the process. This soul then passes through time and materialises into an identical body on the other time plane. Somehow the energy or soul coalesces into his identical human form. He says he can definitely be seen by people in the other time plane and, has even seen his own reflection. So he exists in some form in that time. The fact that he can trigger this and tell us all about it, means we don't need half of the equipment we have here. But, we do have to determine what kind of support we need, to provide for him to stay in the other time plane for much longer periods. To complete my work, I need him to be able to function there for up to maybe an hour. At present just half a minute or so exhausts him, but solving this is a logistical problem. We have the ability to manipulate time and enter a past plane. My theories have always been correct."

Grok is grasping at straws and he knows it, but he pushes on anyway.

"Okay Professor. You have never told me what it is you are searching for, only that this manipulation of time is just a means to an end. Surely, once you have achieved this and proved you can manipulate time…"

"Manipulate *past* time," interrupted the Professor.

"Okay… *past* time," says Grok. "Surely then there is untold wealth to be had. You could conceivably become the richest man in history."

"And you with me of course," says Tetsuya. "Don't worry Grok, I know you have been a loyal supporter of my work all these years. More than that, it is true that without you, or maybe someone like you, I would never have succeeded. I have asked you to do all of those things that I have neither the skill nor the heart for, and I know that on every one of those many occasions you have had to… how shall we say, cull… no, retrench. Yes, retrench people; you have done so professionally and unquestioningly."

He paused.

"And that is why I am surprised that you baulk at just four more *retrenchments*."

"But Professor they are just children. And they have been an invaluable source of funding."

"They're teenagers Mr, Grok."

There it was again *Mr.* Grok.

"And what's more they are thieving teenagers… petty criminals. As they grow older they get harder to manage and more bold. If any of them were to get caught it could destroy my life's work. Also, the odds are narrowing that someone could get caught coming and going from the labyrinth. I think we may have been running on luck for just a little while, and now that we are so close we need to consider who or what is necessary, and who or what isn't."

"They would never talk Professor," said Grok, who really didn't have the stomach for this.

Adults were no problem. Even the nurse had been no problem, but these were just boys. He lived with them, he knew them well. Hell, they were just like him at that age.

"Why Mr. Grok… I do believe you are getting a little sentimental. Or are you just queazy?" he added with a sting in his voice.

"Just get it done Mr. Grok… and quickly. Take them far away from here and ki… no, retrench them. Nobody will miss them."

And with that he stood up, walked around the desk and placed a hand on Grok's shoulder.

"Just think of all that money Mr. Grok," he said and opened the door, standing aside for Grok to leave.

52. RUSH HOUR AT SHINJUKU

The past...

It's not like it was my fault or anything, but once my cuts and bruises had healed it seemed like I was the butt of every train joke that ever was.

My fascination with Japan had begun when I was very young. I was about eleven years of age, when I got a hold of a copy of James Clavell's Shogun. I was immediately hooked, and sought out as much reading matter as I could to feed my habit. I had survived the horrors of boarding school by escaping to foreign lands and adventures with book after book. I had built up a pretty impressive list of 'places to travel', and Japan was creeping up to the top of that list. I had learnt to ski at an early age, and I had played ice hockey, so in February 1998, when the winter Olympics were held in Nagano, Japan, I was glued to the television at every opportunity. The alpine skiing events were regularly postponed due to the weather, and the little travelogue fillers that showcased various regions of Japan were, to me at least, as interesting as the events. I started lobbying various friends... I had to go.

In 1998 I was in a hiatus. I had completed my senior schooling and had to wait a year before entering Art College. So that year I worked in a junior government position that paid well and offered four weeks holiday a year. It took a bit of smooth talking and a few white lies, but finally my department head approved two weeks leave, and at the beginning of August that year, three green and grinning teenagers boarded a 747 for their first Japan adventure.

I recall that our hotel was in Ueno. I remember our travel agent telling us this was the best area to stay. He told us this was where Japanese from other parts would stay when they came to Japan, so it would be an authentic experience. The hotel was pokey and short on facilities, but I guess it was cheap. It was just somewhere to go at night, or early morning, to sleep, and in those two weeks we covered as much of Tokyo and its surrounds as we could jam in.

On about our fourth day we had found ourselves in Shinjuku in the middle of the evening rush hour... talk about a crush! I had read somewhere that a couple of million people a day went through the Shinjuku railway station, and we had all seen footage of railway workers pushing people into the rail carriages like sardines. So, we three fools figured this might be an interesting experience... wrong! We had no idea where we were going, or where we might end up. There was no English signage, it was all in Japanese or Kanji symbols. We bought tickets that we thought might get us back to our hotel and joined the rushing rapids of peak hour commuters, carried along on a tide of shop girls and salarymen. I'm not even sure the platform that we ended up on was the train we had tickets for, but I swear it looked like a thousand people ten or fifteen deep. We were being pushed from behind to go somewhere... anywhere, and the only clear way forward was along the very edge of the platform. There was a yellow strip of tiles, and then a narrow grey tiled area to the edge of the platform; and that's where we were going whether we liked it or not. I could see other commuters making their way along the platform edge, and I could see the crowd surging back and forth over the yellow line. We were about halfway along and trying to turn in so we could make our way to the back wall. The crowd closed the gaps and we were left with no option than to keep moving along the edge of the platform. I felt a shove from behind and turned to see a guy dressed in a black suit and tie, carrying a briefcase and wearing a white surgical mask. Somehow he had got past my friends and was now wanting to push past me.

I felt him push into me again, and as I turned back toward him, the crowd surged forward a foot or so. I was caught off balance and my foot slipped off the edge of the platform. I was scrambling for grip and reaching out for whatever I could grab. I got a hand on to somebody's coat sleeve, but gravity took hold, and I went over the edge sideways, landing hard on the gravel beside the tracks. I had shut my eyes on impact, and when I opened them I could see I had some kind of black mark, like a scorch, on my hand. I remember being unsure about whether the rails were electric, and I was lying half on some kind of flat black conduit or cable box that ran beside the inside rail. I could hear people shouting and yelling and I realised they were screaming at me to look along the line. Panic is panic in any language. A train! There was a little three step ladder thing not far away, but too far to reach in time, so I jumped to my feet, took hold of the edge and hoisted myself up. It felt like about twenty hands grabbed me at once, and dragged me over the edge of the platform. It was all very surreal after that. I was still lying flat out on the ground, while people stepped over and around me to get on their train. As the crowd thinned out, a railway assistant ran towards where I lay with my friends hovering over me. They half carried, half dragged me over to the nearest wall and propped me up against a door.

It had been a pretty close call. My friends told me my feet cleared the train by mere inches. Apart from the burn on my hand and a graze on my stomach and right thigh, I discovered a blister on my finger. I also had a severe case of the shakes. I sat in that doorway for maybe twenty minutes while I calmed down, and then the railway assistant took me to an office where a more senior guy put some yellow stuff and a bandage on my wounds. Then I got a severe dressing down from both of these guys, and even though I didn't speak a word of Japanese, I knew exactly what they were saying!

53. HIKING IN THE MOUNTAINS OF SAITAMA

The past...

It's just another job, it's just another job!

Grok sat at his desk with his eyes glued to the camera feed for the dining room. He had switched it over to manual, and was watching the four boys sitting around the table eating breakfast, talking and laughing. Yesterday he had announced that as a special treat he was taking them on a hiking trip. He had made the trip to Bukousan many years earlier... with a nurse!

. . .

The little group boarded the train at Shinjuku and made the short trip to change trains at Toshima. There was the general air of a holiday trip on the one and a half hour train journey to Ohanabatake. The boys either didn't notice or didn't care that Grok was so quiet and introspective. He never said too much anyway. Grok sat staring fixedly out the window, his reflection, with it's grey floppy bush hat and wrap around sunglasses, stared back at him. Occasionally he reached the inside pocket of his grey parka to feel the solid cool metal of the Browning 9 mm pistol. In the past few days he had gone over this again and again, and had come to realise there was no turning back. He was too deep into this to risk any complications now. But that didn't make it any easier. These boys would take the same one-way journey as the nurse, who was led up here with the promise of a picnic all those years before.

Grok clutched the pistol in his palm, and felt the deadly resolve flow like energy from the cold grey metal. By the time the group piled off the train and made the short walk to Seibuchichibu Station for the final train leg to Urayamaguchi, Grok had come to terms with the task ahead. The Browning would speak today. It would be a shame to have to throw away the pistol, but he had another.

Leaving the station at Urayamaguchi they first headed into a Seven Eleven to buy some food and drinks. They trekked up the hill past a small house with a graveyard and, after about fifty minutes, they reached the trailhead. Climbing steadily, in just under two hours they had came to an open space with a temple. To the left of the temple was a path to the lookout that marks the top of Bukousan. Grok sat on a small wall, and sent the boys off down the path to enjoy the views of Chichibu and the valley below. It was midweek, and they had seen nobody else on the trail. *Be quick... make it quick,* he said to himself. He made his way back to a point where he could see well down the path and finally, when he was content there was nobody else in the vicinity, he ran back up the path, pulling the Browning from his pocket and cocking it in one easy motion.

As he made his way down the path to the left of the temple, he clicked off the safety and, coming up rapidly behind the laughing boys, he dispatched the first three left to right in quick succession, with clean head shots. The fourth boy, Masato had spun round at the sound of the first shot and, after just a split second of frozen terror, had turned to run. Grok's fourth shot had caught him on the side of the neck, but as he ran he presented a nice square target and Grok's fifth shot tore through the back of his head, flinging him face down dead on the walkway. Grok quickly checked that all four boys were dead.

Grok was a professional, and the whole bloody business had taken less than ten seconds. The noise of the shots was part buried in the noise drifting up from the cement quarry below, but could still be heard echoing faintly around the mountain. Grok bent to the task and grabbed Masato's legs, dragging him back along the trail, he heaved his body over the safety fence. The boy's body landed below on a shale landslip and slid down into the trees and out of view. It took Grok about six minutes to haul the other bodies up and heave them over the fence to the same fate. He could have done it quicker, but he was careful to avoid getting blood and brain tissue on his clothes. Breathing heavily, but with the task complete, he took off his parka and rested it across the fence. He peered below to see if there was any sign of the bodies, but they had been swallowed up by the forest at the end of the loose, steep incline.

Breathing steady again, Grok retraced his steps around the path and lookout area, kicking up dust and removing any blood or signs of the ten seconds of incredible violence that had just taken place. Finally content, he pulled on his parka, walked back to the front of the temple, and made his way briskly down the left fork of the path. After about forty minutes he came to a small wooden bridge and a waterfall. Here he paused just long enough to remove the Browning from his pocket. He dropped the magazine out, wiped it as best he could with his handkerchief and heaved it out into the river. Then he wiped the pistol carefully, and threw that out towards the base of waterfall. As he made his way downward, heading for Yokoze Station, he wondered if the mountain would ever give up its secrets. The nurse had never been found and there would be little trace of her after all these years, but four boys in a row... who knows. Anyway, with his floppy bush hat, parka and sunglasses he would be impossible to identify, and apart from today, he had no previous link to the Browning which anyway, now rested like a stone at the base of a waterfall.

At the bottom of the hill Grok came to a paved road with a registration box for hikers. Here he changed his grey floppy bush hat for the red one that he pulled from the side pocket of his parka. Then he shucked out of his parka, turned it inside out, and put it back on. Now with his red hat and burgundy parka, he strode off down the road to find Yokoze Station. Two and a half hours later, after a few train changes, he made his weary way to the lower platform and edged his way near the blind spot and the green door. When the next train departed, he unlocked the door and stepped through.

This has got to stop... he said to himself as he made his way below. *I really am getting too old for all this crap!*

54. JUST A SMALL DETAIL

The present...

Itsuru Oka just sits there shaking his head.

I have just been sitting here thinking about my first trip to Japan. I had remembered the trip and all the excitement of that first visit. Of course I would never forget the accident in Shinjuku Station, but we'd had such a blast, that I had forgotten some of the little details. Details that didn't seem important then, but certainly seem important now.

"So you thought this wasn't important?" says Oka with just the right level of scorn.

"No I didn't," I say defensively. "To be honest I never really thought about it. I mean I've been to Tokyo plenty of times and I can't see why you would expect me to fill you in on the details of each and every trip."

"So why are you telling me about this first trip?" says Oka.

"Well, because of the burn on my hand."

"Oh," says Oka. "Oh... that small detail, hardly worth mentioning really. But now that you have, is there anything else you think might interest us?"

I've come to like Oka, but that doesn't mean he can't be an annoying little prat at times... and this was one of those times. I raise my eyebrows and spread my hands in supplication.

"Are you finished? Good... I'll continue then shall I? Like I was saying, I didn't think it was relevant until I started to recall little details of what happened after the accident. What happened was the railway guy put some yellow stuff, probably mercurochrome, on the grazes and the scorch mark on my hand. Funny thing is I don't remember the scorch hurting at all, just the blister on my fingertip. He dabbed this stuff on with a cotton swab, then wrapped it in a light gauze bandage. He put two bandaids across my fingertip and told me that it would probably be a good idea to go see a real doctor in case there was any chance of infection."

"And you didn't, right?" says Oka.

"Of course I didn't. Hell I was seventeen and in Tokyo to party! I remember as the evening wore on, my right leg and stomach seemed to stiffen up, but I can't recall feeling any more pain from the blister."

I stand up and drop a capsule in the coffee machine. I make them wait while the glass fills.

"When we finally got back to the hotel that night, or sometime the next morning, I checked both the grazes, and they were bloody sore to touch. Then I took off the bandage and the bandaids. There was absolutely no sign of any scorch or burn mark, just a yellow stain. And there was no sign of the blister either."

I take a sip of my coffee.

55. IT'S JUST A THEORY MIND

The past...

On the day following Grok's cull, Tetsuya had provided Grok with a list of staff he required for the next set of experiments.

Sitting in the Professor's office, Grok warily reached out and took the sheet of paper. At least this time it was only one page. One of Grok's problems was that over the years he had found it harder and harder to find the type of people the Professor needed. *I mean let's face it* he thought, they were a dying breed... literally. So Grok was pleased to see the page contained a new cook come housekeeper, and just four other positions. These final four were mercifully from areas that Grok had not yet mined too deeply. The first three were all mathematics related. Doctorates, or at the very least brilliant Masters, but each with slightly different specialties. The fourth position was for a statistician. Grok had no idea what a statistician really did, and he looked at Tetsuya and shrugged.

"Statistician?" he said, almost flinching now at the thought that the Professor was going to deliver him one of those long lectures.

"I'm sorry Professor, I kind of know what a statistician is, but I have no idea how they would fit into your project. Maybe it would make the selection easier if you could give me some more information."

"Well," said the Professor, "thanks to Kioshi's cooperation and our historians, I now have three waypoints."

Tetsuya got up and took a globe from the sideboard. He sat back down and placed it in the centre of his desk.

"I have three actual locations in the world where Kioshi found himself during those experiments. Thanks to a child poisoning episode, we know that the first experiment put him in North Vancouver, Canada."

He tapped the point on the globe.

"The second put him in the middle of a car crash in Tasmania… here."

He span the globe and pointed to Hobart.

"The third experiment landed him right outside the post office in this little village in France… right here."

He turned the globe and tapped on a location in the south of France, then he pushed the globe aside.

"It is my intention to focus all of our resources on what I would call way-point mathematics. You will notice that I have three mathematicians on the list, and it will be their job to each, individually and separately, construct temporal-geographical models."

"Temporal-geographical models," echoed Grok. "Sorry Professor, you've lost me again."

"Okay… let's keep it simple and apply this directly to our specific problem. We have successfully mastered the practical aspect of crossing into a past plane of time. Each time the boy has travelled into the past he has arrived at a different geographical location. If the temporal-geographical location was not a problem, then the boy's, let's call it, *alter ego*, would have shown up in the same room as his true self, only at sometime in the past. But it didn't, so there is a correlation between when we sent him, and when and where he arrived."

Grok looked even more confused.

"Look," he says turning the globe on its axis and pointing at the equator.

"The circumference of the Earth at the equator is 25,000 miles. The Earth rotates once every twenty four hours. Therefore the speed of the earth's rotation at the equator is approximately 1,042 miles an hour. If we multiply by the cosine of our latitude we can see how fast the Earth is rotating right here at our location. That means that we should be able to accurately determine where the boy will turn up geographically on the temporal plane. Think of the boy as a rocket Grok. We should be able to determine that if we launch him from right here at a certain time, he will land at a given spot *exactly* 36 years ago."

Grok ponders this carefully then reaches forward and picks up the globe.

"Now I see what you are getting at Professor, but the speed of the earth thing worries me a bit."

"I don't understand," says Tetsuya, "it's a simple issue of mathematics."

"Yes, but pardon me Professor, I only have a basic high school knowledge of these things, but isn't the earth rotating around the sun at many thousands of miles an hour as well?"

He held up his left hand to the globe and moved the globe off to the right, keeping his left hand stationary where the globe had been.

"Wouldn't that mean that the boy could end up maybe hundreds of thousands of miles out in space?"

"Very good Grok, great question. Yes the earth does travel around the sun at 67,000 miles an hour, but it just isn't a problem apparently."

"But Professor, why isn't it a problem?"

"Well my friend, it may have something to do with the earth's gravity, or the way time bends in the earth's atmosphere. I know it may be unscientific, but I just don't care. I'm just going to assume it's for the same reason that the entire population doesn't get spun off into space, and leave it at that. Somebody else can work that one out sometime. I just know it's not a problem for our purposes. Because the boy always ends up somewhere on earth and that's that. So... let's move along.

Like I said, the three mathematicians will each create a model that should enable us to determine where the boy will land. In an ideal world, all three models would end up identical, but I doubt that will happen. Up until the time that the boy told us about the third experiment having worked, I had come to believe that success was dependent upon some kind of trauma at both the launch point, in other words the trigger, and at the arrival point. This was because we had trauma at the arrival point on the first two experiments. We had the poisoning tragedy in Vancouver and the car crash in Hobart. But, we now know that we had no trauma of any kind near the post office in France... we have researched this thoroughly. What this means is that clearly trauma at the arrival point is not necessary. My personal guess, and that's all it is really... a guess, is that because we are talking about pure energy here, any kind of trauma occurring in close proximity to our landing site could pull the boy off course and into that trauma."

Tetsuya stood up and carried the globe back to the sideboard.

"The thing is Grok, that Kioshi may not have actually *arrived* at a trauma, he may have *caused* it... on both the first two occasions. It could be that his arriving, just appearing out of thin air, would be enough to scare the daylights out of anybody. They said the driver had a heart attack, and that caused the accident in Hobart. In the Vancouver incident, the oldest girl was supposed to be taking care of her younger siblings, but something distracted her long enough for those children to get at the rat poison. Having a young boy appear magically in your bedroom... well that would probably do it."

"But what about the last one, in France?" asks Grok.

"From what Kioshi tells us, it seems the postmaster was asleep in his chair. Not much chance of disaster there, and so there was none. So what we need to do once we have our temporal-geographical models, is to determine whether these trauma events were occurring anyway, and pulled Kioshi off course, or whether that was always the correct landing point and he caused the trauma. The statisticians job will be to take what we can therefore call 'imperfect information' and provide theoretic analysis on each model. Certainly we could just apply the information from each model in turn, but this will be very time consuming. In addition to reducing the testing time, I think the statistician may well value add to the modeling process.

And so... to the initial task. You will notice at the bottom of the sheet I have provided a list of candidates to fill the mathematics roles, and just two candidates for the statistician's role. But Grok, I want to move very quickly on this list."

Grok returned to his office and removed a red, leather bound notebook from his small floor safe. Always a methodical man, Grok flipped straight over to the Ps. Under the heading PIs was a list of about thirty names and telephone numbers. This list was a work in progress, and Grok allocated a certain amount of time each month to updating and maintaining it. The compilation of this list had proven surprisingly easy. Each of the persons on the list was a private detective with a specific set of qualifiers. They were single, unremarkable, had no known family or strong friendships, were alienated, disenfranchised, greedy and unscrupulous. In other words, they would do almost anything for money, and then would not be missed when disposed of. The surprise for Grok was just how many PIs fitted this general profile. Eleven names had been crossed out with a red pen. For this job he would choose two separate PIs. One to deal with the mathematicians, and one for the statistician. Their role would be to sift through the candidates and find any hidden skeletons, or in fact, to find any candidates that resembled their own particular profile.

Grok copied six names and phone numbers at random from his list onto a single small sheet of paper which could easily be disposed of later, then he left his office and made his way up from the labyrinth to the station and a bank of public telephones.

. . .

It took Grok three weeks to identify and wrangle his candidates into a suitable shortlist for the Professor's final interviews. One by one the mathematics candidates were investigated until five threw up possible weaknesses suitable for exploitation. Grok communicated with the PI only by public telephone, directing him on the process of drilling down into the personalities, backgrounds and lifestyles of the candidates. Then following further meetings with Tetsuya, he selected a final three for interviewing by the Professor. Once Tetsuya had interviewed and accepted these three, and they had signed contracts and confidentiality agreements (all window dressing of course), Grok disposed of the PI that he had appointed to the task.

Identifying the right candidate for the role of statistician was, with just a short list of two, relatively easy. The PI allocated the task was named Sugimura and even on the telephone, Grok could sense the obsequious little toad might be a problem. One of the candidates was so squeaky clean you could eat your lunch off him. The other was best described as having a major gambling and drinking problem. Sugimura didn't need to scratch too far below the surface to uncover a combination of heavy drinking and just plain bad judgement. Basically this guy followed a regular cycle. He used his considerable skills to beat the odds gambling. When he lost, he lost big time; there were no half measures with this guy, and when he won he won big time. Then cashed up, he would hole up in a love hotel with a selection of women, and stay there until his money ran out.

Sugimura caught him in the middle of a losing streak, and having provided all the necessary information to Grok, Grok had little difficulty in recruiting him for an interview. Sugimura turned out to be a little more of a problem than Grok had anticipated. Having correctly surmised that Grok's activities were of a clandestine nature, once Sugimura had provided his detailed report to Grok, he took to following the statistician to learn more. On the third day, he witnessed the man meet up with a foreigner in an immaculate dark blue suit, and when they parted, he deftly switched subjects and followed that man onto the Yamanote Line at Shinagawa.

Grok had met the candidate in the grounds of the Tokyo University of Marine Science and Technology, and his sixth sense for these things had alerted him to an unwelcome presence. While the candidate talked, Grok raised his nose in the air and sniffed lightly. Then he settled back on the bench and scanned his surroundings while feigning interest in the candidate's conversation. As he swivelled his head, Grok caught something out of the corner of his eye. A short man in a dirty, baggy suit and scuffed shoes, had taken a seat on the bench further along the path. Instinctively Grok knew this man did not fit the picture. He was an almost exact match for the image that Grok had formed in his mind when talking on the phone with Sugimura. Having completed his arrangements with the candidate, Grok made his way back across the Takahama Canal towards the station. He paused on the bridge to watch a group of rowers, in a white wooden boat, make their way underneath him and as he turned to depart, there was the little, baggy man coming onto the other end of the bridge. Unbeknownst to the hunter, he had become the hunted, as Grok kept the little baggy man firmly in his sights.

Grok took the train as far as Ueno then, making certain he could be seen by Sugimura, he got off the train and proceeded along the road beside Uenoonshi Park, in the direction of the Tosho-gu Shrine. About halfway along, he passed through the old grey Torii gate and up the stairs into the park. He paused at the top of the path to ensure that Sugimura could see which way he was going, then strode off to the left. There was nobody in his immediate vicinity, so he quickly left the path and ducked behind the thick trunk of a mature Zelkova tree, removing his blue and red striped necktie as he went. In a matter of seconds, Sugimura hastened by, his eyes firmly fixed on the path ahead. Grok silently stepped back onto the path and in eight long strides, came up behind the little baggy man and wrapped his necktie around the fleshy neck. He dragged him quickly off the path with the necktie, and pulled him into a thick patch of shrubbery. The little man's eyes popped out as if they might fly from their sockets, part by surprise and part by the pressure as Grok applied one of his base skills. Grok leaned forward to whisper in the detective's ear.

"You were always going to die you greasy little man, but I just want you to know your greed hastened the event."

And with that he dropped the little man down between his knees and applied even more pressure. There was an obscene sucking noise not unlike that of a toilet plunger at work, and the little baggy man's tongue swelled out between his purple lips. Grok felt the last beat of his heart, and allowed the little baggy man to fall flat on the ground. He quickly but thoroughly went through the man's pockets, removing all trace of the detective's identity. He stared at the keys in his hand. He made sure the path was clear, then stepped out and headed quickly back to Ueno Station and, once there, boarded a train on the Hibaya Line for Kita-Senju Station. He had the detectives address, and once out of the station, he quickly located the man's office above a pharmacy a few blocks west. The street was busy, and it was easy for him to get through the door and up the stairs without attracting attention. The second key he tried opened the detectives door, and Grok let himself in. His nose wrinkled at the sour smell of old sweat and cheap cigarettes. Five or six minutes later, Grok was back on the street having removed all trace of his business with the little baggy private detective.

56. THE TAKU AND YAMASHITA SHOW

The past…

Tetsuya Hiroko looked down at the date on his desk calendar. It was August 2007, and he was back in the labyrinth to attend a meeting with one of the mathematicians and the statistician. Grok had called him the day before to tell him that the statistician was very excited about something. He wouldn't share this information with Grok, insisting that he wanted to present it directly to the Professor… it was that important. Tetsuya had been unable to sleep, and so had arrived at the labyrinth early.

As he sat at his desk, he wondered what all the excitement was about. It was less than a year since they had started work on the problem of understanding the modeling of the temporal-geographical equation. The statistician, called Yamashita, came from Kagawa Prefecture on the island of Shikoku. Tetsuya had worked with the man for the best part of a year and, apart from where he came from, he knew very little about him. He did know that he was broke and had massive gambling debts. He knew that he had a whole swathe of bad habits, and that he approached these with a passion. Fortunately for the Professor, he approached his work with the same kind of passion. It wasn't hard to keep him on the 'straight and narrow' while he was locked in the labyrinth, and his results had been impressive, even given his draining a bottle of cheap scotch every day. Tetsuya had to admit the guy knew his stuff. At first they couldn't equate his gambling losses with his undeniable skills as a statistician, but then you factored in heavy drinking with its attendant bad judgement, and you had the answer.

The mathematicians had all produced close models. Two were remarkably similar. If they hadn't been working in isolated conditions, Tetsuya would have been suspicious. But this was the result he had been looking for. A solid model with solid corroboration. Even the third model was very close, sullied only by a small but fundamental error.

Yamashita was only able to work with one mathematician at a time and he had finally chosen to work off the model created by the youngest mathematician, a young Tokyo local with a Ph.D. It had been this man's thesis that had got him across Tetsuya Hiroko's radar in the first place. Grok had told Tetsuya that it was this man, Taku Watanabe, who Yamashita was bringing to the meeting.

A knock at the door roused Tetsuya from his musings.

"Come in."

The door opened and Grok ushered in Taku and Yamashita. Yamashita was about forty six years old and was dressed tidily in black cotton pants and a white cotton shirt open at the neck. The younger man was twenty six and wore cheap sneakers, ragged denim jeans and a long sleeve green t-shirt with a short sleeve red t-shirt over the top. The red t-shirt had a large Totoro character, sitting in a field with an umbrella, on the front. Tetsuya came out from behind his desk and ushered the little group over to the round meeting table. Grok was carrying a small television with a built in DVD player and Yamashita had a great pile of folders and a black plastic DVD case. The young mathematician was empty handed. Grok placed the television on the sideboard beside Tetsuya's globe and plugged it in.

"What is that for?" asked Tetsuya.

"I have absolutely no idea," said Grok. "You'll have to ask our learned friend here. I'm just doing what he asked."

"Let's not worry about that now," said Yamashita rubbing his hands together almost in glee. "It will all become apparent later."

"Well then, shall we get started?" said Tetsuya dropping down in his chair and waving the others into their seats.

Once they were settled, Tetsuya asked Yamashita to make his report.

"You are aware Professor that we have spent the past nine or ten weeks working on Taku's model. The first thing that I should do is repeat or reinforce what I said at the very beginning, when you first briefed me. This is not strictly speaking an exercise in statistics. It is more like the theory of probabilities. We started with a *theoretically* firm foundation of numbers, which are the boy's known temporal and geographical coordinates from each of the first three experiments. We then constructed a comprehensive model, laying out a massively complex matrix of time versus waypoints of latitude and longitude, as a basis for establishing probabilities. However the further we go back in time, the more variants the matrix throws up. In addition to that, we have had to deal with the question of trauma and cause and effect. Cause and effect is the philosophical concept of causality, in which an action or event will produce a certain response to that action, in the form of another event. Simply put, that means we have to factor in whether the trauma was a result of the boy's presence, or the boy's presence was a result of the trauma.

Probability theory is used in order to represent the uncertainty of outcomes, and so we ran this both ways. The outcomes seem to suggest that his presence is both the cause *and* the effect. Confusing I know, but try this on. In all probability, his presence in the car in Hobart in 1962 caused the crash, or trauma. And then from 1998 when you sent him back, he was drawn to that same trauma that he had already caused."

He sat there grinning like a contented cat.

"I think we will call this Yamashita's Law," he said laughing; then noticing the frown on Tetsuya Hiroko's face continued.

"Okay, maybe not. But it means that in all probability, you can use a known trauma to complete the temporal-geographical time jump with accuracy. However, it is by no means necessary.

Applying this information to our best mathematical model, we can project future outcomes within the laws of probability. But with every minute we travel back in time, we increase the conditional probability of geographical error. So here we used Bayes' Law. Put simply, Bayes' Law is a formula for calculating the probability that our waypoints, called 'A', will be true, given a certain set of circumstances, called 'B'."

He stopped and took a long pause for all this to sink in. He had noted that poor old Grok's eyes had glazed over a few minutes back. It didn't matter… he dug into his paperwork and pulled out two or three sheets of paper.

"Of course," he continued. "This is all based on supposition, which is why we call it theory. However as I say, after many long sessions with the boy Kioshi, we have been able to provide a selection of waypoints upon which to not only base our theory, but to test it. We know with absolute certainty, where he has been geographically during each of your previous experiments. And that means…"

And here he paused again for effect.

"That we can determine with almost absolute certainty, and when I say *almost*, I mean with an accuracy of 98.6345 recurring, where he will be during your next experiment."

Tetsuya was silent. Could he possibly be this close.

"So you are saying that using this, this Bayes' Law, that with the corrected matrix we can place the boy exactly where we want within our 36 year cycle?"

"That is now a given Professor, but what I'm actually saying is much more than that. What I'm saying is that with more work, I believe we can place the boy exactly where we want without concern for either your 36 year cycle, or your three year lag!"

Tetsuya Hiroko was rendered speechless. He felt physically ill and dizzy as he heard these words. He realised his mouth was open, and he was staring at the back of his hands as if waiting for something to sprout there. He tried to bring both his thoughts and his breathing back under control. He also realised that the hammering he thought was coming from the next room was coming from his chest. He fought to slow his heart, convinced everybody around the table could hear it.

Yamashita took his silence as doubt. He stood up and went to the Professor's whiteboard. He drew a rough version of Tetsuya's 'pasta' diagram, showing time winding backwards and forwards.

"Professor... on the paper I have given you..."

Tetsuya mentally shook himself like a shaggy dog coming out of a river, and regained his concentration.

"....You will notice your original model displays 36 years on one layer then 36 years back the other way on the next layer and so on. This model cannot be supported by the mathematical information we now have. Or should I say the graphical representation cannot be supported. I think you are correct about the 36 year cycle."

He turned back to the diagram on the board.

"But a true 36 year cycle would look like this."

He drew a red line down either end of the pasta diagram and wrote *18 YEARS* between the red lines.

"This is a true representation of the cycle, where it takes 36 years to arrive back at the starting point... 18 years out, 18 years back. Going back through all the data you have collected over the years, particularly those cases you really investigated thoroughly, like the Ken Hayashi case, seems to support this. To complete the 36 year cycle a subject must pass through this layer."

Now he drew a red line through the top pasta layer and wrote 2009 on the top layer and 1991 on the second layer down and 1973 on the third layer down.

"So I believe that based on our research, you can cross *two* layers, and travel back exactly 36 years, every single year without any trauma required. In addition you can theoretically cross just *one* layer back in time if you have a natural, or seeded trauma with a known temporal-geographical location to aim for. For instance, last year you could aim for 1992, this year, 1991 and next year 1990. Now here's where it gets interesting. I haven't worked out any temporal-geographical waypoints for this yet, but based on our circular cause and effect theory, this year, 2009, you could send the boy back to his own birth moment. How's that for traumatic energy?"

Tetsuya Hiroko was silent and unmoving, but his head was spinning and his mind was racing.

"So," continued Yamashita, "after Grok advised us that the boy can trigger his own event, we looked for a way to prove our corrected matrix. The best way to do this was to send the boy to a specific location where we could gain firm evidence."

Tetsuya Hiroko's eyes snapped from the whiteboard to Yamashita with an almost audible twang.

"You what! I never gave approval for the boy to be sent back," screamed Tetsuya, his face reddening with rage.

"I'm sorry Professor," interrupted Grok, "I tried to locate you, but I was unable to find you. They said they had a very limited window of opportunity. I didn't know they were going to conduct an experiment, I thought they just wanted to do another question session with him," said Grok looking at Yamashita.

"Please calm down Professor," spoke Taku softly; the first time he had opened his mouth. "Mr. Grok was not a party to this. But you will see why it was necessary."

His voice was so soft and pleading that it pulled Tetsuya up short.

The room filled with a heavy silence.

"Now Professor," said Yamashita from the whiteboard. "Using our projections we have established a computer program that uses our location as the constant starting point. Searching back in 36 year increments, day by day, minute by minute, we found what we were looking for, and landed the boy at 34.145400 latitude and -118.39030 longitude… at exactly 12.30pm our time yesterday!"

"And you say you can prove this," snarled Tetsuya.

"Absolutely Professor. Mr Grok, if you would be so kind as to switch on the DVD and load this disc."

And with that he opened the plastic cover and handed Grok a shiny DVD disc. He went back to the whiteboard.

He wrote the latitude and longitude on the board along with a minute, hour, day, week and month in the year 1971. Then he walked over to the television and, using the remote control, set the DVD playing. He turned down the volume and turned back to the Professor.

"Those geographical co-ordinates," he said tapping the board, " are sound stage two at the CBS studio Centre in Los Angeles, California, and at that very time, CBS were filming an episode of a sitcom called The Mary Tyler Moore Show. The year is 1971. Now watch carefully please Professor."

On screen the show's star, Mary Tyler Moore, was arguing with a character called Ted Baxter. With the volume down you could not tell what they were saying, but Ted threw his head back and laughed at something, then dug his hands in his pockets and walked away. Mary Tyler Moore reached for a door handle to her left, and the camera feed changed to a camera on the other side of that door, inside her boss's office. As the door swung open Yamashita hit the pause button.

"There!"

And there, off in the background, but perfectly framed in the door was... Kioshi.

"You can check those co-ordinates Professor, and you can check exactly when that episode was filmed. I have... and I got a near perfect match."

Tetsuya jumped up and grabbed the remote control off Yamashita. He rewound and played, and rewound and played, and froze the scene again and again. Then he switched off the set and slowly put down the remote control. He turned to face Yamashita.

"You mean you planned to get Kioshi on that camera in that episode. I'm sorry, but I believe that's impossible."

"And you'd be right Professor. The variables make that completely impossible. We gave the boy a window of twenty three seconds on the ground, and simply told him to take in as many faces and as much data as possible. We knew we were putting him in the CBS studios somewhere and we were counting on the fact that afterward we could show him pictures of TV stars and see if he recognised anyone. You see, we needed to land him somewhere where there was a high probability that those faces he may see would be readily available for him to identify all these years later. Our list of possibilities included film and television studios, sports events or even political investitures. We went with film and television studios because it seemed a more probable spread. Beyond faces we asked him to look for proof of date and time. We lucked out there. That is until we researched when that episode was filmed.

We knew there were two sitcoms filming at the studios that night and we showed him photos of all the stars involved with both shows. After about half an hour he came up with Ted Knight, who played Ted Baxter in The Mary Tyler Moore Show. Then he identified Mary Tyler Moore herself. He said she walked through a door and he was looking straight into a camera… said he noticed it because there was a red light on it. Can you believe it? A live camera, and our boy caught in the lens like a startled rabbit in headlights. Of course, we figured if he was on camera they would probably have cut him out in the edit suite, but we found out which episode was made that night, got hold of the series set late yesterday and… bingo, there he was.

The odds that this would happen are astounding Professor, but with all the years you have put in on this amazing discovery, I guess you have earned a bit of good luck. I mean we had all the information we needed from the boy's observations but his appearance on this DVD proves something else. There was no trauma and the boy never left my sight during the experiment, but there he is… two places at the same time, and that time is separated by 36 years."

Yamashita stopped talking. The excitement and energy visibly draining out of him as he wilted under the Professor's gaze.

"Two things Mr. Yamashita. First of all I must congratulate you and thank you for this result, but then I must warn you that if you conduct any more time experiments with Kioshi without my permission or presence, not only will you lose this job, but you will lose your whole career."

Grok, who like the Professor, was stunned by what he had just seen, was not so stunned that he couldn't think to himself… *but your whole career will be very short anyway my friend.*

Taku jumped up and bowed deeply to the Professor. The threat of menace was palpable in the room. Yamashita took his lead and did likewise.

Taku spoke.

"We must apologise Professor. It was not our intention to do anything wrong. The magnitude of what you have created here and its potential application is simply unbelievable. I think Doctor Yamashita and I were just swept away in the excitement. Please excuse us Professor, and please understand that we are honoured to be chosen to work with you on this project. We are here only to serve you."

Tetsuya let the silence hang just long enough. He weighed up the value of a meltdown at this stage, and decided that their voluntary cooperation was the more valuable option.

"I accept your apology on the one clear condition that you never again use the boy in any experimentation of any sort without me being present. You have risked control procedures and you may well have endangered his life. Do I make myself perfectly clear?"

Both men bowed again deeply, and their reply of 'yes Professor' was as one clear voice in the silent room.

"Fine. Let us talk no more of this matter. I have some questions," said Tetsuya.

"Let us start with how you chose to time the boy at twenty three seconds."

"Well," replied Yamashita, regaining his animation. "We had the boy act out his previous 'visits' and determined that the longest he had spent in the past was around twenty three seconds, so that became our timing limit."

"Now gentlemen, the next question is pivotal to my research outcomes. It is something that has bothered me for many years. I have formed a theory about this problem, but it remains unsupported by any science or experimentation. It is simply this. If the boy is on the ground in the past for… let us say we use your twenty three seconds as an example, then in that time the planet would turn what? …Three hundred and ninety eight miles or so underneath his feet. So why is he staying put?"

"Taku has a theory about that Professor. Taku, please," said Yamashita, indicating that Taku should speak out.

"Well," said Taku ever so quietly, "I am really not qualified to advance any theories on this matter Professor. I simply feel that it is an issue related to the question of why the boy's travel is not affected by the earth's orbit around the sun. I believe once he is grounded in a location he falls… or his alter ego or whatever it is, falls under the standard laws of gravity the same as you or me. However, and please understand Professor that I am a mathematician. As such I am unable to support this hypothesis, so I would rather call it a hunch than any kind of theory."

He laid his right hand on his forehead and his left hand on his stomach, feigning some sort of dizzy spell.

"I believe that this is related to the dizziness and exhaustion that the boy experiences after each experiment. I think it is an extreme form of inertia or motion sickness, occasioned by either the moment of his arrival or departure. Or, it could be due to the effort of fighting gravity to maintain his position. Let us not lose track of the fact that this is not the boy's actual body, but some form of visible alter ego. I myself suffered badly from motion sickness."

He hung his head.

"Whenever I went in a car, bus, or an aircraft, I would vomit my heart out. It was very embarrassing in my school years. It used to take me days to get over it. Strangely I almost always got seasick on boats and ferries, but as soon as I got off the boat there was no residual sickness, unlike with cars and buses. What this boy Kioshi describes to me is exactly how I would describe my own feelings. As I say Professor, just a hunch."

He folded his hands in front of himself defensively as if preparing for Tetsuya's assault. When it failed to materialise he pushed on bravely.

"There is something called the '*mal de debarquement*' syndrome which, as it turned out, was my problem. It roughly translates as 'arrival sickness'. This simply means that the sickness lasts a few days beyond the normal motion sickness, which normally ends when the motion ceases.

If you want the boy to spend longer in the past, or to travel there more often, then we will need to improve his resistance to both motion *and* arrival sickness. I know that people like NASA have special centrifugal machines that they use for conditioning, but in the absence of access to these things, I think we can maybe look at the standard antihistamine medications. These drugs aim to prevent and treat nausea, vomiting, and dizziness. Drugs like meclizine and diphenhydramine. There's also big advances in the use of other classes of drugs applied via medicated skin patches behind the ear. This medication is slowly absorbed directly through the underlying skin and into the body. All of these drugs are generally more effective when administered well before the motion activity takes place."

57. WHATEVER WILL BE WILL BE

The present...

The next day was stifling. Thick humid air hung over the city, and frequent heavy showers laced the concrete jungle, sending millions of people digging for their umbrellas and raincoats.

In the labyrinth it was the same temperature as always. This far down, the tunnels fell under the influence of the geo thermals. Kioshi had been awake all night. Anticipation gnawed at him like a termite at a wooden beam... incessant, audible. Something was building. He felt that matters, decisions even, were about to be taken from his control. He also thought instinctively, that he should surrender to the feeling. He knew that this feeling had something to do with the musician. Slowly, but inexorably, their paths were converging. He did not feel any form of affection towards this man, rather a feeling of inevitability. He would be freed or he would be destroyed, but neither would happen without the assistance of this man; this musician who wore the mark of Kiochi's soul on his right hand. He remembered that moment in the past, when this man had stooped to help him. The man had been there twice now. Kioshi had no idea how this man was there the first time, only that it was something he, Kioshi, had caused to happen. Kioshi had been there again, on that coarse black road very recently, and this time he had taken the musician with him on purpose. Made him come, forced him to understand.

And now he could sense the air about him slowly charging with positive energy. Something was happening.

Kioshi lay on his bed staring up at the blank learning screen. He knew that he was now eighteen years of age and that he had been in the labyrinth for seventeen of those years. At various places around the city, he had stashes of cash amounting to over fourteen million yen. Five years ago he had successfully escaped the labyrinth but, having done so, he found he had no idea what he had escaped from or, what he had escaped into. He was older now, and he had spent those five years wisely. He had come to terms with life in the labyrinth and, he had even learned to live with Grok. He now knew that there were lots of people like Grok, above or below ground.

Professor Hiroko of course remained an enigma. Kioshi had developed an image of the planet, and of all the people moving around on it, doing things, going places. In this image there were two people that had big giant question marks over there heads... that went with them everywhere they went, whatever they did. One was him, and the other was the Professor. He knew they were somehow headed for the same destiny, and he sensed that the events unfolding around him were speeding up. They would soon pass the point of no return. For the last few days, whenever he left the labyrinth he could feel the air palpably vibrating, humming, buzzing around him.

After two of the mathematicians had left, the Professor had ceased all experiments for about six months. Yamashita and one other mathematician had stayed on... the young one called Taku. Every day Yamashita, Taku and the Professor sat together at computers, analysing data and doing something that Grok referred to as mapping.   At the end of six months, the experiments started up again. Only this time it was different. Now they were aiming to put Kioshi into specific locations, and to have him look for and report certain things, in much the same way as Yamashita had done when he had sent Kioshi to the television studios. They now also had a doctor, and someone that he had heard Grok refer to as a *shrink*, working with them. The doctor had him doing all sorts of strange exercises, and trialling different medications. Initially they had limited the actual experiments to once every 3 months, but they were concentrating on expanding the time that he could comfortably stay in that other place, that other time. Kioshi had lost his advantage with Grok and the Professor. They now knew that he had some level of control over the trigger, when he went and how long he could stay.

It was the nausea, the dizziness, that sent Kioshi into a kind of faint, and that faint or swoon or whatever it was, brought him back. He described the feeling as being pulled rapidly through the air sideways, but not actually moving. He could struggle against it and stay longer, but then it took him days or even weeks to recover. The Professor had nothing if not patience, and he would wait until the doctor advised him that Kioshi was ready to go again. During the last experiment, with the aid of exercises and heavy doses of medication, the monitors showed that Kioshi had been able to spend just over fourteen minutes in that other place. The next experiment was planned for two weeks, and it was apparently the most important of all. Both the doctor and the shrink were monitoring him carefully, to be sure he was up to it. The strain of all this was taking an incredible toll on Kioshi. He was physically pale and drained. Out on the street, he would be mistaken for some kind of serious addict. Mentally he was losing his edge. It was difficult to think, to remain alert. Sometimes when he woke in the morning, or during the night, he was so disorientated, he was unable to tell which world or time he was in. On these occasions, mild panic would grip him, and he would thrust his hand under his bed side lamp, to see if it cast a shadow.

And so now as he lay on his bed considering all these things, he felt no concern for his health. He felt no fear. He knew that only down this dark path, would he find out who he was, and also… who the Professor was.

He swung his feet off the bed and went to find Grok. He found him in the dining room having a coffee with Taku.

"Good morning Taku, good morning Mister Grok," he said, dropping down into a spare seat at their table.

Taku smiled a greeting over the rim of his coffee cup.

"Good morning to you," replied Grok amiably. "Day off today Kioshi. What have you got planned?"

"Well I thought I might go up and get some fresh air. I haven't been out for six or seven days and you know, with all these medications and things I think I could use some sunshine. I thought I might go take a long walk to Meiji Shrine, have a coffee, and watch all the comings and goings. I always find it enjoyable. Would anyone like to come with me?" he said, hoping of course that nobody would.

Taku lowered his coffee cup and looked at the ceiling as if he was looking at the sky through a hole up there.

"Ah, the Shrine. I like to go there and watch the blessings. I have twice now been involved in ceremonies there."

Now he looked back down at Kioshi.

"But not today I'm afraid, I am too busy."

Grok was watching Kioshi carefully. His big nose twitching ever so slightly. Then he slapped his big leathery hand down on the table and stood up, pushing his chair out with the back of his knees. He looked squarely at Kioshi.

"Who knows... I might see you there."

And with that he turned and headed for the door. He stopped.

"Oh Kioshi."

"Yes Mister Grok?"

"Forget about that sunshine. Take an umbrella or wear a waterproof jacket, it's awful wet out there today."

"Oh... I will. Thank you Mister Grok."

Grok paused with his hand on the door frame, then nodded and was gone.

58. KIOSHI CALLS US OUT

The present…

Our little meeting is breaking up. Nick has to head to Osaka to sort out some problems, and our favourite gumshoe says he has a lead to follow down, with the cop who got him all the surveillance photos.

"I don't think there's much more we can achieve here today," says Oka. "I think maybe tomorrow, you should start by going to all the places that you have already seen the boy in the flesh. We'll stay close by, then if you get a reading on your Kioshi meter, you can contact us for support."

"Kioshi meter?"

"That thing on your hand," gestures Oka. "It goes off whenever he's near right?"

"Right."

"And," says Oka. "Even though you feel he is somehow trying to reach out to you, and that he means you no harm, I think we need to exercise caution."

"Okay, well try not to let anything exciting happen until I get back on Wednesday," says Nick and with that, he's out the door and gone.

When the door finally closes behind Oka, I go to the coffee machine and drop in another capsule. I push the short cup button and wince in pain. I feel the blood rush to my head, like I have been spun upside down and left to drain. A strange sense of inevitability comes over me, and I spin back up the right way and turn to Yuka, who is staring at me with a look of concern.

"The boy won't wait until tomorrow," I say quietly, trying to get my head around what to do next.

"What do you mean?" says Yuka.

I hold up my index finger, and display the fierce red blister welling up there. She steps closer and we both watch the black carbon-like stain run down across the heel of my thumb, and up onto my wrist.

She goes to the window and looks down into the street below.

"We should get Oka-san back," she says reaching for her phone.

I step forward and take her phone from her.

"No, I don't want to do anything to frighten him away. It's best I go alone."

I step up to the window and look first left, then right towards the footbridge. There is no sign of the boy, but I know he has just been there. I turn back to find Yuka has pulled on a cheap yellow raincoat.

"Best grab a jacket," she says, "it looks wet out there."

Before I can comment, she steps up, takes her phone from my hand, gives me my suit coat, and goes to the door.

"Let's move," she says, holding the door open.

No point arguing, her mind is made up. I shrug into my suit coat as we head down the corridor to the lifts. We're out on the street in no time.

"Which way?" she says.

59. THE VIEW FROM THE BRIDGE

The present...

Kioshi leaves the south entrance of the Shinjuku Station, turns left, goes down the stairs and across the road, to stand on the corner under the Green Peas Pachinko building. It is Sunday morning and there seem to be people everywhere. He leans against the wall underneath a giant green pea pod. He's part concealed behind a lamp post and, from here, can observe the roadway from the east entrance, and the stairs down from the south entrance, if Grok comes either of those ways. He is well aware that Grok follows him on occasions. Of course Grok may or may not follow him this morning. It seems that one of Grok's main aims in life, is to keep you guessing.

He waits ten minutes, and then as a further precaution, he strolls off under the road bridge in the direction of the Takashimaya Building. He goes up into the ground floor of the Tokyu Hands store, passes out through the rear entrance, and crosses the wide footbridge that spanned the railway tracks. On the other side of the tracks he diverts briefly, and wanders over to the nine trees that grew up here, so straight and formal and perfect. This spot is somehow significant to Kioshi. What are these trees? How did they get here? Where did they come from? Down here, all lined up like green sentinels in a concrete forest. In Kioshi's mind, if they were people, they too would each have a question mark above their heads... but at least they had each other.

He shakes the thought from his head and, reaching out to touch the central tree, he turns and makes his way across the next bridge. From the middle of the bridge he can see the musician's hotel. He can feel his presence. The vibration in his ears seems to ramp up a notch. He leans against the rail, behaving as casually as he can, while he scans around the roadway below. He is looking for Grok, making sure Grok hasn't come this way.

Finding nothing, he pushes off the rail and makes his way to the end of the bridge, then down the stairs and out on to the roadway.

60. HIDE AND SEEK

The present...

Kioshi strolls off down the street past the General Hospital. He does not look back. He keeps walking along the same street and, under Metropolitan Expressway Number Four, he turns right towards the Northern Torii Gate for Yoyogi Park.

The road is lined with large, beautiful trees, and about halfway up he moves behind one of these, and carefully observes the intersection that he has just come through.

Content with what he sees... or doesn't see, he walks up and through the gate, and into the park.

61. THE MAN IN THE TUNNEL

The present...

Yuka and I head off down the street. My right hand holds the umbrella, and Yuka clutches my left arm with both her hands. My right hand tells me where to go. The rain is coming and going in great swathes, that have the exact same effect as throwing water on hot rocks in a sauna. It's very warm and close.

"Do you know where we are going?" she asks.

"Yoyogi Park... I sense that if we go to the same place as the other day, he will find us."

We carry on down the street, and up under the Torii Gate into the Park. We continue down the wide gravel path without stopping. The rain has stopped, and in the quiet you can hear the sweet, musical sound of water dripping off leaves. Soon we can see the main junction of seven paths up ahead. My right index finger feels like somebody is holding a flame to it. I take my hand from my pocket and blow on the fierce red blister. The wide path to the right doubles back, and leads up to the Meiji Shrine. The wide path on the left takes you to a pavilion and car park.

Directly ahead, the main path carries on right through to the Harajuku entrance. I stop and turn around, locating the rock where I had sat just two days before. The air is electric. It is as if a million cicadas have descended upon us, and all the sirens in this great city have started wailing at the same time. I look at Yuka, but can tell she is hearing none of this, sensing none if this. I turn and walk toward the edge of the path, the fear grips me. The air feels as if it will burst into flames. I stare straight at the trunk of a large tree. This is the place. I can feel the flesh melting off the tip of my finger, but I can't look at it. I stare at the tree trunk.

"I see you Kioshi," says a voice that could have been mine.

Everything stops. The fire on my hand goes out. The air cools, and the cicadas and sirens stop, all together in the beat of a heart. A quiet calmness descends upon me... and slowly, the boy steps out from behind the trunk of the great tree.

His hair is three colours; blond on the tips, green in the middle and native Japanese black at the roots. It is teased high on his head, but spills, spear-like down his face, almost covering his eyes. There's a large metal stud to the right side of his bottom lip, and his eyebrows have been shaved off and replaced by two sharp pencil lines peaking at the centre like a child's drawing of Mount Fuji. He's wearing a black hoody with white lining and black formal pants. He's got on a blue t-shirt, with the number 26 printed on a torn, winged heart, and a large silver padlock on a heavy chain around his neck. He looks a little bedraggled from the rain. His eyes are lifeless.

"You are the man in the tunnel." It was not a question.

"I am."

"You are the man who came to me in the road all those years ago... to help me."

"I am."

"The woman... she is with you?" This *wa*s a question.

"Yes, she is with me Kioshi."

This boy, this boy Kioshi, who looks like he would tear your throat out as quick as look at you. This boy comes out of the trees and onto the path. He kneels on the gravel at my feet, his eyes cast down.

"Will you help me now?" he whispers... and raises his head to look at me.

Tears well up in his eyes and flow down his face and neck, creating a river that runs down the path, and out into the city to flood the whole world and beyond.

62. A CURE FOR YOUR BURN

The present...

I am standing on the gravel pathway in Yoyogi Park. Yuka has come up beside me and has taken hold of my left hand. Her grip is so insistent, I can feel the juice being wrung from my fingertips. Kneeling on the ground in front of us is the boy Kioshi. His weeping is now reduced to great racking sobs, and one or two passersby circle wide around us... this strange scene playing out here on the pathway. As the sobs slow, the boy wipes his arm across his face, then pulls down on his own cuffs and uses them to dry his eyes. He finally looks up at me with dead, pleading eyes. I reach out my hand towards him, and I see a small flicker of life ignite behind those eyes, like the tiniest glow of a cigarette at the end of a pier on a black night. He looks at my hand, and I watch as the light in his eyes grows with the decision he takes. He reaches up and takes my hand.

A great spark of electricity jolts through me, and I make to pull my hand back, but the boy holds tighter and gradually, as the electricity sputters and dies, I feel parts of his mind... parts of his story, flowing into me.

I help him to his feet, and I am taken aback when he comes forward and wraps his arms around me to embrace me. After a few seconds he steps back and looks at Yuka. It is a question.

"We are one Kioshi," I say quietly. "This is Yuka, and she has been helping me to find you."

He stands looking at Yuka for six or seven seconds more, then steps forward and embraces her also. She releases the crushing grip on my left hand, and the pain of the circulation returning to my fingers releases me from my almost trance-like state.

Kioshi steps back and looks from Yuka to me.

"I am Kioshi. I do not speak well in English, but I would ask you to help me."

Yuka explains in Japanese that she will help and translate when needed. I am about to speak, but he raises his hand to stop me.

"There is great danger here. Can we go to somewhere... I think it is p... private?"

"We can go to our hotel. I think you know that it is close by."

He almost smiles... almost.

"Yes, I know this hotel, but there is someone else in your room... another man."

"Yes, that is Oka-san. He is a friend. Yuka and I have another room there now."

Kioshi looks around. I can see he is nervous.

"We need to go quickly," he says, "It is best if we do not go together. You must not be seen with me. If you give me the number that is on your room door, and go there now, I will follow in a short space of time."

We tell him the room number, but are hesitant to leave him there. He insists it is necessary, and that he will follow. Then without another word he turns and strides towards the pathway that leads up to the Meiji Shrine.

. . .

We are back in our room at the hotel, and I am flexing the fingers of my right hand. After the boy grasped it and would not release it, I had half expected to see even more burns or blistering. The pain had reached a crescendo and then fallen off rapidly. Now I can see no sign of any burning or injury at all.

On the way back to the hotel, not one word had passed between us; but now we have found our voices.

"I thought maybe we should call Oka-san," says Yuka. "But now I think it is best if we hear the boy's story first. I think we should tell him about Oka-san and how he has helped us, and then he can decide for himself."

"I think you are right. Clearly the boy is very scared, but I get the feeling he is scared for us and not for himself."

"Then why is he asking… I mean, what does he want us to help him with?" she says.

"Well I guess we will know soon enough, but he seems to be mixed up in something pretty weird."

"Well, he is a rent boy," says Yuka, "so I guess it's probably organised crime. Maybe it is about a customer, or maybe he is in trouble with his bosses or his handlers, or whatever they are called."

"I don't think so," I reply. "Actually I don't think he is a rent boy. I mean he certainly looks like one, but I don't think so. There's something not quite right. I mean, think about it. If he was a rent boy who was in some sort of trouble, why would he spend two or three weeks trying to get my attention so that I could help him? And how the hell did he plant that memory or vision, or whatever it was in my mind, all those years ago? Even if we take the easy road, and say what happened to me all those years ago was just a dream, that doesn't help. He was in the dream… he knows he was in the dream. Now, because of that dream, or whatever it was, he thinks I can help him; but help him with what?"

63. A WOLF IN SHEEP'S CLOTHING

The present...

It's rare to see Grok wearing anything other than his immaculate dark blue suit, but then that's the idea... that nobody sees Grok, particularly Kioshi.

Like Yuka Sasaki, he is dressed in a cheap yellow plastic raincoat with a hood. The kind that magically appear on vendor's shelves all over the city on rainy days. With the hood pulled up over a baseball cap and a pair of sunglasses, Grok looks just like any other pedestrian scurrying through the city streets on a wet day.

He has tracked Kioshi from the Green Pea building, where he has luckily spotted him half obscured behind a pole. After the boy had moved off, he has followed at a safe distance up through the Takashimaya building, and out across the railway bridge. There is a close call when he thinks he had lost the boy, and has hurried down towards the next foot bridge. As he walks quickly towards the bridge something catches his eye off to his right hand side.

He looks around to see Kioshi walking out from a group of trees arranged in the small plaza. He has no option but to put his head down and maintain a steady pace ahead of the boy. He crosses the footbridge, and goes to turn down the stairs on the other side. As he does so, he sees that Kioshi has stopped in the middle of the bridge, and is looking back up the road to the north. He continues down the stairs and, clutching the yellow hood closed across his lower face, he walks off in a southerly direction. A little way down the street he goes up onto the stairs beside the hospital, and finds a spot where he can observe the street below the bridge. He has come down the western stairs, but there is a spiral staircase on the eastern side as well.

After a few minutes, Kioshi emerges from the western stairs and heads off in Grok's direction. Grok moves further up and pauses on the landing, leaning on the stainless rail as if catching his breath. He counts off the seconds, and then carefully turns to see Kioshi has walked past him, and is now about twenty paces ahead of him. He heads back down the stairs and, keeping well back, follows Kioshi towards Yoyogi Park.

Now, as the overhead Metropolitan Expressway Number Four comes into view, he sees the boy turn right towards the park entrance. Grok stops to consider things. The boy is going where he said he was, into the park. So far he has been strolling along pretty casually, stopping here and there to look in shop windows and take in the scenery. *Maybe I should forget it and just head back,* thinks Grok. But his nose twitches, and he finally decides to carry on after the boy... *you just never know.*

He rounds the corner under the expressway, and heads slowly up the street. As the entrance to the park comes into view, he sees Kioshi passing under the Torii gate. He follows the boy through the gate but he feels exposed. Probably because it is a rainy day, the park seems empty. He does his best to keep the few people that are on the path, between him and Kioshi. Up ahead, he sees the boy pause and look around him. Grok takes what cover he can behind a park attendant in grey overalls who is wielding a birch broom on the path.

Suddenly the boy steps off the pathway, and into the trees. Grok has no option but to do the same, and while the sweeper is looking the other way, he disappears into the wet undergrowth. He picks his way carefully toward the point where the boy has left the path, but takes a wide arc, deeper into the trees and getting soaked from the waist down. Suddenly up ahead he catches a glimpse of Kioshi standing with his back to a large tree. He moves in as close as he dares, and hunkers down to watch.

There is a man and a woman strolling arm in arm along the path, and they stop directly adjacent to where the boy is hiding. Grok can just make them out from where he is concealed. Suddenly the man turns to face into the trees and says, *'I see you Kioshi'*. Grok freezes on the spot. *Did I hear that correctly? Did that guy say, 'I see you Kioshi'?* He looks back in time to see the boy step out from behind the tree. Kioshi speaks to the man, but so softly Grok cannot hear what they are saying. He watches as Kioshi emerges onto the path, and kneels at the man's feet. Grok tries to move closer, but it is difficult. From where he is concealed in the bushes, he can now only see the man and woman from the waist up. He can hear someone crying. *Who is crying?* After what seems an eternity to Grok, Kioshi rises back into view. He moves forward and hugs the man, gripping him tightly. Then he steps back and speaks to the man. Grok can't hear, but it is too risky to try to move any closer. The boy then embraces the woman. They talk quietly for a short while, but Kioshi is clearly nervous, and his eyes are casting around the whole time. Then suddenly it is all over. The boy quickly turns and heads off. The man and woman watch him go, then turn and walk back the way they have come.

The wolf raises his big long nose, and sniffs the air. He smells trouble, but does he follow the boy, or the man and woman? Clearly he needs to find out who the man and the woman are, so he moves up to the edge of the pathway and checks that it is clear. It isn't, but that's just too bad, thinks the wolf. He steps out of the bushes in front of a startled student, who is busily texting on a phone, and drops into step behind his quarry.

Ten minutes later Grok follows them into the lobby of their hotel. He stands back and watches them board a lift, then steps forward and watches the floor numbers tick off one after the other. Finally the lift stops on a high floor and pauses briefly before heading back to lobby level. He notes the floor where the lift stopped for the first and only time, then heads straight back to the labyrinth.

64. COFFEE WITH KIOSHI

The present...

Even though we are expecting it, the sound of the doorbell startles us both. I look at Yuka and she raises her eyebrows. Her mouth hardens in a tight line across her face, then she takes a deep breath, releases it and opens the door. The boy looks both ways in the hall, then quickly steps in. Yuka closes the door behind him and takes him to the couch.

"Please sit Kioshi," she says to him gently. "Would you like a glass of water or maybe a tea or something?"

"C… could I have a coffee please? Would that be alright?" he stammers.

Yuka smiles and nods to him. The suite has an automatic coffee machine, and Yuka selects a mid strength capsule and drops it in. While the little machine hisses and splutters like an old maid fussing with the silverware, I go and sit opposite Kioshi.

Yuka brings the coffee along with milk and sugar cubes, and then returns and makes me a triple shot. Already she doesn't need to ask. She comes over with my coffee and sits down beside me.

"Well Kioshi," I start, "perhaps you can tell us what this is all about. How is it that we can help you?" I say, trying to keep my voice as normal and level as possible. My stomach is churning, and it screams out for that coffee hit.

Kioshi has been staring at the carpet. Now he raises his eyes to look at me.

"Now that I am here, it is difficult to know what to say, to know where I should start."

I remain silent.

"In the park I asked you if you were the man I had seen in the tunnel, and you said you were. I then asked you if you were the man, the younger man, who came to me on the road in that strange place all those years ago, and again, you said you were. It might help me if you told me what you remember of these things... both of them," he says, relaxing a little and sitting back now that he has made a start.

I begin by describing that strange happening in the tunnel, just a couple of weeks back when all this started. He sits forward and nods, then takes a sip of his coffee. I carry on with a description of the car accident, and when I come to the part where I had tried to touch him, I stop and look at my hand. There is nothing. No blister, no pain, nothing. I finish the story and wait while he absorbs what I have said. He gets up and goes to the window. He spends a long minute or so looking down into the street, or at nothing at all. Yuka and I measure the time by confused glances at each other. Otherwise, the universe is on pause again. Finally he turns and crosses back to the couch.

"Right. The way you say it, is how I remember these things. But you are saying to yourself, how can this be? You must understand that what I am about to tell you seemed normal for me. The people who raised me. The people whose nest I was in."

Here he notices Yuka and I exchange more confused glances.

"I'm sorry, that was how I was taught to call it... a nest. These people did things which I was taught to believe were normal. It was many years before I realised that this was not normal."

He paused again for a sip of his coffee, then laid out the whole incredible story of his life. After almost an hour he seemed drained. I know I was.

"And so," he finished, "that is all I can tell you. I have no idea who I am, or where I have come from. Surely I must have a mother or a father somewhere, or at least did have once. I keep feeling that Professor Hiroko is my father. Then just as quickly I dismiss this thought; but I feel strongly bonded to him. I don't know why I reached out to you. I have been touched by other people at times. I only know that I sense you are a man who can help me. I also know that I cannot leave the labyrinth, until something happens to let me escape. I don't know what that is, but ever since I saw you in the tunnel, I have felt time rushing towards some important event."

Now it was my turn to get up and go to the window. I am trying to digest what I have just heard. This incredible story, recounted by this strange boy who now sits on the couch in my hotel room. I can see his reflection in the window. He is watching me.

"Kioshi," I say. "what you are telling us is that this Professor of yours is able to send you back in time. At least, that is what you think. Mankind has always tried to travel through time, but it has never been possible. I have experienced enough strange events in these last few weeks to believe what you are telling us. But why me and, what do you need me to do?"

"I have nobody outside of the labyrinth or aboveground who can help me, and I have known you in some way since I was a child. Apart from one old man who lives in the Yoyogi camp, I know nobody else. The whole of my life is a question. I have been taught to steal. I steal money, watches, electronics and jewelry… anything small and valuable. I see other people leading a normal life and that is what I want, but I know this can't be. At least not until this thing that is rushing towards me is done. I have money if that's what you want. Lots of money, that I have hidden. It may be that there is nothing you can do to help me, other than hear my story and believe it. Maybe just my knowing that you do believe me, will help make me stronger."

He is becoming agitated.

"Kioshi," I say quietly, "there is no need to worry. We will help you, and we certainly don't want your money. I think what you are saying, is that you need to go back to this *labyrinth* place and see this thing through, knowing that you can escape, or that we can help you escape, when it is over. I think now that I need to tell you some things that we already know. I think these things will help make you stronger, help you understand you are not alone."

He sat forward on his seat with a surprised look on his face.

"It occurs to me that there's probably no way you could know this, but what has been happening to me, or more correctly between you and I, over the past few weeks is not in any way normal. This sort of thing does not happen to people. I had begun to think I was going insane."

"Insane? I don't know this word."

Yuka translates for me.

"Sorry… yes I thought I was maybe uh, sick, crazy or something. These things are not normal. As I have said, travelling back in time is also not normal, but I'd like to come back to that issue later. What I am saying Kioshi, is that I was so concerned about what was happening to me, that I told Yuka here and another friend of mine called Nicholas. Yuka in turn, told a friend of hers. He is a good man, and he has been very helpful to us in finding out what was happening.

Kioshi, this man has found out who you are. He knows about your family. I would like you to meet him, so he can tell you all of this himself."

Kioshi looked a little alarmed.

"Is he a policeman?" he asked. "Because if he is I will not speak with him. The Professor and Grok have told me what the police will do to me if they catch me. I know I have done wrong."

"He is not a policeman Kioshi. You must trust me. Remember you came to me for help, and now we need to work through this. Also, you have been forced to do wrong... against your will, and that is very different."

"When do you want me to talk to this man?"

"Now... well as soon as I can reach him. He is the man staying in my old room, but I think he is out at the moment. If it is alright with you I will telephone him, and have him come here as soon as possible."

The boy looks uncertain. He drops his face into his hands as if to wash away the doubt, then looks up and nods slowly.

"Okay then, that's great," I say getting a hotel pen and writing pad off the desk. "While I am speaking to him maybe you can write the directions for the entrances you spoke of, that get you into this labyrinth."

I place the paper in front of him and dig out my telephone. As I wait for Oka to answer, I watch as the boy stands up and removes his damp hoody. It is getting warm in the room. In fact, I think, things are hotting up all over.

"Musician!" comes the response at the end of the line. "What's happening?"

"Where are you," I ask, "and how quickly can you get back to the hotel?"

"Well," says Oka, "I've been at the police headquarters in Kasumigaseki. I'm on the subway now, but I should be there in say... ten minutes. Why?"

"Because Kioshi is here. In my room."

All I hear after that is a faint click.

While we wait, Kioshi draws details of the entrances and exits he knows. He draws a basic map of the labyrinth, and marks them all on it. He tells us how you can exit from all of them, but that without the special remote control, it is only possible to get in one way and that is via a green door on the lower platform of Shinjuku Station. The green door… this must be the green door from my vision. He tells us that once the door is opened, it appears to lead only into an old disused cupboard, but that if you turn and push on the right hand wall of the cupboard, it slides away with the back wall to reveal the door to a stairway. He shows us the key that he keeps on the thick chain around his neck.

He goes on to describe Grok, and how there is a lot of money and strange documents at this man's house. He asks for paper and an envelope which Yuka gives him from the hotel compendium, and he writes down Grok's address and the details of his hiding places. He also notes the place where *his* money is hidden, and what he wants done with it if he should die. Then he writes the names of some of the people he remembers, that have worked in the labyrinth over the years. He does not know if they are real names or not, but at it is least somewhere to start. Then he puts the paper in the envelope, seals it, and hands it to Yuka.

"Will you please take great care of this for me?" he says somberly. "You must promise me never to open it for at least one year, unless you know that I am dead. If I am dead, you will please open it and do what needs to be done."

I am about to speak… to assure him that he will not die, but he turns to me and says…

"You have not met this man Grok. I think the Professor may be what you called *insane*... sick or something, but Grok... Grok is evil. He has already threatened that he will kill me."

Suddenly there comes both an urgent knock on the door and an even more urgent ringing on the bell. Kioshi jumps up, grabs his hoody, and backs across the room. I tell him it is okay... just our friend. Yuka rises and opens the door. Oka barges into the room as if he'd had a run up. He stops dead just a few feet into the room. Yuka shuts the door and puts the security chain device on.

It's like a Mexican standoff, with all four of us looking at one another uncertainly. I bring my hands together as if in prayer. I try to make my voice as calm as possible.

"Oka-san, that was quick. Oka-san, this is Kioshi. We have just been telling him that you know all about his family, and what happened to him. Maybe we can all sit down and start there?"

Oka takes a chair and motions for the boy to sit. He hesitates, still not certain, still suspicious. Yuka and I sit, and slowly the boy moves back and sits on the couch. I notice his knuckles are white from clutching the hoody in his hands. Oka talks softly, and explains to Kioshi that his mother died when he was born, right outside the hospital, but that his father is still alive somewhere, maybe in Kyoto. He explains that after Kioshi's mother died, his father left his job, and sort of broke down. Oka says he believes he can find Kioshi's father. He goes on to explain how Kioshi was cared for by his grandmother, until he was kidnapped from a doctor's office, when he was just a year old.

Kioshi sits motionless and without expression. A long silence follows, then the boy stands and walks back over to the window. I take the opportunity to fill Oka in on the story that Kioshi has told us. Throughout this whole time, about fifteen minutes, Kioshi stands looking out the window. When I finish, we three sit silently looking at each other, until the boy finally turns from the window.

"There is much more to tell, but I would like to meet this person who you say is my father... and the woman who is my... I am sorry I don't understand this grand..."

"Grandmother," interrupts Oka. "This is how you call the woman who is your mother's mother."

"I would like to meet this woman. But if this man is my father, then who is the Professor, why am I so sure we are connected?"

"The Professor is nobody," says Oka. "He is just a man... a bad man who has kidnapped you, and used you in these experiments for all these years. I mean this is unbelievable, preposterous. Tell me Kioshi, are there any other boys in this underground place?"

"In the labyrinth... yes... well no. I mean there were four other boys, but many years ago, they left the labyrinth to go hiking with Grok, and they never came back. I never saw them again.'

Oka shot me *a this is not good news* look.

"And now," continued Kioshi, "I feel something is about to happen, something that will make sense of all this. As I said, I have spent the last few years learning about the world, and gathering money for my escape. Most of that money I have taken from the man called Grok. He is a dangerous man, and I know he suspects that something is going on. But even though I believe I can escape, and make sure that Grok can no longer harm me or anybody else, I cannot leave until whatever is about to happen... has happened."

"This Grok," says Yuka. "What is his role in the labyrinth?"

The boy considers his answer carefully, then he says...

"He hires people when they are needed, and then disposes of them when they are no longer needed."

"Disposes of them? What does that mean, disposes of them?" Yuka asks.

"He kills them. I know where some of the bodies are, but there have been very many just since I started noticing what was happening. You have some names in the envelope I have given you."

"You could show us where these... bodies are?" I ask.

"Yes I think so, some of them. And maybe at Grok's apartment you will find lots of proof, but now maybe you understand why this is very dangerous for you. Also, Grok has guns. He has one at his apartment, and one almost the same in his office. I know nothing about guns, but I have looked at many pictures in the library. I believe it is something called a Browning Semi Automatic 9 mm pistol. I have made myself as familiar as possible without being able to actually touch it. I was wondering if someone could tell me what it means '*to cock*' this pistol or '*release the safety catch*'."

We all look at Oka-san.

He shrugs.

"Okay, we will have to assume it's a standard Hi-Power single action pistol... What?" he says guiltily, looking at Yuka.

"Didn't they teach you this at your Journalist College?"

"No!"

"Well you should at least be thankful that they did at mine, now shut up and let me try and tell the boy what he needs to know. Like I was saying. With a single action design, you have to cock the pistol before it will fire. You do this by either pulling

332

back the hammer or by pulling the slide to the back and releasing it. I understand that most professionals would have the gun cocked and loaded, and that all you have to do is click off the safety catch then pull the trigger. Do you know where that is on the gun Kioshi? The safety catch I mean."

Kioshi nods.

"So what do you intend to do with this pistol?"

"Well," replies Kioshi, "If I can get it from Grok's office, I will simply hide it somewhere for my own safety."

"Hmmm… well okay then, but you need to be very careful. There's some kind of old saying that you shouldn't pick up a gun unless you are prepared to use it. What do you think of that Kioshi?"

Kioshi held Oka's gaze for a few long seconds, then turned back to me as if waiting for me to say something.

65. THE WOLF REPORTS IN

The present...

"I'm telling you Professor, he was hiding there, waiting for them. The guy knew his name."

"His name?"

"Yes, his name, that's what I'm saying. He called him Kioshi."

Tetsuya said nothing, but thought so hard it hurt.

"Okay, I agree... that's pretty odd. Maybe something is going on. But all we can do is seal Kioshi in, and make sure that he can't get out," says Tetsuya. "We can prevent anything happening until after this next experiment, and then we can get to the bottom of all this. I think it is best to say nothing. If he thinks we know, he may react, and right now my priority is the experiment... we are so damned close Grok. So close."

"Yes Professor."

66. A MUSICIAN'S PLAN

The present…

I am pacing the floor, thinking.

It's probably not much of a plan, but it's all we have, so let's go through it again.

"Oka-san will go with Kioshi now, to establish the location of the green door in Shinjuku Station. Kioshi will give Oka-san the key once he has unlocked the door. If Kioshi is right about Grok being suspicious, then he should not try and leave the labyrinth again. That is unless we can persuade you never to go back there again Kioshi… to stay here now, and not take this risk."

I look at the boy, but can see that I am wasting my time with this argument. He will see this thing through. He will know… must know, who he is.

I touch the drawing on the table. I have opened a Shinjuku & Shibuya Shopping Guide map beside it.

"This map of Kioshi's shows us how to find our way into this secret labyrinth, or whatever we might like to call it, once we are through the green door. Right... so we know that the day after tomorrow at 10.17am, this experiment begins. Yuka will go to the place on the path here… in Yoyogi Park, where she can see if anybody comes out of the concealed entrance you say is by the little wooden bridge. We have mobile phones. If anyone comes out, Yuka will phone me. I will have my phone on vibrate only. I hope the signal works underground."

"Remember Yuka," I say turning to her, "you are not to follow anyone or to take any action. Just stay safe and phone me… okay?Then Yuka will alert Oka-san's friend in the metropolitan police, if we are not back here at the hotel by the appointed time of five o'clock in the afternoon. We will photocopy Kioshi's plans and diagrams, and Yuka will keep them to give the police."

Here I paused. "Kioshi, we give you our word that we will not involve the police, unless it is absolutely necessary."

"You mean unless I am dead?" he says quite abruptly.

It wasn't a question that required answering. Kioshi looked thoughtful for a moment then went back to the table and sat down. He took a pen and paper, and made some more notes. He was almost childlike in his actions. He would stop and stare away in thought, suck on the end of the pen, then bend back to the task of scratching out some instruction or other. Finally content with the result, he folded the sheet of paper in four, placed it in the last envelope from the compendium. He wrote something on the envelope then handed it to Yuka.

"If I die, this one is for my father and only for him. However if you cannot find him, you must deliver it to this grand… sorry… grandmother that you spoke of."

Yuka nods and smiles.

"Right, where was I," I continued. "Yes… Oka-san and I will wait at this green door on the lower platform. If Kioshi does not come out by 11.30am, we use the key and go in, following Kioshi's map. This key also opens the final door into the labyrinth correct?"

Kioshi nods.

When we track Nick down, we will get him back here urgently. If he makes it back in time, he will cover this secret escape route of Grok's in the Shinjuku pedestrian subway.

Oka shakes his head.

"And that's your plan musician?" he asks.

"Do you have a better plan then Oka-san?"

"No no, just wondering. For the record I think any plan that anticipates what might happen if we get into this labyrinth, would be egotistical folly."

"I'm sorry," says Kioshi. "What does this mean, this egotistical folly?"

"It means I think it's time for us to go," answers Oka.

Kioshi looks down at the floor, then once more takes me in a hug. I feel his body shivering, feel the beat of his young heart. After two or three seconds, he steps back and again childlike, scuffs his feet back and forth on the carpet. It might be my imagination, but his eyes, previously flat and dead, seem to have come to life a little.

"I do not understand what has happened, how we came to meet all those years ago but... but."

Yuka cuts him off. She takes him in a motherly embrace and kisses his forehead. She releases him and walks away, not quite strong enough to face him for longer. Oka leads him to the door. Kioshi pauses there and turns to me.

"I see you musician," he intones softly.

"I see you too Kioshi."

And they are gone.

Suddenly Yuka is in my arms. I feel the wetness of her tears through my shirt. I hold her tightly while her sobs subside.

"My god, that poor boy. My heart aches when I think about what he has gone through."

I take her by the shoulders and push her gently back so I can look into her eyes.

"Okay now. Everything will be okay. Stop crying."

"Only if you will," she says suppressing a slight tremor.

And I realise she's right. Rockstar, world traveller, hero to the downtrodden... big giant baby!

67. I WAS HERE BEFORE THIS HERE WAS HERE

The present...

Tetsuya Hiroko's face glows in the green light from the computer screen. Taku Watanabe is shuffling papers on his desk and casting sideways glances at Tetsuya, just waiting for the right moment.

"I think what you are looking for can be found on this time projection," says Taku.

"How the hell do you know what I'm looking for?" shouts Tetsuya.

"Well I don't Professor, although maybe if I did I could be more certain of this. This is just a theory, but I believe that your research is coming to a climax. Having said that, I have no idea why, other than to postulate that your 36 year cycle is a result of an historic event, specific to this particular person... Kioshi. Certainly we know the boy can travel outside the cycle, but those geographical waypoints seem to hold absolutely no interest for you."

Tetsuya is thoughtful. He remembers Ken Hayashi's story. Hayashi's time frames seemed to confirm the cycle... coincidence... maybe. He paces the room with his chin in his hand as if checking the length of the stubble. Finally he spins back to face the young mathematician.

"You know... this is the only subject that we have ever had any success with... I mean that we could control. We know there are others, but we have never been able to establish any trigger mechanism. Could it be that it is only this boy who might ever be able to do this?"

"It's possible but highly improbable," says Taku. "I wish I knew more about how you selected your subjects. I understand there were five boys originally, and that they were all born closely together in Kyoto. Please do not think me too bold Professor, I ask only in the interests of securing you a successful result, why you decided to target these five boys."

Tetsuya remains stock still and fixes his stare on Taku.

"Okay," he says finally, "I can tell you only this. The project grew from a desire to find out more about myself. The selection process came from…"

Tetsuya looked down. He was embarrassed to say this in front of the mathematician. He wrestles with himself and wins. In the end it doesn't matter. This man will never leave the labyrinth. He will be dead soon… possibly very soon.

"Okay… the selection process came from a dream, a recurring dream. I don't know why, but I am convinced that the key to everything, was finding that one boy who was born at that time, in a Kyoto hospital. The details are not important, but the results are. It worked."

Taku let out a long low whistle.

"What?" says Tetsuya.

"Well Professor, it's like I said, pure postulation. I am only a mathematician and this is not my area of expertise, but what if we were to consider that your decision to select these boys was influenced by one very specific event?"

"I'm really not following you. What *specific* event are you talking about?"

Taku paused before answering. He was uncertain if he did this for dramatic effect, or if he feared dire consequences from what he was about to say. Finally he says it anyway.

"The event that is going to happen right here in two days time!"

There's an old saying about it being so quiet you can hear a pin drop. It went so quiet in that room, deep under the city of Tokyo, that you could hear a pin drop on the other side of the planet.

Tetsuya visibly sagged. He seems to crumple down into his chair, his eyes wide with shock. Inevitably the shock turned to concentration, as the gears began turning in his head. He jumps up and goes to the whiteboard. His hands are shaking as he takes a thick black marker from the plastic holder. He writes a time and date on the top of the board.

He pauses before speaking, thinking his voice may come out just a squeak. When he was sure he was calmed, he turns back to Taku.

"This time and date here," he says tapping on the board. "Is the time we next send the boy back from... 10.29am sharp on 23 August 2009. Position Shinjuku."

He draws a line under the date partway down the board and writes another time and date. 9.45pm on 23 August 1991. Position Kyoto.

"And this is where we now hope the boy will end up. In Kyoto General hospital at the time of his birth. This is eighteen years ago. We think the trigger that sends Kioshi back is the moment just after his birth. It is clearly very traumatic and so, based on Yamashita's theory, we hope this matching of energies will pull him down into the same time as he crosses the divide."

"That's right," interjects Taku. "According to Yamashita's table of probabilities. You asked us to find the launch date to get us to the time and place of Kioshi's birth date, and that is what we have done. At least to a very high degree of probability."

Tetsuya pauses with his head down, then rouses himself and draws another line from Kioshi's birthdate, and writes another time and date. 9.45pm on 23 August 1955. Position… and then taking a red marker from the holder, he drew a question mark.

"Now… get on your computer and tell me exactly where that puts us."

"I've already done that," says Taku.

"Well?"

Well Professor, it puts us in almost the exact location where Kioshi was born, only 36 years before of course. That's what I mean about your 36 year cycle being valid."

Tetsuya Hiroko clutches the white board for support, then reaches out and staggers across to his desk. He is as pale as a snowman.

"Would you mind telling me Professor, what is the significance of that date?"

"That date… that date," says Tetsuya. "I am told that I was born sometime on the evening of 23 August 1955 in Kyoto. That date is my birth date."

Now even the young and fit Taku needs to find a chair and sit down.

"What we are about to do here in two days, will cause a rent in time that will affect my whole life. And I guess we know that it has already worked," said Tetsuya Hiroko to nobody in particular.

68. HOME FOR YOUR BIRTHDAY

The present...

"So what do we all think?"

There are five people gathered around the small meeting table in Tetsuya Hiroko's office. Tetsuya, Kioshi, Grok, Yamashita and Taku. Tetsuya has called for this early meeting, based on the hypothesis that he and Taku had discussed the night before.

"Nobody knows the answer to that question Professor. The only person who could even have a crack at answering, is Kioshi here," says Yamashita.

"It has nothing to do with mathematics or probabilities. We now know that all time, in the case of Kioshi here at least, is stacked up in 36 year cycles. Your original explanation of time past as a stack of pasta, applies absolutely. If you push a skewer through the first layer from this point, you will get to August 1991. If you push harder you will pass through August 1991 and into August 1973. And harder still into August 1955... and so on. Kioshi has proven he can make the jump through the first layer. What remains to be seen, is if he can jump from there to the next layer and so end up two layers down. The first jump is all about mathematics and probabilities. It makes the vital correction across the temporal-geographical matrix. In other words, the matrix has provided us with temporal shortcuts, but it seems those shortcuts will rely on a huge traumatic event to draw Kioshi in. If this doesn't work, we will have to wait until the year 2027 to launch Kioshi. The second jump, is less about mathematics, and more about stamina and mindset."

He paused for breath and to let the group absorb this information.

"I understand Professor Hiroko, why you want to land Kioshi at the exact point of his birth. I can see that this will be a defining moment in your research. But I don't understand why you want to try and push through another layer of 36 years."

Tetsuya looked up at Taku whose eyes flickered downwards ever so slightly.

"But whether that can be done," continued Yamashita. "Is a matter entirely for Kioshi to comment upon."

All eyes now turned to Kioshi. He was wary, but he was now well informed. He felt this had to be done.

"I am feeling strong, and I have been training hard. We think we can achieve fifteen minutes on the ground. This I think would be long enough to attempt what you are suggesting. Certainly while I am in the other time space, I can think and function and move around. The only real difference is that I have no shadow, and I am subject to this sickness or dizziness, that you say is caused by motion or inertia. What I am saying is, that I should be able to conjure up the same vision that sets me on my journey. That thing you call the trigger. If I can do that, who is to say that it would not work? The only way to find out, is to try I think."

"Then it is settled," says the Professor.

69. A LONG WAY HOME

The present...

Kioshi lies calmly on the bed. Tetsuya Hiroko stands by his side. Sensor wires run from each of his fingertips, and his head, chest and feet, are covered with electrodes. The only other people present are Taku and Yamashita, who now sit behind the set of monitors on the desk by the wall. The doctor and the psychiatrist have been locked in one of the unused bedrooms, in case they are needed. Grok has locked down the labyrinth... tight, and all is in readiness.

"We'll go over it just one more time," says Tetsuya. "Even though you can visualise the trigger and commence the jump, we will also set the trigger happening from here. You say you are able to keep reasonable track of time. We have estimated that you should be well into your first stage within thirty seconds of seeing the trigger. So when you are ready, or when you need to, you will try to set the trigger again. Do not attempt to hide your emotions. It is important that the monitors show us what is happening. So... when we see on the monitors that you are trying to visualise the trigger for the second time, we will wait fifteen seconds exactly. Then we will set the trigger from here a second time, just in case. At that point, you should jump again to 1955. I have every reason to believe that you will be successful."

He glances across at Taku.

"Once there, move around as much as you can, to see whatever you are able to see. Try to determine a date somehow... a newspaper, anything. Stay as long as the sickness permits. When you return we will be standing by to administer a shot of diphenhydramine and get you straight onto oxygen.

Kioshi just nods.

Tetsuya reaches out and lays a hand on the boy's arm.

"Good luck Kioshi. I think we are about to make history," he says, and opens the cannula to administer the sedative.

Kioshi closes his eyes.

Tetsuya signals to Taku to start the trigger program. He watches as the boy's eyes move about under his lids, then walks over to stand behind Taku and watch the monitors. They leap into life.

Kioshi opens his eyes, and finds himself balanced on a woman's stomach. There is a slight tugging at his waist. A man in a green mask reaches down and tries to place him in the woman's arms. She swats him away, screaming...

"Get them away from me. Get them away from me."

There is a great flash of blinding light, which moves in sync with the echo of the woman's screams. Growing ever louder, ever brighter, the light and sound coalesce into one living piercing pain, that sets him vibrating like a guitar string. The sound splits itself off again, then stops just as suddenly as it has begun. Now there is just the strobing light, now blackness. Suddenly the black becomes white blinding, painful light. He snaps his eyes shut, and feels the spin of the planet force his brain up against the back of his skull. He feels the blood course through his veins and rush up into his fingertips, so that they might burst. He feels himself tilt upward, and sway backwards and forwards. Now a slimy hand reaches down his throat and takes a grip on his bowels, dragging them up through his mouth. It turns him inside out... and then, he feels nothing. His eyes look backwards into his empty skull, and all he sees is a green mist.

When he opens his eyes again, he is in a hospital room. Maybe the same room as before. He is standing back against the wall, and he can see a woman on the bed. Also a nurse and two men. The woman has her legs hooked up over some kind of metal device, and one man, obviously a doctor, is sitting on a stool between the woman's legs. He is yelling at the woman to push. The other man is dressed in a gown, and Kioshi can see that he wears a mask over his nose and face. He stands beside the woman, holding onto her hand, while the nurse stands next to him, watching. Everybody is too busy to notice Kioshi. Unseen, he moves sideways, to be part concealed by the blue curtain hanging from an overhead rail. Suddenly the woman gives a little whimper and Kioshi sees a tiny purple, wet mass, appear in the hands of the man between the woman's legs.

Suddenly, the woman looks directly into Kioshi's eyes. Fear grows there, and then is replaced by resolve. The doctor lifts what Kioshi can now see is a baby, onto the woman's stomach while the nurse ties and cuts the umbilical cord. The doctor tries to place the boy in the woman's arms but, with her eyes fixed directly on Kioshi, she pushes it away and starts screaming.

"Get them away from me. Get them away from me," she screams. Kioshi now understands that the woman means him as well as the baby... *get them away from me!* With a blinding jolt, Kioshi finally understands that the baby is him... and he is the baby.

Through his shock he hears the doctor tell the nurse to take the baby to the nursery.

The nurse hesitates, then takes the tiny boy, wraps him in a sheet and leaves the room. The doctor finishes up what he is doing as the nurse returns. They roll a removable section of the bed back into place and Kioshi, who is now well hidden behind the blue curtain, hears the metallic clicks as the bed locks into place. Through a gap in the curtain he sees the doctor, scowling, unhook the woman's legs from the metal devices. He pulls these out of their slots on the sides of the bed, then turns to face almost directly at the point where Kioshi is concealed. He rips off his surgical gloves and drops them into some unseen container on the floor.

"Take this woman back to her room. I will be there to check on her shortly," says the doctor, and he leaves the room without looking back.

Another nurse arrives and the man beside the bed holding the woman's hand, is pushed aside. With one last horrified look at his wife, he slumps down into a chair, and tugs the mask from his face. As the nurses wheel the bed from the room the woman, who Kioshi now understands is his mother, looks into his eyes, through the gap in the curtain. Her eyes are burning with the hard resolve of knowing.

Kioshi watches as the man in the chair drops his head into his hands, then he slips out into the corridor. He can see the nurses about thirty feet away, wheeling the woman through a set of swinging doors. He follows quickly, and peers through the glass. The doors swing open at his touch, he walks past the room where the nurses had taken his mother, and sits on a red vinyl chair in the corridor. The first nurse comes out wheeling the empty bed, and disappears back through the double doors. Shortly after, the second nurse comes out, and disappears down the corridor in the other direction. Kioshi is starting to feel that he is running out of time. He waits as long as he dares, then steps into the room, just in time to see his mother step out through the door onto the balcony. He starts to move toward her, feeling the beginnings of the dizziness. Through his own struggle, he sees his mother take two steps forward, turn and look pleadingly at him. She climbs the railing, and falls out of sight. He tries desperately to get to the balcony, his heart torn asunder by that last look on his mother's face, but he is overtaken by dizziness. He feels he is blacking out. No... they are setting the trigger again. He takes one last look out the window, but all he can see is a tall white flagpole and the tops of some trees.

Kioshi staggers back against the bed and slips to the floor. The next thing he knows, he is back in the delivery room on his mother's stomach. The second trigger! He passes through the tunnel as calmly as he can. Don't struggle, stay focused, take it easy. His mouth yawns open and his eyes close... then open again. He is on a footpath. It is dark. Something is wrong. He should be in the hospital. There are cars parked beside him on the road, and he notices that they are not like the cars he knows from Tokyo. They are... yes, they are like the old cars he saw in pictures at the library. Stay calm, stay calm. He runs a little way along the road, then doubles over and retches into the gutter. An old drab green ambulance rattles by with a bell clanging, and Kioshi straightens up, takes a couple of deep breaths, and runs after it. He comes around the corner, and sees the ambulance turning into the front of the hospital.

The hospital... he was so close. He runs up to the entrance and finds that one side is blocked off by buildings. The other side of the entrance opens onto a grassed area, with a pathway leading up among the trees, to some wooden benches. He runs in that direction and immediately sees the white flagpole, right in front of him. He continues quickly up the path and stands by the flagpole, looking up at the balconies. They are solid concrete with a steel rail exactly like the one he had seen his mother climb over, just a minute before... no, all those years ago. It's making his head hurt and he feels like retching again, but he fights back the feeling and looks up, trying to estimate what floor his mother's room is on. He guesses it must be around level four or five, but there is nothing to be seen. What does he expect? It is confusing, his head hurts, his stomach churns, but of course there will be nothing there. He realises his mother had jumped off that balcony 36 years into the future. She will not be here.

He feels foolish, there in the dark. He is about to turn and go, it is time to surrender to the dizziness, and leave this place. There is nothing here. Of course there is nothing here, he realises that what he has just witnessed inside, happened 36 years into the future from where he is now. All he can tell the Professor is that yes, he has been to the hospital twice, and that this time, judging by the cars and the ambulance, it was much older... or is that younger. Suddenly, out of the darkness he sees a flash of light, right there near a second floor balcony. There is a small bamboo stand blocking a clear view, so he makes his way around it and, there on the lawn between the bamboo stand and the hospital building, is a woman. It is the woman he now knows as his mother. She is dressed in the same hospital gown, and is struggling to get to her feet.

He is frozen to the spot, as the scene unfolds before him. He watches as she wanders, almost dreamlike, across the grass and into the shadows by the bamboo stand. She seems to come awake, and she looks around her as if trying to figure out where she is. Suddenly she falls sideways onto the grass, clutching her stomach. She rolls onto her back, and Kioshi watches in horror, as another baby slides out of her, and onto the grass. How can this be, these are two different times. He watches horrified as she gives one great rending shudder, and reaches around, to tear the belt from her gown. With one hand she reaches down between her legs, to haul the umbilical cord closer. She cranes her neck down, then ties the gown cord tightly around the umbilical. She strains to get the umbilical into her mouth, then she quickly bites through it; leaving the tiny clump of life squirming on the grass. Kioshi can hear a noise, a far off groan, coming from somewhere not at all human. Then he realised it is coming from within him. He is powerless to stop it, this cry of demons. Wiping her face with the sleeve of the gown, the woman hears the sound and pushes herself upright. She turns her head and looks directly at Kioshi. He looks down at the child and when he looks back to the woman, she is staggering away into the shadows. Finally she stops and turns back to look at the baby on the grass; then after one quick glance at Kioshi, she is gone.

The sudden tug of inertia sucks Kioshi out of his trance. For just an instant he doesn't know what to do. Then, after one last look at this baby squirming on the grass, he turns and runs back towards the hospital entrance. As he pushes through the doors, he fights off extreme exhaustion and motion sickness. It seems his body is spinning one way and his insides another. He pushes past an old man in brown overalls with a yard broom in his hand, and reaches out to the wooden seats in the foyer area. He hauls himself along to the reception counter. As he struggles forward he sees that, in the brightly lit foyer, he casts no shadow. A nurse looks up, alarmed.

"Please," he gasps. "There is a baby... a newborn baby, on the lawn near the bamboo stand."

He hears the cries echo through the hollow space around him, and he sees the old man drop his broom and run out the door. He looks back pleadingly at the nurse, and with a great will and effort says...

"Please Miss, can you tell me what day and year this is?"

The nurse seems scared of him. She rears back and holds up an old fashioned looking desk calendar, on a brown metal base.

"It is Tuesday... Tuesday August 23rd 1955."

He pushes himself back from the counter and half runs, half staggers across the foyer and out through the door. So little time now, he must find the woman... his mother. He manages another twenty or so torturous paces before he goes down on his knees, drops sideways and closes his eyes.

As he surrenders to the darkness, the realisation burns through his brain like a white hot blade. That baby... that baby on the lawn is my brother. My twin brother. I don't understand how, but that baby is my brother. Then the blade twisted in his brain with one last searing thought. My twin brother is the Professor. Professor Tetsuya Hiroko.

Then there is nothing.

Then there is something.

70. WHEN ALL OF THIS IS OVER

The present...

Yuka and I are lying side by side, pretending that we are relaxed, sleeping soundly. I am going through the morning in my head. Nick arrived back last night, and we have brought him up to speed. He wanted to be with Oka and I, or at least protecting Yuka in Yoyogi; but he finally accepted his role and his position watching the pedestrian subway.

Now, as I lie here, I am wishing I had agreed to let him stay with Yuka. I desperately want to stay and protect her myself, but I feel my life is so heavily intertwined with this boy Kioshi, that our very future happiness depends on what happens this day. Our souls have been travelling together forever. I now understand that I did not *come* to Tokyo... I was brought here.

Yuka stirs, stretches out her arms in a giant yawn, and tousles my hair. I turn to look into those huge big eyes.

Her voice is lazy, dreamlike.

"I think we should get up, take an early walk and find somewhere nice for breakfast."

"Hmmm."

"But first..."

The shower in our suite isn't really big enough for two people. I mean for a start, there is only one shower head. But that's okay, we just have to get as close together as possible. The steaming water drives away the weariness, as we discover new things, push out towards new boundaries. Afterwards we cling to each other under the comforting beat of the water.

Out on the street, we stroll hand in hand for an hour or more, before wandering into a small coffee shop. Hot black coffee and genuinely good hot croissants remind me of that life we still have together. All the places we have yet to go, all the things we have yet to do. I leave the coffee shop with a strong, positive resolve.

"You know, when this is all over, and it will be soon, I want us to go somewhere special," I say.

Yuka stops walking and spins around to face me.

"And where would that be?" she asks, kissing me firmly on the lips.

"Mitake," I answer. "The mountains of Mitake. There's somebody there I'd like to meet."

71. MR. BROWNING SPEAKS

The present...

Kioshi wakes in the lab to find the Professor and Taku leaning over him. As the clouds lift from his mind, Kioshi remembers all he has seen. He looks into Tetsuya's eyes with such an intense hatred, that it seems it will ignite the air around him. Tetsuya staggers back under the weight of that hatred and accusal. He quickly turns and hits an intercom button, calls Grok into the lab, his voice shaky. In less than twenty seconds, the door bursts open and Grok blunders into the room. He takes in the situation, sees the look in the boy's eyes, and the unreasonable fear that has invaded the Professor's whole face.

As Kioshi makes to rise from the table, Grok dashes forward to restrain him. While Grok pins down his arms and shoulders, Kioshi thrashes around with his legs. He tries to knee Grok in the stomach, but Grok pulls back easily and avoids the strike. A dull glint of metal catches Kioshi's eye, and he sees the Browning pistol stuck in Grok's waistband, under his suit coat. He bides his time, awaits an opportunity. He pretends to struggle a little more, then calms down and lies still. To struggle is a mistake. To alert them is a mistake.

"I'm sorry," he says weakly. "I didn't know where I was, what was happening. Two jumps is not possible. I thought I was dying."

Tetsuya looks at Yamashita and Taku. They both shrug as if to say, *'there is no way to know'*. Grok's big nose twitches almost imperceptibly, as he sniffs the air... smelling danger.

Tetsuya shudders, and struggles to take control of the situation.

"You gave me a fright boy," he says.

Moving forward he hands Kioshi the oxygen mask, and leans over to turn on the supply tap. He removes the cannula from the boy's right arm, swabs it over, and applies a small dressing. Then he takes a prepared syringe from the stainless tray by the table, flicks it, squeezes out any air, and asks Kioshi to roll on his side. The boy does as he is told. Tetsuya notices his hands are shaking as he places the needle into the boys right buttock, draws back the syringe slightly and injects the Diphenhydramine. He gives the site a quick massage with his thumb, removes Kioshi's oxygen mask, turns off the supply tap, and tells the boy to lie quietly for a moment. He has regained his composure.

"I will shortly have Mr. Grok take you back to your room Kioshi. I am very keen to find out what happened to you, but you are clearly exhausted. I think you should sleep now, and I will come to your room in an hour or so, to see how you are doing then. Mr. Grok, please," he says, gesturing to Kioshi.

Grok goes to the table and helps Kioshi onto his feet, then supporting him by his left arm, he slowly walked him along the corridor toward his room. Twice Kioshi staggers and falls, clutching Grok's waist for support. Finally they make it to Kioshi's room. Grok helps him onto his bed, then goes and closes the door. Kioshi watches him slide the manual lock home, and as Grok turns back, Kioshi sees the eyes of the wolf.

Grok crosses back to the bed, and without breaking stride, reaches down, and grabs Kioshi's neck between his great hairy paws. He puts his big wolf's face hard up against Kiochi's, his foul breath burning the boy's eyes. Kioshi reaches up weakly with his left hand, to try and loosen Grok's grip on his neck.

"I told you once boy, that if you crossed me I would squash you like an ant. I know you're up to no good. You might fool the Professor. He'll believe whatever he wants to in pursuit of his crazy dream. But not me. I think it is time for this whole crazy experiment to come to an end. I think Professor Tetsuya Hiroko's life's work is finally done. That fool will die today as well as you. But you are first," he breathes, grinding his big thumbs into Kioshi's jugular.

Kioshi can just manage to speak.

"I don't think so... Mr. Bronislaw Jasinski," he wheezes.

He feels Grok's grip slacken, sees his red angry face drain of colour.

"What... what did you call me?"

Kioshi whispered the name once more...

"Bronislaw Jasinski."

Now... and only now, Grok feels the muzzle of his own gun, pressing under his ribcage. Too late!

The bullet rips in through his left lung, collects a sizeable piece of his backbone, and exits through his rear right shoulder. He drops back onto the floor beside the bed, and sits quite upright, looking up at Kioshi like a discarded ventriloquist's dummy. An ungodly wheezing, gurgling sound fills the room. Even through his pain, Grog feels a drip of something on the back of his head and, looking up, sees a small part of his own body spattered on the ceiling. He looks back towards Kioshi, and straight into the barrel of the pistol, which barks again, and sends him quickly on his final journey.

There is a banging at his door.

"Grok... what the hell's happening? Open this door." Comes the muffled shout from the corridor.

Kioshi scrambles off the bed and, sliding back the bolt, pulls the door open. Tetsuya Hiroko takes one look at the scene in the room... Grok dead on the floor with half a head, Kioshi with a gun.

"What?"

He turns and runs down the corridor to the main passageway. Kioshi quickly pulls on a pair of jeans and a t-shirt, and is grabbing his trainers, when Taku appeared in the doorway.

"Oh my god!'" he says and adds to the mess and stench by throwing up violently across the floor.

"Taku, did you see which way the Professor went?" yells Kioshi, grabbing Taku by the arm. No answer.

"Listen Taku, the Professor and Grok are not part of some secret government project. They are criminals; killers working to the Professor's own twisted plan. They planned to kill you and Yamashita. A hundred people like you, have come here to work, and never left. Most are buried down here in secret crypts, dropped in lime pits or just left for the rats. You should be safe now, but take Yamashita and go to your room. Do not open the door until I come for you. I have friends who are helping me."

Taku nods; not understanding, but ready to comply.

"Now," says Kioshi shaking him. "Did you see which way the Professor went?"

"I saw him running up the main passageway to the left," answers Taku meekly.

The green door. Without another word, Kioshi takes off in the direction the Professor has run.

72. THIS IS NOT HOLLYWOOD

The present...

Oka and I are on the platform. This is exactly where I fell, all those years ago. We are close by the old green door. Oka is fiddling with the key. Twice now he has dropped it onto the hard surface of the platform, where it rang out like a bicycle bell telling everybody to look our way.

"Look musician, we should get in there as the next train leaves. We are sitting ducks out here. There are cameras everywhere," says Oka switching from foot to foot.

"But the plan was to wait until 11.30, and it's only ten past," I respond.

"What's the significance of 11.30? I say let's go now."

He's right of course. I am feeling pretty vulnerable. Two trains have come and gone, and I can just imagine some zealous station attendant looking at a monitor somewhere and thinking, *what are those guys up to?* It might be fourteen years, but since the sarin gas attacks, railway attendants have good reason to remain vigilant.

"Okay," I say. "Next train."

A few minutes later a train pulls in to the platform. Oka and I look at each other, then as the passengers move forward to board, we edge along, out of the view of the cameras. As the train pulls away, Oka slips the big old key into the lock, and pulls the door easily toward him. With one last glance about, we slip through and close the door behind us. We leave the deadbolt unlatched from the inside. Ignore the light switches that Kioshi has told us about, we use my small high lumen torch, to light the way. The false cupboard has been slid aside, revealing the open door and the first flight of stairs. Down, down, down, ever downwards. We follow the map through dusty old rooms and narrow corridors. We squeeze behind vintage machinery, too heavy to haul out once it broke down I suppose, until finally we come to a dimly lit corridor that leads us into the machinery room marked on Kioshi's map. We find the grey metal lockers, and go directly to the last one on the right. Oka shines the torch down, and refers to Kioshi's map and instructions. Then he reaches behind the locker and pulls it outwards, revealing a white metal door, with a spy hole at eye height. He takes out the key again, and slides it into the lock. It pushes outwards, and swings open to reveal a small room finished in bright, white tiles. The room is sparsely furnished, with only a wooden table and chair. Another white door stands opposite the one that we had just come through.

We pause both for breath, and to listen carefully. All sound from the outside has ceased. We are in the labyrinth. What lies beyond this ordinary looking door?

From somewhere off in the distance, we hear two muted reports. I am about to grab the door handle, but Oka clutches my arm.

"Wait," he says, "that was gunshots."

"Gunshots?" I say, clearly not convinced.

"This is not Hollywood you know musician. This is real life. That is what real gunshots sound like. Just give it a minute."

We wait the minute, but there is no other sound.

"Okay, lets go," says Oka, "but quietly and carefully."

I reach for the handle again, but suddenly the door is pulled open, and a middle aged man, wearing a white lab coat, rushes into the room. He charges toward me, and I hesitate for a split second, then strike out at him with my torch. It grazes across his cheek, opening up a small cut, enough to pull him up, eyes wide open in surprise. Before we can react, he gathers his wits and dives back out the way he has come, slamming the door behind him. Oka rushes to the door, in time to hear the metallic sound of the lock sliding into place. There is no keyhole on our side. We are locked out.

"We have to break it down," says Oka. "I don't think the lock is very strong."

And with that, he backs up as far as the room will allow. He takes a deep breath and spits on his hands, rubbing them together. Don't ask me why! Then he charges the white door, strikes home and bounces back nearly half as far as he'd come.

"Your turn," he says, rolling around on the ground clutching his sides.

I move in front of the door, and jam the bottom of my foot against the spot just below the handle. Nothing. I just keep at it.

. . .

Kioshi rounds the last corner, and there he is. The Professor... leaning forward and breathing heavily, one hand on either side of the passage wall. He drops one arm, and falls back flat against the wall. Smiling at Kioshi, he slides down the wall to sit there on the floor. There is a crash from the door beside him. He looks at the door and shrugs.

"Friends of yours I guess," he says sounding defeated, a small trickle of blood on his cheek. "The cavalry, riding in to save the day. It seems Grok was right about you."

Kioshi says nothing. Letting Tetsuya talk it out. The crashing starts again behind the door. Bang... bang.... bang.

"It doesn't matter anyway. It all came to nothing. If that last experiment didn't work it's all over... right. If I can't reach below that first level, I'll go to my grave never knowing the answer.

Bang... bang.... bang. The door is now shuddering under the onslaught. The timber frame is cracking.

Finally Kioshi speaks.

"No," he says quietly, "you will be going to your grave, and very soon, but you will know the answer. In fact it will be the last thing you ever hear."

He raises Grok's gun and points it at Tetsuya.

Tetsuya scrambles to his feet, and lodges himself as far back into the corner as he can go.

Bang... bang.... bang. The door frame splinters away at the top.

Kioshi steps right up, and pushes the barrel of the gun hard into the Professor's right eye socket. He smells a sharp, sour odour and looks down to see a stain spreading around the professor's tweed pants.

. . .

On the other side of the door, I rest... the sole of my right foot burning.

. . .

"You see Professor, your experiment worked," says Kioshi. A tear rolling down his cheek.

"I saw my mother give birth to me. My mother. I saw my mother... and my father. Then, I saw her jump to her death. She saw me there. She knew I was coming. She knew all this because you caused it. Then I jumped in time again and I saw..." Here he raises his left hand and claws the tears out of his eyes.

"I saw my mother give birth again, only 36 years before... on the grass outside the same hospital."

. . .

On the other side of the door, I steel myself and raise my foot again.

. . .

Kioshi's hand is shaking violently. The tears in his eyes are blinding him. Tetsuya is stunned but alert, he wants the pressure on his eye to end, one way or the other.

"She gave birth to you," continues Kioshi.

Tetsuya's left eye arches and his jaw drops.

"You are my brother," says Kioshi. "My twin brother. Our mother gave birth to me, then jumped off the balcony to her death. Somehow she passed back through time, probably dragged there by me, by your experiment. You and I, we dragged our mother back through time. Then she gave birth to you. You are my twin brother, and these experiments of yours have destroyed our family; destroyed my life. And now I will destroy you."

He is now shaking uncontrollably. He starts to squeeze the trigger.

Bang... bang... bang. The door frame gives way and the door crunches open a few inches.

The first bang distracts Kioshi enough that Tetsuya makes his move. Kioshi fires, as Tetsuya slaps the gun off to the side. The bullet takes a small piece of Tetsuya's ear, as it ricochets off the concrete wall. The pistol clatters to the floor as the door slams open, pushing Tetsuya into Kioshi. Kioshi staggers backwards, and Tetsuya dives on the gun. He comes up on one knee, off balance. He raises the gun, sights with his one good eye, and fires two shots into Kioshi, before I barrel through the door and knock him over sideways. As he falls, I bring my foot down hard

363

on his right wrist. I claw the gun from his hands, and it skids away behind me. He reaches up and grabs my throat, squeezing my windpipe. I feel it collapsing.

There is one last resounding bang, right by my ear, deafening me. In the silence, Tetsuya's grip relaxes and he falls back in slow motion, twitches a few times and lies still. I turn my head in the silence, and see Oka standing wide eyed, with the Browning in his hand. A shocked look on his face.

He throws the gun down the passageway, like it is some poisonous snake. I watch it bounce silently off the walls and skate across the concrete floor. Oka takes three steps, and drops down beside Kioshi. I get to my knees coughing, and clamber over to them.

Kioshi lies on his back breathing shallowly. Oka grabs my arm and shouts something at me silently. There is a faint echo off somewhere in the distance. I point to my ears and shake my head. He waves his arm and points at Kioshi, then makes the universal hand signal for telephone, jumps up and heads off to get help. I sit beside Kioshi and take his hand. I feel the slightest pressure returned.

· · ·

Kioshi lies on his back. He opens his eyes, and sees a face swimming before him, the musician... his friend. His chest burns, and his side. He senses he is lying in a puddle. He strains to look, as he lifts his hand slightly off the floor... there is a shadow.

He will speak to his friend. If it is the last thing he ever does, he will speak to his friend.

"I... I have met my mother," he says.

I press my ear almost to his lips. From far, far away I hear a tiny voice.

"I have met my mother."

I lay down there in that ever expanding puddle of blood, and hold him in my arms.

Now there is nothing.

Now there is something.

73. THE RED CRAB

The present...

It is 11.45 in the morning in Osaka, Japan.

Akira Matsumoto is sitting on a round concrete bench, that wraps around the base of a pole just off the bridge, at the end of Shinsaibashi Suji. A giant red crab scrambles eternally up the wall, on the building above his head. He would sit here for hours watching the crab wage its never ending battle with gravity. He had come here this morning at around 10 o'clock and has been sitting here ever since. He feels strange, like something is happening to him.

At 11.30 he was finding it hard to breath. His chest was constricted.

At 11.40 he thought he was dying.

At 11.44 he felt his heart expanding in his chest. Then he felt a great peace. At last... a great peace.

It is now 11.45... precisely 11.45, near the bridge at the end of Shinsaibashi Suji, under a giant red crab.

Akira Matsumoto slaps his hands hard on his thighs then stands up and says, to nobody in particular...

"I'm going home... my son needs me."